The German Wife

BOOKS BY DEBBIE RIX

The German Wife

Debbie Rix

bookouture

Published by Bookouture in 2022

An imprint of Storyfire Ltd.
Carmelite House
50 Victoria Embankment
London EC4Y 0DZ
United Kingdom

www.bookouture.com

ISBN: 978-1-80019-548-6
eBook ISBN: 978-1-80019-547-9

For my family

'Marriage cannot be an end in itself. It must serve a greater end: the increase and maintenance of the species and the race. That alone is its meaning and its task.'
Adolf Hitler, *Mein Kampf*, 1924

PROLOGUE
CONNECTICUT, USA

OCTOBER 1984

Anna Vogel checked her reflection in the bedroom mirror. At sixty-six she was still considered attractive, with chin-length, thick blond hair, greying a little now. She had always been tall and slender – five feet eight in stockinged feet – and was almost the same weight she had been at seventeen. Smoothing down the skirt of her shirt dress, she leant over the bed to pick up the slacks and sweater she had just discarded, straightening out the eau de nil bedspread. It was a little threadbare in places; she really ought to throw it out, she thought, but something made her hang onto it – a link with the past perhaps.

The bedspread was the first thing she had bought after she and Hans were married. The colour, she told him – as she laid the bedspread out on their large pine bed in the big house in Munich – reminded her of the hotel room in Paris where they had spent their honeymoon.

Hans had smiled slightly, adjusting the collar of his SS uniform, amused by her sentimentality. 'Whatever makes you happy, my dear.'

The bedspread was one of the few things she had brought with her on the long journey to America after the war. She had travelled across the ocean with her baby son, towards a new life in the New World – to move on and forget.

Now, through the sash window of her old colonial-style house, she could see her son's Mercedes sweep up the long drive. Sasha was an architect based in New York, but he'd had a client meeting in the town next to Anna's and had promised to look in on his way back home. She ran downstairs and stood waiting for him on the porch.

'Hi, Mom.' Sasha climbed out of the car, the late afternoon sun catching his tousled blond hair. People always remarked how alike he and his mother were – the long limbs, the same colouring – although his eyes had more of a green tinge, whereas hers were a remarkable shade of turquoise, which changed from blue to green with the light.

Sasha ran across the lawn and up the steps onto the porch, wrapping his mother in his arms and kissing the top of her head. 'How's my favourite interior decorator?' he asked, stroking her cheek.

'Don't be silly,' she said, blushing. 'And I'm almost a retired interior decorator these days.'

'Oh, come on, Mom, you'll never retire. You've got too much talent. Besides, your clients will never let you go... they need you too much. Now, it's such a lovely evening, shall we sit outside?'

'All right, I've got some drinks laid out on the dining table. I'll get them, shall I?'

'No, you sit down on the swing seat, Mom. Let me get them.'

He pushed through the front door to the large central hall that served as a dining room. Anna had laid the drinks tray on a polished mahogany table – a bargain at an auction twenty years earlier. Neatly arranged were bottles of bourbon and sweet vermouth, maraschino cherries, a silver ice bucket, two crystal glasses and a cocktail shaker. *Everything just so*, he thought to himself – as it always was with his mother.

Sasha carried the tray outside and laid it down on the cane table in front of her. 'Shall I mix you a drink?'

'Yes, thank you. A Manhattan would be nice.'

'Why do you love Manhattans so?' he asked, pouring the bourbon into the shaker.

'I don't know...' she began, 'perhaps because I first drank it on board the ship coming over here – after I'd left Germany.'

He handed her the cocktail, which she sipped tentatively, checking the taste was just right. 'Mmm, perfect.' She rocked gently on the swing seat, closing her eyes.

'I like to hear about the old days,' Sasha said, pouring himself a drink. 'How old was I again... when we came here?'

'Just a toddler, really – you were nearly two years old when we left Munich.'

'I can't believe you made a trip like that on your own, with such a young child. You must have been very brave.'

She smiled. 'It didn't feel brave at the time. It felt like... the only thing to do.'

'But to leave Germany, and everything and everyone you knew... that was brave, surely.'

'No, not really. I was an orphan, remember. I had no family, and my husband...' She pulled out a handkerchief from her pocket and blew her nose.

Sasha reached over and touched her hand. 'I'm sorry, does it upset you... talking about Dad?'

'No, it doesn't upset me to talk about Hans. He and I... had already drifted apart. When he died there was nothing left to keep me in Germany. Besides, I hated what Germany had become. As I've told you many times before, I was not supportive of the regime. And immediately after the war the country was in a terrible state – hideous bomb damage everywhere, criminal gangs running wild. You can't imagine how hard it was.'

She glanced over at Sasha, who squeezed her hand. 'I had no idea things were so difficult.'

'But then the Americans arrived,' she said more cheerfully. 'They took charge of our region of Germany and discipline was slowly restored. I got to know a couple of them, and liked what I saw. America just seemed the obvious place to come.'

'Well, I'm glad you came here. I've had a great life, thanks to you.' He grinned, revealing perfect white teeth – the result of several years of expensive orthodontics in his teens. He took her hand in his own and kissed it. 'Shall I bring us something to nibble on – some nuts, maybe? You shouldn't drink on an empty stomach.'

'Yes, good idea. I put some out earlier in a bowl – they're on the table in the kitchen.'

Anna rocked contentedly on the swing seat, gazing at the maples growing along the boundary, glowing scarlet in the early evening light. It was those very trees that had first drawn her to this house. Sasha had been about fourteen at the time; she had been to visit him at his boarding school in Connecticut for the weekend, and was driving back to her small but chic apartment in the Upper East Side of New York, when she spotted the trees. She had stopped her station wagon to admire them, and noticed the 'For Sale' sign. Walking up the long drive towards the house, she found the owner, an elderly widower, raking up leaves in the garden. He had agreed to show her around. He was moving in with his daughter, he told her, and wanted it to sell the house to someone who'd appreciate it.

'I think it's very beautiful,' she said enthusiastically,

admiring its Georgian windows on either side of the front door, and the wide porch that ran along the front, facing the garden. 'If you sell it to me, I can promise I will honour it. I'm an interior designer, and appreciate a house with history. I like to see the world as others have seen it. Also, it reminds me of a house I used to live in.'

Initially she used it only as a weekend retreat, travelling up from New York on Friday evenings. But when Sasha left home and then married, she moved in permanently, only visiting her apartment in the city for client meetings.

Over the years, she had filled the house with antiques bought at auctions. The sofas and chairs had been upholstered many times, but currently she favoured linen in pale colours – beige and cream – with splashes of turquoise here and there. The house contrived to be both traditional and also fashionable. Anna had lost count of how many times it had been photographed by stylists from interiors magazines.

'Here you go.' Sasha put two small dishes of nuts and olives on the cane table between them.

'How's the new project going?' she asked. As a fellow designer, Anna always took a professional interest in her son's work. They had even worked together occasionally.

'Oh, tricky... you know. The clients are constantly changing their minds. They have too much money, I think.'

Anna smiled sympathetically. She had spent her career dealing with demanding and egotistical clients who believed that money could solve any problem.

'Still,' he went on, 'as you always told me, the more drawings I have to do, the more they're going to pay.' He laughed and sipped his drink.

'Try not to let it bother you, Sasha. Each new drawing is a

chance to think of the project afresh. Use the time to improve it. What do they do, the clients?'

'Oh, I don't know what the wife does, but he's a doctor. An interesting guy, actually. Dad was a doctor, wasn't he?'

His mother sipped her drink. 'He was.'

'This man works for a pharmaceutical company – medical research. I think that's what he said.'

Anna shifted in her seat. The conversation was making her uncomfortable. 'Mix me another drink, would you, darling?'

'You sure? The last one was pretty strong.'

She looked at him, her eyes narrowing like a cat.

'Oh, oh... I've seen that look before,' said Sasha warily, 'the last time was when you found me smoking pot in my room. I must have been about seventeen?'

Smiling, he picked up her glass and refilled it from the cocktail shaker. 'You don't really like talking about the past, do you?'

'I don't see the point. What's done is done. It's the future that matters.'

'It's just – and forgive me if I'm wrong – but every time I mention Dad you clam up. I know he died a long time ago, but still... I'd like to know more about him – he was my father, after all.' He handed her the crystal highball glass. 'I didn't think about him much as I was growing up. But since I've had my own children, it seems to matter more – to understand what sort of man he was... what characteristics I might have inherited. Where's that album of photographs of Dad and you, from the old days?'

'Oh, it's in the cupboard in the sitting room.'

'Can I see it?'

'You really want to do this now?' Anna stood up, the cocktails suddenly blurring her senses, and walked slightly unsteadily inside the house. She emerged a few minutes later with a small leather photograph album, scuffed at the edges, and laid it on the cane table. 'There you go... photographs.'

He picked it up and studied the cover. 'I can't remember ever seeing this.'

'Of course you have – when you were younger.'

He opened the album. The front page was blank, just the photo mounts remained. 'What happened to this photograph?'

'Oh... I don't know – it fell out, I suppose.'

He turned the pages, until he found a black and white photograph of his mother standing in the garden of a large grey house, smiling uncertainly into the camera, sun glinting on her hair. 'Where was this taken?'

'That was the garden of our house in Munich. Do you remember it?'

'No, not at all.' On another page he pointed to a rather stout, elderly woman, scowling at the camera. 'Who's this?'

'That's Hans' mother... Elisabetta.'

'She looks so angry.' Sasha laughed.

'Probably because she was... she enjoyed complaining.' Anna smiled at the memory.

Towards the centre of the album was a photograph of Anna wearing a floral tea dress. She was standing next to a man, not much taller than her; he wore a tweed suit, and his hair was combed neatly from a centre parting. 'Is this... Dad?'

She leant across to study the picture. 'That's Hans, yes. We'd only recently been married. It was taken on our honeymoon in Paris. If you look carefully, you'll see Les Deux Magots in the background... it's the famous café frequented by French intellectuals. Hans didn't really approve of them – *too bohemian*, he said.'

Sasha ran his fingers over the photograph. 'You look so happy. You said you drifted apart before he died... what went wrong, if you don't mind me asking?'

'No, I don't mind. Life, I suppose. We had different priorities – that sort of thing. But we were happy enough at the start.'

'I don't look much like him, do I?'

'Not much, no.' She reached across and squeezed his hand. 'You're mine, my darling, all mine.' Draining her glass, she asked: 'Can you stay for dinner?'

'I'm not sure I can. I promised Louise I'd be back. I'm sorry – I hope you haven't gone to any trouble.'

'No, not at all. I made a casserole, but I can eat it myself.' She smiled at him, and patted his hand.

'Oh, Mom, I feel terrible... Look, we could arrange another time. And we'll see you at Thanksgiving. Louise asked me to remind you – we'd love you to come to the city.'

'Yes, I know. It's OK. I do understand you have to get back.'

Anna watched her son drive away, her eyes filled with tears. There was so much she wanted to tell him, so much she held inside. Pouring herself another Manhattan, she pushed through the swing door to the sitting room, sat down on the pale linen sofa, and stared blankly at the fireplace. It had been neatly laid with fresh dry logs and scrunched-up newspaper, in anticipation of his visit. She had hoped they would spend the evening together, watching the flames, feeling their warmth. *I really ought to light it*, she thought. It would cheer her to see a fire – an autumn fire was always a comforting thing – but instead, she drained her glass, feeling the alcohol numbing the pain, and closed her eyes.

PART ONE

THE PRE-WAR YEARS

1932–1935

'The mission of German women is to be beautiful and
to bring children into the world...
In exchange, the male takes care of gathering food,
stands guard and wards off the enemy.'
Joseph Goebbels, Minister of Propaganda, 1929

1

MUNICH

An icy wind whistled through the churchyard as the coffin was lowered into the grave. The priest withdrew to a respectful distance, and Annaliese threw a tiny bunch of snowdrops onto the simple oak box that contained the body of her father. It seemed a cold, cheerless place to spend eternity, she thought, but at least he was now reunited with her long-dead mother.

The gravediggers stood to one side, their hands fidgeting on the handles of their shovels, anxious to fill in the hole. The priest cleared his throat, making it clear the burial was 'officially' over.

'Thank you,' Annaliese told him. 'It was a lovely service.'

The priest shook her hand and walked purposefully across the graveyard, back towards the church. Annaliese glanced down into the grave and was lost for a moment, contemplating her own predicament. Her father's sudden death had left her effectively alone in the world. At seventeen she was now the sole owner of a small grocery shop in a lower-middle-class suburb of Munich, at a time when the country was in the middle of a deep economic depression. Her father had been worried about the viability of the business. Only the day before he died, she had found him sitting at the kitchen table, sighing as he read the newspaper.

'There are now six million people unemployed,' he said, jabbing at the paper with his sturdy finger. 'Think of it, Annaliese, these people are our customers. I pray to God we can keep going, but things will get tough, you mark my words.'

Annaliese – a bright but dreamy girl, more interested in romantic novels than world affairs – had tried to be optimistic. 'But we're a grocer, Papa. Surely people always need food? We'll be all right, won't we?'

Her father looked up into her turquoise eyes. 'I hope so, but I'm already extending credit to so many. Perhaps that new man, Hitler, can make things better.'

Now, as she stared at the oak coffin, Annaliese wondered if the stress of running the shop had been too much for her father. Was that the cause of his heart attack? The weight of responsibility that had now landed on her slight shoulders was only just sinking in. How could she, just a girl, manage a business, and deal with the debts and the creditors? It suddenly seemed overwhelming.

The few mourners, who included a handful of neighbours and fellow shopkeepers, shifted their feet and rubbed their hands in the cold wind, clearly eager to leave.

'Would you like to come back with us?' asked the butcher's wife, taking her arm. She and her husband had driven Annaliese to the cemetery in their van.

'If you don't mind,' Annaliese replied, 'I think I'll walk back home. I could do with the fresh air.'

.   .   .

On the other side of the graveyard an older woman, wreathed in furs, was weeping theatrically in front of a splendid granite tomb. Next to her, holding her arm, stood a younger man wearing a well-cut dark grey suit and a navy overcoat. The man was whispering to the older woman – his mother, Annaliese presumed – and tugging slightly at her arm, as if he wanted to leave. Annaliese walked past the tomb on her way to the churchyard gate, and the man noticed her and smiled a little; she smiled back. At the entrance to the churchyard, she turned around and found he was still watching her. He gave her a wistful look, as if he yearned to be anywhere but standing with his mother at the graveside.

Annaliese hurried down the road past the cemetery, suddenly overcome by waves of conflicting emotions: fear, sadness, and also anxiety. It was almost a relief to experience such feelings, for since her father's death she had been gripped by a sort of emotional paralysis – a habit she had learned from her father. They had buried her mother eight years before in the same graveyard, and had never spoken of it again. It had been his way of coping, she had supposed – to bury his feelings along with the body, and just get on with it. Now, with her father gone, she wondered if his way of grieving had been the right way. Perhaps it was better to let the pain come to the surface and deal with it, head on.

She stopped at the main road and drew a handkerchief out of her pocket, dabbing her eyes and blowing her nose. A tram rumbled noisily past, snaking its way through the traffic. In its wake a troop of Hitler Youth, dressed in their khaki uniforms, marched in unison in the opposite direction. Most of the children in her class at school had joined the youth organisation over the years, but Annaliese had so far resisted. To begin with, it was because she had little free time. Her father had insisted she help in the shop before and after school, and at weekends. But now she was relieved she had never been drawn into it. It seemed to her that Hitler Youth membership made people intolerant. A group from her school had recently attacked some children in the rival Boy Scouts. They had come into class the following day jubilant and boastful. Their behaviour had appalled her.

Waiting for the uniformed boys to march past, she became aware of a large black Mercedes pulling up next to her at the junction. Glancing over, she recognised the man from the cemetery. He was clutching the steering wheel and watching her intently. Unnerved, she pulled her black coat around her against the cold wind, adjusted the angle of her navy-blue trilby hat, and ran across the road, weaving between the cars. As she reached the pavement, she looked back. The man in the Mercedes raised his hand to her in a slight wave, before driving off towards the elegant suburb of Solln.

2

AUGUST 1934

During the two years that followed her father's death, Annaliese made some important changes in her life. She sold the shop to her neighbour, the butcher, and used the money to put herself through secretarial college. Although she still lived in the flat above her father's old shop, she had found a job as secretary to the assistant manager of a bank in the heart of Munich, and yearned to move into the city centre. As she sat on the tram on her way to and from work, she would gaze at the elegant apartment buildings near the Englischer Garten, the huge park in the centre of the city, and fantasise that, one day, she too might live in such grand surroundings.

One warm, sunny morning in August, the tram rumbled to its usual stop near the Baroque church on Theatinerstrasse. As Annaliese jumped off the tram, a newspaper seller was shouting out that morning's headline news: 'PRESIDENT HINDE-BURG DIES! ADOLF HITLER BECOMES FÜHRER!'

It was clearly a momentous event, but Annaliese had to admit she didn't fully understand the implications. She recalled

her father's hope that Hitler might resolve the country's problems, so perhaps it was a good thing. She bought a paper and
tucked it into her basket, intending to read it later.

'You look particularly lovely this morning,' said the assistant
manager, as she settled herself at her desk at the bank. 'That
colour really suits you – what do you call it?'

'Sky blue, Herr Becker.'

'Is it?' he said dreamily. 'Well, it brings out the colour of
your eyes...'

Annaliese suspected Herr Becker was a little in love with
her, but she had so far managed to evade his advances. He
disappeared into his private office and returned with a stack of
files, which he laid in front of her, before perching awkwardly
on the edge of her desk. 'Can you take these to the vault for
me?' he asked, in what he obviously hoped was a seductive
manner.

To get to the vault meant crossing the bank's grandiose hall,
past lines of people queuing at the counters. As she hurried
across the marble floor, weaving through the customers, she
inadvertently bumped into a man who was hurrying equally
fast in the opposite direction. Annaliese dropped the pile of
folders, which scattered across the highly polished floor. As the
man knelt down to help her gather them, she was aware of his
hand brushing against hers.

'I do hope you're all right,' he said, taking her by the elbow,
and helping her to her feet. He seemed familiar, with kind grey
eyes and brown hair. He was not handsome exactly, but he had
a neat symmetrical face, and charming manners. She felt herself
blushing as he gazed at her.

'Yes, thank you – I'm quite all right,' she replied, pushing
her thick blond hair away from her face.

'I think I know you, Fräulein, don't I?' he asked.

'I don't think so... no.' She smiled and hurried back to her office.

Half an hour later she came back out into the hall, carrying another pile of folders. The same man was leaning against the wall, reading a newspaper.

'Oh, there you are,' he said, 'I've been waiting for you.'

'Oh, really?' She found his comment unnerving. Why would a complete stranger be waiting for her? 'Is there something I can do for you?'

'Yes, you can have lunch with me.'

She blushed slightly. 'I don't think...' she began.

'I'm sorry. I've not explained myself properly. You see, we've met before.'

'Have we?'

'Yes, at the cemetery... a couple of years ago. I was visiting my father's tomb with my mother.'

She had a distant memory of a young man comforting an older woman wrapped in furs. 'Oh, yes... I do vaguely remember that. I had just buried my father.'

'I thought you seemed very alone,' he said sympathetically. 'I felt worried about you. And that's why I thought it would be lovely if we sat down and talked – over lunch.'

The man seemed genuine and kind, and what harm could it do, just to have lunch? 'All right,' she replied. 'But I only have an hour, and I have a lot of work to do today.' She held up the pile of files as evidence. 'My boss, Herr Becker, is very strict.'

'We can go to Café Luitpold,' he suggested brightly, 'it's just around the corner. Shall we say one o'clock?'

Annaliese had often gazed longingly through the windows of Café Luitpold, a local restaurant with pretty gilt tables and smartly dressed waiters. Its prices were well beyond her slender means.

'I'd love that,' she replied delightedly. 'I'll meet you there, shall I?'

When Annaliese arrived, she stood anxiously at the entrance to the café, and noticed, to her consternation, that her fellow diners were expensively dressed women and uniformed Nazi officers. She smoothed down her cheap cotton skirt nervously with her hands. A tall man wearing a crisp white shirt, black trousers and a long white apron approached her – the head waiter she presumed.

'Yes, Fräulein?' His tone was haughty and supercilious.

'I'm meeting someone,' she told him.

'Name?'

'Annaliese Altmann.'

'No, Fräulein, the name of your lunch companion.'

Annaliese's palms began to sweat as she realised she didn't know the name of the man she had met in the bank. Suddenly, to her relief, she spotted him, weaving through the tables towards her.

'Oh, it's all right,' she said, 'there he is now.'

'How lovely to see you again, Fräulein,' said the young man, taking her by the arm. 'Thank you, Joachim.'

The waiter bowed obsequiously. 'My pleasure, Herr Doctor – I hadn't realised the young lady was *your* guest.'

'Now,' said her lunch companion, as he guided her to his table, 'you must sit facing out, so you can watch all the comings and goings... everyone who's everyone is here.' He held her chair out for her and snapped his fingers at the waiter once she was settled. 'Two glasses of champagne,' he ordered.

'Oh!' she blushed. 'Champagne... for lunch. It'll go to my head, and I won't be able to work this afternoon.'

'Of course you will,' he replied gently. 'Now... I want to know everything about you. First, what is your name?'

'Annaliese,' she replied.

'Annaliese... that's a beautiful name,' he repeated quietly. 'And I am Hans – Dr Hans Vogel. I am a doctor of medicine.' He reached over for her hand and kissed it, just as the waiter placed two glasses of champagne on the table.

'A doctor,' she said, 'how wonderful.'

He chinked his glass with hers. 'Now, if you only have an hour, I think we should order.'

As the weeks went by, Hans wooed Annaliese. He took her out to dinner, and to the theatre. Sometimes they went for long walks through the parks in the centre of Munich, stopping afterwards for tea or a drink in one of the cafés shaded by plane trees.

Although their backgrounds were very different – he moneyed and middle-class, she from a far humbler background – they discovered they had much in common. Both had felt dominated by their parents, and were searching for their place in the world.

'My father was a doctor, like me,' he told her early one evening as they wandered along the banks of the river which ran through the Englischer Garten. Children paddled at the water's edge, watched anxiously by their mothers. 'Maximillian Vogel was his name,' explained Hans. 'He was high up in the National Socialist Party.' He glanced nervously down at her, as if checking for her reaction. They had never discussed politics and he was unsure of her political inclinations, but Annaliese remained impassive. 'He died about eight years ago,' Hans went on. 'It was a relief, if I'm honest. He was an impatient man, and something of a bully. But I have him to thank for meeting you.'

She smiled. 'What do you mean?'

'Well, if my mother hadn't insisted on visiting his grave every week, I might never have known you existed.'

'That's very sweet of you.' Annaliese flushed with pleasure.
'I'm impressed you go to his grave so often. My father and I only
visited my mother's grave once a year... and then we'd just stand
there, staring. It was awful.'

'I'm sorry,' he said.

'Oh, it's all right,' she replied bravely. 'You said your father
was a bully – was he unkind to you?'

'Sometimes. He could be very domineering, and insisted I
become a doctor.'

'Didn't you want to be a doctor?' she asked.

'I was happy enough to oblige, and I did well at my studies.
But he found my interest in matters "esoteric" rather irritating.'

'What do you mean?'

'I specialised in homeopathy. It held no interest for him and
he told me that I was doomed to failure. But interestingly, it
turns out that he was wrong.'

He smiled.

'How so?'

'Well, a year or so ago, I was persuaded by my mother to
approach the Party – the National Socialists, I mean. She has
connections – friends and so on – who are high up in the local
organisation and, apparently, our new Chancellor is very interested in homeopathy. I'm putting together a research project
that I hope they might take an interest in.'

'Oh, how interesting. What's it about?'

'Malaria, and whether we can cure or prevent it, using
homeopathy.'

'Malaria? But we have no malaria in Germany, do we?'

'There is a little – we had various outbreaks in 1918 both
here and in Scandinavia after the World War. The last outbreak
was just four years ago, in fact. Also that particular illness has
great significance for homeopaths. Samuel Hahnemann – the
German physician who first discovered homeopathy – began his

own research with malaria. If I were to find a cure, it would be a great coup for the German people.'

'And for you too, I expect,' she replied, laughing.

He smiled. 'Indeed.'

'Anyway,' she went on, taking his arm, 'I'm very impressed.'

'Are you? I'm so glad. I do so want you to... think well of me.'

'Of course I think well of you. I think you're marvellous.'

He grinned, clearly delighted, and patted her hand affectionately. 'Now, that's enough about me... tell me all about your family. What were your parents like?'

'Well...' she began. 'My father was a grocer – an honourable man, but very distant. From the moment he got up to the time he went to bed, he worked. It left little time for emotion or feelings. When my mother died, he hardly ever talked about her again.'

'That must have been very hard.'

'Yes it was, and growing up as an only child, it felt very lonely at times.'

He nodded. 'I felt the same. I was sent away to school, and even when I came home I never felt any real affection from either of my parents.' He gazed down at her and took both her hands in his. 'It seems we are two lost souls, wouldn't you say?'

She smiled up at him. 'Two lost souls... yes, I suppose we are.'

As dusk fell, the park emptied. The children playing in the river had long since been taken home, and the only sounds were the buzzing of bees in search of their last nectar before nightfall. The couple appeared to be quite alone.

Suddenly, Hans leant down and kissed Annaliese on the mouth, whispering into her ear, 'I love you, I love you.'

Annaliese, who had never had a boyfriend and never even been kissed, found it intoxicating. 'I love you too,' she replied, caught up in the moment. He held her face in his hands, and tears ran down his face.

One evening, towards the end of the summer, Hans arrived at her flat to take her out for dinner. He was carrying a large bunch of pale pink roses. Their scent filled her tiny kitchen.

'These are so beautiful, Hans. You're really spoiling me.'

'I've only just begun,' he said, dropping to his knees, and taking a small leather box from his jacket pocket. 'Marry me?'

'Oh, Hans.' She opened the box and found a sapphire and diamond engagement ring glistening against the velvet. 'I can't believe it.'

'Say yes,' he begged.

At that moment, Annaliese felt no hesitation. She felt enveloped by his love, and having no previous experience of romance, simply assumed she loved him in return. Hans made her feel safe and cared for – something she desired more than anything. 'Of course I'll marry you... yes.'

As he slipped the ring on her finger, Annaliese convinced herself that Hans was her destiny.

To celebrate their engagement, Hans took Annaliese to the Osteria Bavaria – a Munich restaurant popular with the National Socialist Party elite. As they were guided to their corner table, Annaliese tugged at Hans' sleeve. 'Isn't that Adolf Hitler?' she whispered.

'Yes,' he murmured. 'Try not to stare.'

Hitler was surrounded by a group of high-level officers, interspersed with a handful of young women – all fair-haired and blue-eyed – who seemed mesmerised by their leader. As Hans guided his tall, willowy, blond fiancée past Hitler's table, she couldn't resist glancing over at the Chancellor. His startlingly blue eyes locked with hers, and she felt his gaze following her across the room.

Hans held out a chair for her at their corner table. 'Our new Führer likes you,' he whispered as she sat down.

'Does he?' She felt flattered to have the caught the attention of the newly appointed Chancellor of Germany, but was unnerved by the intensity of his stare. 'Have you ever met him?' she asked quietly.

'Me? No.' He laughed gently. 'I'm not part of those circles... at least, not yet.'

'Would you like to be?'

'I'm not a political animal – I have no aspirations in that area. And to be honest, until recently my attitude to the Party – and the people who run it – was rather negative. I actually think Hitler' – he lowered his voice to a whisper – 'is a bit of a thug.' He grimaced slightly, before shrugging. 'But I'm afraid being a member of the Party is pretty much mandatory these days.'

'What do you mean?'

'Most academics and doctors, in particular, have joined. I would be rather frowned upon if I didn't.'

'That seems rather unfair. Surely, being a good doctor has nothing to do with politics?'

'You're right, of course,' he replied, smiling. 'But it's the way of the world.' He reached across the table and took her hand. 'Are you happy, my darling?'

'Oh, yes – very happy.'

'Tell me something,' he began. 'If we're going to be married I need to know I have your support with my work.'

'Of course you do, Hans.'

'Good. Because, the thing is...' Hans paused, fidgeting with his linen napkin. He looked up at Annaliese, his expression earnest and sombre. 'I'm not sure I can remain a private doctor forever.'

'But why? It's a good profession, isn't it?'

'Yes, it's good enough, and I enjoy helping my patients, of course. But as I've explained before, I have ambition. Medical research is what really interests me.'

'I remember – your project on homeopathy...'

'That's right. Oh, I'm so glad you understand. The problem is, I'm a humble general practitioner, and in order to do research I need to become an academic, perhaps even get a university post. It's been suggested to me, by those in the know, that if I were to join the SS, I might find "our friend" over there rather sympathetic.' He nodded discreetly towards Hitler. 'He has an interest in homeopathy, as I think I told you. I'm told that if I show my loyalty by joining the SS, he might pull a few strings...'

'Well, then you must join,' Annaliese said firmly.

'The thing is,' he went on, 'membership of such an elite group brings many advantages, but there are regulations too.'

'What sort of regulations?'

'About whom one can marry.'

'I don't understand.'

'Members of the SS must be of pure Aryan stock, and they may only marry someone equally pure.'

'I see,' said Annaliese. She felt a twinge of unease. It reminded her of the bullying tactics of the Hitler Youth. 'I really can't see it's anyone else's business who you marry, is it?'

'I know – it's intrusive, and ridiculous. But it's the rule. The problem is that in order to prove our "purity", you and I will need to present the authorities with copies of our ancestors' birth and marriage certificates, going back to our grandparents' generation. I have mine already, which have been accepted, but will you be able to get hold of yours?'

'I'm not sure,' replied Annaliese. 'As you know, my mother died when I was very young and my father was not the best record-keeper. I vaguely remember meeting my grandparents when I was much younger, but they're all dead now, and I have no idea how to get hold of their birth or marriage certificates.'

'I know it sounds complicated.' Hans' tone was apologetic. 'And anyone looking at you can tell you're a pure Aryan woman, but these regulations have been devised by Heinrich Himmler himself, so we have no choice.'

'Is Himmler very important?' she asked innocently.

'He's Hitler's right-hand man,' whispered Hans, nodding towards Hitler's table. 'He's the one wearing glasses, sitting opposite Hitler. He runs the SS, and he calls these marriage rules his "ten commandments".'

Annaliese looked across the restaurant and discreetly studied Himmler. His pebble glasses magnified his tiny eyes, giving him the look of an ugly frog. As Hitler held forth, regaling his audience with a story, Himmler was nodding his silent approval, his mouth grim and unsmiling.

'He looks a most unpleasant man,' said Annaliese. 'But if he makes the rules, I suppose we'd better obey them.'

3

OCTOBER 1934

It took Annaliese several weeks to assemble the documents she needed for her marriage to Hans. She searched every cupboard and drawer in the cramped flat above the shop, and eventually unearthed her parents' marriage certificate in a box in the attic, along with a photograph taken at their wedding. It had been annotated on the back in her mother's neat hand and enabled her to track down a long-lost cousin, who was the only member of the wedding party still alive.

Lena lived in the quaint medieval town of Rothenburg ob der Tauber, and Hans agreed to drive Annaliese there one weekend. The couple was enchanted by the beautiful little town and wandered the cobbled streets together, holding hands, as they searched for Lena's house.

She welcomed Annaliese cheerfully enough, and over lunch revealed as much as she could about the birthplaces of Annaliese's grandparents. On subsequent weekends the couple visited churches and parish offices, obtaining the necessary certificates. Once these had been approved by the

SS authorities, Annaliese's engagement to Hans became official.

The final hurdle in their future together was for Annaliese to meet Hans' mother, Elisabetta. At Hans' suggestion, she invited the couple to tea one Sunday afternoon. Annaliese was filled with nerves at the prospect of this encounter, and spent the whole morning styling her hair and choosing her outfit, finally settling on a pale grey linen suit that she normally wore for work. It was both demure and elegant, emphasising her slim figure, and the colour toned well with her blond hair. As Annaliese stood back to admire herself in the mirror, she hoped it would strike the right note with her future mother-in-law.

'I didn't know what to wear,' she told Hans, as she slid into the leather seat of the Mercedes. 'Do I look all right?'

'You look beautiful,' he said, kissing her on both cheeks. 'And you really mustn't worry. I'm sure she'll love you, just as I do.'

Annaliese smiled bravely, praying her fiancé was right.

Driving through the elegant suburb of Solln – popular with the higher echelons of the National Socialist Party – Annaliese gazed at the houses on either side of the road. 'They're all so elegant,' she said quietly, thinking of the tiny flat where she had been brought up. Panicking slightly, she wondered how she could ever hope to marry into a family so much wealthier than her own.

The car slowed to a crawl. 'Here we are,' Hans announced, turning into a long gravel drive.

As they approached the large white stucco double-fronted house set in extensive grounds, Annaliese's heart began to race. 'It's beautiful,' she said breathlessly. 'What must you think of me and my run-down father's shop?' She glanced anxiously across at Hans as he drew the car to a halt.

'I'm not marrying your father's shop,' he said, kissing her hand. 'I'm marrying you. Now, come on, we should go in.'

'Wait a moment.' She clutched his arm. 'Can I ask you something first?'

'Of course.'

'Are we to live here after we're married?'

He leant back in his car seat and smiled at her. 'Why, don't you like it?'

'I don't wish to sound ungrateful – it's wonderful, of course, but I'd rather we lived alone after we're married. Is that very wrong of me?'

'No, not at all,' he said. 'I'd rather be alone with you too.' He leant over and kissed her fiercely on the mouth. She sensed his pent-up desire as he pulled away from her reluctantly, breathing heavily. 'In fact,' he murmured, 'I already have a plan for where we will live.'

'Really?' she asked excitedly. 'Where?'

'Not yet,' he teased. 'You'll find out soon enough. Now, we'd better get inside. Mother doesn't like to be kept waiting.'

As he reached across her and opened the car door, she stroked the back of his neck. 'Hans... just one more thing. I want you to know I may not have been brought up in a grand house, but I do have a little money left – from the sale of the shop. If we are to get a house, I can make a small contribution. It's important, I think, that you know that.'

'Darling,' he said gently, 'I appreciate the offer, but please don't worry yourself about money. As it happens, I am financially independent of my mother. My father was good enough to leave me a trust fund, which I inherited five years ago. We will have more than enough.' He kissed her again firmly on the mouth. 'Now, come on... let's get it over with.'

A maid ushered the pair into the drawing room. Annaliese marvelled at its opulence: green silk covered the walls, and on the parquet floor was a sumptuous Persian carpet. Through the graceful French windows she glimpsed the garden where a fountain played, surrounded by box-edged borders. But her eyes were drawn to the centre of the room where, sitting on a high-backed, emerald-green chair, was a late-middle-aged woman, her grey hair piled elegantly on top of her head.

Hans kissed the woman's cheek. 'Mama... I'd like to introduce my fiancée – Annaliese.' He took Annaliese by the arm. 'Darling, this is my mother, Elisabetta.'

Hans' mother held her hand out to Annaliese, revealing several diamond rings, which sparkled in the sunlight.

Annaliese took her hand, holding it too tightly and shaking it too vigorously. 'How do you do. It's wonderful to meet you.'

Elisabetta removed her hand brusquely. 'Do please sit down.'

Annaliese perched uneasily on a horsehair sofa, facing her future mother- in-law.

'I gather you are alone in the world,' said Elisabetta imperiously. 'What did your father do?'

'Oh, Mama,' Hans interjected impatiently, 'I've already told you... her father was a businessman. Now, why don't we show Annaliese the garden?'

As the three toured the garden, Hans tried to protect his fiancée from his mother's critical questioning. Annaliese, in turn, did her best to make polite conversation, admiring the magnificent flowerbeds filled with neat rows of summer bedding plants.

'I love these bright pink ones,' she said, trying to sound enthusiastic.

'You know their name, surely?' asked Elisabetta, with just the hint of a sneer.

'I'm afraid not,' replied Annaliese truthfully. 'My family didn't have a garden.'

'No garden?' Elisabetta sounded horrified.

To Hans' relief, the maid suddenly appeared at his mother's

side. 'Excuse me, madam, tea is ready. Shall I serve it on the terrace?'

'Yes, do,' replied Elisabetta.

Hans ushered the two women up wide steps onto the grand terrace, edged with stone pilasters. While Elisabetta poured tea from a silver tea pot, Annaliese sat very erect on a wicker chair, anxiously waiting for Elisabetta to pronounce on her son's engagement.

'Well, I suppose I must give you both my blessing,' she said haughtily. 'And perhaps, Annaliese, you will soon acquire some semblance of horticultural knowledge.' Elisabetta passed Annaliese a china cup; her hand shook as she took it. 'I just hope,' Elisabetta went on, 'that you will not find living in a big house like this too daunting. It will clearly be quite different from what you're used to.'

Hans glanced sympathetically at Annaliese.

'Hans, of course, has his office here,' continued Elisabetta, 'as his father did before him, God rest his soul. Perhaps you might work as his receptionist? I understand you have some experience of typing.' She made it sound like an unfortunate affliction.

'Mama,' Hans began, 'I neither want nor need a receptionist. Besides, we won't live here after we're married.'

'What on earth do you mean?' his mother asked irritably.

'I intend to buy a house of our own, naturally.'

'What is so *natural* about deserting your own mother?'

'I won't be deserting you, Mama,' Hans replied calmly. 'I'll see you as often as possible, but Annaliese and I must set up on our own. When there are children, and so on, it would be too... noisy for you.'

Annaliese was relieved by his show of strength. This one brief meeting with her future mother-in-law had been enough to confirm that she and Elisabetta would never be friends. The prospect of living with her would be unbearable.

. . .

'I hope that wasn't too traumatic,' said Hans as he drove Annaliese back home.

'No,' she smiled loyally. 'But I hope your mother won't resent me. She seemed so disappointed that you're leaving.'

'She's been too used to getting her own way,' he replied, pulling up in front of the shop. 'Since my father died, she's had me all to herself. But she'll adjust.'

'Did you mean what you said about having children?' Annaliese asked shyly.

'Of course.' He took her in his arms and kissed her. 'I'd love to have children with you – half a dozen, at least!' He smiled.

'Half a dozen!' she replied, laughing. 'I don't think so... but two or three would be nice. I'm an only child, as are you, so we both know how lonely that can be.'

'I love you, Annaliese,' he murmured into her hair, 'we understand each other so well. You were sent from heaven to give meaning to my life.'

The wedding was a small affair with just a handful of guests. Annaliese invited Lena, her only living relative, to accompany her. On Hans' side were his mother and her sister Charlotte, a spinster who lived in the family home in Salzburg. Gunther, the best man, was an old friend from medical school, who now worked in public health. He and his wife Ursula gathered with the others outside the Registrar's office.

'That colour suits you very well,' said Ursula, admiring Annaliese's fitted turquoise suit. 'And wherever did you find a hat to match?'

'At a little shop near the bank where I work – Hans helped me choose it,' Annaliese replied shyly. 'He's got a marvellous eye for that sort of thing. Don't you think Hans looks handsome in his elegant new SS dress uniform?'

Ursula glanced uneasily at the sharp black suit, emblazoned with silver buttons and belt buckle. 'Yes, very elegant,' she replied uncertainly. 'I have to confess we were rather surprised to hear that Hans had joined the SS.'

'Yes, he joined a few months ago. He was advised it was a sensible step to take – as a doctor, I mean. Has Gunther never thought of it?'

'Gunther's not a joining sort of person,' Ursula replied quietly.

After the brief ceremony, the party adjourned to a private room at Café Luitpold for the wedding breakfast. Champagne was served, Hans gave a graceful speech, and the 'happy couple' retired to a nearby hotel for their first night together.

While Hans brushed his teeth in the bathroom, Annaliese slipped into a new silk nightgown, which rustled next to her skin, and sat bolt upright in bed, waiting apprehensively for her new husband. When he climbed into the bed beside her, she felt her heart racing – not with passion but terror.

Hans was tender and gentle as they made love, but it struck her that he too seemed nervous – perhaps this might also have been his first time.

The following morning, they boarded a train for Paris. Hans had booked a room in a small hotel on the Left Bank, and over the following days they wandered the streets, eating at fine restaurants and visiting galleries. Annaliese scoured antique shops, admiring the beautiful furniture and *objets d'art*. And when they passed a particularly chic little boutique, Hans had insisted on going inside.

'Let me buy you a dress,' he urged. He sat on a velvet sofa, admiring his pretty wife as she tried on the latest fashions.

. . .

On their return to Munich Hans hailed a taxi at the station, but instead of instructing the driver to take them to his mother's house, he gave him an address near the Englischer Garten.

'Where are we going?' asked Annaliese excitedly.

'You'll see,' he said, squeezing her hand.

As they drove past the tall elegant apartment buildings, interspersed here and there with grand detached houses, Annaliese's heart began to beat fast in anticipation. She had once fantasised about living in one of these apartments. Was her dream about to come true?

When the taxi drew up in front of a large double-fronted house set in its own gardens, she burst into tears.

'Why are you crying, darling?' asked Hans.

'Because I think... you are about to tell me that this is our house. Am I right?'

He nodded shyly. 'Come, I'll show you.'

He helped her out of the car and they stood hand in hand on the pavement. The house was protected from the road by tall metal railings, behind which was a tightly clipped hedge. Beyond it, Annaliese glimpsed a pale and imposing building. As they approached she could see it was painted dove grey, with arched windows edged in white. The walls were decorated with elegant pilasters, which added to its neo-classical elegance. Wide steps led up to a shiny black door, topped by a stained-glass fanlight in bright primary colours – red, yellow and blue. It provided the only colour in an otherwise monochrome façade.

'What a beautiful window,' she murmured.

'Yes, it's a feature of Art Deco architecture,' replied Hans self-importantly.

Above the porch was a stone balcony, encircled by creeping ivy.

Annaliese took his arm. 'That balcony – it's so romantic. Oh, Hans, is it really ours?'

'Yes. The inside needs a bit of work, but I thought you'd enjoy decorating it. You do like it, don't you?' He smiled nervously.

'I love it!' She threw her slender arms around his neck and kissed him several times on the cheek. 'Thank you, Hans, thank you.'

Annaliese was as content as she had ever been, imagining a charmed future living in a grand house. Her early conversations with Hans had convinced her that they both wanted a large family, and she could envisage a happy brood of children running around the spacious garden. The idea filled her with excitement. She would be able to put her lonely childhood firmly in the past, and instead surround herself with love and laughter. Hans gave her a generous budget to redecorate, and she threw herself joyfully into the process, relishing the chance to buy expensive fabrics and furnishings, including an eau de nil silk bedspread for the bedroom, to remind her of the one in their honeymoon hotel room in Paris.

Hans insisted they hire a maid as both cook and cleaner. Several young women were sent by an agency for interview. None seemed suitable until a young girl called Marta arrived. She was a little plump, and of medium height, with shiny brown hair and grey eyes. But she had a friendly smile, Annaliese thought, and when she shyly admitted that this was her first job, Annaliese warmed to her.

'Well... as I have never had a maid before, we shall learn together.'

Hans moved his medical practice into the house, and a new brass plate was put up beside the front door. His consulting room and study now overlooked the garden, and Annaliese ensured there were fresh flowers on his desk each morning. Everything seemed to be going well. To anyone observing Hans and Annaliese, it appeared they had everything they could desire.

But, after a few months, Hans' mood changed. Ignoring his new wife, he spent long hours in his study after his patients had left. Annaliese quickly accepted the situation. She had been used, after all, to her father working long hours. But she couldn't avoid a slight feeling of regret that those early days of chatting happily over dinner each evening had now come to an end. What saddened her further was that Hans seemed so unhappy, despite his hard work.

One evening, she plucked up the courage to talk to him about it, and knocked on his study door.

'Come,' he replied tersely.

She opened the door a crack. 'I'm not disturbing you, am I?'

He looked up distractedly from his work. 'No, not at all.'

'I just wondered if you wanted dinner. It's well after eight o'clock.'

'Dinner? Oh, I'm sorry. I've been so engrossed.'

'May I ask what you're doing?'

'I'm working on my research projects, applying for grants from high-up members of the SS.'

'Oh, I see. But If I may...' she began tentatively, 'I'm worried about you – you seem so wretched all the time.'

'Do I? I'm sorry, darling. It's just... I'm getting nowhere.' He sighed miserably. 'I can't understand it. I'm putting forward such brilliant ideas, but nothing ever comes of it.'

'Perhaps you should try to enjoy what we have,' she suggested. 'We have so much, after all.'

'But what's the point of joining the SS if it does nothing to promote my career?' To Annaliese's surprise, he sounded really anguished. 'I have no interest in being a soldier, or a politician. I am a doctor, and while I love my job, I know I can do more to help society in a significant way – by finding the cures for dangerous diseases.' He paused, gauging her reaction. 'A small part of me, I admit, also yearns to prove to my mother and father that I can be an academic success. They never really believed in me.'

'You are a success already,' she assured him, reaching across his desk and taking his hand. 'And whatever your parents think of you, *I* believe in you, Hans. I feel sure you will succeed – your determination alone will see you through.'

4

_____

April 1935

In spite of the beautiful spring weather, Hans' day did not start well. Waiting for the first of his patients to arrive, he opened his post. Among the letters and parcels was a scientific journal he subscribed to each month. As he flicked through the pages, he found an article about a Dr Claus Schilling of the prestigious Robert Koch Institute in Berlin, and an expert in tropical diseases. According to the article, Mussolini had invited Schilling to Italy to work on vaccines and possible cures for malaria – the very subject Hans had been wanting to research. The article went on to explain that Dr Schilling was to be given access to patients at various lunatic asylums where he could test his treatments.

Hans sat back in his chair. The idea of trialling treatments on people who lacked mental capacity was disturbing – shocking even. But on the other hand, if it helped mankind find a cure for malaria, perhaps it could be justified. Medical research was always a balancing act between potentially harming a few in order to protect the many. And yet the thought of those poor lunatics being used as guinea pigs made him very uneasy. As he reread the article, Hans' initial feelings were soon replaced by another emotion – envy that he had lost out to another doctor. Schilling's career trajectory had been spectacular. He was now in a position to truly test his theories and perhaps, even, become famous for finding the cure for malaria. Had Hans' hard work looking for research grants all been in vain?

'Dr Vogel.' It was Marta knocking on the door. 'Your first patient is here.'

'Show them in,' he called back gloomily.

A quick glance at his appointments diary confirmed that the patient was a middle-aged woman who suffered from a range of menopausal complaints.

'Ah, Frau Fischer, do come in,' he said in his most genial manner. 'Now, how can I help you?'

As the woman reeled off her latest ailments, he found his mind wandering to the serious work he could be doing – if only someone would recognise his potential.

That evening, after his final patient had left, Hans was tidying his desk when the phone rang. It was his friend Gunther.

'I need to see you as soon as possible. I need your help as a member of the SS.'

'My dear man,' Hans replied, 'I will do all I can to assist you, of course, but be under no illusion as to the influence I have. Since I joined the organisation, every idea I've suggested has been completely ignored. I'm not sure anyone high up in the SS has the faintest idea who I am. But you sound very upset, my dear friend, so please come over after dinner and we'll talk.'

Gunther duly arrived, and was shown into Hans' study, where they sat together sharing a bottle of schnapps.

'Now, dear chap,' said Hans warmly, 'what's troubling you?'

Gunther took a swig of his drink. 'There is a policy, which I'm sure you know about, to sterilise people suffering from serious congenital illnesses – Down's syndrome, schizophrenia, that sort of thing. I disapprove, of course, although I know I am in the minority within our profession in Germany, who seem to think that eugenics is perfectly acceptable, even laudable.' Gunther paused, shaking his head in disbelief. 'What particularly concerns me is that the categories of people to be sterilised keep being extended. The other day I was forced to approve the sterilisation of a girl of ten – of *ten*, Hans! She was rather slow-witted, I have to admit, a nervous child, who had been late to speak as a toddler, apparently, but that was all. There was nothing essentially wrong with her, but I was ordered to sign the forms for the procedure to go ahead.' Gunther frowned, swallowing the last of his schnapps. 'There really is only a tiny number of people for whom I could remotely justify such a radical intervention – a chronic alcoholic perhaps, or someone with serious mental disturbances – but a healthy child of ten, Hans!'

'I agree,' Hans replied, refilling Gunther's glass. 'It seems rather over-zealous.'

'I tried to argue with the authorities,' Gunther went on, 'but it was made quite clear to me that refusal would result in me being sanctioned – possibly imprisoned... Prison, Hans, for simply doing my job! What was the oath we took at medical school? "First do no harm." It seems to have been superseded by the oath of allegiance to the Führer, and his crazy, wicked ideas.'

Hans was shocked by Gunther's story. His friend's rage was quite justified, and yet Hans was in a difficult situation. As a member of the SS, he had sworn to serve Hitler and his regime. 'I'm so sorry,' he said, shaking his head sympathetically. 'How did her parents take it?'

'They were hysterical, of course. I'm really worried, Hans. I'm not sure I can bear it any more, but I have no idea what to do about it. If I refuse, I may go to prison, and I'm sure Ursula would never forgive me. But if she knew what I was being required to do at work every day, I'm not sure she'd forgive that either.'

'Now my dear fellow, you must get any idea of prison out of your head – it's unthinkable.' Hans sipped his own drink, musing on how to respond. 'I suppose we all have to see the world through a different lens now.'

'What lens is that?' challenged Gunther. 'One where doctors are required to inflict barbaric treatments on their patients?'

Hans glanced up, taken aback by his friend's anger. 'No, of course not. What you've told me is very troubling, and I'm not saying I agree with it, not in any way, but these are difficult times. I too am wrestling with the complex political structure in which we are working. The Führer, and those around him, have a vision for this country. We may not agree with everything they do, or say, but the argument, I suppose, is that it's better than the poverty and struggle this country went through for over a decade before they came to power.'

Gunther looked at him over the top of his spectacles. 'You don't really believe that, do you?'

Hans flushed slightly. His best friend was confronting him with the reality of the system he had signed up to, and yet he could not bring himself to acknowledge its shortcomings. 'I have to believe that some good will come of all this, Gunther. I am a doctor and, as such, am committed to helping people. But I also have the ambition to advance medical science, which is a profound way of helping society. I have no option but to work within the system. You can see that, can't you?'

Gunther stood up and put his glass down on the table. 'I'm not sure I can, Hans, no. I think you are deluding yourself if you think there is any honourable way of working within this particular "system". I'm getting out – in fact, leaving Germany for good. I suggest you do the same.'

At the door, Gunther stopped and turned back to Hans. 'Beware of selling your soul too cheaply, my dear friend. Goodnight.'

Gunther's words struck home. Hans poured himself a large schnapps and nursed it long into the night. He realised that the line between good medical practice and abuse was certainly becoming blurred. Human experimentation had always been a troubling area of medical research, and yet it was justified by the need to find cures to help the general population. It was, in essence, the suffering of the few for the greater good of the many. That, in the end, was what the government was trying to achieve, and what he must cling to.

A few days later, Hans received a written order to report to the office of Heinrich Himmler at the National Socialist headquarters on Königsplatz. The Brown House, as it was called, was a large neo-classical sandstone building that had been sold to the Party in 1930. Apart from housing Hitler's private office and the Reich press office, it was also the headquarters of the SS leadership under Heinrich Himmler. There were rumours that Hitler's political opponents were imprisoned and tortured in its cellars.

Hans, wearing his new black SS uniform, waited nervously in the grandiose marble reception. Displayed against the end wall was a forest of Nazi flags. Finally a junior SS officer marched towards him. 'Please follow me, Dr Vogel, sir.'

Himmler occupied a huge office which stretched across the front of the building on the first floor. He glanced up as the young officer announced Hans' arrival. Narrowing his eyes, he clicked his fingers. 'Ah, please come in, Dr Vogel.'

The young officer withdrew and Hans advanced towards

Himmler, who was seated behind a large Biedermeier desk at one end of the room, beneath a portrait of the Führer.

'You asked to see me, sir?'

'I did. You may sit – I'll just be a moment.'

Hans sat down gingerly on the edge of the visitor's chair, waiting while Himmler scribbled notes on a notepad. Finally, he looked up and studied the young doctor's face – his pebble glasses magnifying the unnerving squint in his small dark brown eyes.

'I've been hearing things about you.'

'Oh?' asked Hans anxiously.

'Yes... your interest in malaria, for example.'

'Ah!' said Hans, slightly relieved.

'Is that all you can say – "oh" and "ah"?'

'I'm sorry, I'm not quite sure I understand...'

'I want to know everything you know about malaria,' said Himmler impatiently, tapping his pen irritably on his desk.

Hans began to explain his ideas and theories – tentatively at first, but gradually growing in confidence.

After ten minutes Himmler held up his hand. 'Enough. I have a proposition for you – well, it's more of an order really.' He smirked. 'Have you heard of Dachau?'

'Er... yes, I think so.'

'It's a labour camp just outside Munich. We set it up a couple of years ago. We send our political enemies there. It's been quite well regarded – held up, in fact, as a model labour camp. The inmates are put to work, building their own quarters, for example. They are relatively well looked after. We have a doctor to see to their ailments.'

Hans' heart sank. Was he going to be asked to be merely the camp doctor?

'I am interested in developing a medical research facility at the camp,' Himmler went on.

Hans sat up eagerly.

'I need someone to start the ball rolling. Eventually, I anticipate several doctors working there – collaborating on various projects, really breaking the bounds of medical research. Would you like to be among the pioneers?'

'Yes, sir!' Hans declared firmly. If he had any doubts about the regime, he quickly pushed them away. This was the chance he'd been waiting for, the turning point in his medical career. 'I would be honoured, Reichsführer.'

'Good. I shall arrange for you have suitable equipment, staff and premises. Initially, I would like you to concentrate on malaria research. The Führer is interested in homeopathy and how it might further our ability to combat many of these tropical diseases.'

It was as if all of Hans' dreams had suddenly come true. 'Thank you, sir. I'd be delighted.'

'You will need patients, of course, or should I say... subjects.'

'Yes.'

'The prisoners would seem suitable. How does that sound?'

'It sounds wonderful, thank you.'

'I shall expect regular reports, and will inspect from time to time.'

'Of course, I would expect nothing else.'

'Good. You may start next week. You will be promoted to the rank of Sturmbannführer, and assigned an office and a laboratory. I suggest you choose a laboratory assistant from among the prisoners – one or two of them are bound to have scientific backgrounds. You may go.'

Hans stood up, clicked his heels and bowed.

'Oh, and Dr Vogel,' said Himmler, 'I hope you don't have too many scruples. Dachau might be a model labour camp, but we do not tolerate insurrection or disobedience among the prisoners. Punishment is swift, and harsh.'

'I understand, Reichsführer.'

. . .

At home, Hans found Annaliese in the sitting room watering her house plants.

'It's happened, at last!' he said, embracing her.

'What's happened?'

'I've been asked to oversee some important scientific research into malaria – at the local labour camp. It's the opportunity I've been waiting for, Annaliese. It's an SS appointment, and I've been promoted.'

'Congratulations,' she said, throwing her arms around his neck. 'But what about your patients?'

'I'll have to pass them on to another doctor, although I could perhaps continue to see a few of them in the evenings.'

'It seems such a shame that you might have to give up your practice, after all your hard work.'

'Oh, I don't mind. We have a duty to think of what we can do for the Party now, and for the country. You must see how things are going.'

Annaliese shivered slightly, as if something had cast a shadow over her husband's elation, but she saw the excitement in his eyes and heard the joy in his voice, so pushed any negative thoughts to one side. 'Of course, I understand.'

'Besides,' Hans went on, 'I'm hopeful that this work will eventually bring great rewards – perhaps even an important academic post.'

She smiled supportively. 'Well, that does sound exciting. Will they give you animals at the camp for your experiments?'

He looked at her with his pale grey eyes and smiled. 'Something like that... you don't need to know the details.'

'Why?' she asked. 'Is it cruel?'

His thoughts turned to Schiller's experiments on mental patients in Italy and how uncomfortable it had made him feel. But he brushed them aside.

'Don't be silly,' he said dismissively. 'It's medical research, Annaliese – how can it possibly be cruel?'

5

Hans woke just after dawn. It was his first day at Dachau and he was filled with a combination of excitement and agitation. Shaving, he cut himself, and Annaliese woke to find him searching for a plaster in her bedside drawer.

'What's the matter?' she asked sleepily.

'I've cut myself.' Blood dripped onto the white sheet.

'Here,' she said, climbing out of bed. Tearing off a small corner of the newspaper that was lying on the bedside table, she applied it to the cut. 'It will stop bleeding in a few moments.'

He pulled on his new black SS jacket. The stiff collar chafed his neck and his hands trembled as he tried to fasten the silver buttons.

'Let me help you, darling.' The buttons in place, Annaliese stroked his cheek and removed the scrap of paper. 'There, it's all better.'

'It's ridiculous,' said Hans. 'I feel sick to my stomach – just like I did when I was sent away to school.'

'You're bound to be nervous, but this is what you've been

waiting for – the chance to show the authorities what you can do.'

He smiled and kissed her cheek. 'You're right of course... you're so good to me.' He patted his pockets, and smoothed his hair. 'I'd better go.'

'But you've not had breakfast yet... Marta will have it all laid out in the dining room.'

'I don't have time. I have a staff car now. The driver will be waiting for me.'

'Well, have some coffee at least. And I'll get Marta to make your favourite supper.' She kissed him one more time before he ran down the stairs, past the dining room and out of the house, slamming the door behind him.

∼

Converted from an old armaments factory, the labour camp was approached along a narrow road that wove its way through mixed woodland alongside a railway line. On that day in early September, with the sun glinting through the trees, Hans felt he might have been on a pleasant country excursion.

Emerging from the woodland into a clearing, he had his first glimpse of the camp entrance – a white stone gatehouse built in traditional Bavarian style, with a high-pitched, slate-tiled roof, like a romantic castle. As the car approached, a soldier stepped out smartly from beneath a covered veranda into the sunlight, holding a clipboard.

'Sturmbannführer Vogel,' announced the driver, winding down his car window.

The officer checked his clipboard, peered at Hans in the back of the car, and saluted, 'Heil Hitler!' He opened the black iron gates, emblazoned with the words 'Arbeit Macht Frei' – 'Work Sets You Free', and Hans was driven into a large central exercise yard, surrounded on all four sides by long, low buildings.

The car turned down a side road, passing groups of men – prisoners, Hans assumed, judging by their identical beige-coloured jackets – building a new row of huts. They were sawing wood, winching up heavy joists, and installing corrugated iron roofs. It all seemed well ordered and productive. Hans hoped these men found a sense of purpose through their work, and perhaps were even acquiring useful skills for a time when they might be repatriated into society.

The car soon came to a halt outside a building marked 'Administration'. The driver opened Hans' door. 'Obergruppen-führer Eicke, the camp commandant, is waiting for you inside, Sturmbannführer.'

'Thank you,' said Hans.

The camp commandant stood up when Hans was shown into his office. Squat and portly, he held out a pudgy hand. 'Welcome, Dr Vogel.'

'Thank you, sir. Good morning,' Hans replied.

'My name is Theodor Eicke,' said the commandant. His mouth, Hans noticed, was set in a thin, hard line. 'Would you like some coffee?'

'Yes, please,' replied Hans gratefully.

'Good, I always have one around this time. Afterwards, I thought you'd appreciate a little tour.' Eicke sounded almost excited.

'Thank you, Commandant. That would be very useful.'

An orderly brought in a jug of coffee and a plate of pastries, which Eicke ate greedily. Afterwards, the commandant led Hans outside. He adjusted his hat, pulling the peak down over his eyes so that it formed a straight line with his Roman nose, and rubbed his hands with anticipation. 'Right, shall we get started?'

Hans was taken first to the inmates' quarters. Here, wooden

bunk beds were assembled three rows high, each one cheek by jowl with the other.

'How many people sleep in this barracks?' Hans asked.

'About two hundred in all,' Eicke replied.

From there they inspected the workshops and the disinfection barracks. 'The prisoners are full of infestations when they arrive,' Eicke explained.

The neighbouring hut was lined with beds. Men lay on filthy sheets and one or two prisoners shuffled between them, offering mugs of water.

'The barracks hospital,' Eicke announced. 'And you'll be relieved to hear that your services won't be required here... we leave that to the prisoners with some medical qualifications.'

Hans wanted to ask if these 'medically qualified' prisoners had any medicines at all, but he decided to hold back. It seemed wiser not to irritate the commandant on his first day.

Finally, they arrived at the parade ground where a group of about twenty-five men wearing civilian clothes were standing in line.

'Ah, good,' said Eicke, smiling. 'New arrivals. I thought this might interest you. It's our usual introductory procedure – shows them who's boss.'

Hans studied the men. Mostly dark-haired and wearing shabby clothes, they looked terrified. An SS officer was prowling around in front of them, waving a short-handled oxtail whip – its leather 'tails' flicking menacingly. One by one, the men were stripped of their upper clothing, forced to bend over a long table, and beaten.

'Twenty-five lashes per man, to start with,' Eicke explained proudly.

One young man, waiting in line, was sobbing, begging for reprieve. 'Please don't, I couldn't bear it.'

The officer grabbed him, slammed him down on the table and proceeded to thrash him, shouting, 'Fifty for you!'

Hans had never seen a man beaten so brutally before. He had received beatings himself as a child – from his father and teachers at school – but this was something different. The soldier clearly enjoyed inflicting the punishment.

Hans was literally sickened. He felt himself retch, as the pastry he had eaten ten minutes earlier began to repeat on him. His mouth filled with saliva, and aware he was about to vomit, he covered his mouth with his hand and swallowed hard. 'Is this absolutely necessary?' he asked Eicke, as the bile in his throat finally subsided.

'Oh, yes,' Eicke replied firmly. 'It's all about discipline, you see.' He turned towards Hans, and noticed his grey pallor and watering eyes. 'Are you all right?' he asked.

'Yes,' said Hans, wiping his mouth and face with a handkerchief. 'Something I ate, perhaps.'

'Mmm...' Eicke turned back to the beating. 'I've been here since the start – back in thirty-three – and I'm proud to say that Dachau is being hailed as a model labour camp. It is the first of its kind, you know?' He looked back at Hans, clearly hoping for some kind of approbation. 'Himmler is delighted with it.'

'I'm sure he is,' said Hans quietly. 'It certainly looks very... disciplined.' He discreetly turned his head away and closed his eyes, but there was no escaping the young man's screams echoing around the parade ground.

Eicke patted his shoulder. 'Right... time to go to the medical research block. I think you'll be impressed. Follow me...'

'You need to understand,' said Eicke, as they walked down the long alleyway that led to the medical block, 'that the prisoners here are all enemies of the State. They represent a threat to the German way of life, and as such are here to be punished. Many are murderers and thieves, others are "asocials" – like the Sinti and Roma in that group you saw just now, for example. So you shouldn't waste your sympathy on them.'

'I understand,' replied Hans, not very convincingly. He was not clear he knew what an 'asocial' was.

'And as for experimentation – I trust you have no scruples about using the prisoners for that?'

'Oh, no,' said Hans, recovering his composure slightly, as the sound of screaming faded into the distance. 'After all, it's common practice to use prisoners for what are called "challenge trials". The Americans, for example, do it all the time. There are moral issues, of course, but we have to think of the greater good.' It occurred to him that he was possibly convincing himself rather than the commandant.

'Quite so,' said Eicke. 'Right, here we are.'

He pushed through a pale green door into a small outer office. 'This is the office where your assistant will work. The choice of the individual is yours, but we have several scientists here among the prisoners who would be delighted to get the job.' He led the way to a larger room, empty except for low benches around the walls. 'This is the waiting room, where subjects will wait to receive experimental treatments. And through here is the laboratory.'

Eicke pushed open another door revealing a small room with a workbench and some shelving. 'Your laboratory,' he announced. 'You must order what you want in terms of equipment – test tubes, microscopes, that sort of thing.'

Finally, the commandant arrived at a freshly painted door, which he opened with a flourish. 'Your own private office, Sturmbannführer – I hope it provides inspiration.'

Hans stepped inside. The room was empty, save for a desk and a chair. A large picture window overlooked the countryside surrounding the camp. Much to his relief, all Hans could see for miles around were trees.

'Thank you, sir. I think it will do very well.'

. . .

When Eicke had left, Hans sank down in his new chair, still shaken by what he had witnessed. The brutality shown to the men in the parade ground had frightened and disgusted him. He hoped he had not made a terrible mistake. But there was no going back now.

His heart still racing, he removed his SS jacket and hung it on a hook by the door. Opening his doctor's bag, he took out his white coat and stethoscope. As he put the coat on, hanging the stethoscope around his neck, his heartbeat slowed, his breathing regulated. He felt himself again – not a soldier working for an authoritarian regime, but a doctor embarking on important work for the sake of humanity.

He sat at his new desk and wrote out a list of equipment he would need for the laboratory. When he'd finished, he got up and looked out of window, once again admiring the countryside. With luck he would be able to distance himself from some of the crueller practices of the camp, and concentrate on his work. Perhaps he might even be able to introduce a less brutal regime in the medical research block.

It was then that he noticed, on the edge of his vision, a watchtower. At the top was a soldier pacing the four sides of the tower, a gun slung over his shoulder. This was unlike any laboratory Hans had ever been in before, and for the first time he began to doubt whether it would really be possible to help humanity in such a brutal place.

PART TWO
THE WAR YEARS

1942–1945

6

SEPTEMBER 1942

In the late-summer sunshine, Annaliese hurried across Max-Josef-Platz, an elegant square in the heart of Munich. It was dominated on one side by the neo-classical opera house, and on the other by the Residenz – an impressive single-storey palace built for the Bavarian kings. This square, and indeed the whole of Munich, had remained unscathed since the start of the war. Deep in southern Germany, the Bavarian capital was thought to be beyond the reach of Allied bombers. The citizens clung to the idea that the birthplace of National Socialism would remain untouched until the day Hitler and the German people were finally victorious.

Annaliese had arranged to meet her mother-in-law for coffee at the popular Café Opera, which stood opposite the opera house, on the other side of the square. Checking her watch anxiously, she realised that she was fifteen minutes late. She and Hans had had an argument that morning which had thrown her whole morning into disarray. Ironically, the disagreement had arisen over whether to invite Elisabetta for lunch that coming Sunday.

'The last thing I need on my one day off,' Hans had snapped, 'is lunch with my mother.'

'Oh, Hans! I do wish you'd reconsider. Your mother's not exactly my favourite person either, but we've not seen her for months, and I gather she has her sister, Charlotte, arriving to stay with her in a couple of days. We could invite them both over. We haven't seen Charlotte for years – since before the war started, in fact – and you've always had a soft spot for your aunt, haven't you?'

'Oh, all right. Do as you wish.' Hans left the house, banging the door behind him, leaving Annaliese confused and upset.

The truth was that after a few brief months of happiness at the start of their marriage, Hans had changed radically. In the seven years since he had taken the job at Dachau, he had turned from a jovial, sweet-natured man into someone who was permanently in a bad mood, who worked six days a week, and was rarely home before eight in the evening. Then, he was usually tired and short-tempered. He drank a lot, and silently ate the supper prepared by their maid. At night he slept fitfully, and on the rare occasions he made love to his wife, it was wordless and without affection. She had ceased to find any pleasure in it, and now merely endured the experience.

As Annaliese prepared for her meeting with Elisabetta that morning, she suddenly remembered she had promised to sort out some clothes for the Winter Help Fund – a government initiative run by the Party to collect old clothes and repurpose them for German troops fighting on the Russian front. She threw a couple of Hans' old suits onto the bed for Marta to bundle up later, and ran downstairs and out of the house, pulling on her linen summer coat as she raced down the road.

. . .

Elisabetta was waiting for her in one corner of the restaurant, dressed in a haze of lilac – a fitted suit made of lavender wool crêpe, and a matching felt hat, which blended with her grey hair. Even the hat, Annaliese noted, was decorated with little sprigs of lavender. Made of silk, they trembled when she moved her head. Only her black shoes and snakeskin handbag had escaped Elisabetta's ruthless colour coordination.

'Ah, here you are at last,' Elisabetta said impatiently, as Annaliese joined her at the table.

Removing her brown gloves, Annaliese pushed her blond hair away from her face, and felt beads of perspiration trickling down her left temple. Flushing with embarrassment, she took a handkerchief from her pocket and dabbed at her forehead. 'I'm so sorry I'm late. I had to prepare a parcel of clothing for the Winter Help Fund, and I completely lost track of time. When I realised how late I was, I practically ran all the way here...'

Elisabetta flicked her hand, as if swatting away a fly. 'Never mind. I've already ordered.'

The coffee and cakes arrived almost immediately. Elisabetta had a fondness for sweet things, and when the towering cake-stand was set before them, her eyes gleamed greedily. In spite of the wartime rationing, people with sufficient money or influence could always obtain luxurious food.

Ever polite, Annaliese let the older woman choose first, and waited as Elisabetta slid a slice of Prinzregententorte onto her plate. A Bavarian speciality, it consisted of seven thin layers of sponge cake interwoven with butter icing. By contrast, Annaliese chose the smallest offering on the cake-stand – a dainty triangle of wild strawberry tart.

Elisabetta ate her cake with determination, briskly pushing her plate to one side when it was empty. 'So... what are you donating to the Winter Fund?'

'Oh, just a couple of Hans' old suits and a coat of mine that I never wear.'

'I'm glad to hear it. We owe those boys on the Eastern Front our support. It's terrible to think of them suffering out there in the freezing wastes of Russia. I donated the last of my late husband's winter clothes just a few days ago.' She dabbed at her eyes with a silk handkerchief.

'I'm so sorry,' said Annaliese, 'you must miss him terribly.' She reached across the table to pat her mother-in-law's hand, but Elisabetta pulled it away irritably, and helped herself to a large piece of chocolate cake.

'Which reminds me – it's been far too long since Hans visited his father's tomb with me.' Elisabetta plunged her fork into the cake, ensuring it speared not just the dark chocolate sponge but also the cream and thick, sticky cherry jam sandwiched between its layers.

'He's so busy these days, I hardly ever see him myself,' Annaliese explained apologetically, before adding: 'But Hans asked me to tell you that we'd be honoured if you and Aunt Charlotte could come for lunch this Sunday. He knows it's been too long since we saw you both.'

'Lunch? I suppose we could come, yes,' replied Elisabetta petulantly, cramming the final forkful of the chocolate-cherry concoction into her rouged mouth. 'I'm sure Charlotte would appreciate it... I know she finds me dull company. I don't really know why she's coming to stay with me at all.' She glanced down at her daughter-in-law's plate, where the strawberry tart lay virtually untouched. 'Aren't you eating?'

'I've had enough, thank you – the tart was delicious. I'm just not very hungry.'

'You're not pregnant, are you?' asked Elisabetta.

'No. At least, I don't think so,' replied Annaliese, taken aback by the question.

The absence of a child was a constant source of friction between the two women. Annaliese had the impression that her mother-in-law thought her inability to get pregnant was done specifically to irritate her.

'Well, if you don't get on with it, it will be too late,' Elisabetta said acidly. 'You're not getting any younger.'

Annaliese, who was still in her late-twenties, was tempted to answer back, but she said nothing, merely smiling agreeably.

The waitress brought the bill and laid it on the table in a saucer.

'Well, I'd better be going.' Elisabetta put a few Reichsmarks in the saucer and stood up. 'I have people coming for tea later and there's a lot to be done.'

Annaliese followed her out to the front of the shop, where Elisabetta paused in front of a glass case filled with elaborate cakes.

'I need something for my guests,' she said, studying the display. 'I'll take that one there.' She pointed to a chocolate cake, decorated with little coils of cream. 'And make sure you wrap it properly... I don't want it to get damaged on the way home.'

Annaliese marvelled at her mother-in-law's ability to consume cake, noticing she was getting sturdier by the day – the lilac suit was straining over her ample hips.

'Well, I hope you have a lovely afternoon,' said Annaliese, kissing Elisabetta's powdered cheek. 'And we'll see you for lunch on Sunday... about one o'clock?'

Walking back home, Annaliese felt a familiar sense of pride as her elegant house came into view. The maple trees that lined the street were taking on their autumn colours of gold and vermilion. They contrasted spectacularly with the elegant grey house. It still seemed hard to believe that she lived in such an imposing property.

She slipped her key into the lock of the front door and let herself in. Sunlight flooded through the stained-glass fanlight, casting bright colours across the black and white floor tiles of the entrance hall.

Hanging her coat on the rack by the front door, Annaliese could hear her maid Marta singing downstairs in the kitchen. She followed the sound down the set of steep stone steps into the semi-basement, and found Marta on her knees, blacking the range.

'Hello, Marta, were there any messages?'

'No, madam,' said Marta, leaping to her feet. 'Is there anything I can do for you?'

'Did you find the clothes I left out for the Winter Help Fund this morning?'

'Yes... I've wrapped them up – they're in the hall waiting to be collected.'

'Good,' replied Annaliese. 'You carry on. I'm just going upstairs for a rest.'

Her bedroom ran the width of the house and overlooked the back garden. She threw her hat and summer coat onto the chaise longue and stood in the bay window surveying the view. It was a depressing sight. When she and Hans had first moved in, they had completely redesigned the garden. Lawns had been laid, box-edged flowerbeds planted, and a row of espaliered fruit trees established to divide the flower garden from the vegetable plot. But after their gardener had joined the army at the start of the war, they had been unable to find a replacement, and the garden was now badly neglected. The box-edged beds, instead of being filled with colourful annuals, were overrun with dandelions and buttercups, and the espaliered fruit trees were overgrown and in need of pruning.

At Hans' suggestion, Annaliese had approached an employment agency for a replacement.

'I'm afraid gardeners are in very short supply,' sighed the agency manager. 'It's the war, you see – it's made hiring domestic staff almost impossible. Women have all been sent to work in the munitions factories, and any able-bodied man is in the military. But I'll keep my eyes open for you.'

Now, as Annaliese surveyed the overgrown shambles of her garden, she realised it would provide Elisabetta with another reason to find fault with her.

She lay down on the silken eiderdown, reflecting on her encounter with Elisabetta. As usual, she had come away feeling both inadequate and dissatisfied. Her mother-in-law's constant carping was part of it, but the real problem – as she had correctly identified – was Annaliese's inability to have children. She and Hans had now been married for eight years; they still made love – however unsatisfactorily – so why was she not pregnant? With no mother of her own to confide in, nor any close friend who might understand, she was reduced to borrowing books from the library about infertility; these made it clear that an inability to have children was almost always the woman's fault. This saddened her, because she truly yearned to have a child. It would make sense of her life and give her a focus – Elisabetta was right about that.

And yet the one person she could never discuss it with was Hans. His short temper was part of it – that, and his constant preoccupation with work. She felt somehow that her lack of children was her problem alone, rather than something they could share.

But her mother-in-law's comments that morning had given Annaliese the resolve she needed to broach the subject with her husband. He was a doctor, after all, and she hoped, given the right setting, he would be able to apply his calm, rational mind to the issue of her infertility.

Coming downstairs that afternoon, she began to plan a romantic dinner, hoping it would encourage Hans to talk. She set the table with candles and a few flowers salvaged from the overgrown garden. As soon as Hans returned from work that evening, she poured him a drink. 'Let's eat together tonight. We so rarely get a chance to talk.'

Hans, ashen-faced and clearly tired, carried his drink through to the dining room. Marta laid a bowl of parsnip soup in front of him and Annaliese poured him a glass of wine. But to her frustration, he ignored her, opening a newspaper at the table and reading it throughout dinner. She decided to postpone their discussion about children until they were in the sitting room with their coffee.

The evening was chilly and Marta had lit the fire. Hans sat reading an academic paper by the light of a lamp, a glass of schnapps at his side.

'The garden is looking pretty terrible,' Annaliese began, handing him his coffee. 'I asked at an agency again yesterday for a gardener, but they are like gold-dust, apparently.'

'Oh, yes?' said Hans distractedly.

'Darling...' she began. 'I had coffee with your mother today – she's so looking forward to lunch on Sunday, by the way.'

He smiled weakly. 'Oh... good.'

She cleared her throat. 'Your mother brought up a subject that I know we both struggle with... our lack of children.' She studied his face, checking his reaction.

He slapped the paper violently down on the table. 'What's it got to do with her?'

'Well, I know... it's a bit intrusive. But she's right – why can't I get pregnant? It makes no sense. I'm well, I'm fit, I eat properly. You're a doctor... surely you must have some ideas?'

He folded his hands in his lap, with a sigh. 'I didn't realise having a child was so important to you.'

'We always said we'd have children one day,' she reminded him. 'Five or six, you said.' She smiled. 'I'd be happy with one.'

'If it's meant to be, it will happen,' he reassured her. 'It's important not to worry too much about these things. There's a lot of evidence that worry in itself can stop a woman getting pregnant.'

'But Hans – eight years...'

'Look,' he said, 'there is a war on, you know. I wonder sometimes – is this really the right time for a child?'

'So, have you changed your mind?' she asked sadly.

'No,' he replied. 'But when we discussed the subject before, it was a different time. We were young and optimistic then.'

'We're still young,' she retaliated. 'And have you really lost all your optimism?'

He looked across at her with sad grey eyes, as if haunted by something. 'Perhaps, a little.'

'Your work is going well, isn't it?' she persisted.

He stood up and headed for the door, taking the academic paper with him. 'It's a challenge, certainly.'

She held out her hand to him as he walked past. 'Talk to me, Hans. I can see you're not happy. Tell me, what is the problem?'

He smiled down at her. 'There is no problem. Of course we can try to have a child, if that's what you want. Perhaps we should be a bit more scientific about it and try to make love on the right days. You'll need to make a note of your menstrual cycle – can you do that?'

'Yes, of course,' she replied happily. 'I'll start doing it straight away.'

He leant down and kissed her cheek, stroking her hair. 'You're such a good girl – always so kind and supportive.'

After he had gone to his study, she was left with a sense that he was merely indulging her. Something was wrong, she was sure of it, and his refusal to discuss it was driving a wedge between them. It saddened and infuriated her, but what could she do about it? She turned off the lights and went silently to bed.

. . .

Alone in his study, Hans switched on the desk light, and poured himself a large schnapps. He sat at his desk, brooding on his conversation with Annaliese. She was right, of course. He wasn't happy – far from it. But how could he tell her what troubled him? If Annaliese knew about the conditions at Dachau, and the cruelty meted out to the prisoners, she would be horrified, and demand that he give up the job. But the truth was he was trapped. He could never leave his job, because if he spoke out, he would be sent to prison himself – or worse.

Perhaps that was why he struggled with the idea of having a family; why he no longer felt any enthusiasm for it. Children represented hope for the future. He had no hope left. Before the war – when he had first met Annaliese – he thought he had found the perfect mother for his future family. He was filled with optimism then. But the war, and the authoritarian control of his government, had put an end to that. Who in his right mind would bring children into the world Hitler's Party had created. The irony was that SS officers, like him, were duty-bound to father children. Four was considered the magic number – sufficient to replace the couple, plus increase the numbers of good Aryan stock. If the marriage was childless, the prevailing ideology always blamed the woman – refusing to believe an Aryan male might be unable to father children. But as a doctor, Hans knew that the fault could lie with either of them. At university, he had studied animals' sperm under the microscope, and had observed how some samples were of poor quality. Infertility treatment was in its infancy, but gradually theories were being developed. Originally, the size of the sperm's head was thought to be key – the bigger the better. But newer research had concluded that it was the quantity of healthy sperm that was important – too few meant less chance of fertilisation.

As a scientist, Hans knew that he had to confront his own marriage's childlessness head on – by studying his own sperm under the microscope. But shame and fear held him back. If he discovered he was incapable of fathering children, he and Annaliese would have some difficult choices to make. Perhaps to adopt one of the children from the Lebensborn programme? This SS initiative had been set up with the purpose of increasing the pool of Aryan children, and to prevent the abortion of otherwise suitable Aryan citizens. Young unmarried women, who found themselves pregnant, were offered a secure place in a rural 'Lebensborn' nursing home, where they were well cared for, and could deliver their child away from the prying eyes of family and friends. In return for their care, their child could be offered up for adoption. But only women who could prove they were racially pure were eligible to apply to the programme.

Hans had also heard stories of young women from the Hitler Youth being encouraged to have children fathered by high-ranking SS officers. The stigma of illegitimacy had now been so expunged from German society, that these young women were convinced that to produce an 'SS' child was the most valuable thing they could do – for both the Führer and the Fatherland. But Hans knew he would be incapable of such a thing – of effectively raping a young girl in order to father a child. No, he could not imagine himself doing anything so bestial.

The only alternative, equally intolerable, was for Annaliese to get pregnant by someone else, but the National Socialist Party would never condone such a thing. An SS wife must be pure at all times. Besides, Hans recoiled at the thought of Annaliese with another man.

He drained his glass, and realised there was no easy solution to their childlessness. Depressed, and slightly drunk, he switched off the light on his desk, and went upstairs to bed where he lay, wide awake, gazing at his beautiful wife as she slept.

7

Hans woke in darkness; he tossed and turned, before finally giving in to wakefulness. His head throbbed and his mouth was dry. Recalling the bottle of schnapps he had drunk alone in his study the previous evening, he picked up the jug of water on his bedside table, and gulped it down. Anxious not to disturb Annaliese, he got up as silently as he could, and quietly dressed for work in the bathroom. Downstairs, alone at the table in the dining room, he drank a cup of coffee, but couldn't face food. He pushed away the plate of bread and sliced meat Marta had left out for him. A knock on the door outside alerted him that his driver had arrived to collect him. Carrying his medical bag, he closed the front door behind him and settled himself in the back seat of the car.

Bitter experience had taught Hans that it was better to arrive at the camp when the morning roll call, with its routine public beatings, was over. At work he saw little of camp life, remaining in the medical block buried in his research. He even took his lunch most days at his desk, looking out of the window on to the green fields and woods that surrounded the camp. In this way, he almost managed to convince himself that he was much like any other academic, working on important medical research that would one day save many lives.

He spent the short journey studying research papers for the malaria experiment he was due to perform that morning. But as his staff Mercedes drove through the gates of Dachau, Hans could see that the early-morning roll call was still taking place. His heart sank.

'I'm sorry, Sturmbannführer,' said the driver, coming to a halt, 'we'll have to wait.'

On the central parade ground, several hundred inmates were lined up in rows, dressed in their striped uniforms. It seemed to Hans that every day the group got larger, but the prisoners got thinner. As usual, the guards were prolonging the roll call, forcing the men to stand far longer than was necessary. Hans guiltily averted his eyes from the rows of men, and tried to concentrate on his papers, but he was disturbed by angry shouts. Looking up, he watched with horror as a guard viciously kicked a prisoner who had collapsed onto the ground.

'Get up, get up now!' the guard screamed. Hans felt his stomach heave. The wanton cruelty in the camp was becoming ever more extreme. He closed his eyes and prayed the man's suffering would be over quickly.

The roll call eventually came to an end, allowing Hans' car to drive down the alley leading to the medical block. As he climbed out of the car, he was assailed by the stench of burning corpses. Earlier that year, a new block of huts known as Barrack X had been built. Naively, Hans had assumed it was simply further accommodation. But he quickly discovered its true purpose. Barrack X contained four vast ovens, which were used to incinerate the corpses of those who had been executed, or died from disease or starvation.

Hans removed a handkerchief from his pocket and covered

his mouth and nose. Hurrying into the medical block, he felt a combination of horror and shame. This was not what he had signed up for. He had thought he would be allowed to do some good for mankind. But in fact he was just part of a brutal killing machine.

When the camp had first opened, back in the early 1930s, the inmates had been predominantly criminals – murderers and burglars. Hans felt their imprisonment could be justified, even if the punishments meted out were harsh.

But in 1938, after the night of terror known as Kristallnacht – when Jewish businesses were targeted by marauding hordes of National Socialist thugs – there had been a large influx of Jewish prisoners. More than ten thousand men, women and children had poured into the camp. Hans had found the presence of the women and children especially troubling, and had resisted pressure from above to use them as experimental subjects. He was appalled at the idea of inflicting suffering on a child, but kept these sensitivities to himself – instead only using healthy young men in medical trials, according to standard international procedure.

'It would give us misleading results,' he argued to Eicke, the camp commandant. 'The way a child or a woman might react to a drug or procedure can never be the same as the reaction of a healthy man, and that surely is the point of our experiments – to find cures and treatments for our troops, who by definition are all healthy young men.'

Eicke had reluctantly demurred to Hans' professional expertise, but Hans could tell the man was frustrated. He suspected the commandant saw medical experiments as merely another form of torture, while Hans still clung to the idea that his work was for the greater good of mankind.

After a few months, and much to Hans' relief, many of the

Jewish families had been released, on condition they left Germany. Those that were unable to emigrate were moved on to other camps, where Hans hoped their conditions would be less harsh. But standing in the queue for lunch one day, he learned the truth.

'If you think this place is tough,' a fellow officer told him, 'believe me, it has nothing on places like Buchenwald. And don't get me started on Auschwitz. God, that place is brutal. My cousin works there, and basically it's a death camp. Anyone frail or infirm is gassed – women, children, the lot. They dispose of the bodies in ovens. It's all part of the Führer's "Final Solution".'

Feeling faint, Hans mumbled an apology, abandoned his food on the tray and returned to his laboratory. What he had heard was so shocking he could scarcely comprehend it. He'd had Jewish friends at university – clever young men most of them, whom he had admired. The thought that these men and their families could be so wantonly destroyed shook what was left of his faith in the regime to the core. But what could he do? How could one man stand up against the huge Party apparatus?

As soon as the Jews were shipped out of Dachau, their place was taken by thousands of people the authorities considered 'Enemies of the State'. Dachau was no longer a prison in the formal sense of the word – for criminals and reprobates – but a place of severe punishment for anyone the National Socialist regime deemed 'unacceptable'. The camp had originally been designed for six thousand inmates, but that number had quickly risen to over thirty thousand, and the overcrowding inevitably led to disease and death.

The new prisoners were subdivided into different groups, identified by coloured symbols sewn onto their clothes. Hans quickly learned to recognise them, as they all passed through the medical experimentation block at some time or other. The remaining Jews were marked out with a yellow star, but all other categories of prisoner were identified by different coloured triangles. Green triangles were for criminals. Often drawn from violent gangs, they were also open to bribes. In return for more lenient treatment and extra rations, certain offenders were picked out by the SS guards and tasked with keeping the others in check. These men became known as 'capos' and were infamous for the brutality they meted out to their fellow inmates. Sometimes, it seemed to Hans, they were capable of even more gratuitous cruelty than their German masters.

Black triangles indicated the 'asocials' – people the regime considered outside 'normal' society. These included Romanies and Gypsies, mental defectives, alcoholics, drug addicts and beggars. To this group were added prostitutes, lesbians and, for a reason Hans could never quite understand, pacifists. Purple was for Jehovah's Witnesses and other religious sects. Red was for political prisoners – liberals, socialists, communists, anarchists, Gentiles who helped Jews, and Freemasons.

Finally, blue marked out the foreign forced labourers – able-bodied dissidents imported from countries that had been invaded by Germany who were unwilling to collaborate. These included Austrians, brought there after the Anschluss in 1938, but also Spaniards, Italians, Dutch, the Free French and, increasingly, Poles and Russians, who were actively fighting the Germans on the Eastern Front. In all, the camp contained prisoners from over thirty countries.

Brought to Dachau in their thousands, they were forced to become unpaid labour – in effect, slaves – initially being put to work mending roads and working in stone quarries. But the SS soon realised the commercial value of these foreign labourers, and hired them out to German industry. In the Munich area alone over sixty-five thousand prisoners were housed in eighty-five satellite camps around the city – reservoirs of forced labour to support Hitler's Third Reich.

From time to time, Hans was asked to examine these

workers to establish if they were infected with either TB or other infectious diseases. He was due to perform one such examination later that afternoon, but first he had the malaria experiment to perform.

The parade finally broke up and Hans was driven away from the parade ground and into one of the side alleys, coming to a halt outside the medical research wing.

'Thank you, driver,' said Hans, gathering up his notes. He climbed out of the car, and walked briskly into the building, relieved to have finally arrived at the relative sanctuary of the research block. Although it had expanded considerably, with several doctors now conducting their own research into a wide variety of conditions, Hans' office and laboratory were quite unchanged.

He found four patients – he preferred to think of them as patients – in the waiting room, guarded by an armed soldier, as usual. He often wondered why. The chances of any of the subjects escaping his laboratory seemed most unlikely, Hans thought, as they were severely malnourished, almost too weak to walk. They were not, in all honesty, appropriate subjects for a proper medical trial. He knew that to establish the efficacy of a treatment, the only suitable subjects were healthy young men. These men looked almost on the point of death.

He went into his office, closed the door and hung up his grey-green war-issue SS jacket on a hanger. He slipped into his white coat and was aware of his heart rate slowing, of his nerves settling. As a doctor, his life had meaning, his work had value – he had to believe that – otherwise the suffering he was forced to inflict would have been unjustifiable.

He walked out into the waiting room and clicked his fingers at the youngest of the four prisoners. 'You... come with me.'

The young man stood up, glancing down apprehensively at

his fellow inmates. He was tall and gangly, possibly just a teenager, although it was hard to tell someone's age once they'd been at Dachau for a while – emaciation had an extraordinary ability to age people, Hans had observed. Looking at him more closely, Hans noted his neat features, and almost translucent skin. He had no beard – just a fuzz of fair hair on his chin, but the hair on his head was dark, the stubble sprouting thickly from his pale skull. He wore a pink triangle on his uniform, indicating he was a homosexual. Hans feared that even if the lad survived the actual experiment, he was unlikely to last much longer in the camp. The guards despised boys like him.

He led the young man into the laboratory, where his assistant Eugène was waiting. Eugène was a Luxembourger who had been captured while fighting with the French army in 1941. He had been a laboratory technician before the war, and had been singled out by Hans from the ranks of foreign labourers.

He stood up when Hans entered with the boy.

'Good morning, Eugène. Do you have the cage?' Hans asked.

'Yes, Sturmbannführer.'

'Well, get it then.'

Eugène reached up to the shelf running above the workbench and delicately took hold of a small rectangular frame, not much bigger than a box of household matches, covered with fine netting. Buzzing around inside was an angry mosquito.

The prisoner looked alarmed. 'What's that?' he asked in a small, frightened voice. He began to back away towards the door, but Hans tried to reassure him. 'Don't be frightened. Just roll up your sleeve – it won't hurt.'

The boy did as he was told, but was shaking with fear.

'Hold his arm steady, Eugène.' Although inwardly Hans felt uneasy, he went ahead. He strapped the box to the struggling boy's forearm, flipping open a small hatch on the base at the last minute, and releasing the malaria-carrying mosquito. As the mosquito settled, it pierced the boy's skin, producing a tiny pinprick of blood.

'What are you doing?' the boy asked, his eyes wide with terror.

'We are going to test a new treatment for malaria,' Hans explained calmly. 'If it works, you will be fine.'

The boy was taken to the next the room to wait.

By mid-morning, all four prisoners had been exposed to the mosquito bites. It would take Hans a few days to assess their illness and then his proper research could begin – testing a cure for their disease. He was not feeling optimistic, as his experiments had not been going particularly well. And to add to his frustration, Himmler had recently brought Claus Schilling back from Italy to oversee the malaria project – an appointment made behind Hans' back. Schilling had simply arrived one day, demanding to see the results of Hans' latest experiments. It was both irritating and humiliating.

'He's not even a member of the SS,' Hans complained to Annaliese over dinner, 'and yet he's been promoted over me.'

Angered at his apparent demotion, and determined to prove himself the better researcher, Hans decided to begin work on a new project – testing various so-called hallucinogenic drugs as aids to interrogation. The topic had first come to his attention a few years before, when he read about a Swiss chemist named Albert Hofmann, who had discovered that a compound called lysergic acid diethylamide, known as LSD, produced interesting 'mystical', mind-altering effects. Intrigued, Hans had done some further research, and found a report written by an American obstetrician who had used a substance called Scopolamine to ease women's pain in childbirth, and found it produced unusual effects on the mind – making the women 'exceedingly candid'.

A local police chief heard about the experiment and decided to test it on prisoners in his gaol to check if they were telling the truth. The confessions it elicited were 'remarkably accurate'.

Sensing an opportunity, Hans began to research other hallucinogens – in particular mescaline, a naturally occurring substance derived from cactus plants. It had been used by native North and South American Indian tribes for thousands of years, but had also found a recent following among European and American intellectuals.

Hans thought this area could be even more important than his malaria research – not just for the Third Reich, but also for the sake of future prisoners all over the world, as it would surely be a kinder, more humane way to extract information than using torture. Hans hoped that if he could get some initial good results, he could secure Himmler's backing for a fully-fledged research project.

But today Hans had a dull job to do: medical examinations of around a hundred slaves at one of the local armaments factories. Before they were employed, the factory owner had insisted they were checked for infectious diseases.

Hans packed up his doctor's bag, locked up his office, climbed into the back of the car and closed his eyes. After a bad night, he was exhausted. It was hardly surprising he slept so badly these days. He drank heavily each evening to blot out what he had seen during the day, and usually fell into a deep dreamless sleep, before waking at two or three in the morning, his mind overwhelmed with images of suffering and death. His work at Dachau had been a huge disappointment. He had hoped for so much – research success, academic achievement, the chance to help humanity – but the reality was vastly different. Now he had been dragged into a world where he was forced to perform experiments on people who were barely alive.

.   .   .

'Sturmbannführer, sir – we're here.' Hans looked up as the car swept through the gates of the armaments factory.

'Thank you,' said Hans. 'Wait for me here. I'll be a couple of hours.'

Walking into the factory's entrance hall, Hans was directed to the First Aid room. Waiting in the corridor outside, under the watchful eye of a prison guard, was a queue of about fifty men wearing the tell-tale striped uniforms of the concentration camp labour force.

To his surprise, Hans found the factory owner waiting for him. 'Good afternoon,' said Hans, hanging up his jacket and putting on his white coat. 'There's no need for you to be here, really – it's just a basic medical. We'll identify anyone with serious problems and return them to Dachau.'

'No, I'll stay and watch,' said the factory owner darkly. 'I don't want to find I've been sold dud goods.'

'Most of the workers will be fine,' replied Hans reassuringly. 'Some may be infected with tuberculosis, but you need to understand that TB is virtually endemic in the general working population anyway, and most people can carry on working, even if they have it. Typhoid is the one to watch out for. If I find that, I'll remove them from the work detail right away – so there will be no fear of it spreading through your workforce.'

The factory owner appeared satisfied and sat silently while Hans began the examinations. One by one the men entered, wearing just a vest and underpants and carrying their trousers, shirts and boots. A guard announced each one by name, and Hans began his examinations. To his relief they all appeared in moderately good health, albeit painfully thin and often stooped like men twenty years older.

Hans was nearing the end of the session when a tall, fair-haired man stepped smartly into the room.

'Alexander Kosomov,' announced the guard.

'Polish?' Hans asked. He thought the man looked vaguely familiar.

'Russian,' replied Kosomov.

Hans was surprised, as Russians were rarely found among foreign labourers. Intensely patriotic, and fiercely opposed to Germany's fascism, they would rather risk death while trying to escape than capitulate. Only recently, a group of Russians at Dachau had attempted such an escape. Most had been shot as they climbed the barbed wire, but a few had made it into the woods. All had been hunted down and dragged back into the camp, where the commandant had made a great show of their gruesome executions, insisting they were watched by the other inmates.

Clearly this Russian had no such death wish. He was different in other ways too; while most prisoners were cowed and physically weak, this man had strong, muscular arms and stood tall and proud, with an upright bearing. His only physical flaw was a missing big toe on his right foot.

"Put your clothes on the chair please,' Hans asked.

The man obeyed.

As Hans tapped the Russian's chest, and peered down his throat, the man fixed him with a green-eyed stare. There was an air of defiance about him.

Hans put his stethoscope into his ears. 'Turn around, please.'

'Yes, sir – do you want me to breathe in and out deeply?'

Hans was taken aback by the man's almost perfect German. 'Where did you learn to speak our language?'

'My grandparents were German.'

'How so?' asked Hans, listening to the man's breathing with his stethoscope. 'Could you cough, please... louder.'

'They moved to the Baltic States at the turn of the century,' the Russian explained. 'They were landowners... industrialists.

I lived with them as a child. We spoke German most of the time.'

'I see,' said Hans, warming to the man. 'They had land, you say – were they farmers?'

'Oh, yes, they had a big farm, and a beautiful dacha. As I child I helped my grandfather in his garden – it was his pride and joy.' The Russian looked wistful suddenly. 'But then the Revolution happened and life got difficult. My family was fighting on the side of the White Army against the Bolsheviks. All our land was commandeered. I moved away when I was seventeen to go to Moscow University. I've not seen my grand-parents since.'

'What did you study?'

'Architecture – the School of Constructivism.'

The factory owner coughed. 'Are you nearly finished?' he asked Hans irritably.

'Of course. I'm sorry, I won't be much longer.' Hans tapped the Russian's knees, pretending to check for reflexes, eager to continue the conversation. The man fascinated him. 'How did you come to be captured and brought to Germany?'

'I was fighting on the Eastern Front, at Stalingrad.'

That would explain the missing toe, Hans thought. Both Russian and German troops had lost limbs through frostbite. 'You can get dressed now. How long have you been at Dachau?'

'Six months.'

Suddenly, Hans recalled where he'd seen the man before. He was one of a group of Russian prisoners who had been human subjects for a set of experiments conducted by Hans' colleague, Dr Sigmund Rascher. The experiments were designed to test the limits of the human body to survive extreme temperatures, in order to find out how downed Luftwaffe pilots might be saved from hypothermia. The prisoners were submerged in tanks of freezing water until they lost conscious-ness; they were then 'reheated' in varying ways. Many died in the process, but those who survived were 'rewarded' with an early release to one of the sub-camps, and a job in a factory. Clearly this Russian had been one of the survivors.

'Well,' said Hans, 'you seem in remarkably good health, apart from your toe, that is.'

'I don't miss it,' said the Russian, staring straight ahead.

Hans suddenly had an idea. Annaliese was in need of help in the garden – this Russian might be the answer. He was obviously of impressive stock – a 'White Russian', not a Bolshevik; some of his compatriots had even joined the German army, fighting against their communist countrymen. What's more, he was healthy, and looked every inch a German, with his thick blond hair and green eyes.

The factory owner coughed again.

'All right,' said Hans to the Russian. 'You can go and join the others.'

Outside in the yard, the men were lined up in rows. Hans strolled over to the guard in charge of the work detail. 'I want that man,' he said, pointing to the Russian, who stood a good head taller than the rest.

The guard studied his clipboard. 'But... he's down to go to the armaments factory, Sturmbannführer.'

'You have hundreds of others for that,' said Hans firmly, pulling rank. 'I want the Russian to work for me – at my house. See to it.'

The guard marched over to the assembled prisoners, hauled Kosomov out of the line and whispered in his ear. The Russian looked across at Hans, and nodded his head in acknowledgement of this 'special treatment'.

Driving away, it occurred to Hans that his action that day might well save the man's life. It was a tiny act of kindness in a sea of inhumanity.

8

SEPTEMBER 1942

A few days later, Annaliese was upstairs in her bedroom getting dressed when she heard the front doorbell ring. She went out onto the landing, and heard Marta say, 'Go round to the back of the house, and wait for me there.'

'Marta,' she called down, 'who was that?'

'The new gardener. I told him to wait outside in the back garden.'

Hans had mentioned the new gardener to Annaliese the previous evening. 'He'll be here first thing tomorrow. He's not a professional gardener, but he's intelligent – a qualified architect, in fact. He's Russian, but he speaks German well – he had German grandparents, apparently.'

'How interesting. Where did you find him?' she asked, threading embroidery silk through her needle for a cushion she was making for their bedroom.

'In the labour camp.'

'What did you say?' Annaliese looked up from her work in surprise. Hans had assured her in the past that the inmates at Dachau were mostly criminals who deserved to be imprisoned. 'The labour camp! Is he dangerous?'

'No, not at all. He's not a criminal, he's a prisoner of war. He's recently been moved from the main camp at Dachau to one of the sub-camps on the outskirts of Munich. Most of them are being sent to work in the armaments and munitions factories – important war work, you understand,' Hans assured her. 'But it would be a waste of his talents. He's lucky I spotted him, and he knows it.'

'Well, we've been lucky to find him, by the sounds of it,' she replied pragmatically, threading another length of silk through her embroidery needle.

'Many of my colleagues think that Russians are the lowest of the low,' Hans went on. 'In their opinion, as our enemies, and as communists, they deserve no respect or mercy. But I'm pretty sure this man is no communist. His family were wealthy industrialists before the Russian Revolution – White Russians, you know? I wouldn't allow just anyone to work in my home. Nevertheless, I will rely on you, Annaliese, to tell me if he breaks the rules, or is late for any reason. If that happens he will have to be returned immediately to Dachau. Do you understand?'

'Yes, Hans, of course.' Annaliese had learned, through bitter experience, that it was better not to question Hans about the camp or its inmates. To do so made him angry and sullen.

'And he's to be fed the bare minimum – just a piece of bread, or bowl of broth – nothing more. In the summer months, he's to work from seven in the morning, until six in the evening, every day, with just a ten-minute break for lunch. In the winter, he starts at eight. Is that clear?'

'Is it really necessary to be so strict?' she asked, in a rare show of dissent.

'Oh, for heaven's sake,' replied Hans irritably. 'Those are

the rules. If word got out that we were showing any favouritism it would be dangerous – for us, as well as for him. Darling, you've got the gardener you wanted. What more do you want?'

Annaliese, startled by his impatience, accidentally pricked herself with her needle; when she looked down, blood had seeped into the white embroidery cloth.

Annaliese found the gardener standing on the terrace outside the sitting room, waiting for instructions. Hans had warned her he would be dressed in the camp's striped uniform, and that his head would be shaved. Over the top of his uniform he wore an old brown jacket, and respectfully held his striped cap in his hand. His head had indeed been shaved, but a fine stubble of blond hair was already growing back. He had a rather elegantly shaped head, she thought, made more so by his closely cropped hair. She opened the French windows and stepped outside to meet him.

'Good morning,' she greeted him cheerfully.

He nodded. 'Good morning, madam.' He might be a prisoner of war, but he had a certain self-confidence, she thought, and an upright bearing that belied his ill-fitting striped clothes.

'I'm so glad you are able to help us.' She smiled. 'The garden, as you can see, is in a bit of a mess. But I'm sure you'll soon sort it out.'

He gazed into her eyes, a flicker of surprise crossing his face, clearly taken aback by her friendliness. 'I will do what I can to help.'

'You speak our language very well. Your grandparents, I understand, were German.'

'Yes – originally from Berlin.'

Embarrassed at suddenly finding herself in such a position of authority over this handsome, well-educated man, Annaliese blushed. 'Well,' she said, 'let's have a tour of the garden, shall we?'

She led him down the steps onto the lawn. 'The grass is in a terrible state, I'm afraid. And the flowerbeds are full of weeds. I would also like to extend the vegetable garden. With rationing and so on, it seems sensible to grow more of our own food.'

He followed her around as she explained the layout, holding his hands behind his back, like an army officer inspecting his troops.

'We have a shed at the bottom of the garden where the tools are kept, but I'm not sure what condition they're in. The last gardener left us over two years ago, and my husband rarely has time to mow the lawn, or do any sort of maintenance.'

Opening the shed door, they were greeted by the pungent smell of engine oil and old soil.

The Russian followed her inside, and unhooked a garden spade hanging from a nail, inspecting it closely. 'If I can have some oil and a cloth, and perhaps a sharpening stone, I can make these tools look like new, madam.'

'Yes, of course. I'll ask my maid to buy whatever you need today.'

He was squatting down, studying an old mowing machine. 'This needs an overhaul. I can do it, but I need some tools.'

He stood up and rummaged around on the workbench. 'Ah, here is what I want. But I will start with the weeding, and then later will repair the mower.'

'Thank you.' Annaliese was genuinely grateful. 'That all sounds wonderful. Would you like coffee?'

He looked at her, his green eyes wide with astonishment. 'Coffee?'

'Yes... coffee. Most of the time we drink that awful acorn coffee – God knows what it's really made of – but I have just a little real coffee left. I've been saving it for something special.'

'Don't waste it on me.'

'It's not a waste.'

'Are you sure it's allowed, madam – for a slave?'

She was startled for a moment by the word 'slave'. She had not given any thought to the fact that he would not be paid for his work, that he was not there by choice. It made her feel angry and rebellious. 'Well, it's my house,' she said firmly, 'and you're my gardener – so yes, it is allowed. I'll bring you some.'

From the kitchen, she watched the Russian at work. He squatted outside the shed in the sunshine, wiping the tools down with some oil he had found in the shed. He was undoubtedly handsome – beautiful even – with a fine aristocratic head. But he looked painfully thin and in need of food. Whatever Hans had stipulated, a bowl of broth was surely not enough for a grown man working all day. And while she agreed with Hans that the Russian had been lucky to be offered a job in their garden rather than the factory, there was no need to make him suffer.

By the time she returned outside carrying a tray of coffee, he had already dug over part of the old vegetable patch and, from what she could see, had made a good job of it – the brown earth was neatly turned and free of weeds. He had taken off both his brown jacket and the striped prison jacket, which now hung on the branches of an apple tree. He had rolled up his shirtsleeves, revealing muscular arms.

He looked up warily as she walked towards him.

'Here you are,' she called out cheerfully, 'coffee and some biscuits – my maid's speciality.'

She laid the tray down on the ground and offered him a cup. He took it and sipped it slowly – his green eyes closing for a moment, almost ecstatically.

'Good?' she asked eagerly.

'Yes... thank you. I've not had coffee for so long.'

For a moment he relaxed and smiled – a wide, generous smile. He had a perfectly symmetrical face with high cheekbones, but it was his vivid green eyes that fascinated her.

'Well,' she said. 'I'll let you get on. But I'll come out later with some lunch – is soup and bread all right?'

'Yes, thank you.'

'Oh... and you've not told me your name.'

'Alexander, madam,' he said quietly. 'Alexander Kosomov.'

Later that afternoon, she went upstairs to her bedroom. She kicked off her shoes and sat at her dressing table brushing her hair. Alexander had already mended the lawnmower and was now mowing the lawn, creating neat stripes. As if sensing he was being watched, he glanced up at her window and smiled. She smiled back, blushing as she did so.

When Hans came home that night, he stood on the terrace inspecting the garden. 'He's done a good job already,' he said. 'Are you pleased?'

'Oh, yes,' she replied. 'He was very polite and worked very hard. I think he will make a huge difference. Thank you, Hans.'

He leant over and gently kissed her cheek. 'Anything for you, my darling.'

It was a rare moment of intimacy between them, which momentarily surprised her. She could not remember the last time he had kissed her so spontaneously.

Perhaps he was relieved, she thought, that it was Sunday the following day – his one day off. He would sleep better that night, as he often did on a Saturday.

Much later, in the middle of the night, she woke and peered at the small travel clock on her bedside table; it was three in the morning, and Hans, wearing earplugs, lay snoring quietly beside her. Knowing how much he struggled with his sleep, she was relieved to see him lying so peacefully.

Suddenly, she became aware of a faint roaring sound, and sat up in bed, alarmed. Swinging her legs out of bed, she padded across to the window. A full moon illuminated the garden – nothing appeared to be out of place. Relieved, she wrapped a shawl around her shoulders and went out onto the landing. The oak floorboards creaked slightly as she crossed over to the large arched window above the porch. In spite of the silvery moon, a pale orange glow on the horizon suggested something was amiss – a fire at one of the munitions factories, perhaps. Her gardener's living quarters were nearby, she realised. Hoping against hope he was all right, she retreated to the warmth of her bed, and eventually to sleep.

9

Annaliese woke the following morning with the sun streaming through her parted bedroom curtains.

Marta was knocking on the door. 'Good morning, madam. Shall I leave your breakfast outside on the landing?'

'Yes, thank you.' Annaliese climbed out of bed and pulled on her peignoir. Opening the door, she found the tray on the table outside. 'Thank you, Marta,' she called out to the retreating figure of her maid.

She laid the tray on the inlaid table in the window next to her dressing table and poured herself a cup of coffee. To her relief, the gardener was already hard at work. Clearly, whatever had been the cause of the disturbance in the night, he had not been affected.

'Is it breakfast time already?' Hans asked sleepily, hauling himself up in bed.

'Yes. Would you like coffee?'

'In a moment. Let me get dressed first.' Hans went first to the bathroom and then to his dressing room. It was one of a pair

– 'His' and 'Hers'. His was a picture of organisation: tweed jackets were arranged next to informal suits worn only at weekends; formal grey and black suits were hung alongside evening wear – he owned both black and white dinner jackets. In a separate compartment were his uniforms: the everyday grey-green uniform of an SS officer, with its distinctive black collar and red Nazi armband, and his 'mess' uniform – a black double-breasted jacket piped in white. In cedar-lined drawers lay his underwear and shirts – crisply laundered and wrapped in tissue paper. By contrast, Annaliese's dressing room was chaotic. Floral dresses mingled with chiffon evening gowns. Feather boas jostled with fur wraps. Hats were perched on shelves, and handbags hung haphazardly on hooks around the door. Hans often told her that it gave him a headache just to glance inside; it struck Annaliese that their contrasting wardrobes were a metaphor for their different personalities.

Dressed in a light tweed suit, Hans emerged from his dressing room.

'You look very smart,' said Annaliese brightly, 'although I really don't know why you insist on dressing so early. There's no one to see you but me.'

'You know I don't like eating in my pyjamas,' Hans replied. 'It's so... slovenly.'

'You used to.' She smiled teasingly. 'In fact, I remember you eating naked on our honeymoon.'

He frowned, and glanced out of the window. 'How's the gardener getting on?'

'Oh, fine. He seems to know what he's doing.'

'Must have got the mower working – he's mowed the lawn, I see.'

'Mmmm,' she replied abstractedly, as she flicked through the pages of a magazine.

Hans sat down at the table, and spread out the morning newspaper.

'I woke in the night,' said Annaliese. 'I heard something – a noise. I went out onto the landing and there was a strange orange glow in the distance. I wonder what it could have been. Do you have any idea?'

Hans looked up from his paper. 'A glow, you say? I can't imagine.'

'A fire, perhaps?' she suggested. 'At one of the factories, do you think?'

'I don't know,' he replied brusquely, flicking through the pages of the paper. 'There seems to be nothing about it in the newspaper. I'll find out tomorrow, I imagine.'

They sat in silence for a few moments.

'Did you sleep all right?' she asked.

'Yes – not too bad.' He smiled weakly at her.

'The guests will be here at one.' Annaliese reminded him.

'Guests?' His face darkened a little. 'Oh, yes... my mother and aunt are coming, aren't they?'

'Had you forgotten?'

'Possibly.' Hans crunched down on a piece of toast. 'Could you tell the gardener to work at the side of the house during luncheon, so as not to be seen? And not to use the mower – it's too noisy.'

'Yes, of course,' said Annaliese, nibbling on a hard-boiled egg. 'Although, there's nothing to be ashamed of. He's a perfectly nice man.'

'You know my mother – she wouldn't like it. He's a Russian.'

'It seems a shame that he has to come on a Sunday at all.'

Hans put down his newspaper and stared at her. 'What do you suggest he does instead – attend church, and pop out for a drink afterwards with friends? Really! He's a prisoner of war, for heaven's sake. He's lucky to have this job – and he knows it.'

Annaliese felt embarrassed by her naivety. 'I'm sorry Hans, I didn't think.'

'No,' said Hans, retreating behind his newspaper. 'That's often your problem.'

After breakfast, Annaliese bathed and styled her hair. In her dressing room, she chose a fitted navy-blue dress, with matching navy and cream two-tone court shoes. Studying herself in the mirror, she hoped her mother-in-law would approve. Coming downstairs, she was pleased to see that Marta had already laid the dining table with the cream embroidered linen cloth Elisabetta had given them as a wedding present. The table needed some colour, Annaliese decided, so she took a basket and a pair of secateurs, and went outside hoping to find some flowers among the overgrown beds, and give the gardener his instructions about the guests. She found him hauling brambles out of the boundary hedge.

'Oh, there you are,' she said to him. 'We have people coming for lunch today. I wonder... could you work at the side of the house while they're here, so as not to be seen? And try not to be too noisy – no mowing, for example.'

He nodded. 'Of course, madam.' He glanced down at her basket. 'Can I get you something?'

'I just wanted some flowers for the table, but the flowerbeds are in such a state, I'm not sure there'll be anything suitable.'

He took the basket from her, and led her down the garden towards the vegetable patch where colourful dahlias glowed in the sunlight. 'These would look nice,' he suggested. He bent down and cut some long stems, placing them delicately in her basket. He handed it back to her and held out one large, pale pink flower. 'For you,' he said. 'To wear on your dress.'

'Oh, thank you,' she said, blushing. 'The flowers you've chosen are beautiful.'

Back in the dining room, she arranged the dahlias in a silver vase, admiring his choice. The startling clash of colours –

maroon, orange, pink and red – looked stunning set against the pale cream linen cloth. She held the single pink flower up to her dress. He was right about that too. She trimmed the stem and pinned it beneath her pearl brooch at the neckline.

Down in the basement kitchen, she found Marta on her knees, her face red and damp as she checked the pork in the oven.

'Is everything ready, Marta? The guests will be here in half an hour.'

'Yes, madam.'

'And I thought we could serve drinks on the terrace over-looking the garden,' Annaliese suggested. 'Can you put the glasses on the silver tray?'

'I've already done it, madam,' said Marta, now stirring a large pot of red cabbage, her hair frizzing in the steam.

'Oh, good. And you've prepared the canapés?'

'Yes... they're on the table there, covered with the cloth.'

Annaliese lifted the linen cloth and inspected the plate of food. Small curls of smoked trout nestled on beds of creamy-white cheese and horseradish, all on top of slices of Vollkornbrot – a dark seeded loaf much favoured by Elisabetta. Hans had brought the trout back a few days before – a luxury donated by a member of the Party faithful, he had told her.

'Marta, I can see you're awfully busy,' Annaliese said sympathetically. 'Shall I take the gardener his lunch? I'd like to do it before the guests arrive.'

'Thank you, madam – that would be very helpful.'

Annaliese ladled out a bowl of broth from the stockpot on top of the stove and put it on a tray, with a glass of water. When Marta's back was turned, she added a few of the canapés intended for the guests, and covered them quickly with a napkin.

· · ·

Annaliese found the gardener expertly shaping the hedge with shears. She put the tray down on a small stone bird table. 'I brought you some lunch.'

Alexander looked up from his work, beads of sweat on his forehead. 'Thank you,' he said, lowering his gaze. His eyelashes were dark, she noticed, in spite of his fair hair.

'There's a bowl of broth – quite tasty – and a slice of bread, with a little smoked trout.' She removed the linen napkin like a magician's assistant, revealing the delicacy beneath.

Again, there was the familiar flash from his green eyes, and a smile crept onto the corners of his mouth. 'Thank you, madam,' he repeated. His eyes lingered on the flower at her breast. 'It looks very pretty,' he said.

In spite of herself, she blushed a second time. This man may have been a prisoner, but there was something in his bearing – an innate elegance, perhaps – that was deeply attractive. 'My husband tells me you're an architect,' she murmured, trying to change the subject.

'Yes – I trained in Moscow...'

'How interesting.'

He nodded, but he seemed distracted, and kept glancing down at the plate of smoked trout.

'You must be hungry,' she said quickly. 'I'll let you eat. Just leave the plate here. Marta will collect it later. And remember, don't come near the house today,' she warned. 'My husband insists that you stay out of sight.'

'I understand, madam.'

She turned and walked back to the house. When she reached the corner, she glanced back at him. He was eating voraciously; he looked half-starved.

The long clock in the hall chimed one o'clock at the precise moment the doorbell rang. Marta, who had now replaced her cotton kitchen apron for a more formal one made of starched white linen, opened the door. Standing on the doorstep was Elisabetta and her sister, Charlotte.

Marta bobbed a curtsey.

'Where is my son?' Elisabetta demanded, removing her fur wrap and handing it to the maid.

'On the terrace, madam.'

Charlotte, who was more delicate – and far prettier – than her sister, removed her own coat and hung it on a hook by the door, smiling sympathetically at the maid. Marta then led the guests through the drawing room, and out through the long French windows to the terrace.

'Hans... at last,' said Elisabetta, offering her left cheek to her son, who dutifully kissed it. 'Did you hear about the air raid last night?'

'Air raid, Mama?' Hans was genuinely surprised.

'Yes. Bombs were dropped – quite near to where I live. It caused a terrible fire. My friend Hilda rang me this morning. Her house is all right, but another along the same road has been completely destroyed.'

The colour drained from Hans' face. 'I'm afraid I knew nothing about it.'

'Well, what are you going to do about it?' his mother asked tersely.

'Do?' Hans looked bemused, perplexed by his mother's belief that he could somehow prevent foreign aircraft attacking their city. 'I'm a doctor, Mother,' he replied, 'not a politician, nor a tactician. I'm not even a member of the Luftwaffe. What do you expect me to do about it, exactly?'

Annaliese, anxious to defuse the situation, held her hands out to Elisabetta's sister. 'Aunt Charlotte, how lovely to see you again – I'm so glad you could come. Do sit down here, and let's talk.'

Hans joined them, and kissed his aunt's manicured hand. 'How nice to see you again. How is Salzburg?'

'Oh... quiet,' she replied. 'The way I like it.'

'Never mind Salzburg,' said Elisabetta impatiently. 'I thought you always told me, Hans, that enemy planes couldn't get as far as Munich.'

'That has always been the assumption,' he replied patiently.

'Well, the assumption was obviously wrong,' Elisabetta retorted. 'Fortunately, many of them were brought down before they could do much damage. So with any luck, they won't try again.'

Annaliese poured the women a glass of lemonade, and handed her husband a glass of beer.

'*Prost!*' she said, raising her glass.

'I don't think there's much to celebrate,' said Elisabetta pointedly.

Annaliese, flushing with embarrassment, began to offer the plate of smoked trout around. Elisabetta took a piece. 'It's very nice,' she said, sounding surprised.

'What a large garden, Annaliese,' interjected Charlotte cheerfully. 'It must be a lot of work, but I imagine it gives you a lot of pleasure.'

'It's been in a terrible state since the start of the war – when our original gardener was called up,' replied Annaliese, 'but fortunately, Hans has just found a new one...'

'A new gardener?' asked Elisabetta. 'Where did you get him from?'

'The labour camp, wasn't it, Hans?'

Hans looked up, distracted. 'What? Yes... from the camp.'

'He's not a Jew, I hope!' said Elisabetta disdainfully.

'No,' replied Annaliese. 'A Russian.'

'A communist!' spluttered Elisabetta, nearly choking on her mouthful of trout.

'Oh, Elisabetta,' said Charlotte, 'you really are the most prejudiced person.'

'I'm not prejudiced,' replied Elisabetta. 'I discriminate... there's a difference, you know.'

To Annaliese's relief, Marta rang the gong for lunch.

'It all looks very nice, Annaliese,' said Charlotte loyally, as they filed into the dining room. 'You've made the table look really beautiful.'

'Thank you, Charlotte. Please, everyone, do sit down.' Annaliese glanced anxiously at her mother-in-law, hoping she agreed with her sister, but Elisabetta's face remained impassive.

Conversation during the meal was stilted. Charlotte and Annaliese chatted happily enough, mostly about life in Salzburg before the war.

'It's the opera I miss most,' said Charlotte, her bright blue eyes misting slightly. 'The Salzburg Festival used to be such a highlight. But since the Anschluss in thirty-eight, when the Nazis made their power grab, it's become nothing but propaganda.'

'What rubbish!' declared Elisabetta. 'There was no "power grab", as you put it.'

'No power grab?' Charlotte's voice rose in anger. 'That man Hitler marched into my country and annexed it. I don't know what else you'd call it, Elisabetta.'

Across the table, her sister pouted petulantly, as Charlotte went on with her explanation. 'You see, Annaliese, most of the great singers and directors fled – they were too terrified to remain in their own country. Don't you think that's awful?'

Annaliese nodded sympathetically.

'They were no loss,' spat Elisabetta. 'They were mostly Jews, anyway.'

'I beg your pardon?' Charlotte was clearly horrified. 'What *are* you talking about?'

'Well, they were...' replied Elisabetta. 'Those artistic types – they were mostly Jews.'

'What if they were?' Charlotte retorted.

As the two women bickered, Annaliese glanced over at Hans, who was looking increasingly uncomfortable. Hans had enjoyed his visits to his aunt before the war, and shared Charlotte's love of opera. But as a member of the SS, he was in an awkward position. How could he possibly, even in private, denounce the National Socialist takeover of Austria, or the expulsion of Jews from its borders? The unification of the German-speaking peoples was a central tenet of Hitler's master plan and it was Hans' duty to defend it.

Anxious to relieve the tension, Annaliese suggested coffee. 'Let's have it on the terrace – it's such a lovely afternoon.'

'I am too tired,' complained Elisabetta, before turning to her sister. 'I suggest we go home, Charlotte.'

'Well, I disagree,' interjected her sister firmly. 'You go home if you want to, but I'm not tired at all, and I'd adore some coffee – thank you, Annaliese.'

Hans sighed audibly as his wife led their guests out onto the terrace. A tray had been laid with an elegant white and gold coffee pot, and four tiny matching cups and saucers, alongside a plate of delicate chocolate biscuits.

'These are one of Marta's culinary specialities,' explained Annaliese, offering the biscuits around. As she poured the coffee, she suddenly spotted the gardener. He was pushing his wooden wheelbarrow, filled with hedge clippings and tools, across the lawn – presumably thinking lunch was over and it was safe to carry on working, she realised.

Annaliese gently coughed to attract Alexander's attention. He swung round and noticed her guests sitting on the terrace. His face froze in terror. Fortunately, Hans and his mother were sitting with their backs to the garden, and saw nothing. With a discreet flap of her hand, Annaliese shooed Alexander away.

Charlotte, however, had noticed the gardener, but said nothing. She merely winked at Annaliese and smiled, as he hurried up the path and disappeared into the shed.

Coming back onto the terrace, having waved their guests goodbye, Hans sighed deeply. 'I'm going to lie down. Listening to my mother and aunt carp at each other throughout lunch was exhausting.'

'Well, I thought you might have stood up for Charlotte a little. Your mother can be very domineering.'

Hans stared at Annaliese pointedly. 'Once my mother makes up her mind about something, there is no use in arguing. Besides, I didn't think Charlotte needed any help from me. She's quite outspoken enough on her own. But she should be more careful. It's dangerous spouting these kinds of anti-Party sentiments. We wouldn't betray her, of course, but others might not be so lenient.'

'What are you suggesting, Hans? I thought you would agree with her.'

'It's not a question of agreeing or disagreeing, Annaliese. Such ideas, even such thoughts, are not allowed.'

'And you think that's acceptable, do you?' Annaliese's face was pink with exasperation. 'To tell people what they can and cannot say or think? I don't understand you any more, Hans. You weren't like this when we first met. I know for a fact that you had Jewish friends. You told me so.'

'That was then... things are different now.' His tone was resigned.

'You think it's right that Jewish people are persecuted, do you? What's happened to you, Hans? Working at that camp has changed you... and not for the better.'

'I work at the camp because it's the only way I can do my research.'

'That's your answer to everything, isn't it? Everything else can be sacrificed on the altar of your research...'

'I'm a doctor. I'm trying to do my best. I rescued the Russian gardener, didn't I?'

Annaliese realised that further argument was pointless, and irritably began to clear the coffee cups. Hans stood up gruffly, and marched angrily into the house. She heard him clump upstairs and slam the bedroom door. Glancing up, she saw him close the curtains.

Annaliese sat for a while on the terrace, brooding over the lunchtime conversation. Instinctively she agreed with everything Charlotte had said. But she now lived in a strange half-world where her whole existence – their house, their standing in society – was based on a philosophy that she despised. She had once thought that Hans despised it too, but now she could see that he had changed. Or 'they' had changed him.

Picking up the plate of chocolate biscuits, she walked down the steps into the garden. She was intent on defying another Party rule – to feed her enslaved gardener more than his allotted food ration. Looking back towards the house, she checked the curtains in their bedroom were still drawn.

She hurried to the garden shed and knocked on the door. 'Alexander, are you there?' she whispered.

The door opened slightly. There he was, hovering in the doorway. 'I'm very sorry if I upset your guests...' he began.

'Please, don't apologise – it wasn't your fault. You weren't to know they were still here. Look' – she proffered the biscuits – 'I brought these for you. Marta made them. They're very good.'

'Thank you,' he said, his mouth crinkling into a smile. 'You're very kind.'

'It's nothing. I just thought you'd like them,' she replied simply.

The lunch discussion had made her more determined than ever to show the man some kindness. She knew she was powerless to stand up to National Socialism as a whole, but she could be subversive in her own small way, and perform a tiny act of humanity towards an enemy of the Reich.

'Eat the biscuits,' she suggested gently, 'or they will melt.'

He slipped one into his mouth and she watched as his lips closed around it. His eyelids fluttered shut for a moment, as he savoured the sweetness. 'May I keep the others for later?' he asked.

'Of course.' She handed him the plate. 'And I can bring some more if you like.'

'No, this is enough.' He put the plate down on his workbench and took an old tin off the shelf, tipping out the contents – mostly used nails. 'If I may, I'll keep the rest of them in this tin, so I can have one every day.'

She watched him placing the biscuits carefully in the tin, and her heart ached with sadness for him. 'I'll always make sure you have enough to eat, I promise. As long as you work for me, you'll never go hungry.'

He looked at her, his eyes wary. 'You must be careful. It breaks the rules.'

'I don't care about the rules – I'm fed up with them. You're leaving in half an hour, aren't you?'

'Yes. I must be back at my barracks by seven for roll-call. Did your husband like the flower I gave you?'

She glanced down at the pale pink dahlia pinned to her dress. 'Oh, this? He didn't even notice.'

'That's a shame… it looks very pretty on you.'

She noticed his gaze hovering on her neckline. 'I'd better go,' she said quickly.

As he handed back the plate, their hands touched, and she felt a small charge of electricity run through her body.

'I'll see you tomorrow,' she called out as she walked back up the garden path, realising that she was already looking forward to it.

10

Hans' hands shook as he tried to pin his medals onto the lapel of his SS mess jacket. He had been invited to attend a dinner with Hitler himself at the Führerbau – his new headquarters in the centre of Munich – and was inwardly dreading it.

'Here, let me help you,' said Annaliese impatiently. She deftly attached the medals and stood back to inspect him, brushing a tiny piece of fluff from his sleeve. 'You look very smart.'

'Thank you, my love.' He had sensed his wife's irritation over the past few weeks, and was grateful for any flattery, however mild.

'It's unusual for the Führer to hold a dinner here in Munich, isn't it?' she asked, puzzled.

'Yes,' Hans agreed, studying his reflection in the mirror. 'Normally, he's holed up in his mountain retreat in the Berghof, or otherwise in Berlin. But he's back in Munich for a couple of days, and this dinner is the highlight of the visit. To be honest,' he added, turning to look at his wife, 'I was surprised to be invited. I'm certainly not one of his... inner circle.'

'But you're one of his senior doctors, and obviously someone he admires,' Annaliese replied loyally. 'I'm sure he'll be very impressed by you.'

'I don't suppose I'll even meet him. Besides, as you know, I have never been comfortable being part of the National Socialist hierarchy. I am a simple doctor, that's all.'

She kissed him. 'I'm so glad to hear you say that, Hans. I worry sometimes that your appointment at Dachau has changed you, that they are forcing you to do things you don't like. But when I hear you speak like that I can see, I *know*, that they can't change the real Hans.'

'You always understand, darling.' He kissed her hand, before checking his reflection one last time. 'Well, I'd better go. Herr Hitler does not tolerate latecomers.'

Sitting in the back seat of his staff car, Hans watched Annaliese waving him goodbye from the steps of their house. Since his aunt's visit a few weeks before, he had noticed a change in his wife. She had become withdrawn, even a little cool. Perhaps his mother's outburst about Jews, and his own insistence that Charlotte and Annaliese should keep their sympathies with persecuted groups to themselves, had angered her. But he knew she didn't understand the precarious nature of their situation. No one was safe any more – not even an SS officer like him.

As Hans' staff car drove through the quiet streets of Munich towards Hitler's headquarters, he couldn't rid himself of a feeling of impending doom. He'd had it once or twice before – almost like a premonition. He lit a cigarette, trying to brush the thought aside. After all, he was a man of science and should reject such fanciful notions.

'Looks like we'll have to wait, I'm afraid, Sturmbannführer, sir,' said his driver as they neared their destination. Hans looked out and saw a long line of Mercedes, queuing to deliver Hitler's guests to the Führerbau. Completed in 1937, this modern neo-classical building in the centre of Munich had replaced the original Brown House headquarters and was now the inner sanctum of National Socialism in Bavaria.

Hans had often seen it from outside, of course, but had never actually entered its hallowed portals. Now, as he walked up the steps towards the sandstone pilasters, beneath the huge red and black Swastika flag draped from the balcony above, his hand shook as he raised his arm in answer to the armed guard's salute. 'Heil Hitler!' Hans echoed, as smartly as he could.

Inside the marbled hall, a set of glazed doors lay ahead, through which he could see a huge atrium, crowded with uniformed SS officers. His mouth felt dry, a sure sign of anxiety. A soldier saluted him, ushering him through the glass doors. Hans was suddenly assailed by the sound of forty or fifty men talking loudly, their voices echoing beneath the vaulted ceiling. It took a strong effort of will to stop himself from shaking.

He was greeted by a familiar voice. 'Ah, good, here's Hans.' It was Claus Schilling striding towards him. Not being a member of either the National Socialist Party or the SS, Schilling wore no uniform. That evening he was not even wearing a dinner jacket, but an old-fashioned frock coat and floppy bow tie. With his white hair and beard, he looked like a relic from the nineteenth century.

'Good evening, Claus,' Hans replied, his heart sinking. Schilling was the last person he wanted to spend an evening with. Although he had been at Dachau for only a few months, Schilling was already getting better results in his malaria experiments than Hans, and it grated. Hans shot him a barbed comment. 'I had no idea you were coming, Claus. I thought this was an SS event.'

Schilling ignored the snub. 'I was rather surprised to be

invited myself,' he replied smugly. 'But I understand the Führer is interested in some sort of update about Dachau from the medical department. Himmler's idea...'

'I see,' said Hans, irritated that Claus seemed to know more about the evening's agenda than he did.

'Everyone who is anyone is here tonight,' Claus went on. 'The Führer is expected shortly, I understand. Our colleagues are over there – shall we join them?' He led the way towards a group of men in the corner of the room, talking animatedly, glasses of beer in hand. Among them was Sigmund Rascher, the doctor conducting the hypothermia experiments.

'Good evening, Hans.' Rascher bowed slightly, proffering Hans a limp handshake.

Beside him stood Fritz Hintermayer, Dachau's chief medical officer. With a reputation of being brutish and unnecessarily cruel, his main role was to handle the extermination of frail and dying prisoners. He handed Hans a glass of beer. 'Good to see you, Hans. I wasn't sure if you were coming.'

Hans smiled weakly. 'I'm not aware attendance was optional...'

To his surprise and dismay, Hans spotted Himmler carving a path towards them. His hair, closely shaved at the sides, gave him a peculiarly aggressive look; Hans was again struck by how his glasses somehow emphasised the extreme narrowness of his eyes.

'Good, you're all here,' said Himmler coldly. 'The Führer has requested a private word with you all – upstairs.' He made the invitation sound like a command.

The four doctors followed Himmler up the wide marble staircase to the first floor and then down a long corridor. He came to a halt in front of a panelled oak door. 'Before we go in,' he said, turning to face them, 'I must warn you that the Führer is tired and has a lot on his mind. He needs short, simple summaries about your work. No unnecessary scientific jargon, do you understand?'

The doctors nodded and stepped into the inner sanctum of the Führer's study.

Adolf Hitler was standing by the fireplace, his hands resting on the dark green marble mantelpiece. He had his back to the room and was kicking impatiently at the brass fender, as if deep in thought. The fire was lit, and the room was warm. Hans glanced around, quickly absorbing the details of the interior. The room was functional, but elegant, with parquet flooring covered with Persian rugs, and dark oak panelling on the walls. The lighting was soft and low. A lamp with a marbled paper shade cast a gentle glow on Hitler's desk, which stood just to their left, close enough to see the contents of his in-tray – which was empty, apart from an architectural sketch of the mausoleum that Hitler was rumoured to be designing for himself. The thick Persian carpets made the room remarkably silent – the only sounds were the ticking of a clock and the spitting of logs on the fire. In front of the fireplace stood a Bergère sofa and chairs, with rattan backs and sides. They had been fashionable a few years before – Annaliese had wanted something similar, Hans remembered. Behind the sofa stood a table, with a tray of drinks and a set of glasses.

Himmler coughed quietly to alert the Führer to their presence. 'The doctors you wanted to see are here, mein Führer,' he said gently.

Hitler swung round as if startled, glaring at them. Hans had seen him before, of course, but only from a distance – in restaurants or at rallies – but his physical presence, and in particular the intensity of his hypnotic blue gaze, was almost overwhelming.

The men saluted. 'Heil Hitler,' they chorused.

'Yes, yes... come in, all of you.' The Führer sounded tired and impatient. Hans realised he had never heard Hitler's normal voice before. He had heard him give speeches, of course, when he powerfully projected his voice – even shrieked sometimes. But now, here, in his private office, his real voice came as a surprise. It was deep, sonorous and a little monotonous.

Himmler stepped smartly forward. 'They have updates on the medical experiments at Dachau, mein Führer – you said you'd be interested.'

'Dachau? Yes. All right.' Hitler remained in front of the fire while the four doctors stood at the other end of the room, awkwardly shifting from foot to foot. 'Well, get on with it,' said the Führer irritably.

To Hans' annoyance, Claus took the lead. 'My name is Professor Claus Schilling, mein Führer. If I may, we are having considerable success in our experiments with malaria. How to prevent it, predominantly, but also how to cure it. This, of course, is all in aid of saving the lives of our brave soldiers in tropical climes.'

'Go on,' said Hitler.

'We are conducting experiments on various pathogens to ameliorate the symptoms. We hope, eventually, to isolate and prevent the disease through vaccination.'

Hitler's eyes roved around the group. 'You' – he pointed at Sigmund Rascher – 'what are you doing?'

The doctor cleared his throat anxiously. 'We are attempting to find out the limitations of the human body in freezing water. This has implications for our brave airmen, if they have to bail out over the sea, and for the navy too, obviously. We are also examining the limits of the human body at high-altitude flight. We hope—'

'All right, all right,' Hitler interrupted impatiently, turning to Hans. 'What about you?'

Hans was speechless for a moment, unsure how to proceed and disconcerted by Hitler's clear blue eyes holding his gaze.

Himmler coughed nervously, and Hans recovered himself. 'I too am involved with malaria research,' he began, 'using homeopathy to establish a cure. In addition, I'm exploring the use of mescaline as a truth drug – it could be useful in interrogation...'

Hitler put his hand up, as if directing traffic. 'Mescaline, you say... and interrogation? That sounds interesting. Would you like a drink?'

He walked around the sofa to the drinks table and poured some schnapps into a small glass. He held it out to Hans, who stepped forward smartly, clicked his heels together and bowed before taking it. 'Thank you, mein Führer.'

'Sit down here and tell me all about it.' Hitler pointed to the sofa next to the fireplace, and returned to his favoured position, leaning against the mantelpiece.

'Well, mein Führer,' Hans began, perching awkwardly on the edge of the sofa. It felt wrong to be fully seated when the Führer himself was still standing, but he sensed his leader's impatience. 'I've been conducting experiments for a few months and building up a body of evidence. When given mescaline, a compound which is extracted from the peyote cactus, people experience an acute psychotic state – also hallucinations, illusions, depersonalisation, as well as many physical reactions – nausea, tremor, sweating.'

Hitler seemed intrigued and Hans relaxed, warming to his subject. 'There is evidence that in this condition, they will be more susceptible to interrogation, unable to pretend or lie...'

Suddenly, there was a violent noise. Hans swung round, imagining something had been dropped in the far corner of the room. Himmler was already on the alert, giving hushed instructions to a guard, but Hitler remained impassive. Seconds later there was another, much louder crashing sound, and the glass in the windows shook. It was clearly an explosion.

'I must get you downstairs to safety, mein Führer,' said Himmler, hurrying towards Hitler. He took his leader by the arm and shepherded him out of the room. The four doctors looked at each other uneasily and followed on behind. Himmler propelled Hitler to a back staircase, down which ten or twenty other dinner guests were already streaming. In the basement they were funnelled down a long concrete corridor, at the end of which was a huge metal door. A guard was in the process of turning a wheel to unlock it. The door must have been nearly half a metre thick, Hans thought, as it swung open, revealing a gloomy, cavernous space.

Hans was expecting to see some sort of basement cell, but was astonished when the lights went on. There was a comfortable sitting room, carpeted once again with Persian rugs, and furnished with sofas, lamps and even flowers.

The Führer sat down casually on a sofa. Any connection Hans had felt with his leader upstairs in the study had evaporated.

There appeared to be about twenty people in the basement; Hans wondered where the rest of the party guests had gone. Perhaps they were in another bunker. He found himself standing next to Himmler.

'Is it an air raid, sir?'

'Patently,' Himmler replied witheringly.

'Do we know where?' Hans persisted. He was aware that Annaliese was alone in the house close by. He recalled her standing on the steps of the house, waving him goodbye. She had looked so beautiful that evening, wearing a pale grey figure-hugging dress, her thick blond hair falling over her turquoise eyes. It would be unbearable if she were to be killed that night, when they had finally come to some sort of reconciliation. He had a sudden, terrifying vision of her beautiful body lying dismembered on the lawn, the rubble of the house strewn around her. His heart began to race, his palms sweating.

'The suburbs, we think,' replied Himmler. 'But we'll be all right down here.'

'It sounded closer than that,' Hans pointed out.

'A stray bomb, I suspect – nothing to worry about.'

Hans' instinct was to go straight home, but he noticed guards in front of the steel door, barring any exit. Himmler crossed the room and knelt at Hitler's side. The two whispered for some time before Himmler announced: 'The Führer would like you to join him in the cinema to see a film.'

Hans and his fellow doctors looked from one to the other in surprise.

'If you'd like to follow me,' said Himmler, 'I'll take you through.'

One by one they followed him into a smaller room, fitted out with a few rows of plush velvet seats facing a white screen. The Führer was already seated alone in the front row, while the others filed into the seats behind him.

Hans found himself next to Claus Schilling. 'I really shouldn't be here,' he whispered. 'I have a wife at home in a house nearby – what if it's been hit?'

'Don't worry,' replied Schilling calmly. 'They rarely seem to bomb the city centre.' The cinema lights suddenly dimmed and Schilling held his finger to his lips. 'Shh.'

The Führer clicked his fingers and the film projector flickered into life.

11

OCTOBER 1942

When the air raid began, Annaliese had been alone in her bedroom. She had eaten supper on a tray – something she often did when Hans was out – and was reading a book seated in the bay window, when she heard a muffled booming sound, followed by a series of explosions. After the earlier bombing raid in September, she quickly realised what they were. She turned off the light and rushed out onto the landing. A red glare, which soon turned into a sheet of fire, dominated the night sky. Marta, who had already retired for the night, ran down the attic stairs in her dressing gown, her hair in paper curlers.

'Madam, madam... we should go to the cellar – now, madam!'

Annaliese pulled on her dressing gown and followed her maid down to the basement kitchen and through a door that led down a further set of steps into the coal cellar. After the previous raid, Marta had cleared it out and made a small seating area, now free of coal dust.

The two women sat together on a pair of old kitchen chairs, with a candle flickering in the darkness, listening to the bombers flying overhead, braced for the bomb they feared would hit the house above them.

'Oh, madam, I don't want to die.'

Annaliese reached across and took Marta's hand. 'I'm sure we'll be all right. It sounds as if the planes are dropping their bombs further away.'

Marta continued to weep. 'I want to go home to my parents in Augsburg...'

'Now, now,' said Annaliese gently. 'Bombs get dropped there too, you know.'

With Marta still sobbing loudly, Annaliese crept out of the cellar and retrieved a box of biscuits from the kitchen. 'Marta, have one of these, and wipe your eyes.'

Curiously, Annaliese felt no fear for herself. She had faith that the solid grey house would protect them. But she wondered if perhaps the bombers were aiming for Hitler's headquarters at the Führerbau. To her surprise, she realised she felt concerned for Hans' safety. There had been times recently when she had thought she no longer loved him, but after his admission that evening that he felt out of step with the regime, she felt they had arrived at some sort of understanding. She prayed silently he would survive the night.

By one in the morning, it was clear the raid was over. Annaliese pushed open the cellar door, and the pair emerged into the kitchen. Everything was in order; this time they had been spared.

Back upstairs, Annaliese lay restlessly in bed, a cashmere shawl around her shoulders, unable to sleep. By two in the morning, when Hans was still not home, she began to get really worried. Had he been caught in the raid? It wasn't until an hour later that he finally returned, looking pale and exhausted.

'Thank God,' she said, climbing out of bed and embracing him. 'I've been so worried.'

'Have you?' he asked, almost surprised. 'That was kind. I was very worried about you too. I would have come home sooner, but they wouldn't let us leave.'

He put his arms around her and they stood for a moment in the moonlight – each reflecting on what life would have been like if the other had been killed.

Annaliese pulled away first. 'Marta and I were quite safe – we went to the cellar. We heard the planes flying overhead. Do you know where they were aiming for?'

'One of the suburbs, someone said – on the south side of the city.' He removed his dress jacket and draped it on a chair.

'Near your mother, do you think?'

'Oh, I'm not sure... I don't think so. Fortunately, the Führerbau was untouched – although, if the bombers had realised the Führer was in residence, they might have changed course, and aimed for the city centre instead. He's had a remarkable escape.'

'Did you meet him?' Annaliese asked.

'Yes. I was invited to his study. He seemed quite interested in some of my experiments.'

'Did he?' In spite of her innate loathing of Hitler and all he stood for, Annaliese knew he held the key to her husband's future happiness. 'I told you he would be impressed by you.'

'Well, the other Dachau doctors were there too,' said Hans modestly. 'We all had to give him a progress report.'

'What happened when the raid began? Was he frightened?'

'No, not at all,' Hans assured her. 'He was unnaturally calm. As soon as the raid started we were all taken to the basement shelter.' Hans sank down on the bed, still wearing his black jodhpurs and highly polished knee-high black boots.

'You must be exhausted,' Annaliese said sympathetically. 'Here... let me help you.'

She walked around the bed and pulled off his boots, removing his socks, and pulling the eiderdown over his legs.

'The basement bunker was quite remarkable,' said Hans, leaning back against the embroidered pillows. 'It was decorated with elegant rugs, and even had a proper bathroom. The Führer suggested we pass the time by watching a film.'

Annaliese looked bemused. 'Watch a film? How?'

'He has a projection room down there, with all the latest films... it was most impressive and slightly bizarre.'

'What did you watch?'

'*Snow White and the Seven Dwarfs.*'

'You're joking,' said Annaliese.

'No... it's his favourite film, apparently.'

Annaliese climbed back into bed. 'Did you get anything to eat?'

'No. We never got dinner.'

'Aren't you hungry?'

'Not really.' He threw off the eiderdown and put on his pyjamas. In the bathroom he brushed his teeth, and went back to bed. He lay down with a sigh and closed his eyes.

'Try to sleep now,' said Annaliese. 'The bombers won't come back, will they?'

'Probably not again tonight, no.' Hans put in his earplugs, turned over and was soon snoring.

Annaliese was deeply asleep when she was woken by the sound of the telephone ringing downstairs in the hall. Checking her alarm clock, she saw it was only four o'clock in the morning. Stumbling out of bed, she hauled on her silk dressing gown, ran down the stairs and picked up the phone.

It was Elisabetta. 'My house has been bombed. You must come – immediately.' The phone went dead.

Annaliese rushed back upstairs and gently roused her husband. 'Hans... Hans, wake up.'

He opened his eyes, and smiled at her. 'Annaliese...' he said gently.

'Yes. It's me. I'm sorry to wake you, but your mother just rang.'

His smile evaporated. 'What did she want?'

'Her house has been bombed. She's asked us to come.'

It was still dark when Hans and Annaliese drove off to Solln. By the time they arrived, the sun was rising, casting a lilac glow across the devastated suburb. As they drove down Elisabetta's road, it became clear that several of the houses had been completely obliterated; people were wandering around in a daze, wearing only their nightclothes.

Elisabetta's house appeared to have received a direct hit – there was merely a pile of rubble where it had once stood. She was sitting on a stone seat in what was left of the front garden, wearing her woollen dressing gown. Her friend Hilda was fussing over her, trying to persuade her to drink a cup of tea.

'I don't want it,' Elisabetta was saying. 'I want Hans.'

'I'm here, Mother,' he said, kneeling down in front of her.

'Oh, Mama,' said Annaliese kindly, 'you poor thing. Let's get you home.'

Elisabetta glowered at her daughter-in-law, her eyes filling with tears of rage as she gesticulated at her ruined house and garden. '*This* is my home! I've lived here for nearly forty years and they've destroyed it.'

Hans caught his wife's eye, and shook his head. But Annaliese sat down next to Elisabetta and took her hand. 'I'm so sorry... but it's a miracle you're still alive. What happened?'

'I heard a distant roar and came downstairs,' Elisabetta began, her voice trembling. 'I went out onto the lawn, looking around, and saw the planes coming towards us. I ran... I didn't know where to, but I just ran as fast as I could. The bomb exploded behind me when I reached the end of the road. I would certainly be dead now if I hadn't come outside.'

'And your maid?' Annaliese asked, looking around for the girl.

'Oh, her... she's dead, I expect,' said Elisabetta matter-of-factly. 'She was fast asleep in the attic. There's no way she could have survived.'

Annaliese looked up at Hans. 'Shouldn't we at least look for her?' He nodded and together they walked towards what was left of the house. They were shocked to see a crater where the sitting room had once been; the maid's attic room had been above. 'Poor girl,' said Annaliese. 'She had no chance.'

'Well, one blessing is that she probably knew very little about it. It must all have been over in moments. I imagine the authorities will find her body eventually,' Hans added.

'You should write to her parents,' Annaliese suggested sadly.

The garden was littered with the remnants of Elisabetta's life: shattered porcelain, shards of picture frames and fragments of furniture – all were strewn about amid the rubble. Lying abandoned on the pockmarked lawn was the hand-painted face of the grandfather clock that had stood in the entrance hall. The clock had been a present to Elisabetta from her parents on her wedding day, and was one of her most prized possessions. Hans picked up the clock face, wiped it clean with the back of his hand, and tucked it under his arm.

'Come, Mama. You'd better come back with us to our house – there's nothing more we can do here.'

. . .

Back home, while Marta prepared the spare room for Elisabetta, Annaliese helped her mother-in-law bathe, picking the fragments of stonework out of her hair. Then, dressed in a clean nightdress of Annaliese's – which she complained was 'far too small' – she was helped into bed, given a cup of warm milk and was soon fast asleep.

Downstairs, Annaliese found Hans already dressed in his SS uniform, at the dining table, drinking coffee. The radio was on, and the Führer's high-pitched voice echoed around the house. *'We will not let this incident damage our resolve. We will rebuild everything... better than before.'*

Annaliese sat down at the table, exhausted. Hans smiled at her and passed her a cup of coffee – *a rare act of kindness*, she thought. He turned off the radio. 'Thank you for looking after Mama, and inviting her back here,' he said, reaching out to hold her hand. 'I know she doesn't make it easy...'

'That's all right. What else can we do?' She knew they were both thinking the same thing – that Hans had spent his whole adult life trying to escape his mother's influence, and now she was back in their lives, perhaps forever.

Hans checked his watch and stood up, gathering up some notes from the dining room table. 'My car will be outside,' he said quietly. 'I'd better go.'

'Must you go to work today?' Annaliese asked gently.

'Of course. It's my duty.'

'It's just... you look so tired.'

'I'll try to sleep in the car – it's one of the advantages of having a driver.' He forced his mouth into a smile and headed for the door.

'But Hans...' she called after him, 'surely, after what you've been through last night, they can't expect you to go to work as normal, as if nothing had happened?'

He stopped and turned to her, his face set in a grim expression. 'I was with the Führer last night, remember. He showed an interest in my work – in fact, he seemed more intrigued by my research than in any of the others. This is my chance, Annaliese. I am a husband and a son, of course, but I am first and foremost a doctor and a member of the SS. I have a duty to carry on, whatever happens in my private life.'

She stared at him. 'I can't believe what you're saying. I thought we had an understanding... that we agreed with each other. I realise you are constrained by your position, but it's important for me, as your wife, to know that in your heart you and I think the same way, believe the same things.'

He sighed and leant against the door frame, as if standing up was too much of an effort. 'There is an important difference between us. You have the luxury of living here in this fine house, protected, to some degree, by my position in the SS. My job gives us that. I don't ask you to change your views, but I beg you to understand that I must abide by the rules, and go through the motions, at least, of being on their side. And believe me, Annaliese, it's not easy. Every day I must close my eyes to things I find abhorrent. Every day I struggle with the decisions I have to make. And I do this, in part, to protect you, to protect us from those in authority above me. Because I love you.' He smiled weakly. 'I'll see you later.'

12

Within weeks, Elisabetta's presence in the house had become intolerable. Annaliese dreaded going downstairs each morning. Her mother-in-law, she knew, would be waiting for her, ready to criticise the way she ran the house and garden, or managed her maid. Annaliese did her best to endure these daily interrogations with equanimity, but one evening, over dinner, Elisabetta raised the one subject that was guaranteed to infuriate both her and her husband.

'I can't understand,' Elisabetta began, 'why you still have no children, Hans. What on earth is stopping you?'

Hans glared at her. 'Mama, this really isn't any of your business. It's between Annaliese and me.'

His mother snorted. 'Well, that's all very well, but I understood that it is required of officers like you to produce children for the Fatherland.'

Hans stood up abruptly, knocking over a glass of red wine; it pooled on the embroidered cream cloth. 'Mama... I, of all people, know what is required – you don't have to tell me my duty.'

He stormed out of the dining room; a few moments later they heard the door to his study slam shut. He would be pouring himself a large schnapps now, thought Annaliese, pushing a linen napkin under the wine stain to protect the polished table.

'The fact is, Annaliese,' Elisabetta persisted, staring fixedly at her daughter-in-law, 'I'm worried that there's something wrong with you.'

Annaliese blushed, her eyes filling with tears of indignation. 'There's nothing wrong with me, as far as I know,' she replied defensively.

'Well,' Elisabetta went on, 'Hans is a doctor – surely he should at least examine you and see if there *is* something wrong.'

'He's not that sort of doctor.'

'Don't be ridiculous,' Elisabetta replied witheringly.

Annaliese suddenly stood up. 'Elisabetta, would you mind if I removed the tablecloth and took it down to Marta? I'd like to get it in to soak as soon as possible.'

Later that night, as she settled herself in bed, Annaliese was aware of Hans lying rigidly beside her, staring at the ceiling.

'*Is* there something wrong, do you think, Hans? We never talk about it... maybe we should. I know the SS expect you to have children – your mother's right about that.'

He turned to her and glared.

'Why do you look at me like that?' she said. 'I'm not blaming you... it's my fault, I'm sure. I just worry that you'll get into trouble. Besides, I would like a baby.' She had suppressed her feelings for so long about wanting a child, but the truth was she had a visceral desire to hold a child in her arms.

'I don't want to talk about it,' he said, turning away from her.

'But Hans...'

'Enough!' he barked.

Annaliese woke the following morning to find Hans had already left for work. She suddenly remembered their conversation, and felt guilty about pressing him too hard the night before. He had seemed so upset.

She decided to go out and speak to the gardener about cutting down one of their fir trees for Christmas – something to cheer them all up. She dressed in woollen trousers and a sweater, and went downstairs to get her coat from the rack in the hall. Dreading another encounter with her mother-in-law, she crept past the dining room as silently as possible.

'There you are, at last!' Elisabetta's rasping voice came from the dining room.

Annaliese sighed and poked her head around the door. 'Yes, I'm here,' she said as cheerfully as she could. She saw that Marta had laid the table with coffee, milk, bread and some cold meat. 'Do you have everything you need?'

'I suppose so. I've been waiting for you for over half an hour, but in the end, I had to start without you.'

'As I've explained before,' Annaliese said patiently, 'I don't usually eat breakfast. And Hans leaves so early he doesn't have time...'

'Well, you should eat breakfast,' replied Elisabetta curtly. 'I'm not surprised you can't get pregnant.'

Annaliese felt her stomach churning with fury.

'Oh, and I'll be going out shortly,' Elisabetta continued. 'I'm meeting my friend Hilda at Café Luitpold for coffee, and then we're going to her house to play bridge. I'll be back in time for dinner.'

'Oh, that's nice.' Annaliese smiled agreeably and closed the door. Relieved she wouldn't have to endure Elisabetta's presence for the rest of the day, she threw her coat over her shoulders and headed towards the sitting room.

Marta, who had been polishing the side tables, emerged with her cloths and polish. 'Oh, madam,' she said, 'the Winter Help Fund is collecting again today. We need to choose some clothes to give them.'

'Thank you for reminding me – I'd quite forgotten. I'm sure Hans has some old jackets that we can donate. I'll sort something out.'

'And also, madam,' Marta went on, 'you do remember I've got the afternoon off, don't you? I'm going to visit my mother in Augsburg. She wants me to help her choose a new coat. She finally got enough coupons.'

'Oh, that will be nice,' replied Annaliese. 'But what do you mean, "she finally got enough coupons"?'

'Well, she went to the local Party office a week or so ago to get some clothing coupons, but they told her that she could only have them if they first inspected her wardrobe.'

'What?' Annaliese was horrified. 'Inspect her wardrobe? Why on earth would they want to do that?'

'They have to check that people don't already own too many clothes, apparently.'

'Your poor mother,' replied Annaliese. 'How terribly humiliating to have these Gauleiters rifling through one's wardrobe. Still, at least she got the coupons in the end.'

'Only when she first agreed to donate her summer coat and a woollen skirt.'

'Oh, that's wicked,' said Annaliese. She knew Marta's mother was not well off, and losing a coat and skirt would be difficult to replace.

'She begged them not to, madam. She told them it was her only winter skirt, but they wouldn't listen.' Marta's eyes filled with tears.

Annaliese had an idea. 'Look, I've got an old wool skirt I never wear, and a spare summer coat. Your mother could have them. I'll lay them out on the bed later this morning and you can take them to her this afternoon, all right?'

'Oh, madam, thank you! Are you sure?' Marta grinned broadly, her normally pallid complexion flushing with pleasure.

'Yes, of course I'm sure. I'll tell you what – why don't you go in time for lunch, and surprise her?'

'But what about your own lunch?'

'Oh, I'll manage – I can cook, you know.'

'Well, I've already made a pot of soup, and supper is also ready – a rabbit casserole. It will only need heating up.'

'Well, that sounds very efficient. Thank you, Marta.'

Annaliese unlocked the French windows that led to the terrace. Outside, a cold north wind was blowing. Shivering, she pulled her coat about her, and looked around for Alexander. Hearing the rhythmic scratching of a rake against the grass, she found him at the side of the house clearing the last of the leaves. 'Good morning,' she said quietly.

'Good morning, madam,' he replied, without raising his head. He rarely looked at her any more, she thought. After that first flush of interest, when she was sure she had sensed a sort of spark between them, he had retreated from her. Perhaps he was fearful of the possible repercussions. They both knew that any sort of friendship was forbidden between foreign slave labour and employer. Annaliese had heard rumours of a factory manager's liaison with one of his foreign labour workers; they had both been sent to a labour camp as punishment.

'Alexander, I wondered if you...' she began tentatively, 'if you could chop down a Christmas tree for the house? I'm sure there are some suitable fir trees in the little copse at the bottom of the garden.'

'Yes, madam,' he replied. 'How big a tree do you want?'

'Oh... a couple of metres – is there one like that?'

'I think so. I'll bring it to the back door shortly.'

'Thank you.'

Annaliese crossed the garden and headed for the kitchen. Marta was nowhere to be seen; perhaps she was upstairs getting ready for her journey. The soup stood to one side of the range. Annaliese went through to the laundry room and found the cream tablecloth soaking in the old stone sink. The red wine stain was now a pale shade of pink. She picked up a block of carbolic soap and vigorously rubbed it on the stain. Hearing a knock at the kitchen door, she emerged from the laundry room drying her hands, and saw Alexander through the glazed doors, clutching a large fir tree.

'Thank you,' she said, opening the door. 'That looks perfect. Could you bring it inside?'

He looked startled at the suggestion. 'Are you sure I should? I don't want any trouble.'

'It's all right, my husband's at work. I want to put the tree upstairs in the sitting room and I don't think I can manage it on my own. Will you follow me?'

She led the way upstairs to the hall, but Alexander paused anxiously at the top of the kitchen stairs. 'Come on,' she encouraged him. 'There's no one around. It's all right.'

In the bay window of the sitting room, a dark green enamelled pot stood ready. 'Put it in here, please,' she asked.

He bent down and arranged the stump in the pot, wedging it into position with a couple of logs from the fireplace. He stood back, straightening the trunk. 'There, madam. It's done.'

'That looks very nice. Thank you, Alexander.'

'I'll be off then,' he said, fiddling with the catch on the French windows that led to the garden.

'Alexander...'

'Yes, madam?' he stopped and turned to face her.

'Can I get you anything before you go... some extra food perhaps?'

'You shouldn't. It's against the rules.'

'I know... but follow me.'

She led the way back down to the basement kitchen and was opening a tin of Lebkuchen – spicy Christmas biscuits – when she heard Marta's heavy tread on the tiled floor of the hall above. 'Quick,' she whispered, passing Alexander a handful of biscuits, 'put these in your pocket.'

As she shepherded him to the back door, she took his hand. 'Come back at lunchtime,' she whispered. 'I'd like to give you a proper meal. A bowl of broth is not enough. Wait until after one... the maid will have gone out.'

To her surprise, she saw his eyes fill with tears. 'Why are you being so kind?'

'Because I like you – and I can't bear to think of you going hungry.'

After Alexander had gone, Annaliese went up to her bedroom to sort out the clothes for Marta's mother and the Winter Help Fund. Looking out at the garden, she watched him turning the compost heap; it steamed in the cold air. Alexander was never idle, she noticed. Somehow he found something to do every minute of the day – presumably eager to justify his pleasant gardening job, rather than working long hours at an armaments factory. Despite having the shed to retreat to, he was outside in all weathers. His prison-issue coat and shirt were tattered and threadbare, and she worried they couldn't possibly keep out the cold or the rain.

She went into her dressing room and selected a summer coat and a skirt for Marta's mother and laid them on the bed. In Hans' wardrobe she picked up a pile of clothes she had already put aside for the Winter Help Fund – an old coat he never wore and a moth-eaten sweater. As she fingered the soft coat and warm sweater, it occurred to her that Alexander needed them just as much as the men who would benefit from the Winter Help Fund.

The irony of this was not lost on her. That instead of giving clothing to German troops fighting the Russians, she was intending to give a Russian her German husband's clothes. Raiding Hans' wardrobe again, she found a couple of old shirts with frayed collars, and two pairs of warm socks, and added them to the pile on the bed, next to the separate pile of clothes for Marta's mother.

There was a knock at the door, and Marta came in dressed in her overcoat and best hat. 'I'm just leaving now, madam. There's some soup on the range for your lunch. Are you sure you'll be all right?'

'Yes, of course – I think I can manage to heat up some soup.' Annaliese smiled. 'Give my best to your mother – and don't forget to take these.' She handed Marta the coat and skirt.

'Thank you very much – I'm sure she'll be most grateful.' Marta glanced down at the second pile of men's clothes. 'Are these for the Winter Help Fund? Shall I take those downstairs and store them until the collection?'

'Oh... no, thank you,' said Annaliese hurriedly. 'I'll do it. Oh, and Marta – is my mother-in-law still here?'

'No, madam, she left over an hour ago.'

Annaliese was annoyed with herself that Marta had seen the pile of Hans' old clothes, as there was now a chance she would notice Alexander wearing them in the garden. That had been careless. Giving clothes to a slave was against the rules and it wasn't unknown for maids to denounce their employers. But surely Marta would not be that vindictive? She'd been with them for such a long time and had never been shown anything but kindness.

Annaliese took the clothes downstairs to the kitchen, and put them on the dresser. She heated up the soup on the range and laid the table for two. To her surprise she felt a sense of anticipation, as if she was expecting a special friend for lunch. She knew, of course, that to fraternise with a slave was illegal. Alexander was technically an 'Enemy of the State', and yet she felt drawn to him.

Just after one o'clock, she went out into the garden to call Alexander in for lunch. She found him filling the wheelbarrow with piles of fallen leaves.

'The soup is ready – would you like to come to the kitchen?'

'Are you sure, madam?' he asked.

'Of course. Everyone's out, it's quite safe. Come on, put the rake down and follow me.'

He did as he was told, but stopped at the back door. 'I shouldn't really come inside. Perhaps I should take my food back to the shed.'

'Don't be silly, it's far too cold. Besides, I'm all alone... please come in.'

He stepped inside, anxiously looking around the kitchen, as if he didn't really believe her, and began to untie his muddy boots. Standing in the doorway in his stockinged feet, she noticed his socks were full of holes.

'You can leave your boots by the door,' she instructed him. 'I promise we're alone. Now... sit down.' She held a chair out for him at the kitchen table.

He removed his old jacket, revealing his torn and tattered shirtsleeves. Annaliese retrieved the bundle of clothes from the dresser, and laid them on the table in front of him. 'I've dug out a few things that my husband doesn't wear any more. I thought you might like them – your jacket doesn't look nearly warm enough.'

Alexander touched the soft cloth of Hans' coat with his soiled hands and looked up at her. 'Are you sure? Isn't it against the law for you to give me anything?'

'Yes, technically, but no one need know. They're your gardening clothes. I thought you could keep them in the shed, and change into them when you arrive. Then, at least you'll be warm enough while you work.'

'What about your husband – won't he mind?'

'Oh, he won't even notice. Besides, he's at work all day. Would you like to wash your hands before lunch?'

Soap was rationed – even Annaliese struggled to get hold of it sometimes. She suspected there would be none at all in the labour camp barracks. Alexander scrubbed his hands with a brush, scraping under the fingernails and washing his forearms. He leant over and inhaled the scent of the soap, relishing the experience.

'Does that feel better?' she asked as he dried his hands on a towel.

He nodded, folded the towel carefully, and silently sat down at the table as she ladled the soup into two bowls. She cut a thick slice of bread and put it on his plate with some butter and a hunk of cheese.

'Can you spare that much?' he asked, wide-eyed.

'Yes. We get extra rations because of my husband's job.'

'Ah...' he said, picking up his spoon.

He ate the soup quickly, and then buttered the bread. 'It tastes wonderful,' he murmured.

'Do you want some more?' He nodded shyly and she refilled his soup bowl. It felt good to be able to feed him. He ate the second bowl more slowly – his appetite sated a little – and they sat in companionable silence for a while.

Annaliese was the first to speak. 'Can I ask you something? How did you meet my husband? How did he find you, I mean?'

His green eyes were alert suddenly, like a fox. 'Has he not told you?'

'Not really. He said you were supposed to go to the factory, but he thought you'd do well as a gardener, working for us.'

'Yes, that's true.'

'He tells me very little of what goes on in the camp. I know that you were there because we are at war with Russia. But he said you had German ancestry.'

'Yes. My grandparents emigrated to the Baltic States at the end of the last century. They owned a lot of land and factories – most of it was lost during the Revolution.' He put his spoon tidily in his bowl, and stood up suddenly, bowing slightly. 'Thank you for lunch, madam.'

'No... don't go yet.' She reached up and took his hand in hers; there was that spark again – like electricity running between them. 'We have time,' she said gently, 'everyone's out this afternoon. Please stay. I'd like to know more about you. I feel so ignorant sometimes. Hans tells me so little.'

He sat down reluctantly. 'What do you want to know?'

'Well, for example, before the factory, what job did you have in the camp?'

'I'm not sure I should say.'

'Why, was it a secret?'

He glanced at her – that fox-like stare again. 'I don't know... in a way.'

'Then I insist you tell me.' She put her spoon down and crossed her hands in her lap as if waiting for someone to tell her a story.

He paused, biting his lip. 'I'm not sure you will want to hear it.'

She felt her heart beginning to race – with anxiety, but also mild irritation. Why was he being so defensive? 'I think that's my decision, don't you?' she insisted. 'Tell me, please.'

'I was part of the experiments.'

'The experiments?'

'Yes... you know about them, of course.'

'I know they do medical experiments – searching for cures for diseases. Did you help the doctors in the lab? I thought you were an architect, not a scientist.'

A faint smile flickered across his face. 'It wasn't that sort of help.'

'I don't understand. I know my husband has an assistant called Eugène – were you a laboratory assistant too?'

'No. I wasn't there as an assistant... I was an experimental subject.'

She frowned, not understanding. 'A subject?'

'They use the prisoners to experiment on.'

'What?' she asked, her heart racing. 'No, no, no... that can't be right. Hans told me they use animals.'

'The only animals in the lab are the mosquitoes that they use to infect people with malaria.'

Annaliese stood up suddenly, and agitatedly started to clear the plates, stacking them clumsily one on top of the other.

'I'm sorry... I've upset you.' He leapt to his feet. 'I shouldn't have said anything. Thank you so much for the lunch, and for the clothes.'

She was standing with her back to him, placing the dishes in the sink, turning on the tap. 'What experiments were you made to do?' she asked in a quiet voice, her head spinning.

'I shouldn't say. You're upset.'

She swung round to face him. 'I'm asking you. Tell me – now.'

'Thermal experiments.'

'What do you mean?'

'They put prisoners into deep tanks of iced water to see how long they can survive, before they die of hypothermia.'

The bowl she was holding slipped from her fingers. It fell to the stone floor with a clatter, smashing into little pieces. He rushed over to her side, and began to pick them up.

'Leave it,' she said quietly, 'it doesn't matter. Tell me about the experiments. I want to know.'

He took her arm, and guided her back to her chair, sitting down opposite her at the table.

'All right, I'll tell you.' He began slowly, watching her reaction. 'The ice baths usually render people unconscious, which is when they're removed from the tank... hopefully before they die, but the doctors don't always get the timing right. They monitor the heart rate and temperature, of course. They then heat them up in various different ways to see which technique works best. If they do it too fast, people die anyway. I was fortunate – I was part of a group who were warmed up quite slowly. I did several experiments before they released me. Going to the factory was my reward for surviving.'

'Who runs these experiments?' she whispered. 'My husband?'

'No, it was a doctor called Rascher. Your husband is involved in other work, I think. I heard stories about malaria and certain types of drugs.'

'Do you know if people also die in his experiments?' she asked.

'I don't know, but I suspect so. Many people disappear. They go into the lab and never come out again. Russians, Poles, homosexuals, priests – we are all considered expendable.' His face was pale and drawn, and he fiddled anxiously with his water glass.

She reached across and covered his hand with her own. 'I'm so, so sorry... I didn't know,' she whispered, her eyes filling with tears.

The thought of Hans being involved in the sorts of experiments Alexander had described seemed unimaginable. That her husband – who had always been so gentle and mild-mannered – could be experimenting on human beings was horrific.

'I'm sorry if I upset you,' said Alexander, gently squeezing her hand.

'Please, please,' she said, weeping openly now, 'you have nothing... nothing to apologise for.'

'I should go.' He stood up abruptly and bowed again. 'Thank you for these.' He picked up the bundle of clothes and let himself out of the kitchen.

Distraught, Annaliese abandoned the kitchen and the dirty dishes, and retreated upstairs to her bedroom. Her head throbbed as she reflected on what Alexander had told her. Glancing out of the window, she watched him raking leaves, the new coat lying on the bench next to him.

Exhausted suddenly, she sat down heavily at her dressing table and studied her face in the mirror. She felt angry, but also impotent, trapped in a marriage with a man she no longer recognised. A man who had concealed from her the hideous work he was involved in – a man who had become a monster.

Casting her mind back to the start of their relationship, Hans had been a good man then, doing his best to help people and save lives. But he had clearly changed: to treat human beings as no more significant than laboratory mice was so horrifying she simply couldn't comprehend it. How could she love someone who was capable of such cruelty? How could she contemplate having a child with such a man?

She resolved to confront Hans when he got home that evening and demand that he stop such evil research work immediately; how would she live with herself otherwise? But gradually it dawned on her that any confrontation would simply put Alexander in jeopardy. The only way she could have found out about her husband's work was through speaking to the gardener, and if Hans knew they had been discussing it together, he would have him arrested and sent back to the camp – or worse, executed.

She realised she had no choice but to remain silent, and do her best to help Alexander in secret. It was the only sensible thing she could do.

13

FEBRUARY 1943

Hans climbed silently into the back seat of his staff car early one morning, and laid out his paperwork on the black leather. He had spent the previous few weeks focusing his attention on mescaline research. A new set of subjects had been selected from among the prisoners, and that morning the cactus extract would be administered to them in three different ways – one by injection, another would eat it and a third would drink it as a tea. A fourth subject would be given a regular amphetamine, which also had mind-altering effects, and would act as the experimental control.

Once at the camp, Hans went first into the laboratory searching for Eugène, but he was nowhere to be seen. He opened the door to his private office and was surprised, and not a little shocked, to see Heinrich Himmler sitting behind his desk.

'Ah, here you are,' Himmler said cheerfully. 'I've been waiting for you.'

'I'm so sorry, Reichsführer – if I'd known you were coming,

I'd have got here earlier.' Hans hung up his jacket with trembling fingers, and slipped into his white coat. His doctor's uniform put him at ease and created a distance between himself and Himmler. He was no longer the junior officer, but a professional doctor.

Himmler remained in Hans' chair, lolling slightly, swinging from side to side. 'The Führer has asked me to follow up on your experiments with mescaline. Science bores him as a rule, but he wanted a little more information, so I thought I'd come and see how you are getting on. I am hoping for great things from these experiments of yours.' He stared intently up at Hans. It was unsettling, particularly because Himmler had wrong-footed Hans by sitting at his desk.

'Yes, of course, Reichsführer,' Hans stuttered. Without his notes in front of him, his mind was blank.

'Well, get on with it,' Himmler demanded.

'Well, I have done one or two preliminary studies, and today we are proceeding with experiments on three different modes of administration, to try and establish which produces the fastest or most potent mental effects.'

'Good,' said Himmler, 'I'd like to see those results.'

'Yes, of course, Reichsführer – as soon as they're ready. It won't be today, though – the analysis takes a little time.'

'Oh, I didn't mean today,' said Himmler dismissively, waving his hand in the air. 'Get a little further down the road with your work and I'll come back. I'm really here today to meet with Sigmund Rascher. I have been closely involved with his work on the development of a treatment for sepsis. Do you know about his experiments?'

Hans nodded. He had certainly heard about the sepsis experiments. When he wasn't immersing prisoners in ice-cold water, Rascher was busy testing a new 'wonder drug'– something to rival the British penicillin, or so he told everyone. Trials had begun during the summer. Prisoners were first injected in the thigh with pus to provoke blood poisoning, after which they were given either Rascher's new wonder drug, or the standard sulphonamide treatment. Hans had heard that those treated with the new drug had invariably died. In spite of his lack of success, Rascher had relentlessly continued with the experiments, and the death toll was now considerable. It was also rumoured that Rascher's lab technicians were secretly handing out sulphonamide to the most recent intake of subjects, making a mockery of the experiments. But Hans couldn't blame them; the new 'drug' was an utter failure.

Knowing this was a pet project of Himmler's, Hans refrained from making any negative comments. 'Dr Rascher's work sounds very interesting and important, Reichsführer,' he said quietly. 'I'm sure it will be a success... over time.'

Himmler narrowed his eyes suspiciously. 'You don't sound very enthusiastic, but perhaps you could offer him some support. You have a certain scientific rigour that might be useful to him.'

Hans was about to decline, arguing that he was far too busy with his own work, but Himmler continued. 'You should know Sigmund and his wife Karoline are good friends of mine. They have just had their third son, and Karoline is sure it won't be long before they have a fourth.' He stared at Hans with his cold blue eyes. 'You and your wife... you have no children yet, do you?'

'Er... no,' Hans began, somewhat bewildered by this change of tack. 'Not yet, Reichsführer.'

'Then I advise you to get some,' said Himmler, finally standing up. 'There really is no excuse. You are a member of the SS. You have sworn to do your duty to the Führer, and part of that duty means producing children – males, in particular – for the Reich.'

Himmler briefly held Hans' gaze, then briskly raised his right hand in salute. 'Heil Hitler.'

'Heil Hitler,' responded Hans, as smartly as he could.

After Himmler had gone, Hans paced his office, worrying about the implications of their conversation. He despised Rascher, and was appalled by the thought of working with him. But more alarming was to have been compared with the man, and found wanting – at least as far as his lack of children was concerned.

There was a knock on the door. Fearing it was Himmler returning, Hans took a deep breath and opened the door. Eugène was standing outside.

'Yes?' Hans asked irascibly, resenting the intrusion. 'What do you want?'

'Should I assemble the subjects now, Sturmbannführer?' Eugène asked.

'Oh, yes, I'm sorry.' In his agitation Hans had almost forgotten the experiment. 'Are the doses ready?'

'Yes, everything is prepared.'

When the last of the subjects had been given the mescaline preparations, they were placed in locked cells for observation. It would take up to two hours before the substance took hold, and Eugène was standing by to monitor and record any initial reactions.

Hans retreated to his office. Brooding on Himmler's veiled threat about his childlessness, he made a decision: to establish whose fault it was – his, or Annaliese's. He was a scientist, after all, and must find the evidence and confront the truth. He locked the door and pulled down the window blind. He took out his microscope and put it on the desk. He sat down, and concentrated his thoughts on Annaliese. He visualised her wandering around their bedroom in her peignoir, it slipping off her shoulders, revealing her firm breasts and tight stomach.

Eventually he had a sample and transferred it to a small petri dish. He washed his hands and turned on the strong desk light. As he peered at the sample beneath the microscope's lens, his heart sank. Just one or two active sperm were crawling feebly across the glass. How could he break the news to Annaliese?

Back in the laboratory, Hans went through Eugène's notes detailing the mescaline subjects' reactions to the various modes of drug administration. They had all initially experienced nausea, trembling and sweating, and a rapid heartbeat, but their subsequent symptoms varied slightly. Those who had eaten or drunk the mescaline tea reacted faster than the subject who had been injected. The mechanism, Hans deduced, was that mescaline was absorbed most quickly via the intestinal tract. But it was clear that all the subjects experienced various types of hallucinations – causing some to scream, others to tear at their clothes, others simply to sit and stare.

'Thank you for the notes, Eugène, I'll go and take a look at them. The drug should be wearing off by now.'

Hans walked down the line of cells, peering through the peephole in the metal doors. 'How are you?' he asked each of them by name, hoping they were still alive. Hans was relieved to see each one look up from their grubby mattress and acknowledge him.

But when he arrived at the final cell, there was no reaction at all from the inmate – a young man of no more than eighteen. 'Guard, unlock the door,' Hans ordered. He went inside, and found the boy slumped against the wall, his head lolling to one side. Hans placed his fingers on the boy's neck, but there was no pulse. Instinctively he manoeuvred the boy onto the floor and began resuscitation, pounding the boy's chest. 'Guard, fetch Eugène from the laboratory... now.'

His lab technician was there within seconds. 'Oh, no,' he gasped. 'Is he dead?'

Hans gave up his pounding. He listened for the boy's breathing and checked his pulse. 'Yes. I'm afraid he's gone. I thought you were watching them.'

'I did... I was. I only left them alone for short while. I'm sorry.'

'How was he the last time you checked?'

Eugène flicked through his notes. 'He was having breathing difficulties about an hour ago, sir.' He looked guiltily over at Hans.

'You should have called me then.'

'I tried to, sir... but your door was locked. I didn't like to interrupt.'

Hans flushed slightly, before collecting himself. 'Well... it's not your fault. These things happen. Who knows what under-lying medical issues he had. He may have had a weak heart, for example.' He closed the boy's eyes, and stood up. 'It's such a pity, Eugène. I had thought there would be little long-term risk to the subjects from this set of experiments. Please arrange for the body to be disposed of.'

As he wrote up his notes that afternoon, Hans was unable to rid himself of a vision of the boy, lying slumped against the wall. People died in the camp all the time – from dysentery, starva-tion or sheer brutality. One or two had even died as a result of his malaria experiments – although he had strived to save them. But this boy's fate seemed less acceptable. He had effectively poisoned him to death.

It was late when he called for his driver. On the way home, he was haunted by the face of the dead boy, but also tormented by what he had discovered about his own fertility. Perhaps it would have been better not to know. How could he and

Annaliese have a child now? The only route open to them was to adopt as part of the Lebensborn programme. But that would simply compound his sense of failure.

He arrived home and hung up his overcoat on the coat-stand in the hall. The dining room was dark; Annaliese and his mother had obviously finished dinner. He could hear music coming from the sitting room at the end of the corridor. Perhaps they were listening to a concert on the radio.

'Good evening,' he said, opening the door.

Annaliese looked up from her embroidery. 'Your supper is in the kitchen.' Her tone was cold. Recently, she had been increasingly offhand with him, he had noticed – snapping at him about the slightest thing.

Elisabetta reproached her sharply. 'You should go and get it for him, Annaliese. The poor man must be worn out.'

'No, it's all right, I'll fetch it myself,' said Hans, not wishing to irritate his wife further.

Marta was sitting at the kitchen table, polishing silver.

'Good evening, sir,' she said, leaping to her feet. 'Your supper is keeping warm on top of the range. Are you happy to eat it here in the kitchen, or would you rather I set it upstairs for you in the dining room?'

'No, thank you. I'll eat it here.'

Back in the sitting room after his solitary meal, Hans found his mother alone, the fire flickering in the grate.

'Is Annaliese not here?' he asked, throwing a log onto the fire.

'No... she went upstairs twenty minutes ago. Hans dear, do sit down. You look exhausted.'

He sat down on the sofa opposite her, and gazed forlornly into the flames. 'Yes – I am rather tired... In fact,' he said, standing up suddenly, 'I think I'll go up to bed too. Goodnight.'

Their bedroom was dark as he opened the door, but through the gloom he could see the outline of his wife lying in bed. He crept past her and into the bathroom, shutting the door. He turned on the light and studied himself in the mirror. He looked haggard – racked by a devastating combination of shame and guilt. He was a bad doctor and a worse husband. He quietly put on his pyjamas, and slid gently into bed next to Annaliese, who moaned and turned over to face away from him. Was she really asleep, he wondered, or just pretending?

Sometime in the middle of the night they were woken by rumbling engine noise overhead. This was followed by the distant sound of explosions, and the faint whine of a siren. Annaliese sat up, rubbing her eyes. 'Are the bombers back?' she asked sleepily. 'Should we go to the cellar?'

Hans was already out of bed, and peering between the curtains. 'There's a raid going on, but it looks like it's a few miles from here, in the suburbs. I think we'll be all right.'

'Why do they keep attacking the suburbs?' she asked.

'To destroy our industries and break our spirits. Try to go back to sleep.'

Hans woke early the following morning, and lay for some time watching his wife sleeping. She finally opened her eyes and smiled. But as soon as she noticed him gazing at her, her smile disappeared.

'Annaliese... what's the matter, darling?'

'Nothing,' she replied irritably. 'I'm just tired after last night. Tired and frightened.' She swung her legs out of bed. 'I'm going to have a bath.'

He lay in bed for a while, listening to the sound of running water. Determined to confess his infertility, he got up and tentatively opened the bathroom door. He found her lying on her back in the water, her hair fanned out behind her.

'You are so beautiful,' he said, sitting on the chair next to the bath and gazing at her.

'What do you want?' she asked brusquely, covering her breasts modestly with an arm. 'Can't I have a bath alone?'

'Yes... yes, of course. I'm sorry. I'll leave you.'

She soon emerged from the bathroom, draped in a towel, and found him lurking by the door. 'What do you want, Hans?'

'Nothing... nothing at all.'

As Annaliese sat down at her dressing table, Hans quickly retreated into the bathroom and locked the door. As he shaved, he considered his predicament. Perhaps now would not be the best time to tell Annaliese what he had just discovered about his fertility. She already seemed so angry with him; such a revelation would only make an already tense situation much worse.

Coming out of the bathroom, he found Annaliese had already left the room. As he began to dress, he glanced out of the window. He could see Annaliese at the bottom of the garden talking to the Russian. The man was wearing an overcoat which looked strangely familiar. 'That's my old coat, damn it,' he muttered angrily to himself. Surely Annaliese could not have been so foolish as to give it to the Russian? Did she not realise that giving gifts to a slave was illegal?

Hans watched the pair for some minutes, analysing their body language. They looked well matched – both were tall, blond and striking. And there was an intimacy in the way they related to one another. At one point, the Russian must have said something amusing, because Annaliese laughed, tossing back her head coquettishly.

His instinct was to rush down to the garden and separate them; to have the Russian arrested and sent back to Dachau. It would be easy enough – indeed, if he reported the man for stealing his coat, he would be executed on the spot. And, judging by the way his wife was gazing up him, the Russian would deserve it, for it looked like he *had* stolen something – something far more significant than a coat. He had stolen her heart. Everything suddenly became clear – her emotional distance from him, her angry outbursts, her reluctance to make love – it all made sense. The Russian had seduced his wife behind his back, in his own house, and she had fallen for him. How could he have been so blind, so foolish?

Seething with jealousy and rage, Hans put on his SS jacket and pistol belt, and headed downstairs to confront them. But he suddenly stopped in his tracks, struck by an idea. Might his wife's affection for the Russian be the solution to his fertility problem, rather than the cause of a marital disaster?

As soon as the idea entered his head, he tried to expel it. Clearly, it was absurd, and yet... was it? Gradually his thoughts crystallised. However much it hurt him that his wife might care for someone else, the Fatherland required sacrifices from everyone, especially senior SS officers like him who had sworn a personal allegiance to the Führer. In particular, his failure to produce at least one child was already putting both him and his wife at risk. Himmler's veiled threats that morning had made that quite obvious. If Hans could keep a clear head and control his emotions, might the Russian, in fact, prove his salvation?

He went to his study to collect his research papers, and glanced out of the window into the garden. His beloved, beautiful wife was still chatting gaily with the handsome Russian. The pain Hans felt was almost physical – like a stab in the heart. But that morning, in the car en route to Dachau, he made up his mind to turn the situation to his advantage – his own future depended on it.

14

MARCH 1943

The winter months of 1943 were intensely cold. Even as the spring bulbs nosed their way through the frozen ground, ice formed on the insides of the windows overnight. Annaliese stayed in bed as long as possible after Hans had gone to work. She would eventually get up, wrap up in her warmest dressing gown and scrape the ice off the windows. Alexander was always hard at work digging over the rock-hard ground. She worried about him in these harsh conditions, but was relieved to see him wearing her husband's overcoat.

Ever since Annaliese had learned the truth about Hans' experiments at the camp, she found it hard to mask her true feelings about him. She no longer saw him as the kindly man who had rescued her from relative poverty, whisked her away to Paris on honeymoon, and fretted about her during a bombing raid. Now, all she could see was a monster, who treated human life with contempt.

Hans had never really discussed his work, and now she knew why. She realised that ever since he had worked at

Dachau he had become secretive, deflecting any questions. Thinking back to their earliest conversations about the camp, it was she who had presumed he would be doing experiments on animals – an impression Hans had done nothing to alter.

Increasingly, they lived in their own private worlds, rarely speaking. He usually left for work so early that there was no time to talk, and when he did come home, he was sullen and preoccupied. Of course, the continuing presence of Elisabetta made everything worse – although fortunately her mother-in-law was so self-obsessed that she seemed not to notice her son's deteriorating relationship with his wife. Or maybe it suited her – she had always resented her daughter-in-law.

The real problems began at bedtime. Hans' physical presence repulsed Annaliese and she found any intimacy unbearable. She tried to avoid it by going to bed early, and pretending to be asleep when he came upstairs. But sometimes he followed her upstairs, and when she came out of the bathroom, he would be lying in bed waiting for her.

During the day she managed to distract herself by planning improvements to the garden. She began to design a new border and spent hours studying gardening books she had borrowed from the library, and sketching out ideas. Armed with her drawings and lists of plants, she would seek out Alexander in the garden. To her delight, his face would light up when he saw her. Sometimes, when both her mother-in-law and Marta were out, she would bring him a flask of coffee or hot soup, and they would sit together companionably in his shed. They talked about everything – their ambitions before the war, and what they hoped for when it was finally over. They spoke too of their early lives, including how she and Hans had met.

'Perhaps I was naïve,' she said, after telling the whole story. 'Well, I'm sure I was... but I met Hans when I was so young, just eighteen. My parents had both died, and he was more like a father figure really. I have lived a life of privilege ever since, a life that many would envy. But I swear I had no idea what was being done at Dachau. I thought Hans was saving lives, not taking them.' She reached out, taking Alexander's hand in hers. 'You do believe me, don't you?'

'Of course,' he said compassionately. 'What they are doing is too horrific for an outsider to imagine. How would you ever guess what was going on? But you know now.'

'Yes,' she said, 'I know now, and I'm ashamed.'

Gradually, in Annaliese's mind at least, their friendship grew into something more profound. She thought about Alexander all the time, and began to plan her days around seeing him. After sending Marta off around town on long errands, she would encourage Elisabetta to go out and meet friends – anything to be alone for a precious hour or so with Alexander. Was she in love with him? She began to believe she was. Of course, she had once thought she loved Hans, but this felt different. Her love for Hans had not been based on sexual passion; he had made her feel safe, almost like a child with a parent. When she discovered the truth about his work, that sense of being protected had evaporated, and with it the love she had once felt for him. Now, her affection was directed towards Alexander. He provoked in her a sort of raw passion which was quite novel and exciting. She had butterflies in her stomach at the prospect of seeing him. When they were together, she felt breathless and craved his touch. She had never felt that way with Hans.

Did Alexander return her feelings? If he did, he kept them to himself. He had never been anything other than meticulously polite and courteous, had never done more than take Annaliese's hand. How would he react, she wondered, if she kissed him, or tried to make love to him?

Eventually, the desire for him – the sheer physical need to feel his arms around her – made her reckless. One afternoon, when Elisabetta was out, Annaliese despatched Marta to the shops. Watching from the landing window, she waited until her maid had reached the end of the road, and then ran downstairs, pulling on her overcoat. She hurried down the garden path towards the shed, her eyes gleaming with excitement.

'I only have a minute,' she said grinning, pulling Alexander into the shed and closing the door behind her. 'I just had to see you.'

He looked nervously back towards the house through the grubby side window.

'It's all right,' she reassured him, 'my mother-in-law is out, and I sent Marta to the shop on the corner. But she'll be back soon, so we must be quick.' She took hold of his hand, reached up and kissed his cheek. 'You're so cold,' she murmured. 'Let me warm you up.'

'What are you doing?' He pulled away, frowning. 'Someone might come.'

'No, they won't. I told you, we're alone.' She gazed up at him. 'Don't you want to kiss me? I want to kiss you so much...'

He hesitated for a second, before lowering his head towards hers. Their lips just grazed at first, but then he wrapped her in his arms, and kissed her with such passion, she felt herself floating. 'I think I love you... I love you,' she whispered as he released her.

He stroked her cheek. 'You shouldn't say that – it's too dangerous. I fear for you, for us.'

'But it's true,' she said. 'When Hans makes love to me, it's you I think about. It's the only way I can bear it.'

She kissed him again, but he pulled away. 'You should go,' he whispered, 'before the maid gets back.'

'All right,' she reluctantly agreed.

Walking back to the house, Annaliese felt her heart racing and her body surging with adrenalin.

Making time to be with Alexander soon became an addiction. The moment she woke up, she began to plot how to be alone with him. To her frustration, it was a cold, damp spring, which made Elisabetta reluctant to go out. Instead, she would occupy a chair in the sitting room, sewing or reading, with a perfect view of the garden, making it impossible for Annaliese and Alexander to meet.

One afternoon Elisabetta stopped Annaliese in the hall. 'Oh, there you are. I was coming to find you. The sun is shining at last, and although it's cold, I'd like to go out into the garden.'

'Please do,' replied Annaliese.

'But I would like *you* to accompany me. It was frosty this morning and the steps might be slippery.'

Annaliese suppressed a sigh. 'Yes, of course – if you insist.'

Elisabetta glared at her. 'You can be very rude sometimes, you know. I would have thought you would want to help me – you have nothing better to do, after all.'

'Yes, of course... I'm sorry, Elisabetta, I wasn't thinking. I'll just go and check on the weather.' She hurried into the sitting room, and looked out on to the garden, searching for Alexander. She spotted him, working on her new border, halfway down the garden. To her horror, she realised he was wearing Hans' old coat. If her mother-in-law saw it, she would be bound to recognise it.

She came back into the hall. 'It looks a bit like snow, Mama. Are you really sure you want to go out now?'

'I need some air,' insisted Elisabetta impatiently. 'If it's cold, perhaps you could bring my fur?'

Outside on the terrace, Annaliese coughed loudly, alerting Alexander to her presence. To her relief, he moved silently away, pushing the wheelbarrow towards the compost heap behind the shed.

Elisabetta soon emerged wearing her coat, and Annaliese

guided her down the stone steps. They stopped at the bottom to admire the winter border; it was filled with snowdrops and the beginnings of purple crocuses, mixed with winter-flowering shrubs. The two women began to walk slowly up the garden.

'What's going on here?' Elisabetta asked, stopping by a patch of bare earth.

'I'm making a new border,' replied Annaliese. 'Eventually it will be full of spring bulbs, but later in the year I'll plant some roses, and perhaps lavender – I've not quite decided.' Alexander, she noticed, was peering out from behind the shed. Discreetly, she shook her head at him.

'Where's the gardener?' Elisabetta asked darkly.

'I don't know – by the compost heap, perhaps.'

'Good, I don't want to see him – filthy Russian.'

'I really think we ought to go back inside now,' Annaliese suggested, 'it definitely looks as if snow is coming...'

She guided her mother-in-law back towards the house and up onto the terrace. As Annaliese was trying to open the catch on the French windows, Elisabetta turned around to have a last look at the garden.

'Oh, there he is, the Russian,' she exclaimed, spotting Alexander appearing from behind the shed. 'But why on earth is he wearing Hans' coat?' She swung round and glared at Annaliese.

'Oh, I don't think it's Hans' coat, is it? Come on, let's get inside.'

Elisabetta stood her ground. 'That *is* Hans' coat,' she insisted. 'I'd know it anywhere – I bought it for him.'

'Oh, yes, of course – *that* coat. Well, it was my idea. Hans never wears it any more, so I gave it to the gardener. He's out in all weathers and his own coat was falling to pieces.'

'How dare you give that filthy wretch my son's coat?' shouted Elisabetta. 'Go and get it back – now.'

'I really can't do that,' said Annaliese plaintively. 'The gardener needs it and Hans doesn't.'

'Now listen to me. If Hans no longer wears the coat it should be donated to our brave soldiers on the Front, who are losing their lives fighting people like him,' Elisabetta shouted again, pointing a bony, manicured finger at Alexander.

'I can donate another coat to the Winter Fund,' Annaliese suggested brightly. 'One of mine – they get remade for the men, anyway. There's really no reason to take it away from him, is there? That would just be cruel.'

But Elisabetta wasn't listening; she had already marched back down the steps and was striding purposefully up the garden. 'You... you there,' she shouted at the gardener. 'Take off that coat at once.'

Annaliese ran as fast as she could to overtake her, and stood defensively in front of Alexander. 'Please, leave him alone. I gave him the coat – it's not his fault.'

'How dare you defy me!' Elisabetta slapped Annaliese's face. 'I shall speak to Hans about this.' She marched away up the steps and into the house through the French windows.

Alexander took off the coat and handed it to Annaliese. 'Here, it's not worth it. If she reports you, we're both in trouble.'

'She wouldn't dare. Hans would be furious with her. She'd never do that. Please keep it, I insist.' Annaliese looked up into his troubled face, and felt a wave of passion for him. She wanted to take Alexander in her arms, and kiss him there and then.

'You should go now,' he said quietly. 'She will be watching you.'

Annaliese briefly touched his hand. 'I'll bring you some food later.'

Annaliese returned to the house to find Elisabetta shaking with fury. 'How dare you?' she hissed. 'How dare you demean Hans and this family? How dare you break the rules? Who are you to behave in such a way? You're nothing but a common little grocer's daughter. You were never good enough for Hans. I warned him at the time. You can't even get pregnant. He should divorce you immediately. I will speak to him when he comes home.'

Annaliese spent the rest of the afternoon alone by the window in the sitting room, watching Alexander working in the garden. Hans' coat, she noticed, had been folded carefully and placed on a chair outside on the terrace. When she went out to collect it, he glanced up from his work briefly, but not a flicker of recognition crossed his face. At dusk, as the light began to fade, he gathered up his tools, putting them away in his shed. He emerged a few minutes later, wearing his prison shirt and old brown jacket, and walked down the path, heading for his barracks. In the fading light, as the moon rose over the garden, he looked up at her just once more. She blew him a kiss and he was gone.

That evening, she was sitting gloomily at her dressing table, when Hans burst into the bedroom. 'What the hell's been going on here? My mother is incandescent – talking about me divorcing you.'

'Oh, we went out to look at the garden and she saw I'd given the gardener an old coat of yours. She made a terrible fuss, and insisted he gave it back, which he has.'

'You do realise how foolish that was, don't you?' Hans was pacing the room, his face white with anger. 'To give him anything was madness. It's illegal, Annaliese. I thought I'd made that quite clear when I brought him here. No gifts, no favouritism, only basic meals. My mother is threatening to report you. Do you understand what that would mean?'

'She wouldn't dare,' Annaliese replied petulantly. 'It's ridiculous. Why can't I give him the coat – you never wear it.'

He pulled her up roughly from her chair. 'Don't you understand? You could go to prison. Do you really want that? Of course not. I know what these prisons are like...'

She glared up at him, yanking her arms free of him. 'Do you? Do you, Hans? What are they like, then?' She could feel fury welling up inside her and all her resolve to stay silent evaporated. 'What is it that you do exactly in these prisons, Hans?'

He looked at her through narrowed eyes; his voice suddenly became measured and calm. 'I do medical research – you know that.'

'What sort of medical research?' She could feel the blood rushing in her ears. There was a sort of madness to her defiance, as if she were on the edge of something cataclysmic.

'I research cures for illnesses. I've already told you...'

'Yes, you've already told me, but was it the truth?'

'What exactly are you trying to say?' His tone was cold and clipped. His grey eyes studied her face, penetrating deep inside her very being. For the first time ever, she was frightened of him.

Tears came into Annaliese's eyes as she realised she had come dangerously close to losing control. Confronting her husband with what she really knew was impossible – it would serve no purpose and put Alexander in danger. She took a deep breath and tried to calm herself. 'Nothing,' she replied meekly. 'I'm not trying to say anything. I just... I just don't understand why everything and everyone has to be so cruel!'

'If you are referring to the Russian, do you think it's cruel of me to offer one of our nation's enemies a job in our garden? Don't you think he'd rather work here than in a factory twelve hours a day, or be back locked up in Dachau? Don't you think I've actually been quite kind to him?'

Annaliese felt trapped, aware that at any moment she risked betraying Alexander's confidence. 'Yes,' she murmured. 'You have been very kind to him. I'm sorry... I apologise for what I said.'

She sank down onto the chair, trying to think of a plausible excuse for her outburst. 'I think perhaps it's the strain of your mother living with us,' she said. 'I feel her watching me all the time... it's exhausting.'

Hans stood behind her with his hands on her shoulders, looking at her reflection in the dressing table mirror. He was smiling now – the old Hans once again. 'You are a silly girl, sometimes. I will talk to Mother and make her understand that she must try to be more considerate, for all our sakes. But I wonder if it would be better for everyone if the Russian were to leave.'

Annaliese felt a tightening sensation in her chest, verging on panic. She had risked everything, and now risked losing Alexander himself – all for the sake of a coat.

'Don't do that, darling,' she said gently, trying to keep her tone light and carefree. 'He's just beginning to get the garden organised. I've been planning a new border, and he's already dug it out.' She smiled happily, looking up at her husband. 'I'll be more careful, Hans, I promise. And I'll be nice to your mother, and I'll be a better wife. Just, don't send him away. None of this is his fault.'

Hans kissed the top of her head. 'All right, if that's what you want. But try to be more careful.'

15

MAY 1943

Heinrich Himmler arrived unannounced at the Dachau medical block one afternoon. After a tour of the various experiments, he ordered Hans to join him for a private meeting in his office. As usual, he took Hans' chair behind his desk, leaving Hans standing awkwardly on the other side.

'The last time we met I suggested you offer some support to Dr Rascher,' Himmler said briskly. 'He has too much on his plate and you are the obvious person to assist him. For some reason that help has not been forthcoming. Can you explain?'

Hans flushed with embarrassment. He had deliberately avoided making contact with Rascher, infuriated at the idea of 'supporting' him, hoping Himmler might forget his instruction. 'I apologise, sir,' he began hesitantly, 'and am grateful, obviously, for your faith in me – but as I think I explained at the time, I am in the middle of my own experiments. In fact, I'm at a rather critical stage.'

'Yes, yes... I'm sure,' Himmler replied irritably, 'but I'm also sure that you can find some time to support a colleague. He is running two projects, remember. First, the Luftwaffe cold-water exposure experiments, which now require statistical evaluation, but also his work on sepsis. That is the imperative now, and I expect you to drop what are you doing and help him.'

'If I may make so bold, Reichsführer,' Hans began tentatively, 'I should perhaps point out that I am also running two sets of experiments – malaria research, but also mescaline – something in which, I had thought, the Führer had taken a personal interest.'

'I am perfectly aware of your workload, Dr Vogel.' Himmler's eyes narrowed. 'As for malaria, Dr Schilling has already taken charge of that project and he tells me that your personal involvement is now less important. We have plans... ideas for how to make use of his research. We are considering using malaria as a form of biological warfare in North Africa.'

Hans was taken aback. 'But with respect, sir, how could that possibly work? There would surely be a risk of infecting our own troops.'

'Dr Vogel, I am surprised that you question my judgement.' Himmler's tone was icy.

'I'm not questioning it, Reichsführer, sir,' replied Hans hurriedly, regretting speaking out. 'But as a scientist, I am simply pointing out the inherent flaw in such a proposal.'

'I am not interested in your opinions, Dr Vogel,' said Himmler, slapping his hand on the desk. 'From today, you will cease your work on malaria, and support Dr Rascher with his sepsis research – starting next week. You may continue with the mescaline experiments when you have time. Is that clear?'

Hans realised any dissent was futile. 'Perfectly clear, Reichsführer.'

To his relief, Himmler stood up, indicating the meeting was over. 'Good, that's settled,' he said, patting his pockets and heading for the door. Halfway through the doorway, Himmler turned around. 'Oh... and how is your wife?'

'My wife?'

'Yes, your wife. She is still not pregnant, I understand.'

'Not as far as I know,' Hans replied, disconcerted. 'But we are trying.'

'Well... you should try harder. When I next drop by, I expect results not only from the sepsis trials, but also some marital results from you.'

Himmler swept out, and Hans sank back down into his chair. He loathed Rascher, and the prospect of having to work as his assistant filled him with resentment. The man was a sadist, and anyone could see he had no talent for science; it was hardly surprising his experiments were going so badly. What Hans found particularly frustrating was that his own experiments on mescaline were beginning to pay dividends. He resolved to write up his notes as soon as possible, in order to present them to Himmler the next time he 'dropped by'. Perhaps then he would see what a fine researcher Hans really was.

He called for his car, and sat slumped and dejected in the back seat as they drove through the streets of Munich in the moonlight. The Führerbau, he noticed, had been swaddled in huge camouflage nets since his last visit – presumably to disguise it during enemy air strikes.

He thought back to that curious evening when Hitler had showed such interest in his work. Naïvely, Hans had hoped his future was assured after that encounter; how wrong he had been.

When Hans arrived home, the hall and dining room were in darkness, but a light shone beneath the sitting room door. Realising that Annaliese and his mother must already have finished supper, he went down to the kitchen where Marta laid out his food on the kitchen table.

When he'd eaten, he joined his family in the sitting room.

'Ah, Hans – there you are,' said his mother. 'I thought I heard you coming in earlier. Have you had supper, darling?'

'Yes, Mother.'

Annaliese was sitting on the sofa near the fire, sewing buttons onto an old jacket. Hans sat down next to her.

'I had a visit today,' he began.

'Oh, yes.' Annaliese didn't look up.

'From Heinrich Himmler.'

'Oh, Hans... how marvellous,' interjected Elisabetta. 'What did he want?'

'He asked me to support the work of a colleague.'

'That's splendid,' said his mother. 'He must admire you very much.'

'Perhaps,' replied Hans doubtfully. He looked across at Annaliese, who studiously avoided his gaze. 'Well,' he said, rising. 'I'm tired. I'm going up to bed. See you in a minute?' He reached across and touched Annaliese's shoulder. She flinched visibly.

'Yes...' she answered sharply. 'In a minute.'

Hans was still awake when Annaliese came in. She took her bathrobe from the behind the bedroom door, went into the bathroom and locked it behind her. She often did that nowadays, he noticed, avoiding undressing in front of him. Emerging a few minutes later, wearing her nightgown, the bathrobe wrapped tightly round her, she wordlessly sat at her dressing table, brushing her hair, and rubbing cream into her face.

'Did you have a nice day?' he asked gently.

Annaliese flicked him a look in the mirror. 'It was all right. Your mother insisted I took her to Café Luitpold for lunch.'

'That must have been nice?' he suggested.

'Not really,' she replied sullenly.

'Why?' he asked. 'Please tell me...'

She turned and looked at him. 'You really want to hear about my day?'

'Yes... I do.'

She put the pot of cream down on the dressing table. 'Well, it was a sunny day, so we sat outside. I hadn't realised before that the café is opposite the Gestapo headquarters. A van turned up as we were drinking our coffee and suddenly the doors were thrown open, and a horde of foreign labourers – girls as well as men – were pushed unceremoniously out of the van, onto the pavement. I recognised a couple of them – one was a waitress who works at Café Opera, and beside her was the manager. He's a nice man – do you know him?'

Hans shook his head.

'He's very kind,' Annaliese went on, 'the manager... always very jolly. Anyway, the soldiers pushed them violently into the building. I dread to think what was going to happen to them.'

'I think we can guess, can't we?' Hans replied gently. 'They must have broken the rules somehow.'

She shot him a look. 'Rules! There are so many rules now. You can't breathe for rules.'

'I know it's hard, I understand, I really do. We all live with these rules, Annaliese – me more than anyone.'

'Are you asking for my sympathy?' She turned back to the mirror and began brushing her hair vigorously.

'No, I'm asking for your understanding. I know you're upset with me because of what I do, but I'm under orders. If I disobey I will die. It's that simple. Himmler is putting me under pressure – not just to get results in my work, but even to have a child.'

'What's it got to do with him?'

'He made the rules... his ten commandments... that's what. He as good as told me that I'm finished as an SS scientist, if we don't have a child.'

She swung round on her stool and stared at him. 'You are not serious?'

'Perfectly serious, darling.'

He hadn't called her *darling* for months.

'What are we supposed to do?' she asked quietly. 'Am I in danger too?'

'Possibly.' He paused, steeling himself. 'Listen, my love, I have to tell you something important – something I've avoided telling you for some time.'

'Go on.'

He paused and breathed out deeply, as if calming his nerves. 'Annaliese, it's my fault we can't have children. I've done the tests... I know it's me. Do you understand what I'm saying?'

'Yes, I think so.' She was listening intently.

'We have two options,' he went on calmly. 'We either adopt a child, or... you have to get pregnant in some other way.'

Annaliese stared at him, open-mouthed. 'How do you suggest I do that?'

'I think we both know the solution, don't we?'

She looked at him blankly.

'Come, my dear,' Hans went on. 'I've seen the way you look at him.' He had a momentary flash of panic that he had been mistaken – that perhaps she didn't like the Russian at all. But the flushing on her cheeks told him his suspicions were correct.

'Are you suggesting that I—'

'—sleep with the Russian?' Hans interjected. 'Yes.'

'I can't believe you want me to do that! I mean, I...'

'I know you like him – that you're attracted to him. Maybe I'm mistaken... but tell me it's not true.'

He looked across at her, his face pained, as if he dreaded her answer. She turned back to her dressing table. 'I don't know what you mean,' she said evasively.

'Annaliese... I've known for a long time how you feel about

him. And, while that hurts me more than I can say, in many ways it makes what I'm about to suggest simpler – because I couldn't ask you to sacrifice yourself to someone you disliked. And it's the only way out, Annaliese. Even adoption from the Lebensborn programme would, I fear, be frowned upon. Being unable to produce a child of my own would seriously count against me. Himmler is already forcing me to work for that idiot Rascher. He's lost faith in my work.'

'Is this really about your professional pride?' Annaliese asked angrily.

'No! Not at all.' He paused momentarily. 'Well... it is, in part, of course, but I genuinely fear for us both if we remain childless.' Hans came over and put his hands on her shoulders. 'Besides, it would be wrong to deny you something you want so intensely. I know you'd love a child... we used to talk of having three, do you remember?'

'Of course I remember,' she spat back. 'But that was before...'

'Before what?'

She wanted to reply '*Before I discovered I was married to a monster*', but she held her tongue. 'Before the war,' she replied calmly. Breathing deeply, she studied herself in the mirror. 'If I did agree to your idea – and I'm not saying I will – what about Marta, what about your mother? How do you expect me to seduce someone with them watching me all the time.'

Annaliese observed how he flinched slightly when she used the word *seduce*. She should have been more clinical, she realised – even the word upset him. And yet, bizarrely, that was what they were discussing – her being asked to seduce someone – almost on her husband's orders. Images of Alexander making love to her flooded her mind and she shook her head, almost as if she were trying to shake the thoughts away.

'I'll think of something,' Hans replied quietly. 'I'll suggest Marta visits her mother in Augsburg for a night or two. And I'll take my mother away somewhere – next weekend perhaps, or whenever the time is right... in your cycle.'

'In my cycle? Oh, I see, yes. Let me think... my period was a couple of weeks ago, so, yes, next weekend should be fine.'

'I know,' said Hans gently. 'I'd already worked that out.'

She stared at him, surprised by his attention to detail. She picked up a pot of hand cream. 'What if I don't get pregnant the first time?' she asked, rubbing the cream into her hands.

'Then we continue until you do.' He sank down and sat on the end of the bed, his head in his hands.

She swung round on her stool, and studied him closely. 'Are you really sure about this? Do you understand what you're asking?' The idea that she was being given licence to have an affair seemed extraordinary. Perhaps he envisaged sex taking place like one of his experiments – as a purely clinical exercise – done without emotion, without passion. But, of course, as far as she was concerned, emotion and passion were at the heart of it.

'I understand perfectly what I am asking,' he replied. 'And I can assure you I'm not at all happy about it, but I can't see another way out. I've racked my brains, and this is really the only solution.'

It felt as if they were making a pact with the devil. They both knew that what they were planning was a crime punishable by death. Almost every month there were stories in the newspapers of slaves being hanged for sexual liaisons with German nationals.

'What if we're found out?' Somehow voicing her fears made them more tangible. 'I'm frightened, Hans,' she whispered.

'I'm frightened too,' he replied. 'But really, it's a choice between the lesser of two evils...' Tears were streaming down his cheeks.

She looked deeply into his eyes. 'I'm relieved somehow. For you not to be frightened would make you... almost inhuman.'

He took her hand in his and kissed it tenderly. 'Come to bed, darling.'

They lay down, and for the first time in months she laid her head on his chest and allowed him to wrap her in his arms.

'We live in extraordinary times,' he murmured into her hair, 'where morality, duty and human decency are in short supply. I am surrounded at work by immense cruelty and it's because of what I see each day that I feel this is the only sensible course of action. I love you more than life itself, and it's because I love you that I can bear this. Just try... not to love him too much – and come back to me when it's done.'

She nestled against his chest. 'I'll try, Hans. I promise.'

16

MAY 1943

Hans lost no time in making the arrangements. Over dinner the following evening, he broached the subject of them all taking a weekend break.

'Mama...' he began. 'I was thinking, we should go and visit Aunt Charlotte sometime soon – maybe next weekend.'

'Go all the way to Salzburg to visit my sister? Why the sudden rush to see her now?'

'Because the last time she came to see us I was very busy and didn't give her enough attention. She's a nice old soul, and our only relative. I worry about her living alone.'

'Oh, don't worry about Charlotte,' said Elisabetta. 'She's always got precisely what she wanted – our parents' house, for one thing.'

Hans smiled benignly. 'Now, don't be like that, Mama. The poor thing never married – where else should she have lived? Besides, I like Charlotte – and so does Annaliese, don't you?'

'Yes... oh, yes,' replied Annaliese enthusiastically. 'I'm very fond of Charlotte.'

'And, as it happens,' Hans went on, 'I could do with a break. You're always telling me I work too hard. And Salzburg's only a few hours away and would be lovely at this time of year. We'll all go, won't we?'

He looked conspiratorially at Annaliese, who nodded eagerly. 'Oh, do say we can go,' she encouraged Elisabetta. 'Hans really could do with a weekend away. He's been working so hard.'

'Well,' said Elisabetta doubtfully, 'if you both insist, I'll write to her this evening. I admit the countryside around her house is very charming at this time of year.'

Charlotte's letter arrived by return, saying she would be delighted to welcome the three of them the following weekend.

On Saturday morning, Annaliese packed a bag for Hans. 'Are you sure this is going to work? And what about Marta? Is she really happy to go away for the whole weekend?'

'Yes, I told you. She said her mother was looking forward to it.'

'All right.'

He came over and wrapped her in his arms. He sensed her flinch slightly. 'By tomorrow evening this will all be over,' he murmured into her hair. 'Now,' he said briskly, 'have you remembered the plan?'

'Yes,' she replied. 'I'll call out to you just before you leave and tell you I'm feeling unwell.'

'Good.' He kissed the top of her head and went downstairs to the hall, carrying their suitcase.

Moments later, there was a knock on the bedroom door.

Annaliese found Marta standing on the landing in her best hat and coat, a small suitcase at her side. 'Yes, Marta?'

'I'll be off now, madam,' she said. 'But I'll be back tomorrow, after church.'

'Oh, there's no need. Why not stay with your mother for lunch,' Annaliese suggested. 'You really don't get to see enough of her – and we won't be back till late in the afternoon.'

'Well, if you're sure, madam – thank you very much.'

She watched as her maid went downstairs and left the house. Retreating to her bedroom, Annaliese heard Elisabetta calling Hans. 'Could you come and get my suitcase, darling?'

She listened as Hans came upstairs; heard the door of Elisabetta's bedroom being closed, and then the sound of them both going downstairs to the hall. Only then did Annaliese open the bedroom door and cross the landing. She stood watching as Hans helped his mother on with her coat.

'Hans...' she called out, 'could I have a word?'

He ran up the stairs and followed her into the bedroom. A few minutes later, he went back downstairs with a deliberately pained expression on his face. 'The poor girl is not well, Mama. Some sort of stomach upset, and she was awake most of the night. I've suggested she stays here and has a quiet weekend... it would be the best thing for her.'

'But she was the one who insisted we should go,' Elisabetta argued.

'I know,' said Hans, 'and it's a shame, but she suggests we go anyway. She doesn't want to spoil everything.'

'But how will she cope, with Marta away?'

'I'm quite sure Annaliese can manage to look after herself for one night,' said Hans calmly. 'Come, Mama, let's get going.'

Standing at the landing window, Annaliese watched Hans help his mother into the car. He opened the driver's door and glanced up at her, grim-faced. She raised her hand for a moment to wave goodbye, before he too climbed into the car, and accelerated away down the road.

Back in her bedroom Annaliese ran a bath. She lay,

soaking in the warm water, her heart racing with a combination of nerves and excitement. It was clear she was beginning to fall in love with Alexander – the signs were all there. Now she yearned to feel him inside her, to have his skin close to hers.

Climbing out of the bath, she stood, draped in a towel, and wiped the steam off the basin mirror. 'This is the face of a woman who is about to commit adultery,' she said to herself. She had been brought up to believe in the sanctity of marriage, and somewhere deep inside felt that what she was about to do was a sin. The fact that it was sanctioned – even encouraged by her husband – didn't alter that fact. Would God punish her? Or would He leave it to the authorities? If they were discovered, Alexander could be executed, and she imprisoned. It was one thing for an SS officer to sleep with any willing girl to produce a child – quite another for a respectable Nazi wife to take a slave lover.

Sitting at her dressing table, brushing her hair, she could see Alexander was already at work. She felt a rush of excitement, imagining his arms around her, his firm chest pressing against her breasts.

She chose a pale blue summer dress, which emphasised her neat figure, and went downstairs, relishing the peace and quiet of an empty house. In the kitchen she made a pot of coffee and placed it on a tray with two cups and a plate of biscuits. She walked out into the garden sunshine. Alexander was in the vegetable plot, forking over the soil. 'Hello,' she called out, 'I've made us some coffee.'

Alexander leant on his fork for a moment, a smile flickering across his face. 'That was kind, thank you.' He looked anxiously up at the house.

'Don't worry, everyone is away for the weekend. Shall we sit down?' She went over to the wooden bench which Alexander had built next to the shed, overlooking the vegetable garden.

The bench was hidden from prying eyes – both from the house and any neighbours.

He seemed reluctant to join her. 'They're away, you say? You mean your husband has left you alone with me? Why would he do that?'

'I was supposed to go away too, but I... pretended to be unwell.'

'That was risky,' he said, finally sitting next to her. '*Are* you unwell?'

'No, not at all.' She poured the coffee and handed him a cup. His hand shook as he drank it, she noticed. She reached out, took the cup from him and squeezed his hand gently. 'It's all right. Even the maid is away for the weekend. Let's finish our coffee and then come inside... please?'

He frowned. 'I shouldn't. Don't ask me, it's too dangerous. You must know it would be madness.'

'Don't you want me?'

He looked deeply into her eyes. 'It's not that simple.'

'Yes, it is,' she replied. 'It's absolutely that simple. I want you... and you want me.'

He buried his head in his hands. 'I wish it were that simple. But can't you see that I must do everything I can to stay alive? My whole being is focused on survival. I should have died back there in that tank of freezing water, but I didn't, and I'm not going die now, not even for you.' He took the cup from her, drained it, and placed it back on the tray. He smiled, squeezed her hand, picked up his garden fork and returned to the vegetable plot.

She felt a rising sense of panic; she hadn't foreseen that he would refuse her. She had thought the prospect of making love to her would be enough. 'We may never have another chance,' she said gently. 'Are you telling me that you really don't want to make love to me? I'm falling in love with you – I thought you felt the same.'

'I do... like you,' he said, jabbing his fork into the ground, and looking her straight in the eyes, 'and I'm grateful to you for your kindness. But, Anna, think of the risks – to you, as well as me.' His green eyes were alert, flashing left and right, as if searching for an enemy. But Annaliese felt no fear – she was relishing that he had called her by her name for the first time... not her full name, but a diminutive – Anna.

She stood up and held out her hand. 'Please, I'm begging you – come with me... now.'

He followed her in through the kitchen door. Once inside, she pulled down the blind over the window overlooking the road, and in the gloom pulled him towards her and kissed him.

He resisted at first, but then he responded. Kissing her, he picked her up, pulling at her dress, moaning as he felt between her legs. He sat her on the kitchen table. It was over in moments.

'I'm sorry,' he murmured into her hair. 'It's been so long.'

'It's fine,' she panted, laughing a little. 'We have plenty of time...'

She made him an omelette and served it with a thick slice of bread. He ate it with relish. She poured him wine and he drank, savouring every drop. Then she took him upstairs and ran him a bath. He soaked in it, luxuriating in the warm water. She soaped his back and washed the blond stubble on his head, stroking it with her hands.

'Get in with me,' he said.

'I don't think so.' She laughed. 'Look at the colour of the water! It will take me hours to clean the bath.'

He climbed out and tied a towel around his waist. He was tall and very thin, but tanned from the sun.

'Sit down,' she suggested, pointing to her dressing table stool, 'and I'll brush your hair.' She pulled off her dress and stood behind him, naked, combing his thick bristly hair, and kissing the back of his neck. He watched her in the mirror, then swung round, pulled her onto his lap and kissed her.

'Come to bed,' she murmured. He picked her up, and carried her to the bed. They made love... over and over again.

Hours later, as the sun was setting, he pulled himself away. 'I must go. I can't be late back – I have to report to the police each evening at six o'clock before I go to the barracks.'

'I understand. I'll be waiting for you tomorrow.'

'Are you sure?'

'Of course I'm sure,' she said, kissing him. 'No one will be back until the afternoon.'

She accompanied him back down to the kitchen, and stuffed his pockets with slices of bread and pieces of ham. 'Here's something to eat on the way back to the barracks.' She laughed, and watched him walk away from her, down the path and out onto the road.

The following day she woke early, with the sun glinting through the bedroom curtains. Worrying that Alexander might have found some excuse to stay away, she pulled on her peignoir and looked out of the bay window. She was relieved to see him already working in the garden.

Down in the kitchen she made coffee and toast, and took it outside on a tray.

'You came back, then?' she teased.

'Of course,' he said, smiling. 'I am your slave... what else could I do?'

'That's right. You must always do as I ask.' She laughed, entwining her fingers with his. They sat together on the private bench in the sunshine, eating toast with blackcurrant jam and drinking coffee.

'I know so little about you, Alexander. You never discuss your family – tell me about your parents.'

'My father is a doctor and he works at the hospital in Moscow, but he and my mother spend their summers at the family dacha in the country – at least, they did before the war. That's where I learned to garden... with my grandfather.'

'You must miss them terribly.'

'Yes, I miss them, but I don't miss Russia. There is terrible cruelty in that country, since the Revolution. I don't think I will ever go back.'

'Then where will you go, when the war is over?'

'I like your optimism... that I will survive till the end of the war.' He smiled.

'Of course you'll survive. I've never met anyone with such a strong survival instinct.'

'I will go somewhere beautiful,' he said dreamily, 'where no one cares who you are, or where you came from. America.'

'America! Is that really where you'd go?'

'Yes,' he replied. 'That's my dream. A country where I could be free to work – a big, open country filled with nature and life and energy.'

'That's a beautiful dream,' she said, kissing his cheek.

'Yes, it's a beautiful dream – like you, Anna.'

She kissed him again, then stood up and held her hand out to him. 'Come back inside...'

They made love again – urgently now, finally falling apart, bathed in sweat. 'I love you, I love you, I love you,' she murmured.

'And I love you,' he replied tenderly, kissing her forehead.

They must have fallen asleep, because Annaliese woke with a start, hearing the sound of footsteps on the stairs to the attic. She shook Alexander awake. 'There's someone here,' she whispered. 'It must be Marta.' She glanced at her bedside clock. 'She's early – she wasn't due to come home till later this afternoon.'

Annaliese slid out of bed, pulling her peignoir around her shoulders. She crept out onto the landing. 'Hello?' she called.

Marta appeared at the top of the attic stairs. 'Madam! I thought you and the master were away.'

'I didn't go in the end,' said Annaliese, 'I didn't feel well.'

'Oh, I'm sorry to hear that,' replied Marta, clumping down the stairs, dressed in her kitchen apron. 'Can I get you anything? A cup of tea perhaps?'

'No, thank you, I'll be all right.' Annaliese quickly retreated into her room, closing the door behind her and leaning against it, breathing heavily. 'What are we going to do?' she whispered urgently.

Alexander was already up and pulling on his trousers and shirt. 'Where are my boots?' he whispered.

She blanched. 'In the kitchen... by the door! You took them off this morning when you came in. I'll go and fetch them. But how can we get you out of the house?'

Alexander was already peering out of the window. 'I'll climb down from here onto the terrace.'

'No,' she whispered, 'she might see you. I'll have to send her on an errand to buy something.'

'But it's Sunday,' he said. 'Won't the shops be shut?'

'Oh, God... of course. What are we going to do?' She paced frantically around the room.

'You go and distract her,' he said, 'while I leave by the window. It's the only way. Go...'

Annaliese ran downstairs into the hall. Marta was busy dusting some ornaments by the French windows in the sitting room. If Alexander climbed down from the bedroom above she would certainly see him.

'Marta,' she called out from the hallway.

'Yes, madam?'

'Could you come here a minute, please?'

As Marta walked towards her, Annaliese saw Alexander's legs dangling outside the French windows behind her. He dropped silently onto the terrace and disappeared.

'Could you come into the dining room – there's something I want to show you.'

She racked her brains, trying to think of something to detain her maid, and then remembered the stained cream cloth. 'While everyone was away,' she began, 'I took the opportunity to do a sort of inventory of household linen and so on, and I noticed there's still a stain on the cream embroidered cloth – the one my mother-in-law gave me. Could you get it from the linen drawer and bring it down to the kitchen?'

'Very good, madam,' replied Marta, looking puzzled.

Annaliese ran swiftly down the kitchen stairs to retrieve Alexander's boots. She found them by the back door and moved them outside, behind a plant pot.

When Marta appeared, carrying the cloth, Annaliese guided her into the laundry room overlooking the front of the house.

'This carbolic you use,' she said, picking up a slab of soap, 'for cleaning linen and so on – I really don't think it's up to the job. Open the cloth out and I'll show you.'

Marta laboriously unfolded the cloth. A faint remnant of the wine stain that Hans had made all those months before remained in the centre.

'There – do you see? It's unusable as it is.'

'I can see the stain, and I'm so sorry, madam,' said Marta. 'I thought I'd got it all out... I could try to bleach it, I suppose, but I was worried about taking the colour out of the cloth – it's not pure white, you see.'

'Yes, I realise it's difficult,' Annaliese went on, 'but that's your job, Marta – to do these things correctly. When you next go to the market, I suggest you buy a better-quality soap.'

'It's so hard, madam,' said Marta, tears welling up. 'What with rationing and so on.'

'I do realise how hard life is,' replied Annaliese brusquely. She was struggling to think of any other reason to detain the girl, and praying that Alexander had found his boots. To her relief, she heard a faint knocking at the back door. 'What can that be?' she asked innocently.

They went out into the kitchen together, and saw Alexander through the glazed kitchen door, holding up a cup. He was wearing his boots.

Marta opened the door.

'I found this cup outside,' he said, holding it out. 'I'm sorry – I must have forgotten it yesterday.'

'Thank you,' said Marta curtly, closing the door in his face.

Annaliese went back upstairs to her bedroom and looked down at her lover, walking back up the garden. She had promised Hans she would try not to fall in love with Alexander, but it was already too late. She ached for him.

He turned around when he reached the shed and, sensing she was watching him, looked straight at her. She smiled, but his face registered nothing – neither affection, nor even recognition. He opened the door of the shed, went inside and closed the door behind him.

17

A couple of weeks later, while Hans was dressing for work, Annaliese came out of the bathroom. 'I'm sorry,' she said gloomily, 'my period has come.'

'That's disappointing,' he said, adjusting the collar of his SS uniform. 'I was hoping for a quick resolution of the whole business.'

'Yes, me too, but I suppose we need to give it a bit more time. Perhaps it was unrealistic to imagine I could get pregnant straight away.'

Their conversations, she thought, were becoming more and more bizarre. To even be discussing such a thing with one's own husband seemed extraordinary. And yet Hans appeared almost blasé, concerning himself only with the practicalities.

'We'll have to find another opportunity for you to get pregnant. The problem is, I will run out of reasons to take my mother away. Besides, I can't spare another weekend – I have too much work to do. Himmler has insisted I help Rascher with his experiments. The man is an idiot – Rascher I mean – and making sense of his figures is proving very difficult.'

Annaliese vividly recalled Alexander's graphic descriptions of Rascher's cold-water experiments. The thought of Hans being involved appalled her, and yet she felt compelled to ask him about it, if only to find out if he was prepared to be honest with her. 'What is Rascher doing, exactly?' she asked nervously, dreading the answer.

'Oh, it's all rather complex,' he replied, smoothing down his hair distractedly. 'He's working on two different experiments. I'm only helping him with one of them – exploring a possible treatment for blood poisoning.' He glanced nervously over at his wife. 'If it works, it could be transformative for mankind.'

'That sounds impressive... And the other?' She held her breath for the answer.

'Various issues to do with pilot survival,' Hans replied airily. 'I think the research process is almost complete, but the results need some work, apparently – statistics are not Rascher's strong suit.'

Annaliese felt a wave of relief that her husband wouldn't have to be directly involved in the revolting process of freezing human beings. She quickly changed the subject. 'So, what are we going to do about me getting pregnant?'

'Well, there's nothing we can do until you are next fertile, so you can forget about it for a couple of weeks. In the meantime, I'll see what I can arrange about my mother...'

Annaliese thought it extraordinary that her husband had never enquired about her encounter with Alexander. He exhibited neither jealousy, nor interest. It was as if he regarded the whole process as a scientific undertaking: *Laboratory rat no.1 mates with laboratory rat no.2. The experiment will be considered a success if lab rat no.1 gets pregnant.* Did it not occur to him that, after her romantic weekend, she might now be in love with Alexander? That the idea of waiting until her next fertile window before she could make love again was absurd? She couldn't keep him out of her mind, and constantly yearned for his touch.

So, far from avoiding Alexander for the next fortnight, she threw caution to the wind and concocted a host of reasons to be with him outdoors – planting seeds, arranging pots, pruning roses. It didn't go unnoticed.

'You're always out in that garden these days,' Elisabetta said pointedly over lunch one day.

'Well, it's the summer – the best time to be in the garden, surely.'

'What exactly are you doing out there?'

'Planting seeds, getting my new border ready.'

'Can't the gardener do that?'

'He could, of course, but he's busy doing the heavy work. Besides, I like to plant things – to see them grow. It's good for me to have a hobby.'

'Hmmm... it seems to me that you don't so much need a hobby. You need a child, Annaliese.'

'Yes,' said Annaliese, standing up abruptly, 'I know, and I am trying... we are trying, believe me.'

She left the room and picked up a few packets of seeds along with her gardening gloves from the hall table. It had a notepad and pen and she quickly scribbled a message for Alexander.

'Both Marta and my m-in-law are around today but I'll try to persuade them to leave the house tomorrow, and come to you.'

Outside, she found Alexander at the end of the garden, hoeing the ground, his jacket hanging on an apple tree. Surreptitiously, she slipped the piece of paper into his jacket pocket.

When she turned around, she was horrified to see that her mother-in-law was settling herself on the terrace, watching her.

Annaliese pulled on her gardening gloves and sprinkled a few flower seeds on the ground where he had been hoeing. It was torture having him so close, but being unable to touch him. They worked silently side by side, she listening to his breathing as he dug over the soil, inhaling his scent. After a few minutes, he threw some tools into the wheelbarrow and began to move off to a different part of the garden, but she called him back.

'Could you dig this patch of ground over here – I have some more seeds I'd like to plant.'

'Yes, of course, madam,' he replied.

And as he leant down to dig the ground, she whispered: 'Let's try to meet tomorrow at three... I love you.'

He barely reacted.

The following morning after breakfast, Annaliese set about putting her plan into action, and tried to persuade Elisabetta to go out that afternoon. 'You haven't seen your friend Hilda for such a long time – you could meet her at Café Opera, perhaps?'

'Oh, I don't want to go into town,' argued Elisabetta. 'The bomb damage is too depressing. I don't know why they don't get the slaves to work harder clearing the rubble and bricks cluttering up the roads – it's disgraceful.'

Not to be discouraged, Annaliese tried another tack after lunch. 'You look rather tired, Elisabetta. Why don't you lie down?'

'Maybe I'll close my eyes on the terrace,' Elisabetta suggested.

'Oh, you would be far more comfortable upstairs in bed,' Annaliese suggested. 'Hans always says a nap is better if you're really lying down.'

To her surprise, Elisabetta agreed. Annaliese stood at the

bottom of the stairs watching her go upstairs to her room. As soon as she heard Elisabetta's bedroom door close, she ran down to the kitchen.

'Marta,' she called, 'I wonder if you could go to the haberdasher's for me?'

'Yes, madam, what do you need?'

'I need... I need some thread to mend a skirt – a peacock-blue colour. You know that colour, somewhere between blue and green?'

'Do you need me to go now, madam? I was about to clean the kitchen.'

'Yes, now please – you can clean the kitchen later.' She opened her purse and handed the maid a few coins.

When Marta had gone, Annaliese ran upstairs to listen at Elisabetta's door. Her mother-in-law was snoring gently. Delighted, she raced back downstairs and out into the garden. She found Alexander in the shed, cleaning his tools. 'We're alone,' she declared. 'Hold me!'

They embraced and kissed, and there up against the wall of the shed, he made love to her, his hand over her mouth as she moaned with pleasure.

Her mother-in-law's afternoon naps gradually became a habit, and every day Annaliese found new reasons to send Marta into town – an unusual style of button was required for a jacket, a new book by her favourite author needed collecting, or they had run out of brown paper to wrap up clothes for the Winter Relief Fund.

As soon as she was alone, Annaliese would run to Alexander in the shed, where they would make love, lying on an old potato sack on the hard, unyielding floor.

'I love you, I love you,' she murmured one afternoon, her head resting on his chest. 'I want to be with you forever.'

'I know you think that,' he replied.

'It's true, you must believe me. Don't you love me?' She yearned to hear the words.

'Of course I love you,' he said, pulling her towards him. 'But I fear for us both too. If we are discovered, we're finished.'

'We won't be discovered.'

'How can you be so sure?'

'I'm careful, that's why. The old woman is asleep, and the maid is out. We have another half-hour at least.'

He propped himself up on his arm and looked at her, tracing his finger around her mouth. 'What if you get pregnant... what then?'

She guiltily bit her lip.

'What's the matter?' he asked, as if he sensed she was concealing something. 'What are you not telling me?'

'Nothing,' she said casually. 'If I get pregnant, Hans will think it's his.'

'You still make love to him?'

'Yes, of course – I must. You understand, don't you? Otherwise I'd alert him to something. I don't enjoy it, and never did. It's not the same as it is with you.' She reached up for him and pulled him towards her, kissing him. 'I'm sorry it has to be this way,' she murmured. 'Sometimes, I think about a time when the war is over. Do you?'

'Every second of every day.'

'We'll be together then, won't we?'

'Will we?' he asked, stroking her hair.

'Of course!'

'I am not just a distraction for you, then?'

'How could you say such a thing?' She kissed his cheeks, his chin, his lips. 'I love you. I want to be with you always.'

'You do?'

'Yes. When I lie in bed at night, I imagine what it would be like to sleep next to you. I think of us together in a little house of our own – perhaps in America...' She lay her head on his chest, inhaling his scent.

'Anna...' he began.

'What?'

'Don't let your dreams run away with you.'

'Why – why shouldn't I? What aren't you telling me?'

'My darling, we are in the middle of a war. I'm a prisoner, you're married to an SS officer. It would be naïve to imagine life could ever be normal for us...'

She began to weep. 'Don't say that. Please don't say that – it's the only thing that keeps me going.'

'Look,' he said, 'you should go. You've been here nearly an hour...'

'I don't want to.'

'Anna, don't be childish.'

Admonished, she stood up, adjusting her clothes and tidying her hair. To her horror, through the dusty window overlooking the garden, she saw her mother-in-law walking briskly up the garden path towards them.

'My God,' she whispered, shrinking down beneath the window. 'It's Elisabetta... She's coming this way.'

Alexander leapt to his feet, buckling his trousers, and grabbed a couple of large hessian sacks from a shelf. 'Lie down there and don't move,' he said, throwing the sacks over her. He opened the door and, glancing back, noticed one of her feet was peeking out from beneath the sack. He kicked it and she retracted it instantly.

Holding her breath, her heart racing, she listened to the muted conversation between her mother-in-law and her lover.

'Good afternoon, madam,' Alexander said politely.

'Have you seen my daughter-in-law?' Elisabetta demanded.

'No, madam.'

'That's odd. The maid said she was in the garden.'

'Oh... well, she was, but she left a while ago. I don't know where she went, I'm sorry.'

Annaliese heard the sound of Elisabetta's retreating steps, then felt the potato sacks being pulled off her. Alexander reached down and held out his hand to pull her up. 'She's gone,' he whispered. 'But she's in the sitting room, looking out at the garden.'

'How am I going to escape without her seeing me?' Annaliese asked frantically.

'We'll just have to wait,' he said calmly. 'I'd better get back to work, or she'll report me to your husband. I'll tell you when she moves away from the window.'

Over an hour passed before Annaliese, trapped alone in the shed, heard a knock on the door. It was Alexander. 'She's gone. Come out now.'

She crept out of the shed, keeping a close eye on the house. The sitting room appeared deserted. She walked briskly back up the garden, but instead of going up onto the terrace and in through the French windows, she went round the side of the house and out onto the street, where she strolled to the end of the road and back, before marching back up the front steps and ringing the bell.

'Madam,' said Marta, opening the front door, 'what are you doing there? Have you lost your key?'

'Oh, no – I just felt like a walk down the road, and then realised I didn't have the key with me. I'd have come round to the kitchen door, but I thought it might be locked, and my mother-in-law wouldn't hear me knocking down there – she was having a nap upstairs when I left.'

'Oh, not any more,' replied Marta. 'She went out about half an hour ago.'

'Oh, I see. Did you manage to buy the thread I asked for?'

'Yes, I found it quite easily at the haberdasher's on Marien-platz. I put it into your sewing basket in the sitting room.'

'Thank you,' said Annaliese, suddenly worried. *Had Marta seen her coming out of the shed?*

The following Saturday morning, Hans got up early and dressed in his country tweeds rather than his SS uniform.

'Aren't you going to work today?' Annaliese asked.

'No... not today. I took the day off. It's... your time, isn't it?'

'My time?' She looked confused. 'Oh, my fertile time, you mean?'

'Yes. So I've arranged for Marta to spend today sorting clothes at the Winter Relief Fund – I'd heard they were asking for volunteers. And I'm taking my mother to visit her old neighbour in Solln.'

'You didn't say...'

'No, I only organised it last night. You were asleep when I came up.'

Increasingly, she found this managing of her 'love life' infuriating, but she suppressed her sense of indignation. 'Very well,' she said sweetly. 'I'll see what I can do.'

'What I hope you can do is to get pregnant,' he said, adjusting his tie in the cheval mirror. 'We'll only be away for the day. Will that give you enough time?'

She blushed, remembering those moments of ecstasy lying on the potato sacks in Alexander's shed. *Yes*, she thought. *A whole day will be fine, but sometimes a few minutes is all it takes.* 'I imagine so,' she replied coolly. She found his questions increasingly intrusive. The whole situation was becoming intolerable.

'Let's pray it works this time.' He left the room.

As soon as the house was empty, Annaliese ran into the garden to find Alexander. 'Come inside now,' she begged, dragging him towards the house. 'We have all day – well, several hours, at least.'

But he pulled away. 'Anna. We shouldn't. I worry so much – every day, I worry. What if they came back early? We've nearly been caught twice now. It's too risky.'

She felt caught between the two men in her life – one ordering her to have sex, the other now resisting. It felt humiliating to be in this position, but she had no option. Taking Alexander's hand, she kissed his fingers one by one. 'Darling Alexander – we have so few opportunities to make love in a bed.'

She took hold of his hand, and slid it gently inside her dress; he cupped her breast and gasped. 'Oh, Anna...'

'Come,' she murmured.

He followed her into the house. Upstairs, she removed her dress and lay down on the bed, watching him as he took off his shirt and undid his belt buckle. She felt the familiar ache of anticipation. He lay down next to her, his hands stroking her body. He did not linger, as he often did, but instead pushed inside her quickly. She called out his name as they climaxed.

Afterwards, he lay panting next to her, his fingers just touching hers. She rolled onto her side, and stroked his body – his belly, his chest – but he suddenly removed her hand and sat up, swinging his legs out of the bed.

'Where are you going?' she asked.

'I'm going back to work now... they could return any time.'

'No... we have all day. Stay – don't you want to?'

He turned and looked at her, stroking her face. 'Get dressed, Anna. Make the bed.'

'Are you frightened?'

'Always. Aren't you?'

She wanted to admit their plan there and then. 'No,' she wanted to say. 'No, I'm not frightened, because my husband arranged this – it was his idea.' But instead, she lay silent, feeling guilty that her relationship with Alexander was based on a lie: taking something from him... something he hadn't agreed to give her.

He stood up and pulled on his trousers. 'Why not come outside in a little while and do some gardening. All right?'

'Yes, all right.'

They were working together in the garden – he digging, she dead-heading roses – when Marta suddenly appeared.

'Good afternoon, madam. I'm back now, is there anything I can get you?'

'You could put some lemonade out on the terrace – the others will be back soon.'

Marta disappeared inside the house, and Annaliese smiled at her lover, entwining her fingers with his. 'I'd better go and wait for Hans,' she said, kissing his cheek.

As Alexander moved away down the garden, Annaliese settled herself on a wicker chair. A few minutes later she heard Hans' car draw up outside, and Hans and Elisabetta joined her on the terrace.

'Did you have a nice time?' she asked them.

'Yes, it was very pleasant to see Hilda,' replied Elisabetta.

'And how about you?' asked Hans tentatively.

'Oh, I've been busy,' Annaliese replied enigmatically. 'I think I've achieved everything I set out to do...'

Climbing into bed that evening, Hans put his hand on Annaliese's arm. 'I pray it has worked this time,' he said. 'I'm not sure I can bear the thought of you with that man any more.'

His confession worried her. Up till now, Hans had studiously avoided any reference to his emotions, but his obvious distress at her relationship with Alexander was a new development. He had gone from pragmatist to jealous husband in a few weeks. It was hard enough managing her own emotions, and those of her lover, without her husband's jealousy as well.

Hans lay watching her, his eyes roaming hungrily over her body. He touched her breast through her nightgown.

'Hans... no – please.'

'Sorry.' He kissed her on the cheek and rolled away from her in the darkness. She lay, caught between her two worlds – her deepening love for Alexander and her growing fear of what Hans, in his new emotional state, might do. Sometime in the middle of the night, she woke to find him quietly weeping.

18

AUGUST 1943

On Monday morning, as Hans approached the gates of Dachau, the guard stepped out from his post, flagging the car down. Beyond the gates, Hans could see a line of soldiers barring the way.

Hans tapped his driver's shoulder. 'Tell the guard to open the gates. I have important work to do.'

The driver wound down the window and spoke to the guard on sentry duty, before turning back to Hans. 'He says they can't open them yet – a punishment beating is taking place in the yard. We'll have to wait.'

'That's absurd,' said Hans. 'They can't impede my work for some minor punishment.' He climbed angrily out of the car and demanded the guard open the gates. He strode towards the wall of soldiers, in search of a senior officer. Beyond them in the parade ground, he could see prisoners standing in rows, the regulation three feet apart. In the centre of the yard, spread-eagled face down on a table, was a half-naked man. While two guards held him firmly by his hands and feet, two others took it in turns to beat him with long sticks.

'What is that man being punished for?' Hans asked.

'I don't know, Sturmbannführer,' replied a soldier, shrugging. But the man standing next to him did know. He leant across to Hans, smirking. 'They found a dirty finger-mark on his locker when they did the inspection this morning. He hadn't cleaned it properly.'

'A finger-mark?' Hans asked incredulously. 'Is that all? Is that really worth a beating like this?'

'They are the rules, Sturmbannführer. Prisoners have to keep the place spotless, or standards start to slip, don't they, sir?'

Hans retreated to his car, feeling both incensed and distressed. He had a sudden flashback to an incident in his childhood. He had been on a country walk with boys from his school. A farm dog had snarled at the group, who retaliated by kicking the dog to death. Hans had lacked the courage to speak out, or stop them, and had been mortified by the sight of the poor mongrel lying bloodied and broken. He felt the same way now – unable to speak out and prevent this blatant cruelty from taking place in the prison camp square. His only act of defiance was to insist the gates were opened wide enough to let his car through.

The driver edged the car forward slowly, nudging the soldiers out of the way, and finally swept down the side alley to his office.

His research assistant was waiting for him in the outer office. 'Good morning, Sturmbannführer.'

'Good morning, Eugène. Are the subjects ready for today's mescaline experiment?'

'Yes, sir. Four prisoners have been selected. They will be here at ten o'clock.'

'Call me when they get here.' Hans was about to go into his office, when he paused. 'Eugène...'

'Yes, sir?'

'I would like to ensure that the subjects are properly supervised this time.'

'Yes, sir.'

'Keep an eye on their heart rate, breathing and so on.'

'Of course, sir. I'll prepare the medication and knock on your door when the first subject is ready.'

Hans went into his office and shut the door. As usual, he removed his SS jacket and put on his white coat; he smoothed his hair, sensing his heart racing. The beating he had witnessed that morning disturbed him. The man's body had been covered with bloody weals, and his tortured face now haunted Hans. To his relief, the loudspeakers in the yard began to play martial music, indicating the beating was over. Was the man still alive? he wondered. And if so, would he be taken to the medical wing for treatment? Research doctors like him were forbidden from treating the sick, leaving the task to prisoners with medical qualifications. The problem was they had neither drugs nor proper dressings – a state of affairs that troubled Hans.

He closed his window, muffling the sound of the music, and did his best to concentrate on his work. But alone, in the quiet of his office, his mind flooded with other disturbing thoughts – in particular, of his wife having sex with the Russian. He imagined her lying on their bed, moaning and calling the man's name. She had done that once or twice with him in the early days of their relationship.

'Please God,' he whispered to himself, 'let her get pregnant... let it be over soon.'

To whom he was praying, he couldn't say. Hitler despised religion, and had forbidden the worship of the 'Jew', Jesus Christ. But Hans had been brought up in the Christian Church – had been a choirboy even – and still retained a deep-seated belief that God might be there, might just be listening. But would he help a sinner like him? A man who had witnessed violence and cruelty and said nothing, had done nothing? A man, who, unlike the Good Samaritan, had 'passed by on the other side'. A man who had even injured and killed people himself.

His tortured thoughts were interrupted by a knock at the door.

'Yes,' he called out impatiently.

'Sturmbannführer, sir – Dr Rascher has asked to see you.'

Hans emerged from his office and found Eugène hovering outside. 'He rang just now, asking if you could go over there. I explained we were about to start some experiments.'

'It's all right,' said Hans wearily. 'I'll go and see what he wants. I won't be long.'

Rascher was waiting for him in his laboratory. A large metal water tank had been filled with water and blocks of ice, in readiness for an experiment.

'You asked to see me?' Hans asked, glancing apprehensively at the water tank.

'Ah, Dr Vogel, good. I wondered if you might give me some help with the pilot survival research.'

'Yes, of course,' replied Hans warily. 'But I had understood that the practical side of your work was completed, and the only help you needed involved pulling the results together – is that not correct?'

'It *was* correct,' said Rascher, 'but I've just been informed that there are some Russians who have recently become available. They tried to escape last night, and were due to be executed this morning, but I suggested they would instead prove useful experimental subjects. It would be good for you to observe the whole process from start to finish – from a scientific perspective.' He smiled. 'They can always be executed later. So, I've just ordered the tank be refilled with ice...'

'I'm afraid I am about to start some experimentation of my own,' Hans said firmly. 'I shall be busy for the rest of the morning.'

'That's all right... we can do the experiments any time,' replied Rascher. 'Come back after lunch. We'll begin then.'

Hans normally avoided the officers' mess at lunchtime. He found his colleagues poor company. His habit was to collect his food on a tray and return to his office, where he ate alone. That day, as he queued up for a bowl of lentil soup, he heard someone calling his name. 'Hans, come and join us.' It was Rascher, sitting at a table of Dachau doctors, Claus Schilling among them.

'Oh, thank you,' Hans replied, 'but I ought to get back to my office. I have a lot of work to do before I see you this afternoon.'

'Oh, don't be ridiculous – join us.'

Hans sat down reluctantly, and began to eat his soup.

'I've put in a request for more subjects for the malaria experiments,' Schilling was saying. 'Himmler is very keen for me to consider how we might use the disease against the enemy. What do you think about that, Dr Vogel?'

Hans looked up, surprised to be asked his opinion. 'I think it will present some serious challenges,' he suggested diplomatically. 'I presume he has some kind of biological weapon in mind?'

Schilling looked annoyed. 'You are no longer working with malaria, I understand?' It was a superfluous question, as he knew very well that Hans' work had been shut down due to the success of his own experiments. His comment was designed merely to humiliate Hans in front of his peers.

'Indeed. I'm working instead on a project in which the Führer has taken a personal interest.'

'Oh, mescaline, you mean.' Schilling's tone was dismissive.

'I can't see that being particularly useful. No drug can really take the place of a good beating if you want to get the truth out of someone.'

The other doctors laughed.

'Well, I really must get back to work,' said Hans, standing up. 'I'll see you at two o'clock, Dr Rascher.'

Hans arrived at Rascher's laboratory to find a group of Russian prisoners being dragged into an ante-room by a pair of capos. The Russians were struggling and shouting; the capos responded by slamming the men up against the wall, punching them in the stomach, even hitting one young man around the head.

'Is this violence really necessary?' asked Hans.

Rascher looked up absent-mindedly from his laboratory bench. 'What?'

'These beatings... are they necessary?'

Rascher shrugged his shoulders. 'All right,' he shouted to the capos. 'That's enough. Get them ready.'

The Russians were stripped, and made to wear Luftwaffe uniforms and life jackets – just as airmen would be dressed if they had parachuted into the sea. They were then forced, kicking and screaming, into the tank of icy water.

'Take this,' said Rascher, handing Hans a clipboard and a stopwatch. 'Make as many observations as you want – timings obviously – at what time after insertion they stop struggling, how long until they become unconscious – anything, really. Please note at the top that the water has been cooled to a temperature of two degrees, all right?'

Hans had already witnessed men dying. Even some of his own malaria 'patients' sadly hadn't survived. But a part of his brain had shut out his culpability. He had been able to convince himself that they were ill and he was doing what he could to make them better. This, though, was different. There was something horrific about watching these young men shivering and whimpering, begging for mercy, before finally lapsing into unconsciousness.

One young man grabbed Hans' hand as he took his pulse. 'Please, please,' he cried, 'let me out – I have a wife and a child.' The man's heart rate was already slow, his skin ice-cold, his face deathly pale. Hans knew he should pull the man out, there and then, but it was impossible. Rascher and the capos were watching him. So, instead, he closed his ears and his mind to the man's entreaties, focusing on his stopwatch, the temperature gauges, the blood pressure readings, and noting the figures on his clipboard – anything to avoid the man's terrified gaze.

Gradually, the young man and the rest of the subjects grew docile, until they finally sank into unconsciousness, bobbing on the surface of the water, protected from drowning only by their life jackets.

'Right, get them out,' shouted Rascher.

The men's bodies were dragged from the tank and laid out on the floor of the laboratory, like corpses in a morgue.

'Record their final temperature, heart rate and blood pressure,' Rascher instructed.

Hans did as he was told, opening the jacket of the young man who had begged him for mercy. He placed his stethoscope on the man's freezing chest, but there was no heartbeat. Fighting to keep his emotions in check, he called across to Rascher, 'This one is already dead.'

'Oh, well, mark it on the clipboard,' said Rascher casually, as if the man's death meant nothing. 'What was the last heart rate you recorded?'

Hans consulted his notes. 'Thirty-five beats a minute.'

'Mmmm,' said Rascher abstractedly. 'Interesting. All right, please observe the resting body temperature of the other three subjects. I usually find that it continues to drop after they've been removed from the water. Then, let's get them warmed up. Put that one to heat up fast,' he said, pointing to a dark-haired young man, sprawled unconscious on the floor.

A tank of very hot water stood nearby, its steam filling the room.

Hans knew at once that such a rapid change in temperature would result in certain death. He decided he must at least try to save this one life. If allowed to warm up naturally, the man might just survive and, at that moment, this man's survival seemed of paramount importance. 'Do we not already know that putting a man into near-boiling water will certainly kill him?' Hans pleaded. 'Surely we could skip that step...'

Rascher stared at him, his black eyes cold and unfeeling. 'Skip it, you say? I don't think that would be a good idea, do you? The experiment has been designed in a certain way. We can't change the protocol now. We must continue with the criteria we've already established. If the subjects die, they die, but at least we can show in the figures that we've been thorough – comparing like with like.'

The dark-haired man had begun to regain consciousness and was moaning quietly.

'Throw him into the tank,' Rascher ordered the capos.

They ripped off the man's uniform and threw him naked into the steaming tank. His screams were so horrific that Hans wanted to run from the room. It took all his effort to keep his feet firmly planted on the ground. To his shame he couldn't look at the man, but instead turned his head away and closed his eyes. After a few more agonising minutes the man fell silent. Hans allowed himself to breathe.

The two remaining prisoners, who had been placed in warm water, gradually regained consciousness. Their temperatures, heart rate, pulse, skin quality and pallor were all noted. Finally, they were re-dressed in their prison uniforms and dragged outside by the capos.

'What will happen to them now?' Hans asked. 'I had heard that they were sometimes offered a reprieve, in return for surviving...'

'Oh, not any more,' replied Rascher carelessly. 'We used to release them to the factories. But I suspect these two will be hanged – as an example to the others. They had tried to escape, after all.'

Hans felt faint. The sheer brutality and inhumanity of it all sickened him. Rascher had turned the laboratory into a torture chamber; it was obscene. He remembered the young man's final words: *I have a wife and a child.*

'It just seems unnecessarily harsh,' he said to Rascher. 'Haven't they suffered enough?'

Rascher looked at him, perplexed. 'I am not interested in their suffering. I am a scientist.'

Hans' reaction surprised even himself; he was not a violent man, but something about Rascher's basic lack of humanity made him want to hit him hard in the stomach, there and then. The man was simply a monster. But he held back, and merely replied, 'The two things should not be mutually exclusive, surely?'

Rascher frowned. 'I'm not sure I really understand your point.' He looked down at his clipboard. 'Well, we'd better get on with collating the figures. I'm told you have a particular skill in that area.'

'Really,' said Hans, still haunted by what he had seen and heard. 'Who told you that?'

'My friend, Heinrich Himmler,' Rascher replied smugly, leading the way to his office. 'Come in and sit down.'

As Hans sat down in the visitor's chair opposite Rascher's desk, he was struck by the thought that only a few months before he might have been pleased – proud even – to be recommended by Himmler. But now he felt nothing but shame – shame at being part of this sick, evil nightmare they had created together. He suddenly remembered his friend Gunther announcing he was leaving Germany. What had he said to him all those years ago, before he left? *'Beware of selling your soul too cheaply, my friend.'*

Is that what he had done?

'Dr Vogel!' Rascher, sitting on the opposite side of the desk, was staring at him. 'Are you all right? Can you hear me?'

'Yes... yes, of course, I'm sorry. I was just thinking.'

'Not about the experiment, I hope. You need to divorce yourself from your emotions if you are going to be a successful scientist – surely you know that?'

Hans felt a visceral fury at being lectured by this man.

'We all have emotions,' Rascher went on. 'We all have people we love, but we leave all that behind when we arrive here.' He pointed to a framed photograph on his desk. It was of a stout, middle-aged woman with three little boys.

'Your mother?' asked Hans asked innocently.

'No! That's my wife, Karoline.' He sounded aggrieved and angry. It was the first time Hans had heard any emotion in Rascher's voice.

'Oh, I'm sorry, I just assumed...' Hans mumbled. 'Three boys,' he went on, 'that's impressive. How old are they?'

'The eldest is three,' said Rascher, recovering his composure. 'We've been most fortunate.'

Hans studied the photograph again. *The woman must be nearly fifty*, he thought. Surely the fact that she had managed to give birth to three boys under the age of three in her late forties was nothing short of a biological miracle? 'Have you been together long, Sigmund?'

'Oh, ten years or more – Himmler introduced us, in fact. He and Karoline used to be... close.' Rascher smiled knowingly.

'She must be most remarkable,' Hans observed, 'to be so fertile – three boys under three...'

Rascher snatched the photograph away. 'She is remarkable, yes. We're hoping for a fourth soon.'

'How wonderful,' murmured Hans. *They made a strange couple,* he thought – *the dumpy blond woman and tall, dark-haired Rascher.* In spite of his vile personality, the man could be considered good-looking. He had neat, even features, and an elegant nose, but dark, cruel eyes.

'My wife and I are also hoping for a child.' Hans regretted this admission as soon as he'd made it. Somehow sharing any private information with this monster seemed wrong.

But Rascher appeared not to have heard him. He picked up his notes. 'Well, enough of that – to work...'

They spent some hours writing up the details of the iced water experiments. When they had finished, Hans stood up to go. 'I really ought to get back to my lab and my own experiments.'

'If you must,' said Rascher casually.

Standing at the door, Hans paused. 'This work we do... do you ever wonder if it's worth it?'

Rascher stared at him. 'Worth it? What sort of question is that?' He stood up and pointed to a small, framed letter on the wall behind his desk. 'I suggest you read this. It will give you the perspective you need.'

Hans walked round the desk and studied the letter, which was addressed to Rascher. Underlined in the text were these words:

> *'I regard those who still reject these human experiments,*
> *and instead would rather let brave German soldiers die*
> *from the effects of freezing, as traitors.'*

The letter was signed, 'Heinrich Himmler, Oct 24, 1942'.

. . .

Returning to his office, Hans locked the door, stood in the corner of his office with his face to the wall, and sobbed. There had always been violence at Dachau, and of course violence was an unfortunate but natural part of human existence. But the sheer brutality of his colleagues was becoming unendurable. It was getting harder and harder to justify, harder to ignore. The entire National Socialist ideology, he realised – especially the use of science to justify abject cruelty – was an abomination. It was a contradiction of everything he had been taught; in particular, it contravened the Hippocratic Oath he had taken the day he qualified: 'First do no harm.' At Dachau, doctors were harming their fellow men every hour of the day.

He removed his white coat – the symbol of his medical qualification, and something of which he had once been proud – and hung it on the peg at the back of the door. As he did so, he glimpsed himself in the small mirror that hung on the wall. Before the war he had considered himself a success – well-off, married to a beautiful woman, with a fine house and a promising career. Now, as he stared into his dead grey eyes, all he saw was a sad, middle-aged man whose wife loved someone else, and who had lost his way as a doctor. He could no longer claim to have saved lives. Instead he had stood by and watched, helplessly, as people suffered and died.

He put on his SS jacket, but felt sullied by his uniform now. He locked his office and went out into the alley, where his driver was waiting for him. As he climbed wearily into the back seat, it struck him that future generations would look back on this period in medical history with horror. And, to his shame, he was part of it.

19

OCTOBER 1943

Annaliese was sitting at her dressing table, going through her diary. For many years she had been in the habit of marking the day her period came, as it had never been particularly regular. Flicking through the gold-edged pages, her heart began to race as she went through the entries. There was nothing five weeks ago, nor six. Finally, she found a mark – it had been eight weeks since her last period. Her long years of childlessness had taught her to be cautious. There had been long gaps between periods before, during which she had become excited and convinced she was expecting a child, only to have her hopes dashed when her period returned soon after.

Nevertheless, her hands went instinctively to her belly, stroking it. She stood up and watched Alexander digging over the vegetable patch, clearing it for the winter. It was already chilly – frost had settled on the mown grass – but in spite of the cold air, steam was rising from Alexander's warm back. The heat and energy he was emanating seemed to symbolise his virility, and she wanted to rush outside and tell him, there and then, 'I think I'm pregnant with your child.'

Sadly, she knew that was impossible. He still believed she was having sex with her husband, and unless she was prepared to reveal the truth – that Hans was infertile and had planned the whole thing – Alexander would never be convinced the child was his. Besides, he had avoided her in recent weeks.

When she had last visited him in the shed, pleading with him to make love to her, he had refused.

'It's too risky,' he whispered into her hair. When he kissed her, she clung to him, begging him to change his mind. But he was implacable. In her heart she knew he was right. What future could there be for a German wife in love with a Russian prisoner? The only chance they had of ever being together was if the war was to come to an end.

Desperate for accurate information on the state of the war, she had begun to listen to foreign news broadcasts – in secret, of course, because it was illegal. But it was the only way to get news of what was truly happening in her country. From these news bulletins she learned that the war was not going well for Germany. They were losing on all fronts – North Africa, Italy, Russia. And even Munich had not escaped, as she well knew. Allied planes were now hitting the ammunition factories around the edges of the city with relentless regularity. And the city centre was also coming under attack. A few weeks before, a stray bomb had landed on a house just a few doors away. Hearing the commotion, Hans and Annaliese had shepherded the household into the coal cellar and had spent an exhausting few hours listening to Elisabetta complaining about how the Allies were destroying her beloved city.

Annaliese slumped back down at her dressing table and turned her attention to Hans, and how he might react to the news of a child. Would he be happy? She hoped so – after all, it had been his idea. But a nagging fear lodged itself in her mind. If she were pregnant, would he now forbid her from seeing the man she loved? Hans had been very distracted recently. He seemed permanently on edge, angry even. If she told him of her pregnancy now, he might do something rash. She decided to keep it a secret from both of them, at least for now.

She spent the morning quietly in her room, only venturing downstairs at lunchtime. To her relief, she found Elisabetta standing in the hall, dressed to go out.

'Annaliese, I'm meeting Hilda at Café Luitpold,' she said. 'We'll play bridge afterwards at her house but I'll be back in time for supper.'

'Oh, that will be nice,' said her daughter-in-law distractedly, wondering how she could also get rid of Marta; then she would be able to spend the afternoon alone and listen to more news on the radio.

Sending Marta to the shops on another errand, Annaliese went into the sitting room and turned on the radio. She tuned the dial until it picked up the BBC German Service frequency.

This is the BBC in London. Here are the headlines: Allied troops have landed in Italy, entering Naples two days ago. The German army, in retreat, destroyed the university, as well as the famous Teatro di San Carlo.
On the Russian Front, the Second Battle of Smolensk has ended in victory for the Soviets.
And in France, General de Gaulle has taken over leadership of the Committee for National Liberation, paving the way for a post-war government.

It seemed to Annaliese that the end of the war really was in sight. Keen to give Alexander the news, she went down to the kitchen, heated a little milk and made two cups of acorn coffee. Then, dressed in a warm coat and boots, she went outside.

She found Alexander at the bottom of the garden, digging up the spent dahlia corms.

'I thought you looked as if you needed warming up.'

Automatically, he glanced up at the house, checking they were not being observed.

'Don't worry,' she reassured him, handing him a mug of coffee. 'The house is empty... everyone has gone out. We have an hour at least.'

He smiled faintly. 'All right. And thank you for the coffee.' He warmed his hands on the mug, and blew on the liquid to cool it down.

'Let's sit on your bench,' she suggested.

They sat together, their legs pressed against one another, and she leant her head on his shoulder. 'I've missed you so... do we have time, do you think?'

He put his arm around her and kissed her hair. 'No, I don't think so – not for that. Let's just be together and enjoy the winter sunshine.'

'I've been listening to the news... from London.'

He suddenly pulled away from her and shot her a look. 'Isn't that illegal?'

'Yes, but I don't care any more. Don't you want to know what's going on – what's really going on? Not the lies and propaganda we get here in Germany.'

He narrowed his eyes suspiciously. 'Yes, I suppose so – tell me.'

'We are losing the war,' she said excitedly. 'It might all be over soon.'

He smiled ruefully. 'That's a nice dream.'

'It's not a dream,' she insisted. 'The Allies are already in Italy, and our troops are being defeated everywhere – Russia, North Africa.' She reached across and took his hand. 'Just imagine – when it's all over, we'll be able to run away and live in America with our...' She stopped suddenly, realising her mistake. She must not mention the baby. Instead she sipped her coffee.

'With our what?' he asked, puzzled.

'With our love,' she murmured, kissing his hand. 'I was thinking... we could run away, even now. You could easily pass for German – you speak the language so well. We could escape to Austria and live in the mountains, and wait until the war is over.'

'It would be madness, Anna. I have no papers. They would track us down and execute us.'

'But my husband is a senior SS officer – a doctor at Dachau. Surely they wouldn't dare...'

'That's exactly why they would come after us. Dear, sweet, innocent Annaliese, do you have no understanding of the depths to which your people will go to punish those who disobey?'

'But all I want is to be with you,' she replied, her eyes filling with tears. 'I would go anywhere with you.'

'Let me tell you a story,' he said, putting his cup down on the grass. 'When I was first brought to Dachau, I was with three men I'd served with in the Russian army. They were crazy patriots, and wild – heavy drinkers, you know. As we were dragged into the prison, one of them shouted to the guards, "Just wait till the war is over – then we will kill you, like the animals that you are."

'I knew it was a stupid thing to say. One of the guards hit him, and then dragged him out of the line, along with the man standing next to him, and marched them up to the officer in charge. They were taken out into the parade ground and we were all made to stand and watch them being half beaten to death – laid out on a table, with soldiers on each side beating them with sticks. But that was just the beginning...'

Annaliese began to weep and put her hands over her ears. 'Don't tell me any more... please don't.'

'You need to hear it,' he said, pulling her hands down by her sides. 'Once they were unconscious, the guards dragged them to the gallows, and placed a rope around their necks. When their bodies dropped, I heard their necks snap. I realised then that one of those men could have been me. I was standing right next to that idiot who taunted the Germans. They could have grabbed me, but they chose the man on the other side. I had a lucky escape. And I made a promise to myself that day, that however much I hated the Nazis – and believe me, I hate them – I would keep my head down and I would survive, whatever they did to me. All I've ever wanted was to get through the war alive. And running away with the beautiful wife of a Dachau doctor can only end one way – with getting myself hanged.'

He stood up and picked up his garden fork. 'Thanks for the coffee, but I must get back to work.'

Annaliese felt her world spinning out of control. She wanted nothing more than to confess to the man she loved that she was pregnant with his child. In return, she wanted only commitment – a promise they would be together once the war was over. Suddenly, all the months of self-control, the secrecy, the lies, fell away and she reached up and grabbed his hand.

'What if I told you something that might change your mind?'

'What could you possibly say?'

She took a deep breath. 'I'm pregnant.'

He gasped. 'Pregnant?'

She nodded.

'Why would you tell me this? Do you want my sympathy, or my congratulations?'

'Neither.' Her eyes began to fill with tears. 'I want your love. It's your... it could be your child.'

'Well, if it is, I'm sorry for it. It could also be your husband's, remember. How will you ever know?'

She began to weep.

'Anna... look, I'm glad for you, if that's what you want. You'll be a wonderful mother.' He helped her to her feet. 'You should go back to the house now – your maid will be back soon. Dry your eyes and let's not take any more risks, all right?'

She sensed him withdrawing, as if their affair was already over. Clinging to his hand she cried out: 'And what if I could prove to you that the child is yours?'

'How could you do that?'

'Dates, times... I haven't had sex with Hans for several weeks.'

The colour drained from his face. 'What are you telling me? You told me you still slept with him. He's a doctor, Anna, he'll work it out. He'll have me shot.'

'No!' she insisted, 'that won't happen. He wouldn't do that. I'll convince him, you'll see. He's always wanted children. He'll be happy about it, I promise you. It will be all right.'

'No, Anna – it won't be all right. Don't you see? We must end our relationship now. If you have any love for me – any love at all – you must give up this fantasy of us being together. Let me go on working here quietly. And you must go back to your husband... back to his bed. He must believe that the child is his... please Anna, I beg you.'

His voice was shaking with fear, and she saw in that instant that he was right. She had been selfish, fantasising about running away with him. And now she had risked everything. He must be terrified, she realised. He had told her so often of his determination just to survive. Why couldn't she just be grateful for what she had, and let him think the child was her husband's? The war would come to an end soon enough, and then they could be together.

'I shouldn't have told you,' she sobbed. 'I'm sorry. Please forgive me.'

She stumbled back to the house and ran upstairs to her room, weeping, just as her maid returned.

'Madam?' Marta called up the stairs. 'Are you all right?'

'I'm fine!' screamed Annaliese, slamming her bedroom door behind her.

When Hans returned home, he found her lying on the bed in the darkness, covered with a rug. He turned on the bedside light, and stood over her.

'My mother says you are unwell. What's the matter?'

'Nothing,' she said, turning her face away from the light.

'Clearly, that is not true. Something is wrong.' He sat down next to her on the bed and took her hand. 'Annaliese... tell me.'

She turned and looked at him, her eyes red-rimmed. 'I can't.'

'Is it something about a child? Have you perhaps... lost a child? Were you pregnant, but it has been lost – is that why you're upset? Tell me, Annaliese, I beg you, tell me.'

'No! I've not lost it. I think I *am* pregnant.'

She started to sob, while he stared at her in wonder, kissing her hand tenderly. 'Oh, my darling – how wonderful! But we must be sure. I will arrange for an obstetrician to take a look at you tomorrow. Then you will have the best of care. Oh, Annaliese, you have no idea how happy you have made me.'

He lay down next to her, taking her in his arms, but she froze, repulsed by his presence. This was not the love she had dreamed of. He was not the man for whom she yearned. That man was a foreign prisoner, locked up in a prison barracks – and in fear of his life. And that was her fault.

Hans duly arranged for her to be examined by a specialist, who pronounced that she would give birth in the spring. Both Hans and his mother were "ecstatic", they told her.

Elisabetta's attitude towards Annaliese changed dramatically. 'Come and sit down,' she insisted that evening in the sitting room. 'Hans dear, get her a cushion for her back, and that little stool for her feet – swollen ankles, as I know to my cost, are a great burden for the expectant mother.'

'Thank you,' said Annaliese irritably, 'but I'm quite well. And I don't need a stool. Please, Hans, do stop fussing.'

Hans and his mother sat on the sofa gazing at her throughout the evening. It was exasperating. 'Please stop doing that,' she begged them. 'You're both looking at me as if I were the Virgin Mary herself. Can't we just get back to normal?'

It was not her husband's approbation Annaliese wanted, but Alexander's. Ever since she had told him about her pregnancy he had avoided her. One afternoon, when the house was empty, she ventured into the garden. He was nowhere to be seen, so she guessed he must be in the shed. She gently knocked on the door.

'Yes?' He sounded wary, frightened even.

'It's me,' she replied. 'Can I come in?'

'Are the family at home?'

'No, everyone's out.'

He opened the door. His tools were laid out on the bench. He had an oily rag in his hand. 'I'm cleaning up... for the winter,' he explained.

'Oh, that's nice.'

'Was your husband happy with the news?' he asked, almost indifferently.

'Oh yes, very happy.'

'Did he not say anything – about the timings?'

'No,' she replied. 'He didn't mention it. He's just so delighted.'

He shook his head. 'He must be a fool.'

'I love you, Alexander,' she suddenly declared.

'Don't say that. You mustn't love me. It's over, Anna – you

must see that. If you have any love for me at all, then leave me alone now. Have your child, be a good German wife.'

'You don't really mean that?' she begged him.

'I do. I've already explained. Survival, Anna. That's all that matters now, for you, me and the child.'

～

As the months went by, Annaliese became more and more wretched. The pain of Alexander's rejection was almost unbearable. Christmas was approaching, but she could take no joy in it. As her pregnancy developed, she became short-tempered with everyone, snapping at the slightest provocation. At mealtimes she was sullen, and after dinner, when Elisabetta fretted and fussed over her, Annaliese frequently lost her temper. 'Leave me alone!' she shouted. 'I'm not an invalid, I'm just pregnant.'

The atmosphere in the house grew increasingly toxic. With Elisabetta constantly occupying the sitting room, Annaliese spent more and more time in her room. Each morning, before he left for work, Hans would find her sitting at her dressing table, looking miserably out of the window.

'You're obsessed with that garden,' he muttered. 'There are more important things to think about – our child, for example. Why don't you concentrate on decorating the nursery? Choose some wallpaper – doing that used to make you happy.'

She looked at him with a tear-stained face, wanting to scream, *What is more important to happiness than love?*

As her misery overwhelmed her, she became obsessed with Alexander, searching him out in the garden each day, desperate for reassurance that he still loved her. But as soon as she appeared, he would walk away, deliberately avoiding her.

Dejected and confused, she finally confronted him one day in the shed: 'Why are you ignoring me?'

'Because it's too dangerous. I've explained already – please, Anna, please try to understand...'

As the weeks went by, she stopped going outside and retreated once again to her room. The pain of Alexander's rejection was so intense, she took to closing the curtains, so she couldn't see him. It didn't go unnoticed.

'The garden seems to have lost its allure,' observed Hans one morning before leaving for work.

'Well, as you've already pointed out, I have a lot to think about now,' she replied, cradling her swelling stomach. 'I can't do up my skirts any more. So I'm going into town today, to buy some bigger clothes – and to choose wallpaper for the nursery.'

'I'm so glad,' said Hans, kissing the top of her head. 'I'll see you this evening.'

The sky was grey, filled with the threat of snow, as Annaliese walked into the centre of town wearing her fur coat and boots. At the department store, she produced her ration stamps and was able to buy a light wool dress that would see her through to the end of her pregnancy, plus one rather basic skirt. In the men's department, she found herself picking up a soft woollen emerald-green jumper, thinking how well it would suit Alexander; it would match his eyes perfectly. But of course giving him clothing was illegal, and would only exacerbate the danger she had already put him in. Regretfully, she put it back down.

Her shopping complete, she decided to have a coffee at Café Luitpold. The snow was starting to fall, so she hurried inside. In spite of the war, and the bomb damage all around, the café was full of women, like her, taking a break from their Christmas shopping. Rationing had limited the choices of cakes, but she treated herself to a small slice of stollen. She observed the male waiters – mostly foreign labour – gently flirting with the female customers. *Perhaps Alexander would have been safer working in a café like this than in our garden*, she thought. She could imagine him there, charming the old ladies with his perfect German and handsome, blond looks. Had she been wrong to seduce him? Surely, love could never be wrong, and in any case, he had genuinely returned her love. She was sure of that, at least.

But for now, she resolved to be responsible and assure Alexander that she understood his predicament. She must leave him alone, give birth to their child, and hope that the war would soon be over.

20

DECEMBER 1943

Hans sat dejectedly at his desk at the camp, struggling to concentrate. He was supposed to be writing up his notes on Rascher's sepsis experiments, but his mind kept wandering to his wife's unhappiness. She seemed unable to take any joy in her pregnancy. It was bewildering to a rational man of science like Hans, and he decided to 'review the evidence'.

Annaliese was finally impregnated, he reasoned to himself, meaning that the Russian's job was effectively done. She had been desperate for a child – so the pregnancy should make her happy. What, then, was the cause of his wife's misery? Hans could only conclude that it was the continuing presence of the Russian. The solution, therefore, was clear – he should be removed as soon as possible. Nothing must get in the way of the health and happiness of his beloved wife and unborn child.

Unable to concentrate on his work, he called for his driver. 'I need to go back home,' he told him. 'There's something I have to deal with.'

'Of course, Sturmbannführer.'

. . .

Snow began to fall from a grey sky. It came in flurries, not quite
settling on the slushy pavements. Looking out from the back
seat of his staff car, Hans had a momentary rush of anxiety that
he was about to make a monumental mistake, but he pushed it
aside. He had made a rational decision and couldn't go back on
it now.

'Wait for me here,' he told the driver, as they pulled up
outside the grey house. 'We'll have to make a detour on the way
back.'

He strode up the steps and into the house. 'Marta, is my
wife here?' he shouted.

Marta rushed up from the kitchen. 'No, sir, she went into
town.'

'Good,' said Hans. 'I want you to order a three-metre
Christmas tree – and have it delivered today. I'd like it to be a
nice surprise for Annaliese when she comes home. Can I leave
that with you?'

'Yes, sir, of course.'

Hans found Alexander turning the compost heap. 'Ah, here
you are.'

'Yes, sir, here I am,' Alexander replied warily. 'How can I
help you?'

'By coming with me.'

'Coming with you – where?'

'Don't question me,' said Hans, removing a pistol from his
belt. 'Just come now. And don't make a fuss.'

Hans pushed Alexander down the path, the pistol pressed
into the small of his back. He noticed him glancing up at the
house, where Marta was standing wide-eyed at the French
windows, watching the Russian being frog-marched up the
garden.

'She won't save you,' said Hans, pointing to Marta, 'and

neither will Annaliese – she's not even at home this morning. And before you ask, she doesn't know that you're leaving. You think I didn't know what's been going on? Don't worry, I'm not having you killed, although I'd be within my rights. You're just going back to where you came from, back where you belong.' He pushed Alexander round the side of the house and into the road, towards the waiting car.

'Open the passenger door for my prisoner,' Hans ordered his driver. He pushed Alexander into the front seat, and sat behind him, the pistol pressed against his head.

'Take us to the Volkswagen factory,' Hans instructed. 'Do you know it?'

The driver nodded. 'Yes, sir.'

The black Mercedes drew up outside the factory – a vast concrete structure with four towering chimneys that dominated the skyline. It was protected from the outside world by tall metal fences and stainless steel gates.

'My name is Sturmbannführer Vogel, from Dachau,' Hans announced to the guards. 'Open the gates now.'

The gates duly opened, and the car drove up to the factory entrance. Pressing the pistol against his neck, Hans pushed Alexander out of the car and marched him through a pair of glass doors into the spacious entrance hall. 'This man is my prisoner,' Hans barked at a guard. 'Don't let him out of your sight. I need to speak to the manager.'

He returned ten minutes later, accompanied by two further armed guards, who pinioned Alexander's arms behind his back. Hans addressed him in a calm but firm voice. 'You are being returned to the factory. You will live in the same barracks as before, just doing a different job.'

Alexander said nothing; he simply stared blankly over the top of Hans' head, impassive and unblinking. Hans found his reaction disconcerting; he had expected resistance, or at the very least an argument.

'I think you'll agree,' said Hans quietly, putting on his black gloves, 'that I've dealt quite fairly with you, in the circumstances. Good luck.'

In the car, on the way back to Dachau, Hans sighed with relief. He felt almost liberated, knowing he could put the whole experience behind him. He had freed the Russian from the factory, and was now simply returning him there. He had nothing to reproach himself for.

Settling down to work once again in his office, Hans studied Rascher's notes and figures with a growing sense of disbelief. It seemed that the sepsis experiments had not only been poorly executed, they had also delivered disappointing results. There had been several problems: the anti-sepsis drug was almost impossible to administer – each 'patient' had been forced to take more than 280 pills at five-minute intervals throughout the day and night. And of the forty cases of sepsis treated with the new drug, ten had died, while the remainder had become severely ill. It was a disaster, and no amount of massaging the figures could turn it into a success.

Hans decided that Himmler should be shown the results as a matter of urgency. Perhaps then he would realise which of the two doctors was the better research scientist. And he had another reason to feel cheerful – he was looking forward to seeing Himmler's reaction when he told him that Annaliese was expecting a child.

～

The snow had begun to settle, as Annaliese walked up the road to her house. Her day out had revived her. She felt curiously optimistic that things would work out.

Marta met her in the entrance hall and took her shopping bags. 'Did you have a nice time, madam?'

'Yes, thank you, very nice. I think it was what I needed. I bought some new clothes, and ordered wallpaper for the nursery – yellow with animals and flowers. I also bought a couple of little presents... I'd almost forgotten that it's Christmas next week. I must ask Alexander to cut down a Christmas tree, like he did last year. Could you get that big china plant pot ready in the sitting room?'

'You don't need to do that,' said Marta hurriedly. 'The master arranged it – I've already put the tree up, but I left the decorations to you.'

'Hans arranged it?' said Annaliese in surprise. She walked through to the sitting room, and there was the tree, standing in its pot by the window, the boxes of decorations laid out on the floor. She opened the French windows and stood for a moment on the snowy terrace searching for Alexander. She wanted to tell him that she had come to a decision: to do as he asked – to leave him to do his job and concentrate on her child. Then, when the war was over, perhaps they could be together.

Snow had settled on the tops of the box hedges, forming neat geometric shapes across the garden, as she walked towards the shed. She imagined Alexander tidying away his tools – perhaps oiling the spade, cleaning the tines of the garden fork. Pulling her fur coat around her, she knocked on the door, but there was no reply. Pushing it open, she found the shed empty.

Panicking, she ran around the garden, searching for Alexander, but he was nowhere to be seen. Back inside the house, she called for Marta. 'Where is he?' she demanded.

'Who, madam?'

'You know who – the gardener, of course.'

'Oh, him... he's gone, madam.'

'Gone?' Annaliese felt light-headed, her heart racing. 'What do you mean? Gone where – was he ill?'

'No. The master dismissed him earlier today. While you were in town, he came back and took him away.'

'Took him away – where?'

'I'm afraid I don't know, madam. Shall I help you with the decorations?'

Annaliese stared at her. 'What?' she screamed. 'No!' She ran upstairs, and into her room, slamming the door behind her.

When Hans returned home that evening, he found his mother sitting by the fire in the sitting room. 'Good evening, Mama. Is Annaliese not with you?'

'I've not seen her this evening at all. She's upstairs, I think.'

Hans climbed the staircase and pushed open their bedroom door. 'Annaliese...' he called out softly into the darkness. He walked around the bed and turned on the bedside light. Annaliese lay, fully dressed, beneath a rug, her head buried in her hands.

'Go away,' she mumbled, rolling away from him.

He sat down next to her and rested his hand on her back. 'Darling...'

'Don't,' she said, shrinking from his touch. 'I hate you.'

'Darling...'

'How could you?' she whispered. 'How could you do that?'

'If you're upset about the gardener, all I've done is send him back to the factory where I found him. He's quite safe, darling. He has work, food, and a place to sleep. I could have been much harder on him.'

She sat up in bed, glaring at him, her eyes puffy from crying. 'Where is he?' she demanded. 'You must tell me!'

'I told you – he has a good job at one of the factories.'

'When did you plan this? How could you keep it from me?'

'Because I realised you would never agree to him leaving. But when I saw how unhappy you were, I did what any husband would have done in the circumstances.'

'You must have forced him to leave? Did you hurt him?'

'No. He left quite willingly.'

She glared at him. 'I don't believe you. You could have let him keep his job here, or found a way of rewarding him – by getting a pardon for him. He gave you a child, Hans – a child! He's saved your career, maybe your life, and you've punished him. I will never forgive you, never! Now get out.'

Hans stood up, running his trembling hands through his hair. 'In time, you will come to see that I have done the only sensible thing. The Russian understood the danger you were both in, better than you. I suspect he withdrew from you, scared of the implications of what you had done, and that was making you unhappy. I understand completely. To be so close to someone you love, and have that love rejected, is mental torture.'

She stared at him. 'How would you know that? How could you possibly know how I feel?'

'I see it in your eyes every day. And I know how you feel because I feel the same way – about you. I love you, you see. I always have, and always will, but I realise my love is not returned. I just hope you will learn to replace the love you feel for the Russian...'

'He has a name!' she hissed. 'He's called Alexander Kosomov. He is an architect. His father is a doctor – like you. They had an estate outside Moscow. He is a better man than you will ever be. And I'm glad he's the father of my child, and not you!'

Hans recoiled as if he'd been punched in the face. He took a deep breath and looked into the turquoise eyes of his wife – they were filled with hate. 'I just hope,' Hans repeated patiently, 'that you will learn to replace the love you feel for the Russian, with love for your child.'

Annaliese threw herself back down onto the bed, weeping loudly.

'I'll leave you now,' Hans said quietly, 'and I'll tell Marta that you're unwell. She'll bring some supper up for you. I'll sleep in the spare room tonight. Goodnight.'

21

MARCH 1944

Throughout that winter and into the following spring, Annaliese tried everything she could to persuade her husband to reveal where Alexander had gone – she begged, nagged, raged and pleaded – but Hans was implacable.

'No good will come of you knowing where he is,' he endlessly repeated. 'But I can assure you, he is perfectly safe. He works twelve hours a day in a factory, after which he returns to his barracks. If he works hard and doesn't step out of line, he will come to no harm. And from my knowledge of the man, that's all he wants – to survive. Leave him be, Annaliese. If you have any concern for him at all, let him alone. You will only endanger him by trying to contact him.'

Annaliese knew Hans was right, but her heart dictated otherwise: discovering Alexander's whereabouts became an obsession. Hans had given her a clue – her lover was in a factory somewhere, presumably in Munich. Determined to find him, she bought a map of the Munich area, and a trip to the library yielded a list of all the factories in the city. Hans had already

told her that the major manufacturers of cars, steel and pharma-
ceuticals had been repurposed to produce goods for the war
effort – mostly employing slave labour. She marked their loca-
tions on the map, and set out on the hunt for Alexander.

Every morning, she chose one area of the city, and took the
tram there, visiting every factory that might be employing slave
labour. It was not without risk; an obviously rich woman in a fur
coat and hat was conspicuous in the rough industrial parts of
town. She couldn't go inside the factories, of course, nor ask to
see a list of their employees, so instead she waited outside by the
perimeter fences. When the workers came outside for their
breaks, milling around the yard behind the fences, she would
call them over.

'Do you know a man called Alexander Kosomov? I need to
find him urgently.'

At factory after factory, the answers were always negative,
accompanied by suspicious looks at the rich pregnant woman
on the other side of the wire. For her part, Annaliese was
shocked to find women and children – no more than eleven or
twelve – working in the factories alongside the men. They all
looked exhausted and hungry, and their clothes were in tatters.
The German people had been told that foreign workers were
happy and well looked after – at least, that was what was
reported in the press. Newspapers often ran stories explaining
that, while the brave workers of Germany were away fighting
for the Fatherland, foreign workers were willingly filling the
gaps. But Annaliese knew otherwise. They were slaves, just like
Alexander.

Slowly she began to build up a picture of the slave labour
situation. For example, the camera manufacturer Agfa-
Commando was turning out timing devices for bombs. Clinging
to the wire at the Agfa factory one lunchtime, she beckoned to a

young female factory worker. The girl, who was no older than twenty, came suspiciously to the wire. 'What do you want?' she asked.

'I'm looking for someone.'

'Who?'

'A Russian man name Alexander Kosomov.'

'There are no Russians here, and no men either. We are just women – all from Poland.'

'Just women?'

Their conversation was interrupted by a guard. 'You there,' he called out to the girl. 'Get back to work.'

She scowled at Annaliese. 'Now you've got me into trouble.'

'I'm so sorry.' Annaliese watched helplessly through the barbed wire fence as the woman was frog-marched back inside.

One evening, Hans returned from work and, as usual, found Annaliese in her bedroom, brushing her thick blond hair at the dressing table. He laid a stiff white card in front of her; it was embossed with gold lettering. 'Good news – we've been invited to a party next month,' he said cheerfully. 'The bad news is that it's at Dr Rascher's house.' He smiled, trying to make a joke of it.

Annaliese pushed the invitation to one side and carried on brushing her hair. 'You go if you want to, but I'm not going. My pregnancy will be so far advanced by then, I'll be too uncomfortable to spend all evening standing up at a party. Besides, I have nothing to wear – at least nothing that would fit.'

The truth was she was appalled at the idea of spending time with her husband's colleagues.

But Hans persisted, with just a hint of sarcasm: 'Not too uncomfortable to spend your days wandering the city, however.'

'What do you mean?'

'Oh, come now,' he said calmly, 'my mother and Marta have

told me – you go out each day, and you're away for hours. I can guess what you're doing. You're looking for him, aren't you?'

'What if I am? I love him. I need to know he's all right.'

He was surprised by her honesty, but also distressed. He had hoped she had accepted the situation, and come to terms with it. She had seemed so much calmer in recent weeks, preparing the nursery, getting things ready for their child. But he now realised that her devotion to the Russian was unbreakable.

'My love,' he began gently, 'I've told you before... he's alive and well, but you'll never find him. There are hundreds of factories. Just give up. Forget him. Concentrate on the child. That's your duty now.'

'Don't tell me my duty!' she shouted, glaring at him in the mirror. 'I have no duty to a country which makes slaves of innocent men, women and children. Nor to a husband who tortures people in the name of science!'

Hans blanched, as he absorbed the implications of what she was saying. Clearly the Russian had told Annaliese what was going on in the medical wing at Dachau. But there was nothing he could do about that now. Annaliese threw her hairbrush down on the dressing table with a clatter, and flopped, sobbing, onto the bed.

Hans sat down beside her. 'Darling, I'm sorry for everything. I know you're suffering, but you must do as I ask and stop looking for him. It's too risky – both for you and him, let alone the baby. You could be arrested for what you're doing.'

She turned over and looked at him. 'Why? Am I no longer allowed even to go for a walk?'

'Of course, but not to search for foreign workers – surely you can see how that might look. It's your safety I'm thinking about.'

She turned over and studied his face. 'You really believe that, don't you?'

He nodded. 'I don't believe it – I know it.' He tentatively reached out and stroked her hair. She was too exhausted to resist. 'Now, about this party,' he said, briskly changing the subject, 'we really must go. Himmler will be there, and to refuse would be a black mark against us both. Apart from anything else, I want you to meet him – for him to see you in all your glory, blooming and pregnant. You must buy a new dress for the occasion. I understand that Rascher's wife is pregnant too – you could share your experiences, perhaps? It might be helpful to spend time with another woman in the same situation.'

Annaliese rolled away from him, and closed her eyes. As usual, argument was pointless. It would be easier just to agree. 'Fine,' she replied quietly. 'I'll go to the party.'

∼

The Raschers lived in an elegant enclave on the outskirts of Munich. All the houses were substantial and set in large gardens. A manservant opened the door to the Vogels, took their coats, and ushered them through to the drawing room. It was a vast room running the whole width of the rear of the house, and was packed with guests – mainly SS officers in dress uniform and their wives... or at least so Annaliese presumed. Most of the women were wearing traditional Bavarian dress – dirndls, paired with low-cut peasant blouses. Annaliese glanced down at her new outfit – a slender column of dark green velvet, cut low over the bosom and stretched over her neat bump – and hoped she was dressed appropriately. The room was elegantly furnished, and lit with chandeliers. There were bowls of fruit arranged around the room – an extravagance that Annaliese hadn't seen since before the start of the war. Even with Hans' extra rations, they never had enough to buy a whole bowl of fruit, let alone display one.

'Ah, good – you're here,' said Rascher, pushing through the

crowd towards Hans and shaking his hand. 'And this must be your beautiful wife, I presume?' He took Annaliese's hand, bowed low and kissed it. 'How lovely you look, Frau Vogel,' he murmured.

Annaliese smiled politely, but instinctively recoiled from the man. He had an unusually high forehead with a receding hairline and dark malevolent eyes that seemed to bore into the depths of her being.

'You must come and meet my wife,' he said, pointing to a statuesque fair-haired woman, obviously heavily pregnant. She was chatting to a man Annaliese vaguely recognised.

'That's Himmler,' Hans whispered to her, as Rascher escorted them across the room. Annaliese watched fascinated as the woman threw her head back and laughed gaily at something Himmler had said, shaking her blond curls. It was a curiously coquettish gesture for a pregnant, middle-aged woman, she thought.

'Heinrich,' said Rascher, 'may I introduce Dr Vogel's wife, Annaliese?'

'Enchanted,' replied Himmler, kissing Annaliese's hand. 'It's about time we met the elusive Frau Vogel. I can see why Hans has kept you hidden, my dear – for fear one of us might steal you away.'

Annaliese smiled wanly.

'Have you met our hostess for the evening?' Himmler asked grandly. 'May I introduce Karoline Rascher. She is a good friend, and a most talented singer.'

Karoline blushed a little. 'Oh, Heinrich, you're too kind.' She turned to Annaliese. 'Do call me Nini – everyone does.'

'Frau Vogel,' Himmler continued, 'Nini, like your good self, is a loyal National Socialist wife. She's soon to have her fourth child.'

'Congratulations,' said Annaliese, struggling with this information. *The woman must be nearly fifty*, she thought. 'How wonderful,' she went on. 'Are the children here? I'd love to meet them.'

'Oh no, they're all in bed,' replied Karoline briskly, 'but I can show you their photographs.'

She led Annaliese to an elegant grand piano, where a group of silver picture frames were ostentatiously displayed. There were pictures of the Rascher family on country walks, and driving a horse and cart; a photograph of the couple in evening dress with Himmler, and another with the Führer himself and Eva Braun – clearly taken at the Berghof, Hitler's mountain retreat. But in pride of place, at the front of the display, were individual silver-framed photographs of the Rascher children.

'This is Rudi,' explained Karoline, picking up the largest photo frame. 'He's three and a half, and such a character! And here's Otto – he's just had his second birthday. And the little one, shy of the camera, is Klaus.'

'Gosh,' said Annaliese, 'three boys under the age of four. That must be hard work. And when is the next one due?' she asked.

'Oh, in a week or two,' Karoline replied airily. 'And you?'

'Soon – a few more weeks. But I feel awfully uncomfortable already.'

'Oh, I know,' said Karoline conspiratorially. 'These men don't how lucky they are. But I'm glad for you – I know it's something you and your husband have struggled with for a long time.'

Annaliese found this last comment disconcerting. How did the woman know? The idea that her marriage – and more especially, her lack of children – had been discussed in the higher echelons of society came as a shock.

The evening went well enough. There was plenty of food to eat, and elegant cocktails to drink, but Annaliese felt alienated. The other guests appeared boorish and self-satisfied, as well as being foolishly over-confident. They all insisted that the war was winnable, and that the Allies would soon be on the run. Annaliese, having listened to the foreign news, knew this was extremely unlikely. She also wondered if these elegant women knew what work their husbands really did during the day.

She made polite conversation but secretly yearned to leave, and was on the point of asking Hans to take her home, when she saw Himmler stand up on a chair in the centre of the room.

'I want to make an announcement,' he shouted. The chatter immediately stopped and everyone turned towards him.

'I'm delighted to be here this evening, at the kind invitation of my good friends Sigmund and Nini. As we all know, Nini is not only a talented singer but has also produced three children in as many years, with a fourth expected soon. In that context I have two announcements to make. Firstly, you will doubtless have seen their family photographs on the piano. I intend to make millions of copies of one of these photographs and distribute them around the country. This remarkable family is a shining example of the perfect German family – producing fine Aryan boys for the Fatherland.' There were murmurs of approval around the room, but Himmler held up his hand and continued. 'My second announcement regards scientific research. Because of his wife's remarkable fecundity, Dr Rascher has generously offered to allow his wife to be studied by scientists. She is, I think you'll agree, the perfect example of German women's genetic superiority. I'm sure Nini won't be offended if I mention that she is approaching her fiftieth birthday and yet is about to give birth to her fourth child. She is literally a living medical miracle.'

The guests now applauded rapturously.

Himmler beamed at Nini, who bowed to the crowd, smiling weakly. 'Now everyone,' he added, 'get back to having fun.'

Annaliese sidled over to Hans. 'I'd like to go now – please?'

'Not yet,' he said, 'I need to talk to Himmler about something. Try to be patient.'

Annaliese left the drawing room and went upstairs in search of the bathroom. The first door she tried led to what appeared to be a dark, empty bedroom, but as her eyes became accustomed to the gloom, she realised it was the nursery, because against the wall stood four cots in a row. Intrigued, she crept inside. Each cot had a child's name painted on the headboard: 'Rudi', 'Otto' and 'Klaus'. The children were fast asleep, but Annaliese was struck by their different hair colours – one dark, one blond and one redhead. She noticed the fourth cot was empty, but its headboard bore the name of its future inhabitant – 'Heinrich' – named after Himmler, she supposed. *How odd*, Annaliese thought, *to be so confident of the sex of your unborn child*. What would they do if they had a girl – change the name to Helga? The room felt more like a school dormitory than a children's nursery. Her own baby's room had recently been wallpapered, and decorated with pretty yellow curtains and rugs. But this room was bare apart from the four cots, and a chair and a single light bulb hanging from the ceiling.

Annaliese was about to leave, when one of the children woke up and began to cry. Blond-haired Otto sat up, sucking his thumb and whimpering. 'Hello there,' she said gently. 'Are you all right?'

He scowled and began to cry lustily.

'Now, now,' she said, bending down to pick him up. 'Don't cry.' She rocked him gently in her arms and he began to relax. His thumb fell from his mouth and his eyes closed dreamily.

The door suddenly flew open. 'What are you doing in here?' It was Karoline, her blue eyes flashing. 'Why have you woken him up?'

'I didn't,' said Annaliese, laying him gently back in his cot. 'I was just walking past – looking for the bathroom – and I heard him crying. I only came in to check on him.'

'Well, you've done that now,' replied Karoline coldly. 'You can go.'

'They're lovely children and all so different, aren't they?' Annaliese remarked, as she pulled the covers back over Otto's little body. 'Their hair colour, I mean.'

'Yes... well, I'm blond, and my husband's dark... shall we go?' said Karoline, propelling Annaliese out of the room.

Back downstairs in the drawing room, the hostess plunged into the crowd to talk to her other guests, leaving Annaliese by herself. She spotted Hans on the other side of the room standing next to the mantelpiece with Himmler, having what appeared to be a heated but muted conversation. Intrigued to find out what they were talking about, Annaliese sidled towards them, positioning herself nearby, pretending to study a book from one of the shelves.

'I would be very careful, if I were you,' Himmler was saying, 'about criticising a man in whom I have placed such considerable faith. Dr Rascher is integral to my whole scientific programme, and so is his laboratory.'

'I do understand, Reichsführer.'

'Your role, Dr Vogel, is to ensure that the statistics and methodology are correct. It is you I shall hold responsible for any errors... is that understood?'

'Completely, Reichsführer.'

In the car driving home, Hans brooded. As he turned the corner into their road, his wall of silence finally broke. 'It's outrageous. Himmler is completely blind to Rascher's incompetence. The more I investigate his research, the more appalling it appears to be. His methodology is inconsistent – and worse, the placebo group and treatment group have been muddled. Suffice it to say, the work is completely flawed and now, it seems, Himmler is going to blame me for his results. It's intolerable.'

'Did you tell him what you thought of Rascher?' asked Annaliese, wondering if Hans had had the courage to criticise Rascher's experiments.

Hans pulled up outside their house, and glanced across at his wife. 'You must understand, there are limits to what I can say. The problem is Himmler wouldn't hear a word against his friend.'

So he hadn't confronted him, she realised.

Back inside, they went through to the sitting room where Hans poured himself a large drink and sank down onto the sofa.

'I thought Rascher's wife was odd, didn't you?' said Annaliese. 'I find it almost impossible to believe she's had so many children. Why didn't she have them earlier? Why wait until you're forty-seven if you're so fertile? It doesn't make sense.'

'You're right,' replied Hans, 'it is odd – particularly, as they've been together for years. Although I've heard rumours that she and Himmler were once... you know... close friends.'

'Oh, that doesn't surprise me,' said Annaliese. 'The way they had their heads together throughout the evening. But it was the way she behaved towards her children that worried me – she wasn't very loving.'

'How do you know?'

'I was in their nursery. I was looking for the bathroom and one of the boys started crying. I just went in and picked him up. Karoline arrived and was furious. She made no effort to take the boy from me and comfort him herself. It was odd. In public, she seemed so proud of them, but when she was actually with them, she was cold and rather aloof. I thought they looked so sad in their little dormitory.'

'Dormitory?'

'Yes – four cots next to one another, and the room completely bare – no toys, no wallpaper, no pictures. The rest of the house is so beautifully decorated, it just seemed odd...'

'Mmm,' said Hans. 'How interesting.'

A few days later, Hans returned from work early, in a state of heightened excitement. 'Marta,' he called out from the hall, 'where's my wife?'

Marta hurried into the hall, carrying a duster. 'She's having a nap upstairs, sir.'

Hans took the stairs two at a time, bursting into their bedroom and shaking his wife awake. 'Annaliese, Annaliese... you'll never believe what's happened.'

'What is it?' she asked sleepily.

'Rascher and his wife – they've been arrested!'

'Arrested? What on earth for?'

'Well, it seems your suspicions about them and their children were well-founded.'

'What do you mean?' She hauled herself up in bed.

'Karoline has been arrested in Munich railway station. She was caught trying to steal a newborn baby!'

'You're joking!'

'I'm not... I'll tell you the whole story.' Hans sat down next to her, looking almost gleeful. 'It seems that the mother had left her baby in a pram outside the café while she went in for a coffee. She chose a table in the window so she could keep an eye on the child – which was lucky, because she actually saw Karoline Rascher grab hold of the pram and walk off with it. Fortunately, she was quick off the mark, ran outside and caught up with her. Sounds like she was lucky to get the baby back.'

Annaliese was dumbfounded, but her mind was racing. 'Well, that explains it...' she finally replied.

'Explains what?'

'There was a boy's name on the empty cot in the nursery – Heinrich, as it happens.'

Hans laughed. 'How ironic.'

'I thought it was odd – to assume you would have a boy. I mean what would you do if you had a girl...? Oh, never mind about that... go on with the story.'

'Well, Karoline tried to deny it, of course – saying she thought the child had been abandoned, but the woman made such a huge fuss that the police were called, and arrested Karoline. This all happened a couple of days after the party, apparently. I had noticed Rascher was in a foul mood at work – he must have been frantic with worry. Then today I was sitting in his office, working on the figures of his terrible experiments, when two guards came in and arrested him.'

'My God!' said Annaliese.

'Himmler's absolutely furious. He'd just distributed millions of copies of the Rascher family photograph – the perfect German family – and it turns out that all the children were stolen!' Hans sniggered. 'It's priceless!'

'All of them?' said Annaliese, appalled. 'You mean all those little boys belong to someone else.'

'Exactly! They were all stolen. All over Munich – families who've lost children are being contacted.'

'Oh, that's awful,' said Annaliese. 'Unforgivable, really.'

'That's exactly what Himmler said. He came into the lab and was screaming at everyone. "That bastard Rascher – after all I've done for him. He'll be made to suffer".'

'They must have been really desperate to do something like that,' said Annaliese quietly.

'You surely don't feel any sympathy for them, do you?' asked Hans incredulously.

'In a way,' Annaliese admitted. 'We are all driven to extremes of some kind, aren't we? Driven by fear, or a desire for acceptance or promotion.'

'I think you'll find, my dear, that Rascher was driven by a far more unpleasant emotion – pure greed. He's going to get what he deserves and I, for one, am delighted.'

Annaliese lay back down, her hands stroking her swollen stomach. The baby was really beginning to kick hard now. Unlike Hans, she could take no pleasure in Rascher's disgrace. In fact, it made her feel even more anxious. She too was deceiving the authorities – an adulterous wife carrying the child of a Russian slave. How long might it be, she wondered, before her secret was also exposed?

22

April 1944

The news of Rascher and his wife spread rapidly among the senior officers at Dachau. Karoline had been arrested and sent to Ravensbrück concentration camp – even her once 'close relationship' with Himmler was not enough to protect her. Meanwhile, her husband, had been despatched to Buchenwald as a 'special prisoner'.

'I hear Himmler feels utterly betrayed and, as such, will never forgive them,' Hans told Annaliese a few days later. 'He's determined to make an example of them. There's even talk of execution...'

'Doesn't that frighten you?' Annaliese asked him, shivering slightly.

'Not really. Why should it? We haven't stolen any children.'

'Isn't what we've done just as bad, if not worse? We stole something from Alexander to make our child. I think the parallels are rather striking.'

'Don't be absurd. That was quite different. No! We were right to do what we did.'

But she was not so sure.

Annaliese woke in the middle of the night to the sound of an air-raid siren. Clambering out of bed, she hauled on her dressing gown and found Hans already outside on the landing.

'It's a raid,' he said. 'Let's fetch my mother and Marta and go down to the basement.'

'It's intolerable,' Elisabetta complained, once they were safely installed in the cellar, 'this constant bombing in the middle of the night.'

'I know, Mama,' said Hans gently. 'Just try to be patient, and I'm sure it will all be over soon.'

The raids had recently become more frequent. Marta and Annaliese had tried to make the cellar as comfortable as possible. A few months earlier, they had dragged a couple of old mattresses down from the attic, along with blankets, candles and card games. But there was no card-playing that night – the bombing was too insistent. At one point, the house juddered violently and coal dust flew through the air, making everyone cough. Suddenly, a massive explosion ricocheted through the house; the joists above their heads trembled, and the women screamed. Hans instinctively threw himself across Annaliese, covering her body with his own.

'Did it hit us?' Annaliese asked eventually, when the dust had settled.

'No, I don't think so,' said Hans. 'But it landed somewhere quite close. Are you all right, my darling?'

'Me... yes, I'm fine.' Annaliese lay back exhausted on the mattress. Her thoughts turned, as they often did, to Alexander. Was he being bombed now, too?

'Annaliese, Annaliese!' Hans was shaking her. 'You are all wet, darling... I think your waters have broken.'

She calmly reached between her legs. 'You're right. The baby must be coming.'

'It's the shock of the bombs,' said Elisabetta. 'It's brought on her labour. Hans, you must do something.'

'All right, Mama,' said Hans quietly, 'let's not panic. As it's her first child, the chances are it will be a long labour.' He turned back to Annaliese. 'Once the sirens give the all-clear, we'll get you back to bed. Marta, the telephone line is bound to be down, so please go to the obstetrician's office first thing in the morning – it's just behind the Hofgarten. His name is Dr Hartmann. Tell him Dr Vogel's wife needs him – and bring him back here.'

Stumbling out of the cellar at dawn, they climbed up the stairs into the kitchen. Annaliese gasped as she looked out at the garden: the central lawn was now a crater of brown earth. 'Oh my God!' she said. 'Look at the garden…'

'I thought the bomb was close,' said Hans. 'It's a miracle we weren't hit. Let's get you upstairs. Marta, make some tea and then run to the doctor.'

Annaliese's contractions were getting more painful, and Hans was pacing anxiously around the bedroom, when Marta finally returned, rushing upstairs, out of breath. 'I'm afraid I couldn't reach the doctor's office, sir. It's chaos out there – three houses in our street have been hit. There were roadblocks everywhere. I tried to push through them, but the soldiers wouldn't let me.'

Annaliese looked panicked. 'Hans – what are we going to do?'

'It's all right, darling,' said Hans. 'I am a doctor, after all. Marta, go down and boil some water, then bring me some towels and my doctor's bag from the study.'

Annaliese's labour lasted for the rest of the day. She found the pain eased slightly if she walked around the room, but Elisabetta knew better.

'She shouldn't be standing up. Make her lie down, Hans,' she instructed.

'Please,' Annaliese begged her, 'I know you mean well, but could you just leave us alone?'

'Come, Mama,' said Hans, guiding his mother out of the room. 'We've all had a long night. You're tired, why don't you go to your own room and lie down? There's nothing you can do here.'

It was early evening when Annaliese felt the contractions getting closer together.

'Maybe you should lie down now,' Hans suggested. 'It won't be too much longer.'

'I need something for the pain.'

'I have very little I can give you,' he said. 'Any sort pain relief is discouraged by the Party – it's considered a sign of weakness. You must try to be strong, Annaliese.'

'You try and be strong,' she screamed, as another contraction hit her.

At seven in the evening, after fifteen hours of labour, a tiny boy slithered out into the world and screamed lustily.

Annaliese, although exhausted, was filled with a hormonal surge of pure joy. As she took her child in her arms and laid him to her breast, she murmured, 'Thank God,' while at the same time privately thanking the man who had made it possible – the man she still loved – Alexander.

The tiny blond boy had the dark blue eyes of every newborn. But how long would it be before they settled on their true colour – and would that be turquoise like hers, or green like his father's?

'Little Sasha,' she cooed, as she held him to her breast.

'What's that you're calling him?' Hans asked, as he tidied away his instruments.

'Sasha... it's short for—'

'—I know exactly what it's short for,' he interrupted fiercely, 'and you cannot, in all honesty, expect me to allow that, can you?'

She shook her head sadly. 'No, I suppose not.'

'The child will be named after my father,' Hans insisted.

'Your father? Why not my father?'

'That can be his second name, if you like.'

She acquiesced, knowing it was pointless to argue, and the following day the baby was registered as Maximillian Pieter Vogel. But at night, or when she nursed him alone, she reverted to her own name for him – little Sasha, son of Alexander.

Over the long hot summer of 1944, the bombing of Munich continued unabated. The Allies seemed determined to destroy Hitler's favourite city and the factories supporting the war effort.

At night, raids flew over so frequently that the Vogels slept down in the cellar, only creeping out after the sirens gave the all-clear at dawn. Annaliese was nervous during the raids for herself and the child, but was more frightened for Alexander. There were no bomb shelters for slave labourers, and the newspapers were full of stories of direct hits on armaments factories.

By day, in spite of having an infant to care for, Annaliese continued her search for Alexander. After feeding the baby, she would put him in the pram and prepare to go out – 'only for a walk,' she told her mother-in-law.

Predictably, Elisabetta objected. 'Are you sure? After the bombing, the streets will be virtually impassable. It can't be safe.'

'I like to walk,' Annaliese would answer, armed with a variety of excuses: 'It's good for the baby to have fresh air'; 'We just sit in the park – what's left of it'; 'I can't stay here, just looking at the garden. I can't bear it, knowing how beautiful it was last summer.'

'But Hans has said he'll get some men to fill in the hole,' Elisabetta argued.

'Well, until he does, I shall continue to take the baby out with me.'

One morning, towards the end of September, Annaliese left the house pushing her son in his pram, a map of Munich hidden beneath the baby's covers. She had three factories to visit that morning: Siemens, Krupp and Volkswagen. The first two drew a blank, and it was lunchtime by the time she arrived at the VW factory.

The baby was hungry and grizzling; she jiggled the pram, wondering if she should abandon her search that day and find somewhere quiet to feed her son. But just then, the lunchtime siren went off, and the workers began to filter out into the exercise yard for a few moments of respite in the sunshine. They filed out, slowly at first, in groups of ten, but then gathered pace, until hundreds of men were shuffling around the yard, watched over by armed guards.

'Just a few minutes more, Sasha,' she murmured to her son, rocking his pram. As she cast her eye over the throng of workers, suddenly there he was – about forty metres away, leaning against the wall of the factory. He held a grubby cap in one hand and was wiping his shaven head with the other. He looked thin, she thought, but there was something about the way he held his head that showed he was still proud, still defiant.

She wanted to call out, but she knew that her voice would

alert the guards, so instead she pressed her face against the wire fence, willing him to notice her. A young man joined him, and offered him the end of a cigarette. Together, they began to walk slowly in her direction, chatting. Alexander inhaled the cigarette, and as he exhaled, he saw her. She smiled, tentatively raising her hand, and pointing to the pram. He muttered something to his companion, before sauntering casually towards her. But as soon as he got to the wire, he turned his back on her, staring into the yard.

'What are you doing here?' he asked, through clenched teeth.

'Looking for you. I've been looking for months – I've been everywhere. I can't believe I've actually found you.'

'Well, now you have, you should go.'

'Not yet... I wanted you to meet your son.' She lifted the baby from the pram and held him up to the wire. The child wriggled and mewled, screwing his eyes up against the sun.

Alexander began slowly to walk away.

'Alexander,' she called out, 'don't you even want to look at him?'

He stopped in his tracks. 'He's not mine,' he said flatly.

'But he is,' she pleaded. 'Just look at him, and you'll see the likeness.'

Only then did he turn around. 'No. I can't see it. It's just a baby.'

'I'm showing him to you, to give you something to live for,' said Annaliese, clutching at straws. 'When this war is over, I'll be waiting for you. *We'll* be waiting. The three of us will start a new life together, away from this awful place.'

'I don't need a baby to live for. Just go home, Annaliese, please.'

'But he's yours,' she sobbed. 'Don't you understand? You have a son.'

'How can you be so sure?' he asked suspiciously.

'Well, he looks like you,' she began.

'Babies all look the same.' Alexander turned and headed back towards the factory.

Annaliese realised this was her last chance – she must make him understand. She had to tell him the truth. 'My husband can't have children,' she cried out. 'He's infertile.'

He swung round, and glared at her, the colour draining from his face. 'What are you saying?'

She clutched the baby to her breast. 'Hans can't have children,' she said softly, almost under her breath.

'So, let me understand – have you always known this was my child?'

She nodded guiltily.

He banged the wire between them hard, with his fist. 'Oh, now I understand – was that the plan all along? Was that what it was all about? You couldn't have a child, so you get your husband to bring back some suitable slave from a factory, and screw him?'

'No!' she cried out. 'Well... yes, partly. But I did love you... do love you – you must believe that.'

'How can I believe anything you say?' he replied coldly. 'I'm not surprised your husband wanted me out of there. It must have been torture for him – knowing we were screwing in his own bed, in his house. Go, and don't ever try to find me again.'

'But I love you.' She began to sob.

'No, Annaliese – you love yourself. You risked my life to get that child. I could have been executed for what we did – I still might. How can I ever forgive you for that?'

He turned and strode away across the yard, rejoining his friend.

She watched them put their heads together, resuming their conversation. His friend turned and stared at her. She wondered what had Alexander told him. How he must hate her. Holding the baby with one arm, she clung to the wire with the other. 'Alexander, Alexander, I love you,' she whimpered.

∾

Over the following months Annaliese slowly began to accept that Alexander would never forgive her. In many ways she saw it as justice. After all, she had gone along with Hans' plan; she could have refused to sleep with Alexander but she had been a willing participant. Equally, she could have left Hans when she discovered what he was doing at Dachau – making her disapproval, her revulsion, very clear. But instead, she had chosen the line of least resistance and had stayed. She had heard rumours of brave young people in Munich who opposed the regime and were standing up to Hitler. They were prepared to go to their deaths for what they believed. She could have followed their example; she could have been noble and pure. Instead, she had chosen comfort and security. And worse, what she had done was a sin – a repudiation of her marriage vows, and the wanton seduction of a man who had no choice.

Annaliese was not a religious woman, but with no one in whom she could confide, she took to visiting her parents' grave in the little churchyard where she had first met Hans. She would take the tram and then wheel little Sasha down the long road to the churchyard. Each week, she would put new flowers in the glass vase on the simple grey stone that marked their resting place. What would her father think of her now – rocking her bastard child in his pram? Would he be disappointed, she wondered, or would he understand? What would he have said? Not much perhaps – he had been a man of few words at the best of times. He had taught her the importance of hard work, but little else; had given her no moral compass with which to guide her life. She had worked that out for herself, and made a bad job of it.

On the way home, she would wheel the pram past the bombed-out shops and homes, past families in makeshift shelters by the side of the road. In spite of her privileged position, she shared their crushing sense of despair. As the chance of winning the war slipped away, the people were impatient for it all to be over. Suddenly the sacrifices – the shortage of food, clothes and daily comforts, the loss of life, the bombing, the destruction – seemed utterly pointless. It had all been a terrible waste.

The only light in Annaliese's life was her son. In spite of it all, he grew strong and healthy, his strawberry-blond hair and green eyes drawing admiring glances from people in the street. 'What a beautiful boy,' they would remark, peering into his pram, and Sasha would reward them with a broad smile.

To Annaliese's surprise, her husband appeared to genuinely care for the boy. He picked him up if he cried, and kissed him if he was hurt. He read him stories and even built a little cart for him to sit in, which he pulled around the garden, making the boy scream with delight. To any casual observer, Hans was a devoted, loving father. Indeed, there were moments, in that last year of the war, when Annaliese would watch them together in the garden, and could almost imagine they were father and son. But she could never rid herself of the memory of Alexander standing behind the barbed wire of the factory, hating her. And her guilt – at how she and Hans had manipulated him – wormed its way into her mind, poisoning any delight in her son.

She withdrew into herself, deliberately restricting her life to her child, her house, her husband. That, after all, was all she deserved, and she was lucky to have even that. Operating like a kind of automaton, she arranged meals, weeded the garden, grew vegetables and cared for her child. She even allowed Hans back into her bed. She didn't enjoy his attention, but in some strange way, she felt it was a just punishment for her part in their wickedness. She had lied to Alexander, had used and betrayed him. She had made her choice and now must live with it. But throughout it all, she thought every day of the man she still loved, the man who had now rejected her, and was filled with regret.

23

Events were moving fast. The Allied armies – American, British and Russian – were advancing inexorably into Germany. Hans and Annaliese discussed it one morning in their bedroom before he went to work.

'I have heard,' said Hans, buttoning his shirt cuffs, 'that while Berlin was falling to the Soviets, Hitler was quietly celebrating his birthday in his bunker at the Reich Chancellery, still fantasising about victory. Can you believe it?'

'I don't know what to believe. What's going to happen, Hans?'

'I don't know either... but the end is in sight. Hitler's senior officials are fleeing Berlin with their families, and heading this way – to Bavaria and the mountains.'

'Escaping, you mean... actually running away?'

'What else can they do? Hitler is mad... trapped in his own delusional mind.'

'What about Himmler? Is he with him?'

'No, he's abandoned the Führer. I wouldn't put it past him to be doing a deal with the Americans.'

'Really?'

'Himmler's a survivor,' said Hans. 'I've heard a rumour that he's promised to release over seven thousand Jewish prisoners being held at Ravensbrück concentration camp, and hand them over to the Allies – in return for being allowed to run the country when Hitler's gone.'

'Well, I agree that he's self-serving, but it would still be a good thing to release all those people, surely?'

'If they're even alive,' said Hans, putting on his jacket, 'which I doubt.'

'You think he's lying.'

'Of course he is. Himmler would do anything to save his own skin. Meanwhile, he has issued orders that every SS officer must stand and fight. The hypocrisy is breathtaking.'

'Stand and fight – does that mean you?'

Hans combed his hair. 'Perhaps.' He smiled, not wishing to worry her. What he couldn't tell her was that anyone questioning Himmler's orders was at risk of severe punishment. Only the day before, one hundred and sixty SS officers who had dared to disobey Himmler had been brought to Dachau and imprisoned in a special cell block reserved for elite prisoners, known simply as 'The Bunker'.

'So what will happen to you?' Annaliese persisted. 'Are you really expected to resist the Americans when they arrive?' She felt scared for him, she realised, and it surprised her. She had thought she had no love left for him.

'Try not to worry about that,' he replied, kissing her cheek. 'I'll work something out... see you later.'

On his journey to work that morning, Hans reflected on their conversation. There was so much he couldn't reveal to his wife.

And as for her question – what would he do? – the truth was, he didn't know. Not yet. But, like Himmler, he was determined to do whatever he could to survive.

At Dachau, a black cloud of smoke hung over the camp, and the air was acrid with the stench of burning corpses. Dr Hintermayer – the 'gas man' as he had become known – had been bragging for days about the hundreds of prisoners who had been successfully 'terminated'.

'Basically, we're getting rid of anyone who's too feeble to go on the long march,' Hintermayer told Hans casually, as they stood in the queue for lunch in the officers' mess. 'The plan is to herd any able-bodied prisoners as far away as possible from the advancing Allied forces.'

Hans merely nodded at this information. It seemed absurd to remove prisoners now. Where were they taking them, exactly? German defeat was inevitable, so why not just abandon the prisoners to the invading forces? But he kept these thoughts to himself.

After lunch Hans retreated to the relative sanctuary of his laboratory. He was keen to write up the last of his mescaline experiments, but was interrupted by a knock on the door.

'Sturmbannführer, sir.'

'Yes, Eugène, come in – what is it?'

'I thought you'd like to know that Dr Rascher has just been brought back to Dachau.'

'Brought back here?' Hans leapt to his feet. 'Has he been released, then?'

'No! He's been put into The Bunker.'

'The Bunker – you mean he's a prisoner?'

'Yes, sir. On the orders of Reichsführer Heinrich Himmler himself.'

'My God,' said Hans, 'how the mighty are fallen. What's going to happen to him – do we know?'

'No, sir.'

'Well,' said Hans firmly, 'I'd better go and say goodbye.'

Hans had done some wicked things in his time – had infected young men with malaria when he knew they couldn't possibly survive the disease, and triggered psychosis in patients through the use of mescaline, killing one or two of them. Every death had distressed him, and he had always tried his best to keep any suffering to a minimum. But the sheer sadistic pleasure that his fellow doctors appeared to derive from torturing and murdering prisoners had sickened him to his stomach. As he walked towards The Bunker, he reflected on Rascher and how he had come to such an ignominious end, imprisoned in his own concentration camp. Himmler was punishing him for stealing children – for making a fool of him and his 'Ten Commandments', but his real crimes were the hideous experiments he had performed on hundreds of innocent men. There were even rumours that his house contained a collection of saddles and lampshades made of human skin. The man was clearly delusional, perhaps even insane. He was a sadist and a brute who had tormented, abused and murdered, and if there was any justice in the world, he deserved to die.

The Bunker was at one side of the square exercise yard. Hans approached the guard on duty at the entrance. 'I must speak to Dr Rascher.'

'I have orders not to let anyone through, Sturmbannführer.'

'I am a fellow doctor – we have important research work in common. It's vital I speak to him,' said Hans convincingly. 'Heinrich Himmler himself is waiting for the results of our work.'

The guard reluctantly let him pass. 'He's in cell number seventy-three, at the far end, sir.'

Hans walked down the long concrete corridor, past cells filled with men in SS officer uniforms; each man looked up at Hans with dead eyes, as if they already knew their fate. It appeared that Himmler had finally gone mad, lashing out at his own men.

When Hans arrived at Rascher's cell, he peered through the small barred window in the door. Rascher was sitting in the corner, rocking slightly, his head in his hands.

'Sigmund,' Hans said quietly.

Rascher looked up. 'Hans! Get me out of here... please,' he gasped.

'I'm afraid I can't do that,' replied Hans.

Rascher leapt up and clutched at the bars, his fingers reaching out for Hans' face. 'Please... I beg you. I'll give you anything – money? Do you want money?'

'I don't want your money,' said Hans impassively. 'I have enough of my own.'

'Women, then... I know lots of women.'

'I don't want your women, either. What happened to your wife, by the way? I'd heard they arrested her too.'

'Himmler had her shot,' Rascher said, his eyes filling with tears.

'I'm sorry.' Hans was surprised to see Rascher showing any emotion at all.

'Why are you here?' Rascher asked suspiciously.

'I just wanted to take one last look at you. To remember you as you really are – not as the sadistic monster you will go down as in history, but as the powerless, simpering creature you are now. I hope you rot in hell.'

Hans turned on his heel and began walking smartly back up the concrete corridor, as a pair of SS soldiers marched past him. He turned to see them unlock Rascher's cell and drag him outside.

Hans walked briskly away, out into the yard, where he

waited just out of sight. He saw Rascher being manhandled into the centre of the yard, where three soldiers stood ready with their rifles. Rascher collapsed onto his knees, begging for mercy. Within seconds he was hit by a hail of bullets and fell face down into the dirt.

So, Rascher is dead at last, thought Hans – but it had been too humane an end for such an evil man.

For the rest of the day, Hans retreated to his office to plan his next move. The distant sound of gunfire gave him a sense of urgency. The Americans must be close. He gathered together all his research papers on mescaline, collated them into three bulging folders on his desk and slid them into his leather brief-case. Still wearing his white coat, he walked across to the camp records office. To his relief, he found it unguarded – perhaps record-keeping had ceased to have any importance now the Americans were only a few kilometres away. He first opened the wooden filing cabinets containing the records of SS officers serving at Dachau. He found his own file and removed it, intending to destroy it later. On the other side of the room was a row of cabinets containing details of every prisoner who had lived or died in Dachau.

He flicked through the meticulously arranged filing cards until he found what he was looking for – a man in his late thirties who had been imprisoned in 1938 for being an 'Enemy of the State', but who had died the previous year from typhoid. Otto Werner was an Austrian, and a member of Freies Österreich, an illegal underground organisation seeking to liberate Austria from German control. Fortuitously, he was also a doctor, and in looks and age was not dissimilar to Hans. In the envelope with Werner's identity card were his personal effects, meticulously preserved by the filing clerks: a fob watch, with his initials carved on the back, and a black and white photograph of a pretty young woman smiling into the camera. Written on the back was her name: 'Mimi, Vienna, 1937'. Hans slipped the envelope into his inside pocket.

Back in his office, he wrote a letter to the Americans, explaining that his research assistant Eugène was a prisoner who had had no choice but to support the work of the lab. He propped the envelope up against the phone on his desk, took off his white coat and hung it on the peg behind the door. He put on his SS jacket, picked up his leather briefcase and went out into his outer office, where Eugène was still working diligently.

'I'm going home now,' said Hans. 'Is my driver out there?'

'Yes, Sturmbannführer.'

'Good, I'll see you in the morning.' Hans paused at the door. 'You've been a good chap, Eugène. I'm sorry for all the terrible things you've had to do.'

As Hans was driven through the gates of Dachau, he made the sign of the cross – something he had not done since boyhood. '*God forgive us for what we have done,*' he prayed silently.

They drove through the country lanes and on into Munich. The streets were filled with rubble from hundreds of collapsed buildings destroyed by Allied bombing. But as they drove past the Führerbau – Hitler's headquarters – he could see that the building had remained miraculously unscathed. It seemed ironic to Hans that the Allies had not once managed to hit this most iconic of buildings. Carefully negotiating the bomb damage, the driver finally deposited Hans at home.

'Good night, Sturmbannführer.'

'Good night,' replied Hans. 'See you in the morning.'

Hans wanted to speak privately to Annaliese. Standing in the hall, he softly called out her name, but got no response. He opened the door to the sitting room and found her with his mother, watching the baby crawling around on the rug.

'Annaliese,' Hans said gently, 'I'd like a word with you. Could you come upstairs to our room?'

'Yes, all right, give me a moment. I'll bring the baby – it's nearly his bedtime, anyway.'

Within minutes Annaliese was at the door of their bedroom, carrying the baby. Inside, she found Hans dressed in his tweed suit. His SS uniform lay in a crumpled heap on the floor. A small suitcase was flung open on the bed, surrounded by neat piles of clothes.

'What are you doing?' she asked.

'I'm getting out of the country, and I want you and the child to come with me. We'll take the car and just go.'

'But how on earth will you manage that? Aren't there check-points everywhere? You'll never get away with it – the Americans are nearly here.'

'That's why we have to leave now. I'm not waiting around to get arrested at Dachau. I'm as likely to be executed by my own side as by the enemy. Even Himmler's gone mad – he's like a crazed animal lashing out at everything and everyone. Rascher's already dead, and his wife too. Come with me, Annaliese – we'll make it work, I promise.'

Annaliese paused, considering how to respond to her husband's extraordinary suggestion. 'No, Hans,' she said finally, clutching the baby to her more tightly. 'I'm staying here.'

'But why?' He looked bewildered, distraught even.

'Because I've not committed any crimes – I'm not even a member of the Party. Besides, how would we all survive, living on the run like that? You go if you like, but leave me and the baby here. Please, I beg you.'

'All right,' he said quietly, his voice catching with emotion. 'Is there nothing I can say that will make you change your mind?'

She shook her head.

'Life could get difficult for you – the Americans are bound to come looking for me and may interrogate you, or even put you on trial.'

'What for? I've done nothing wrong.' Annaliese was defiant, but Hans heard the fear in her voice. 'Let them come... I'll tell them the truth – that I don't know where you've gone.'

Hans closed the catches on his suitcase and ran his fingers through his hair. He looked agitated. 'If you really won't come... you'll need money.' He took a wad of notes out of his pocket. 'This is all I can give you at the moment. But I've transferred this house into your name.'

'Really? When did you do that?'

'A little while ago... I could see what was coming.' He took her face in his hands. 'Listen, darling. Things won't be easy, but somehow we'll get through it. From now on, you and I can't have any contact – they'll be watching you.' He pulled a key from his trouser pocket and handed it to her. 'Take this – it's the key to the safety deposit box at the bank. The deeds of the house are in there, and one or two other things.'

'Is this how it ends, then?' she asked gently. 'After all this time?'

'Yes, for now...'

'What do you mean, for now?'

'Who knows what the future holds,' he replied, stroking her cheek and ruffling the baby's hair. 'I will miss you both. I had thought we'd get through it. I was rather naïve, wasn't I?'

He kissed them both and picked up his suitcase. At the door, he turned back and gazed at them. 'I shall hold this image in my mind,' he said gently. 'Try to be kind to my mother. I know she's a difficult woman, and you two have never really got on. But my father left her very comfortably off, so don't feel guilty if you decide to ask her to leave – she has more than enough money to buy another house. And I'm sure she will be generous to you – just let her see the baby from time to time, and don't disillusion her about where he came from.'

'Of course,' she replied.

'And, Annaliese...' His eyes filled with tears. 'I have loved you very much. I hope you know that. And I'm sorry, for everything.'

24

The following morning, Annaliese woke with a knot of anxiety deep in the pit of her stomach, still struggling to make sense of Hans' departure.

She gazed enviously at the baby sleeping peacefully in his cot next to her bed, his legs splayed and his arms thrown up above his head. He looked so relaxed and happy, unaware there had been a seismic shift in their lives. Climbing out of bed, she leant over him and kissed his soft cheek. He briefly stirred, sighed and went back to sleep. She pulled open the curtains, letting the sun stream in. The bomb crater had been filled in over the winter, and was now turning green, new grass seeding itself over the surface. The borders she had created the previous year with Alexander were flourishing. The bulbs were in full bloom – military-red tulips jostled for space with summer-flowering perennials. All were nosing their way through the crumbly brown earth.

She paced the bedroom nervously, and assessed her situation. Hans had gone, perhaps forever. He had given her the house and whatever was in the safety deposit box. That, plus the money he had given her – now hidden away in her underwear drawer – meant she was to some extent, at least, master of her own destiny, possibly for the first time in her life.

Leaving the baby to sleep, she put on her dressing gown, and went downstairs. The table in the dining room had been laid, as usual, for Hans' breakfast, and Marta was in the kitchen, scrubbing the sinks.

'Good morning, Marta. Please clear away the master's breakfast. He won't be needing it.'

'I saw he hadn't eaten, madam. Did he leave very early?'

'He left late last night. He won't be coming back.'

Marta looked up from the sink in surprise. 'What do you mean, madam?'

'He's gone... for good. I'm in charge of the house now.'

'Gone, madam? I'm not sure I understand.'

'Don't worry,' replied Annaliese. 'I'm sure everything will be all right, but what with the war coming to an end and foreign troops taking over...'

Marta began to weep. 'Are we all going to be killed in our beds by the Russians?' she sobbed.

'No, of course not!' said Annaliese, patting her shoulder. 'The Russians are miles away, near Berlin. It will be the Americans who come to Munich. Perhaps we ought to listen to the news?'

She led the way upstairs to the sitting room and fiddled with the dials of the radio until she found the BBC's German Service. Marta, hovering in the doorway, looked startled as the news headlines were read out. 'Isn't it illegal to listen to foreign news?' she whispered.

'Not any more,' said Annaliese. 'Come in... let's hear what they're saying.'

The lead story was about Dachau. The Americans had

broken through the German lines, and liberated thousands of starving prisoners.

Marta interrupted the broadcast. 'Is the master still at Dachau?'

'No,' replied Annaliese. 'I don't know where he is.' She continued listening intently, fearing a story about her husband: *Dr Hans Vogel – a doctor from Dachau – has been arrested, attempting to cross the border into Switzerland.*

Is that what he intended to do? It seemed the obvious escape route.

The second news story was all about the hunt for Hitler. The Russians, as she had suspected, were in Berlin and fighting their way through to the Führerbunker.

'Will they capture the Führer?' asked Marta, her eyes wide with fear.

'I suppose so,' said Annaliese. It seemed extraordinary to think of the man who had dominated their lives for so long – all her adult life, in fact – being hunted down like an animal. She wondered what life would be like without him. It was almost unimaginable.

The news bulletin included a report from northern Germany. The bodies of a thousand or more slave labourers had been discovered in a barn, burned to death. It appeared the barn had been deliberately set on fire. Annaliese went cold. What if something similar were to happen to Alexander?

'I don't see how that can be true,' said Marta defiantly.

'What do you mean?' asked Annaliese.

'That story – about slaves being burned alive. No one would do that. Especially not in Germany. That's why we should never listen to foreign news – it's all lies.'

'No, Marta,' replied Annaliese patiently. 'I'm afraid you're wrong. I fear they are telling the truth – it's our government who have been lying.'

At that moment the baby started to cry upstairs in his room. 'I should go to him,' said Annaliese, switching off the radio.

'Was that the radio you were listening to? Elisabetta called out from the sitting room door. 'What's the latest news?'

'Marta, could you get the baby up for me?' asked Annaliese. 'Elisabetta,' she said gently, 'I think you'd better sit down.'

'Why? I don't want to sit down.'

'It's about Hans.'

'What... what about Hans?'

'He came home last night, packed a bag and has left.'

'Left? Where's he gone?'

'I don't know. He didn't say and I didn't ask. He's run away.'

Elisabetta sank down onto the sofa, her face pale. 'Run away. No... he'd never do that. He's an officer and a gentleman... and certainly no coward.'

'I'm afraid it is true. He was under orders to stay at Dachau and fight, but he didn't have the heart for it, and I can't say I blame him. He hated everything about that place. He tried to persuade me to go with him...'

Elisabetta flinched visibly.

'...but I turned him down. I couldn't take the baby on such a difficult journey. Besides, I have nothing to hide and, if I'm honest, I can see no long-term future for us, as a couple.'

But Elisabetta wasn't listening. She was pacing the room. 'His father would have been horrified. How could Hans do this to the Führer?'

'I'm sorry,' murmured Annaliese, 'but there's really nothing else I can say.' She left the room, and slowly climbed the stairs. Halfway up, she heard her mother-in-law beginning to wail below her.

Upstairs, she found Marta bathing the baby.

'Thank you, Marta. I'll manage now. Perhaps you should go and make my mother-in-law a cup of tea? She's had a bit of a shock.'

Annaliese took off her nightgown and climbed into the
bath beside her child. He giggled and smiled, his cheeks rosy
from the warm water. She lifted him out and wrapped them
both in a big towel. She dressed him in a nappy and romper
suit, and put him on the floor to play; then took a floral dress
from her wardrobe and laid it on the bed. Sitting at her
dressing table in her underwear, she put on a little make-up
and some perfume, and made a plan for the day. If the war
was nearly over, surely slave labourers would soon be
released. If she could just get to the factory, and convince
Alexander of her love, perhaps they still had a future
together?

Downstairs in the kitchen, she sat the baby in his high chair
and fed him the last of the eggs.

'I'm going out now,' she told Marta. 'If my mother-in-law
asks for me, tell her I'll be back later.'

Outside in the street, Annaliese pushed the pram purposefully
towards the tram stop, her heart racing with excitement. In
places, the streets and pavements were blocked with rubble, and
Russian slave women had been formed into chain-gangs,
passing shattered bricks and pieces of masonry from one to
another in a long line, clearing it into neat piles at the side of the
road. It seemed extraordinary, Annaliese thought, that the
world was just carrying on, as it had done before, and yet everything was about to change.

She tried to imagine Alexander's face when she told him
Hans had gone and that they could be together at last. But then
she had a moment's panic that he might already have been
released, and quickened her step.

Sitting at the front of the tram, the pram by her side,
Annaliese gazed proudly at her son. Sasha looked around
eagerly, giggling, his green eyes sparkling, as if he shared her

excitement. When they arrived at her stop, her heart was racing with anticipation, as she manoeuvred the pram out of the tram.

The Volkswagen factory loomed over the surrounding buildings, its tall chimneys soaring into the sky. At the steel gates, she boldly approached the guard on duty. 'I would like to speak to the manager.'

He looked dubiously at the pram, but opened the gates and directed her to the reception through the impressive metal double doors.

Annaliese was surprised by the elegance of the entrance hall. Her heels clicked on the marble floor as she approached the reception desk.

'I have come to see the manager,' Annaliese confidently told the receptionist.

'I'm afraid that won't be possible,' she replied.

'Why not?'

'He's not here. There's no one here – just a few people, like me, left behind.'

'What do you mean?' asked Annaliese. 'Where are the workers?'

'Oh, they were taken away two days ago. I don't know where.'

'Taken away?' Annaliese cried out. 'Where – where are they? I have to know... my baby's father is among them.'

'Well, I'm sorry,' the receptionist replied dismissively. 'Soldiers came for them – I think they're being marched somewhere. They are prisoners, after all.'

Annaliese backed away tearfully. Once outside the factory, she wandered aimlessly through the industrial streets, past the bomb-damaged factories, pushing the pram forlornly in front of her. All her optimism for the future had evaporated. She had hoped that with the war nearly over, and Hans gone, she and Alexander would at last be free to be together. She had convinced herself that she would talk him round... make him see how much she loved him. But it seemed he had been taken from her again, and now there was a chance he would be murdered, like those slaves in the north.

She returned home hours later, just before dusk, and let herself into the hall. As she lifted the baby from his pram, the sitting room door flew open, and Elisabetta emerged, her face puffy from crying. 'We need to talk, Annaliese.'

'Not now,' Annaliese replied. 'I'm sorry, but I must see to the baby and then go and lie down.'

'You're upset too, of course you are,' said her mother-in-law. She reached out to Annaliese in a rare moment of kindness. 'Let me take the baby for you.'

'No thank you,' said Annaliese, clinging to her son. 'I'll deal with him. We could both do with some sleep.' She pushed past Elisabetta and ran upstairs.

She changed the baby and put him in his cot, where he waved his hands and feet happily, before quickly falling asleep. Exhausted and tearful, Annaliese walked across to the window and looked down at the garden. Suddenly, in spite of her tiredness, she felt compelled to be outside – in the place where she and Alexander had been most happy. She ran downstairs, and opened the French windows onto the terrace. The garden had been their space – hers and Alexander's – where she had felt safe, wrapped in his arms. She walked past the flowerbeds they had planted together, remembering happier times as they tended the fruit trees and vegetable plot. At the far end of the garden, she opened the door to the shed and looked longingly at his tools, so neatly polished, hanging from hooks on the wall. The workbench was scrubbed down and tidy, just as he'd left it. The potato sacks were folded neatly in a corner – the place, perhaps, where their son had been conceived. She collapsed onto the sacks and sobbed.

Marta knocked on the door. 'Madam... madam...? Are you all right?'

'Yes,' Annaliese called back feebly.

The door opened a crack. 'Is there anything I can do for you?'

'Nothing, Marta – thank you. I'm just sad, that's all.'

'About the master?'

'No, not that.'

'About him... the Russian?'

Annaliese looked up at her, startled. 'So you know. Are you shocked?'

'Not really, madam. I had my suspicions. You just have to look at the baby, don't you? He looks just like his father. Did you find him... on your walk?'

'No,' Annaliese replied sadly. 'He's been sent away on a long march – I don't know where.'

'Come back inside, madam,' said Marta, holding out her hand.

It's the first act of real friendship between us two, Annaliese thought, as Marta helped her up.

They walked back up the garden together.

'I won't tell anyone,' whispered Marta, as they went inside. 'I promise.'

'Thank you, Marta... I appreciate that.'

Back upstairs, Annaliese checked on Sasha. He lay peacefully, yawning and murmuring in his sleep. 'Shhh,' she said, 'sleep, little one. Everything will be all right. We'll find your daddy, I promise. He'll survive, I know he will. It's not over yet.'

It occurred to her that she could be speaking about either one of the men in her life. Both Hans and Alexander were survivors: neither one would give in easily. Her eternal triangle of emotional entanglement was not over – perhaps it never would be. Exhausted, she lay down on her bed, covered herself with the eiderdown, and slept.

PART THREE
THE AFTERMATH

1945–1946

25

MAY 1945

On 8 May, the war was declared officially over. In Munich, Allied bombing had obliterated entire neighbourhoods. The city's elegant centre had been destroyed, with just the skeletons of buildings left standing, as mountains of rubble were piled up by the side of the road.

But in spite of this destruction, many in the crowds greeted the American troops as liberators – cheering, waving white handkerchiefs, and even throwing flowers in their path. Although Munich had been Hitler's spiritual capital, and its occupants among his most ardent supporters, all were now weary of war and his false promises of a new dawn.

Annaliese, although struggling with depression, joined the well-wishers welcoming the American troops. She looked into the faces of those young foreign soldiers as their tanks rumbled through the streets, and liked what she saw. They were the victors, it was true, but they behaved with grace – smiling cheerfully, accepting flowers and kisses from young German girls. News of what the Americans had found at Dachau was already filtering out to the local population, and many felt an overwhelming sense of shame. It was as if the people were emerging from more than a decade of propaganda and mind-control.

Annaliese listened to snatches of the crowd's conversation as they watched the Americans arrive. Few seemed to regret the passing of Hitler and his National Socialist Party. One boy, who just a few days before would have been an enthusiastic member of the Hitler Youth, muttered to his friend, 'Now the Americans are here, perhaps we'll get some decent food.' She heard only one dissenting voice: a boy of no more than eighteen stood up and shouted, 'Hail to the Führer', but few paid him any attention. It was as if Hitler, and all he had stood for, had been completely forgotten.

For the first time in weeks, Annaliese felt some stirring of optimism.

But within days, there was a breakdown in law and order. Mobs of newly released slaves roamed the streets, looting and stealing. Marta returned home one afternoon in a state of terror.

'I was in the haberdasher's,' she told Annaliese tearfully, 'buying those buttons you wanted, when some young men came running down the road and smashed the shop window. They burst inside and threw over the display table – there were ribbons and threads all over the place. We were terrified. Then they carried on looting shops further down the street, and stealing food and drink. It was awful.'

'It does sound frightening. Who were they, do you think?'

'Polish labourers,' Marta replied angrily. 'I recognised a few words... my brother told me all about them. He says they're not to be trusted.'

'I think that's rather unfair. I agree they shouldn't steal, but maybe they were starving? They've been kept in camps, remember, with very little to eat.' She recalled how hungry Alexander had always been.

'That's no reason to loot and steal, is it?'

'No, I suppose not, Marta.'

The American authorities quickly took control, introducing curfews to reduce the threat of violence, and pacifying the population with donations of food.

One morning, Marta returned from another shopping expedition and, with deep suspicion, laid a large tin on the kitchen table.

'What's that?' asked Annaliese.

'It's grapefruit juice – a gift from the Americans. They were handing it out at the grocery store. My friend Horst says they only give it to us because it tastes so bad their soldiers won't drink it.'

'Well, I'm sure that can't be true,' said Annaliese, piercing the lid with a tin opener. 'Let's at least try it.'

She poured a little into two glasses and they tentatively sipped the juice.

'Mmm,' Annaliese said, 'it's quite sharp, but delicious.'

In spite of her earlier wariness, Marta agreed.

'It must be full of vitamins,' suggested Annaliese, 'so we should save some for the baby. And it's good of the Americans to provide food, don't you think? We need all the help we can get.'

Annaliese had become increasingly anxious about her finances. Hans had given her the house and the contents of his safety deposit box, but she had no idea what the box contained. Her most immediate concern was ready cash. What little money she had inherited from her father was long gone, and Hans' Reichsmarks were already running low – and rapidly becoming worthless. Without money, how could she afford to live?

Annaliese knew she had to confront the situation head on. One morning, she came down to the kitchen wearing her best coat and hat, with the key to the safety deposit box in her handbag.

'I'm going to the bank now,' she told Marta. 'I've been putting it off for weeks, but I have to face the future with my eyes open. If I have no money, I have no idea how I'll even pay you.'

'You know I'll stay as long as I can, madam. Shall I watch the baby for you?'

'Thank you, that's kind, but I think I'll take him with me. He could be useful... the manager might be more sympathetic if he sees a child.'

The bank stood on a wide boulevard in the centre of Munich, and was one of the few buildings still intact after the bombing. The marble entrance hall was busy with customers, queuing at the counters.

Annaliese approached one of the reception clerks. 'I'd like to open my safety deposit box,' she told him, showing him her key.

The clerk looked dubiously at the pram. 'You won't get that down to the basement, madam,'

'That's all right, I'll carry the baby.' She picked Sasha up, who wrapped his sturdy legs around her waist.

'Follow me, madam,' said the clerk, parking the empty pram by his desk. The safety deposit boxes were housed in the basement behind a pair of reinforced metal doors. The clerk unlocked them and ushered Annaliese through. The room was empty except for a table in the centre, covered with felt. The walls were lined with small metal cabinets.

'Here is your locker, madam,' said the clerk. 'You open it with the key – the box is inside. The same key opens the box.'

'Yes, I know,' replied Annaliese. 'I used to work here.'

The clerk raised his eyebrows quizzically, and retreated to a discreet distance while she unlocked the box. She didn't know what to expect: jewellery, gold or foreign currency, perhaps? But it contained only folded sheets of paper. The first ones she opened were the deeds to the house. She saw that Hans' name had been removed and her own written in its place, just as he had promised. The other papers were mostly share certificates in all the great German industrial companies: Volkswagen, Krupp, Agfa, Group Auto Union and Mercedes. She made a rough count. There were over a hundred thousand shares – at one time, a small fortune.

Back in reception, she put the baby in the pram and wheeled it to a teller's counter. 'I'd like to withdraw some money,' she said to the girl behind the grille, filling out a cheque on the countertop. 'A hundred marks should be enough.'

The girl took the cheque and studied it. 'Excuse me, madam,' she said. 'But I need to check the account records.' A few minutes later she returned, slightly flushed. 'I'm afraid there's a problem, madam.'

'Why... what?' asked Annaliese, flustered.

'The account has been closed.'

'But there were several hundred thousand marks in there just a few weeks ago.'

'I'm afraid the money appears to have been withdrawn.'

'I see,' said Annaliese. 'I'd like to see the manager... as a matter of urgency.'

After a short wait, she was shown into an impressive office at the front of the building, overlooking the street. The manager wore an old-fashioned frock coat and his hair was parted in the centre, giving him the appearance of a silent film star from the 1920s. He stood up and welcomed her warmly.

'Ah, Frau Vogel, may I introduce myself? Franz Assel, at

your service. Do please take a seat. Is the baby all right in his pram?'

'Yes, quite all right, thank you.' She settled her handbag on her lap and cleared her throat nervously. 'I'll come straight to the point, Herr Assel. There appears to be a problem with my account – or rather, my husband's and my account. It has been closed.'

The manager flushed slightly. 'Ah, yes... Herr Doctor Vogel came in recently and transferred it all. He said it was for an emergency.'

'Transferred it – where?' she asked.

'I'm afraid I am not at liberty to tell you. But he left instructions that the contents of the safety deposit box were at your disposal. The property deeds and the shares have all been transferred to your name.'

'I know... I've just seen them. Can I ask... when did he do all this?'

'A couple of weeks ago, madam.'

'I see.' Annaliese was startled by this revelation. Hans must have prepared carefully for his departure. 'Herr Assel, the problem is – I'm just not sure what I'm supposed to do without access to the account. How can I live with no money?'

'I'm sure we can sort something out,' the manager replied silkily. 'An overdraft can be arranged, using the deeds of the house, or your shares, as security. Alternatively, I can arrange to have some of the shares sold, if that would help. But now is not a good time to be selling equities. Prices are rather jittery, as you can imagine, and most shares are on the floor. If you can afford to wait, I would advise it.'

'Very well,' said Annaliese. 'If you can arrange a loan or overdraft, I'd be most grateful. And in the meantime, I'll just have to get a job, I suppose.'

. . .

As she walked home, Annaliese felt a strange kind of excitement at the prospect of being in charge of her own life, and of working for a living. Hans had left her a beautiful house and a considerable number of blue-chip shares which, although they currently had little value, would – if she had the courage to wait – one day be worth something. Since her marriage, she had lived her life as a powerful man's charming adornment – the outwardly perfect German wife. Now she had a chance to prove to herself that she could be truly independent.

She decided to make an immediate start. The house belonged to her now, and the thought of continuing to live under the same roof with her mother-in-law was unbearable.

She broached the subject at breakfast the following morning. 'Elisabetta, I know you're still in shock about Hans. I am too, but I do really think it would be better if you were to find somewhere else to live.'

Elisabetta stared at her blankly across the table. 'And where am I supposed to go, I'd like to know?'

'I thought your friend Hilda might help, initially. You'd be back in the neighbourhood you know best, among friends – your bridge partners and so on. And I know that you have enough money to buy another house – something smaller, perhaps, where you could live more conveniently.'

'How can you possibly know anything about my finances?'

'Before he left, Hans explained to me that your late husband had left you very comfortably off. Obviously, I don't know the details, but he made it clear there would be enough to buy another house, and live a good life.'

'And what about seeing Max, my grandson?'

Every sinew of Annaliese's body strained to blurt out the truth – to tell Elisabetta that Max, as she insisted on calling him, was not her grandson. But this would be dangerous and reckless. There would be time enough for that revelation. 'Well, of course there's no problem with you seeing him. I can bring him over to you, or you could come here.'

Elisabetta reluctantly agreed. Over the next few days, Hilda was persuaded to put her up until a new house could be found. Elisabetta packed what was left of her belongings into two suitcases, and three weeks after Hans' disappearance, she stood with Annaliese on the stone steps of the grey house. As a large taxi drew up outside, honking its horn, Marta carried her suitcases down the steps of the house, and loaded them into the boot.

'Well, I'd better go,' Elisabetta said sharply, pulling on her leather gloves, and turning to her daughter-in-law. 'You have surprised me, Annaliese. You have more steel in you than I had ever thought possible.'

And with that, she walked smartly down the steps and into the taxi, leaving a trace of lavender scent behind her.

26

MAY 1945

Hans had remarkably little trouble crossing the border into Austria. Dressed in his tweed suit, and with a jaunty Tyrol-style hat, he looked every inch the respectable Austrian family doctor he purported to be. Nestled in his waistcoat pocket was Dr Otto Werner's fob watch, along with the photograph of his wife, Mimi. At the border, he had wound down the car window, showed Dr Werner's identity card, and explained he was on his way to visit a relative. The guard waved him through without a second look. Hans realised that his unremarkable looks – neither handsome, nor ugly, just ordinary – could turn out to be a valuable asset. He might not have the stunning features of his Russian rival, but his plainness rendered him unnoticeable, even forgettable.

His destination was Salzburg, and the house of his mother's sister, Charlotte. She was no fool, and would be curious about his visit, so he spent much of the journey constructing a cover story. By the time he arrived in the outskirts of Salzburg, he had decided on a version of the truth, rather than the truth itself. He knew that, when fabricating a lie, it was always better to stick as closely as possible to reality.

Despite Austria's takeover by Hitler's Germany, Salzburg still looked much as it had before the outbreak of war. There was bomb damage here and there, but compared to Munich it was relatively unscathed. As he drove across the river, Hans looked up at the striking rocky outcrop that dominated the city. Halfway up that outcrop was his Aunt Charlotte's house, accessible only via a footpath. Her charming white-painted cottage was one of a row of similar houses that nestled against the dark rock face. It was this remoteness that made Charlotte's house the perfect place to hide out, at least for a few days.

It was already getting dark when Hans parked his car at the bottom of the hill two hundred metres below her house, and set off on foot up the narrow path that led to her cottage. In one hand he carried his brown leather doctor's bag, containing his medical equipment, and in the other a small overnight bag, with his research files and a couple of changes of clothes. He was deliberately travelling light to avoid suspicion, and hoped he looked like an Austrian family doctor on a routine home visit.

Charlotte's house stood in the middle of the row of houses – all well-tended, with neat front gardens. Hans paused outside her house, and stood looking down over the city. He felt, for just a moment, as if he were on top of the world – liberated at last from the past years of servitude to National Socialism.

He pushed open the ornate metal gate and walked up the narrow path to the oak front door. He rang the bell-pull, looking anxiously around him, checking he had not been followed.

'Hans!' Charlotte exclaimed, as she opened the door. 'What on earth are you doing here? Is it Elisabetta?'

'No, no – Mama's quite all right. May I come in?'

'Of course, dear boy.'

Charlotte led the way to the sitting room – a pretty, low-ceilinged room, which had changed little since her parents' day.

She and Elisabetta had been brought up in the house, and Charlotte – whose only love had been killed in 1917 during the war – had remained with her parents until their death twenty years earlier. Hans glanced around the room; it was quite unchanged from the last time he'd visited. Family photographs were still displayed on the baby grand piano, including several of the two sisters, Charlotte and Elisabetta. They couldn't have been more different: Hans' aunt, pretty and fine-boned, and his own mother, heavy-jawed and, even in her twenties, prone to fat.

'Sit down,' Charlotte suggested, pointing to one of the plump chintz sofas on either side of the fireplace. 'Have you driven here from Munich?'

He nodded.

'Have you eaten?'

'No, but I would like to. I've not eaten all day.'

'Well, you must stay for dinner. I'll tell the maid to lay another place.'

When she returned from the kitchen, she poured them both a drink, and sat down opposite him. 'Now, dear boy, I think you'd better tell me what's going on.'

Over the course of the evening, Hans explained his situation, tempering reality just a little. He had been forced to work at Dachau – against his will, he told her. He had gone there initially in good faith, but had soon discovered the horror of the place. He had been unable to leave, for fear of losing his life and of putting his wife in danger.

Charlotte listened intently, nodding throughout, and appeared to find his story plausible. In so many ways it was true, he convinced himself. As the evening wore on, Hans gradually relaxed, increasingly confident that despite his aunt's keen intelligence, she had completely accepted his story.

After dinner they went back to the sitting room, and Charlotte poured each of them a cup of coffee and a small glass of schnapps. 'What are your plans now?'

Hans lounged comfortably on the plump sofa and sipped his coffee. 'The thing is, Aunt,' he began tentatively, 'I still feel I have a lot to offer to the world of medical research. To give myself up to the Americans now – to be imprisoned, or possibly even executed – would be a waste. I'd like to think I can do some good in the world, but what good can I do if I'm dead?'

'Yes... I can see your reasoning,' Charlotte replied dispassionately. She stood up and wandered over to the window. The lights of Salzburg glowed beneath her. 'You know, Hans... I've lived here all my life. I've seen rulers come and go... the king emperors, of course – Franz Joseph and his great nephew, King Charles. I watched with sadness as the Austro-Hungarian Empire collapsed, and the Republic was established. Since then we've had the revolt of 1927 – a shameful period in our history – and the civil war in 1934. But none of these episodes have been as dark and as evil as the domination of our country by Hitler and his wicked, wicked ideology.'

She turned around to face him. 'Hans, I do not approve of what you did at Dachau – whether you were forced to or not. But I will help you because you are my nephew and, after Elisabetta, the only relative I have. You may stay here for the next few days, until we make other arrangements. The safest place for you would be in the mountains. I have a chalet in a tiny village called Alpbach. Your mother and I used to go there as children in the summer to play in the fields, and in the winter months to ski. Elisabetta never liked it – she's always been an urban, sedentary creature. You will be able to almost disappear up there... the authorities would never find you. Do you have the appropriate papers?'

'Yes, I do,' replied Hans, somewhat chastened by her outburst, and surprised by how knowledgeable she seemed. 'I have another identity card.'

'How prescient of you,' she said acerbically. 'What about

your wife – did she not want to come with you? And your child – I heard you'd had a son.'

'Annaliese decided to stay in Munich,' Hans replied matter-of-factly. But beneath the surface, he had a brief moment of regret at how he and Annaliese had parted, and her stubborn refusal to go with him. Would he ever see her or the child again?

'Very wise,' said Charlotte. 'A life on the run is no place for a family. But how will she manage financially? I presume you have made arrangements?'

'Yes... to a degree,' he mumbled, 'although it's complicated.'

'How complicated?'

'I've left her the house and some shares.'

Charlotte snorted. 'Shares? But they're worthless at the moment, aren't they? How will she live... buy food, feed your son?'

Hans flushed. 'The bank will offer her a loan against the house... I arranged it before I left. There's nothing more I can do, as it's vital that there is no communication between us. It's better for her, from a security point of view, if we are completely separated. That way she can't come to any harm. Besides, I'll be back one day, perhaps quite soon.'

Charlotte stared at him. 'You really think that will be possible?'

'Yes,' he replied calmly. 'I'll stay out of sight for a while and eventually it will... blow over.'

'Your optimism is astounding,' said Charlotte, yawning. 'But I'm too tired to argue with you. You can sleep in the spare room at the top of the stairs – the one with the blue wallpaper. Good night, Hans.'

A few days later, Hans boarded a country bus heading for the Austrian Alps. He had decided to abandon his car near Charlotte's house, fearing its German number plate might give him away up in the mountains.

Just outside Salzburg, the bus came to a halt at an American checkpoint. Two US soldiers climbed aboard and began checking the passengers' papers. Hans' hand shook involuntarily as he handed over his stolen identity pass.

'Herr Werner – ah, you're a doctor, I see,' said the soldier. 'Where are you going?'

'Alpbach,' Hans replied.

The soldier quickly checked Hans' face against his identity photo, seemed satisfied, and moved on up the bus.

Once they were on the move again, Hans relaxed a little. As the bus rumbled up the winding narrow roads, he admired the view from the windows, impressed by the deep gorges and tumbling rivers, white with froth. The bus lurched violently as it negotiated the hairpin bends, stopping every few kilometres to let passengers off at tiny hamlets en route. By the time the bus drew into the village of Alpbach, Hans was the last remaining passenger.

Charlotte had drawn a small map showing the location of the chalet, which was up a mountain road just outside the village. Hans set off, carrying his doctor's bag and suitcase, quickly leaving the houses behind. He studied Charlotte's sketch-map again, and continued up a steep dirt track past a grassy field of goats, the bells around their necks clanging melodiously. Finally, the track ended at a wooden chalet. As instructed, he felt behind a stone on the right of the porch and found the key.

Charlotte had told him she hadn't visited since before the war, and as he opened the door, the house smelt strongly of pine and damp. On the kitchen table was a solitary candle in an old wine bottle, and oil lamps hung from hooks in the ceiling. Clearly, there was no electricity. He quickly inspected the rest of the accommodation: two sparsely furnished bedrooms, a bathroom, a kitchen and a living room. It was all perfectly adequate, he thought to himself.

He reached into his jacket pocket and pulled out another sheet of paper with instructions from his aunt.

Turn on the water – the stopcock is under the sink in the kitchen.

The range is a wood-burner; you should find some logs stacked up on the porch at the back.

Hans gathered a basket of logs, and laid the fire, but when he tried to strike a match found they were too damp.

The kitchen cupboards were bare, so he took a basket from the dresser and walked back into the village. There was one general store, and he bought a few basic supplies – a box of matches, oil for the lights, milk, eggs, bread and beer – but when he got to the counter to pay, the shopkeeper demanded his ration stamps.

'I'm sorry, I've lost them all,' he told him. 'It's a long story. But I have money...'

The shopkeeper tutted, but took the money anyway, and handed over the goods. Back home, Hans lit the range, made himself an omelette and then sat with a glass of beer, considering his future.

A few weeks went by. Initially, Hans kept a low profile, only going into the village for food. But gradually, the locals began to recognise him, nodding morning greetings to him. He grew bolder, reasoning that he would be less likely to arouse the villagers' curiosity if he socialised a little; he began to visit the bar each day, to drink coffee or beer with the locals.

The bar owner was a man in his fifties – ruddy-faced, like many of the villagers – with a pot-belly from drinking too much beer. 'Werner, you say, is your name? How do you know Charlotte, then?'

'She's a distant cousin,' Hans replied.

'We haven't seen her up here for years. She and the whole family used to come, regular as clockwork, winter and summer. I've known her since I was a boy. Nice woman.'

'I think it was difficult for her to get here during the war years,' Hans explained.

'What brings you up here, then?' the owner asked.

'I find myself temporarily homeless. Cousin Charlotte was kind enough to suggest I use her house for a bit. It's been a life-saver.'

'Why was that? Your house bombed, was it?'

Hans paused, wondering how to reply. He decided to persist with his alibi, in line with his new identity. 'I was recently released from a prison camp called Dachau,' said Hans. The bar owner started, clearly shocked. 'I'd been imprisoned for most of the war,' Hans went on, 'for being a member of the Free Austria movement.'

'Communist, are you?' asked the bar owner warily.

Hans suspected that communism was probably a worse crime than being a Nazi up there in the mountains. 'No!' He assured him. 'No, I'm not a communist and never have been. I'm a patriot... an Austrian patriot.'

'You did well to survive,' said the owner, looking Hans up and down. 'From what I've heard, Dachau was a terrible place. You look pretty well on it.'

'I managed to get work as a clerk in the medical wing. I got better rations.' Hans hoped his explanation sounded believable.

'A medic, are you?'

'I'm a doctor by training.'

'We don't have a doctor here,' said the bar owner. 'The nearest one is down the mountain in the valley. You could be useful. I'll put the word round.'

'Of course,' said Hans. 'I'd be happy to help. Everyone here has been most welcoming.'

. . .

As spring turned to summer, Hans became a regular at the bar, where he would keep up with the news. The papers were filled with stories of senior Nazis being tracked down – many of them hiding, like him, in the Austrian hills. Heinrich Himmler himself was arrested in Austria by the British, and taken back to Lüneburg Castle in Germany, where, on the twenty-third of May, he committed suicide by taking a cyanide pill.

'Good riddance to bad rubbish,' said the bar owner, reading the headline upside down. 'A bad lot, that Himmler.'

'Yes, he was, wasn't he?' murmured Hans.

A few days later, another headline caught his attention: '*Austrian war criminals indicted*'.

'What do you make of that?' asked the bar owner, pointing to the paper.

'Well, it's good that they've been discovered,' said Hans. 'Let's hope their trials reveal the truth.' He glanced up at the bar owner, hoping he sounded convincing. But the man was looking at him quizzically.

Austria, like Germany, had been divided up between the four Allied victors – America, Britain, France and Russia. News began to emerge of refugees pouring into Austria from the east, pursued by vengeful Russians.

'They're mad as hell, those Ruskies,' said the bar owner. 'Raping and looting... that's all they do. Even in Vienna, no woman's safe. I've got a cousin who spends the night locked in her cellar she's so terrified of them.'

Hans smiled sympathetically. 'I'm so sorry – that must be awful.'

'You married?' asked the bar owner.

'A widower, sadly,' said Hans. He delved into his breast pocket, and brought out the photograph of Mimi, laying it on the counter.

'Pretty girl,' said the bar owner. 'I'm sorry – you must miss her.'

'Very much,' said Hans, thinking of Annaliese.

The bar owner's questions were becoming irksome. Hans was concerned that what he had originally taken to be friendly interest might be something else.

Salzburg, and the surrounding area, was now in the American zone. There was talk of the Americans searching the mountains for runaway members of the SS. How long would it be before Hans was discovered? How long before he was given away?

He began to plan his future. The only solution, as far as he could see, was to negotiate some sort of deal with the Americans. Hitler himself had seen the value in his medical research, and surely every country – every police force and secret service – would be interested in the potential of a 'truth drug' like mescaline. Each evening he took out his research documents and laid them on the kitchen table, collating and recollating them, checking and rechecking the figures, writing and rewriting his findings. Could this bundle of papers, which he had hurriedly packed into his briefcase at Dachau, be his passport to a long and happy life?

27

JUNE 1945

Annaliese was woken by the sound of loud knocking on her front door. Wrapping her dressing gown around her, she went downstairs and found Marta hovering nervously in the hall.

'Why haven't you answered the door?' Annaliese asked.

'There are soldiers outside – I saw them from the kitchen window,' Marta whispered. 'They looked like Americans.'

'Well, we've done nothing wrong. There's nothing to fear.'

She opened the door. Standing on the steps were three men in American army uniforms.

'Frau Vogel?'

'Yes.'

'Get dressed please, and come with us.' The soldier's German was quite good, but with a strong American accent.

'Why, what have I done?'

'I'm not at liberty to say. We'll wait for you here. Don't try to escape – we have all the exits covered.'

Marta began to weep.

'I'll go and get dressed,' answered Annaliese, surprised at how calm she felt.

Sasha, now aged fourteen months, had a room of his own. He was standing up in his cot, rattling the bars. He held his arms out to his mother, demanding to be liberated. She picked him up and took him to her own room, where she dressed hurriedly.

Carrying her son on her hip, she went down to the hall, and handed Sasha over to Marta, who was still snivelling. 'Marta, do please calm down.'

'I'm frightened,' Marta complained. 'What if they arrest me too?'

'They won't,' Annaliese assured her. 'Just look after the baby, and I'll soon be back... all right?'

Marta nodded uncertainly.

'I hope this won't take too long,' said Annaliese firmly to the soldiers. 'My son is just a baby... he needs me.'

The first soldier looked at her sympathetically. 'I'm sure we'll have you home in no time. It's about your husband.'

'I see,' said Annaliese. 'Well, I could save you a lot of trouble – I haven't seen him for weeks and have no idea where he is.'

'I'm sorry, ma'am, but our orders are to take you to headquarters.'

Annaliese put her hand on Marta's shoulder. The girl was still sobbing.

'Do stop crying, Marta, you're upsetting Sasha. Take him to the kitchen and give him breakfast. I'll be back by lunchtime... and don't worry.'

Annaliese's mind worked feverishly as she was driven through the streets of Munich in the American army jeep. She felt confident that she had nothing to tell these people; she genuinely had no knowledge of Hans' whereabouts, but would they believe her? She had heard that the senior officers at Dachau had been rounded up by the Americans, but there had been no word of any of their wives being punished. So far, only Rascher's wife had been executed, and that was the work of Himmler, not the Americans. Himmler's own wife had been captured too, somewhere in northern Italy – but then she had been on the run, and probably deserved it.

For the first time in weeks, she thought about Hans. She was relieved that he had not stayed and fought, as Himmler had ordered. She was glad he'd escaped just in time, even if she couldn't forgive him for his work at Dachau. Would she denounce him to the Americans? She decided she would not, but she wouldn't defend him either – she would simply tell them the truth.

The jeep drew up at a building on Beethovenplatz. A soldier opened the passenger door and helped her out.

'Frau Vogel for Major Miller,' announced the soldier to the receptionist.

'He's expecting her. I'll give him a call.'

Within a few minutes, a young American officer came bounding down the stairs, holding out his hand to her. 'Frau Vogel?'

'Yes.'

'I'm Major Miller of the CIC.'

'The CIC?'

'US Army Counter Intelligence Corps.'

She nodded, her stomach fluttering with nerves. 'Counter Intelligence' sounded sinister. Was she going to be detained, or worse – imprisoned? What would become of her beloved Sasha, alone in the house with just her maid to look after him?

For the first time since Hans had left, she felt real fear.

'Frau Vogel, please follow me.'

Major Miller's office was on the first floor. He ushered her past his secretary's desk, and through to his private office.

'I don't want to be interrupted,' Miller called back to his secretary, and closed the door. 'Do please sit down.' He pointed to the chair in front of his desk. His German was excellent. 'Can I get you anything – coffee? We bring it in from the States.'

Annaliese smiled. 'Yes, thank you. I'd like that.' It had been some time since she had tasted real coffee, and besides, she was keen to appear helpful and friendly.

Miller pressed his intercom button. 'Two coffees please, Marion.'

He leant forward casually on his elbows. 'You're probably wondering why we brought you here.' He had a gentle face, with soft brown eyes and wavy hair. He didn't look intimidating, but she had learned that appearances could be deceptive.

'I was told it had something to do with my husband.'

'Yes. He was a doctor at Dachau, we understand.'

'That's right.'

'And a member of the SS.'

'Yes, but a reluctant member.'

'Really?' He looked into her eyes. 'Are you also a member of the National Socialist Party?'

'No,' she replied firmly. 'I despise them.'

'And yet you were married to a senior member of the Party for... how long?' He consulted his notes.

'Ten years.'

He raised his eyebrows. 'That's a long time to live with someone you despise...'

The sentence hung in the air, like an accusation. Annaliese blushed, uncertain what to say, or how to justify herself.

'You may have read in the newspapers that we are gradually rounding up all the senior SS officers at Dachau to put them on trial.'

'I don't read the papers,' Annaliese replied truthfully. 'It's too upsetting.'

The secretary came in with the coffees. Miller handed one to Annaliese. Her hand shook as she took it.

'What is it that you find upsetting? The idea that your husband might be arrested?'

'No, not that,' she replied. 'I just can't bear to think about it any more. I just try to get through each day, for my son's sake.'

'You and Dr Vogel have a child?'

'*I* have a child, yes.'

Miller quickly made a note. 'How old is the child?'

'Fourteen months.'

'That's a nice age. But it must be hard... being on your own.' His voice was soft, gentle.

'I survive. Many are having a far worse time.'

'I wanted to ask about that... how you survive, I mean. You have a child, so I presume you don't work. How do you live? We have access to your bank records, so don't try to lie.'

'I won't lie,' she replied. 'I'm not sure how I'll live, to be honest. There are very few jobs available. The bank has offered me a loan against the house.'

'Your husband didn't leave you any money?'

'No, not really – just a little cash. It's nearly gone now,' she replied.

'Mmm, leaving no tracks, I suppose,' said Miller, almost under his breath.

His tone changed suddenly. 'I have to ask you now about the events that led up to your husband's disappearance. Have you any idea where he is?'

'No.'

'When did he leave, exactly?'

'I can't quite remember – at the end of April, I think. Yes... it was a few days before Hitler killed himself. I heard about that on the radio.'

'And he didn't tell you where he was going?'

'No. He told me he was running away – I knew that much. I

presumed he meant to Switzerland, or perhaps Austria. He asked if I would come with him, but I refused.'

'Why?' Miller leant forward eagerly.

'Because, I'm just a wife and a mother. And *I*'ve done nothing wrong.' She stared back at the major defiantly.

'Did you know the nature of his work at Dachau?'

'No, not at first. For many years I was naïve – stupid, you might say. I thought he was involved in medical research for the sake of humanity.' She smiled thinly at the irony of it. 'You must think me very foolish.'

'You expect me to believe that?'

She was startled by his response. He had seemed so mild-mannered up till that point. 'Yes, I do. I genuinely didn't under-stand at first what they were doing there. You could argue I didn't choose to look – to see what was in front of my eyes – but my husband hid the nature of his work.'

'But eventually you found out what was happening at Dachau?'

'Yes, eventually – and I told Hans I despised him for it. I thought it was abhorrent, immoral... appalling.'

'How did you find out?'

'I met someone who had been in Dachau – a prisoner.'

'How did you come to meet a prisoner?'

'My husband brought him to our house as a gardener.'

'What was this man's name?'

'Alexander Kosomov.'

Major Miller made another note. 'And what did he tell you, this Kosomov?'

'That he had been the victim of certain... medical experi-ments – not involving my husband,' she added hurriedly. 'Hans was mainly working on cures for malaria, whereas Kosomov was forced to undergo barbaric experiments involving iced water – hypothermia experiments, I think they were called.' She felt tears pricking her eyes.

'And where is this Kosomov now?'

'I'm afraid I don't know,' said Annaliese, pulling a handkerchief from her handbag and dabbing at her eyes. 'My husband sent him away, and he was put to work in one of the armaments factories. I went looking for him, but he'd been taken somewhere – on a long march, they said. I don't know where he is, or if he even survived. You hear such terrible things...'

Major Miller nodded. 'Yes, any able-bodied camp prisoners were sent on the long march – they were pushed east, away from our forces. It was a terrible business.' He sighed, replaced the cap on his pen, and laid it down on the desk. 'Well, I think that's all for now. You've been very helpful, Frau Vogel. You are free to leave, but we may need to contact you again – our investigations are not over. No one who worked at Dachau will be allowed to escape punishment. Do I make myself clear?'

'Perfectly.'

'And as you are the wife of someone who held a senior position at Dachau, you will remain under observation.'

'I understand,' she replied quietly. 'Although you must believe me when I say that I don't know any more than I've already told you.'

Major Miller studied her face for some time. 'I've met several SS wives now,' he said. 'Most either leap to their husband's defence, or try to convince me that they were on the side of the Resistance all along. I've only met one woman, whose husband is also on the run, who admits to being a proud Nazi.'

'Did you arrest her?' Annaliese asked.

'No, but I admired her honesty,' he replied. 'You, on the other hand, don't fit easily into either camp. I find your frankness refreshing and rather surprising, but if I find you have been telling me lies, I will deal with you harshly. Do you understand?'

She nodded.

'And, needless to say, if your husband gets in touch, you must let me know.' He handed her his card.

Major James E. Miller
430th detachment
US Army Counter Intelligence Corps (CIC)
Beethovenplatz, München

As she left the American headquarters, Annaliese felt a combination of anxiety and guilt: anxiety at the idea of being 'observed', and guilt about her ignorance. As a grown woman she ought to have been more knowledgeable about the world around her. She picked up a newspaper from the stand on the corner of the street and walked back home, glancing at the headlines. The papers were full of stories about SS officers on the run.

Hans had warned her the Americans might come looking for her, and he'd been right. Could they charge her with anything? Technically she had done nothing wrong, apart from not actively opposing the National Socialist regime – but very few Germans had. She was simply an ordinary German wife and mother. Her thoughts turned to Hans: where was he now? Had she been right to mention Austria, or Switzerland? Although she was fairly sure Hans would have gone to his Aunt Charlotte in Salzburg, perhaps she should have said nothing. The last thing she wanted to do was get Charlotte into trouble – she was such a nice woman, and so unlike her sister.

When Annaliese got home, she found Sasha in the kitchen with Marta.

'Here I am,' she called out cheerfully. 'I said I wouldn't be long. Can you get lunch started, Marta? I'm just going outside into the garden. I'll take the baby with me.'

The garden had always been the place where Annaliese felt safest and most at peace. While Sasha played at her feet, she sat on the bench behind the shed and considered her predicament.

Hans was gone from her life, perhaps forever. Somehow, she felt sure she would never hear from him again. What surprised her was how easily she had accepted his disappearance from her life. He had given her a home and comfort when she needed it, but now she wondered if she had ever truly loved him.

Alexander's disappearance, on the other hand, was a different matter. Now, looking around at the garden, Annaliese almost imagined she saw him there, digging the borders, turning the compost, his jacket hanging from the fruit trees. But that was just a dream. The reality was that he had disappeared, and that thought tormented her. Had he died on the long march east, or had he managed to escape? Was he even now starting a new life in a different town or country? Or was he a displaced person, lost and alone? The last seemed most unlikely – Alexander was nothing if not a survivor. But if he was free, why didn't he come to her?

The papers were full of stories of Russian prisoners of war who had returned to their home country, only to be sent to gulags as punishment – as if it was a crime to have been captured and made a prisoner of war. Of all the scenarios that played in an endless loop in her mind, none gave her any comfort.

As she looked into the green eyes of her child, her heart ached for his father and she prayed she would have the strength to live without him.

28

Autumn was in the air, and the house was always cold in the evening. Annaliese went out onto the terrace carrying a basket to fill with logs for the sitting room fire. Alexander had chopped down a couple of fir trees the previous winter, and had stacked the wood neatly outside by the sitting room doors. The pile, she noticed, was running low; she would have to ration herself if they were to get through the cold winter. Firewood was at a premium in the city – she had even heard rumours of people breaking into other people's gardens and stealing their supplies. She loaded up her basket, and brought it back inside, where Sasha was playing on the floor with his toy bricks, piling them one on top of the other. She laid the fire with old newspaper and kindling, lit a match and watched the flames take hold.

At that moment, she heard the doorbell ring. Going out into the hall, she opened the front door and found Major Miller standing on the steps.

'Good evening, Frau Vogel,' he said, removing his cap. 'I'm sorry to disturb you, but I wondered if I might come in.'

'Yes, I suppose so,' she answered nervously, already dreading his questioning.

'It's all right,' he said, sensing her fear. 'I'm alone, and I'm not here to arrest you.' He smiled encouragingly. 'I just wanted to talk a little more.'

She showed him through to the sitting room, where Sasha, seeing their visitor, stood up and toddled across to the major, gripping his legs.

'And who's this?' asked Miller, stooping down to stroke the boy's head.

'Oh, I'm sorry,' said Annaliese quickly. 'This is Sasha – short for Alexander. He's just beginning to walk.'

'Well, hello there, Sasha,' he said, picking the boy up and cradling him to his uniformed chest.

Sasha giggled, and patted the major's face affectionately.

'Sasha, stop that,' said Annaliese, rushing forward, arms outstretched. 'Let me take him. I'm sure you didn't come here to play with a baby.'

'That's true, but he's delightful, nevertheless,' said Miller, handing the child back to her. 'He reminds me of my own son at that age.'

'Please do sit down,' she said, pointing to an armchair by the fireplace. She threw a log onto the fire, and sat down on the sofa opposite the major, with Sasha safely by her side.

'Thank you,' said Miller, taking a notebook and pencil from his top pocket. 'I thought we might talk a little more about your husband. Our last conversation was rather formal, and frightening for you, I suspect.' He leant forward, looking her straight in the eye. 'Frau Vogel, I do believe you when you say you didn't know what was going on at Dachau. But my job is to find the people who've done wrong and bring them to justice.'

'I understand.' In spite of herself, she felt nervous, and was keen to get him on her side. 'Would you like a drink, major? I was about to have one.'

'I shouldn't when I'm on duty, but thank you, yes.'

'I can't offer you much of a choice, I'm afraid,' she explained. 'There are so many shortages these days, but my husband had quite a good cellar at one time and there are a few bottles of wine left.'

'A glass of wine would be very nice.'

She hurried down to the kitchen, returning with a bottle of Riesling, a corkscrew and two glasses. 'Could you open this for me?' she said, handing him the bottle. 'I'm not very good at these things. And do please call me Annaliese. Whenever you say "Frau Vogel", I think you mean my mother-in-law.' She smiled, hoping he appreciated the witticism.

He poured the wine and handed her a glass, raising his own with a smile.

'Cheers, Annaliese. And please call me Jimmy.'

'Cheers, Jimmy.'

'Where does your mother-in-law live?'

'Solln – it's a suburb of Munich, popular with the Party hierarchy. I don't see her much these days. We were never really close. I don't think she ever thought I was good enough for Hans.'

Miller sipped his wine. 'Mmm, delicious,' he said appreciatively. 'Now, if you don't mind, to get back to your husband...'

'I'm not sure there's much more I can say.'

'You made it quite clear last time that you didn't approve of his work.'

'I didn't know about his work until the end, and then, of course I didn't approve at all. I was horrified.'

'Did you ever meet his colleagues – the other doctors at Dachau?'

'I met a man called Dr Rascher once. We went to a party at his house. Himmler was there.'

Miller looked up, clearly impressed. 'You met Himmler?'

'Yes. I got the impression he was often hanging around the

Dachau doctors. Hans loathed him. As for Rascher, in my opinion he was crazy – literally insane, both he and his wife.'

'Oh?' said Miller, refilling her glass. 'What makes you say that?'

Annaliese took a large sip of wine, and felt herself relaxing. She began to blurt out the whole story. 'Rascher's wife was nearly fifty when they had their fourth baby! It seemed incredible and, as it turned out, it was. They had stolen all four of their children, and passed them off as their own – presumably to satisfy Himmler's mad demands that SS officers should have as many children as possible. I suppose they must have been desperate to do such a terrible thing, but how could they live with themselves?'

She glanced down at Sasha, and stroked his blond hair. 'Himmler had them both sent to concentration camps,' she went on. 'She was executed last year, but Rascher was only killed a few days before your troops arrived at Dachau, at the end of April.'

'He had them both executed?'

'Yes,' she replied simply. 'For fraud, I think my husband said. It was a matter of honour, I suppose.'

'Honour!' Miller snorted. 'I doubt that Himmler even knew the meaning of the word.' He put his glass down on a side table, and opened his notebook. 'Do you mind if I take notes?'

She shook her head.

'When we last met, you mentioned a Russian who had worked for you and your husband. What happened to him?'

She blushed.

'I get the impression that you liked him,' he said softly.

'Yes... I loved him.'

Miller picked up the bottle and refilled her glass. 'That must have been difficult. If your husband had found out, he would presumably have been arrested and...' His words tailed off.

Annaliese took a large mouthful of wine, and wandered over to the French windows, gazing out into the night. 'I'm not sure what else I can tell you... he disappeared, that's all.'

'Please try to give me some detail – I just need to understand.'

She turned to look at him. He had such a kind face, this American, and such a gentle manner, she felt sure she could trust him. Besides, why not tell him? What harm could it do now? She turned back to face the moonlit garden. It was easier somehow, when she couldn't see him, and vice versa.

Slowly she began to tell her story: of Hans' infertility, their fear of being persecuted for having no children, and finally Hans' 'solution' – that Alexander, a Dachau prisoner, and victim of Dr Rascher's hypothermia experiments, should father her child.

She turned back to face Miller, tears now streaming down her face. 'You're shocked, aren't you?'

'I can hardly believe a man could ask that of his wife!'

'Hans did love me, very much. But he was a very controlled man – it was the scientist in him, I suppose. I think he imagined that I would have sex, get pregnant and that would be that. And I desperately wanted a child, so I went along with it. But I quickly fell in love with Alexander. I felt we were kindred spirits in many ways. He was younger than Hans, more artistic, more exciting. And in spite of the terrible things he had endured in prison, he retained a calm intelligence. I adored him. Hans was devastated when I fell in love with him, of course, but he was prepared to sacrifice his own feelings in order to get a child. It was survival, really, like the Raschers. But at least we weren't taking a baby from someone else. Can you understand?'

'Yes, I suppose so.' Jimmy nodded towards Sasha, now fast asleep on the sofa. 'Is this...?'

'Alexander's son? Yes – he looks just like his father. I'm

amazed that people can't see it. Not even my mother-in-law, who thinks Sasha is her perfect grandson.'

'Oh, yes, your mother-in-law... Do you think she has heard from your husband?'

'I don't imagine so. I'm sure she would have told me if she had. She was furious with him for deserting us, which surprised me rather, but she still adores him. They have a complicated relationship. But I can't see him appealing to her for help, if that's what you mean.'

She went and stood by the fire, feeling its warmth against her legs. 'I don't really know why I'm telling you all this, Jimmy,' she said, looking down at him, 'but something about you makes me feel you will understand. You do understand, don't you?'

'Of course, Annaliese. But what happened to the Russian?'

'After I got pregnant, my husband sent him away. I was so angry with Hans, and broken-hearted. I searched everywhere for Alexander, and finally found him working at the VW factory. I showed him the baby, but he didn't want to believe Sasha was his. He was angry with me. He felt betrayed, you see. He thought I'd used him – which I had, to a degree. As soon as your troops arrived in Munich, I tried to find him again, but the factory workers had all been marched away. I still don't know what happened to him, or if he's even alive.'

She slumped back down on the sofa, curling her legs beneath her. They sat in silence for while in the gathering gloom.

'War does terrible things to people, Annaliese,' said Jimmy finally. 'It makes them behave in strange ways.'

'Indeed... Have you visited Dachau?' she asked.

'Yes. I was part of the advance party with General Eisenhower. I arrived on the twenty-ninth, the day Hitler killed himself, and I have to say I was appalled by what I found. The conditions were indescribable.'

'Could you tell me what you saw?' she asked quietly.

'You must have read it about it, surely?'

'I told you before, I try to avoid the newspapers. But I can't keep my eyes closed forever. Tell me what you saw... what they did there.'

'It's such an ugly story,' he said quietly. 'It reveals the worst in humanity.'

'Then I should hear it... every German should. We may have been ignorant at the time, but ignorance is no defence, isn't that what they say?'

Jimmy paused. He looked deeply into her turquoise eyes, now red-rimmed with tears. 'Well, if you really want to know...' he began, draining his glass of wine. 'The first thing we found was a train parked in a siding beside the camp. It had kind of a bad smell all round it. It wasn't like a normal passenger train, you understand, with doors and windows – but more like a cattle transporter with wooden doors held in place by steel bars. When we forced those doors open we found bodies – hundreds of them. Men, women and children, all piled on top of each other... looked like they'd been there for days. It was as if the train had arrived and no one had bothered to let them out. They'd either suffocated, or starved, or both. Some of my men were so angry, they rushed out and grabbed hold of the first uniformed Germans they could find, and shot them dead. I should have tried to stop them, I know, but their actions seemed justified in that moment. I mean, how could those guards allow that to happen? Were they sadists, or simply following orders?'

Annaliese, whose face had first registered shock, then horror and disgust, shook her head in disbelief.

'Inside the camp,' Miller went on, 'we found thousands of people who were just managing to cling onto life. God... they were just skin and bone. And yet, as we marched in through the gates, they cheered, like they were really happy. It made me feel so ashamed.'

'Why should you feel ashamed? You were rescuing them.'

'I guess I was ashamed of just being alive, and well fed. Suddenly just normal life – my own existence – felt like a luxury... like I'd been born the luckiest guy alive.'

'Did you go into the medical block?' Annaliese asked tentatively, fearing the answer.

'Yes...'

'What did you find there?' Her voice was almost a whisper now.

'Enough to piece things together. There were huge tanks of water that people had presumably been submerged in, and cages full of mosquitoes. There was a young Belgian guy – Eugène was his name...'

'He worked with my husband,' Annaliese interjected.

'Right, well, he talked us through the experiments. Did your husband really never explain what was going on?'

'No. I couldn't have stayed with him if I'd known.'

'So you literally had no idea.'

'Not until Alexander told me a little of what went on. After that, I found it hard to reconcile the kind man I'd married with the cruel one he had obviously become, working in that place.'

The room fell silent, with only the sound of Sasha breathing and the fire spitting.

'Well, I should be off now,' said Miller eventually, standing up, cap in hand.

Annaliese shifted her son's head gently off her lap, and rose to join him.

Miller looked down at her kindly – almost with affection. 'Thank you for your honesty tonight. I appreciate this is very hard for you. It's clear you're innocent of any crime, and we won't be bringing any charges against you. But we will track your husband down – you can be sure of that.' He held out his hand. 'Goodbye, Annaliese. I hope we meet again.'

'Goodbye, Jimmy. Do call round any time.'

'Oh, and one other thing... do you have a photograph of your husband you could let me have?'

'I'm not sure. Perhaps... somewhere.' The truth was that she had destroyed most of the photographs of Hans after he'd gone. It had been a sort of purging of their life together. All that remained were a few photos from their wedding and honeymoon in Paris. In happier days, she had mounted them in an album, and kept it in the drawer of the bureau. Somehow she couldn't bring herself to destroy all those memories.

She took out the album, opened it on the desk, and pulled off the photograph on the first page. It showed Hans in his SS dress uniform, arm in arm with his young wife, wearing her new summer suit and hat. They looked so innocent, smiling for the camera. Now, she realised, she couldn't bear the sight of him in that uniform.

'Here,' she said, handing it to him. 'Take this.'

'That's rather a special one,' he said. 'Don't you have another? What if I lose it?'

'I really don't mind,' she said calmly.

'And do you have a photograph of Alexander?' he asked.

'No, I'm afraid not,' she replied sadly, kneeling down beside her son and kissing the top of his head. 'I have nothing to remember him by, except for Sasha...' She looked up at Miller, her eyes glinting with tears.

'I understand,' Miller said gently. 'I'll see myself out.'

29

OCTOBER 1945

As autumn came to an end, Hans began to relax. Winters could be harsh up in the mountains, with drifting snow blocking the roads, reinforcing the village's isolation. As each day passed, Hans felt more secure. If the Americans hadn't found him by now, perhaps they never would. His life in Alpbach was dull, of course, but he had acquired a small and loyal coterie of patients who seemed grateful for his medical care. In his alias as Dr Werner, Hans treated all the regular complaints – influenza, bronchitis, even an outbreak of the measles. The doctor's medical bag he had brought with him from Munich contained a few basic surgical instruments, and one or two simple drugs – even some morphine. Although originally intended to bolster his cover story, it came in useful for rudimentary surgery. He had extracted a rotten tooth or two, and even taken out a ruptured appendix on his kitchen table. He'd turned the spare bedroom into a consulting room and the sitting room into a waiting room. Sometimes, there would be as many as two or three people waiting to see him. The villagers paid him promptly, and he began to seriously envisage spending the rest of his life there, as a country doctor. He set up a medical supplies system, ordering what he needed from a Salzburg wholesaler, which the bar owner collected for him on his regular visits to the brewery. It meant Hans would remain safe, never having to leave the village. He even began to imagine a time when he might be reunited with Annaliese, and they could live together up there in the mountains. It would be a wonderful place to bring up the child.

In November, the first of the snow began to fall. Within days, the summits of the mountains were covered in a thick white layer, which sparkled in the sunshine. One morning Hans woke, shivering with cold. Pulling on a jumper over his pyjamas, he looked out of his bedroom window, and noticed the mountains were enveloped by a dark grey cloud, bringing snow to lower ground.

He pulled on his trousers and boots and went outside to collect wood for the range. As he loaded the basket, he spotted what looked like a military jeep driving slowly up the track towards his chalet. He retreated inside and locked the door, his heart beating fast. He dropped the logs and gathered up his Dachau research notes, already stashed some weeks before in a kitchen cupboard. He slid them into his briefcase, and then went through to his bedroom, where he washed quickly in a basin of water, before putting on his tweed suit. It seemed important, somehow, to be properly dressed if he was to meet the enemy.

He was just tying his shoelaces when he heard boots clattering outside, and a loud knock on the door.

'Dr Werner... Otto Werner... open the door, please.'

He hung back nervously, wondering for a brief moment if he could make a run for it out of the back door, but he spotted a face staring at him through the small kitchen window at the back of the house.

He opened the front door, to find two men in US Army uniforms.

'Dr Otto Werner?'

'Yes.'

'You are to come with us.'

'Where? Why? What do you want?'

'We have reason to believe that you have knowledge of activities at Dachau.'

'I was a prisoner there – so, yes I do.' His tone was defiant but his heart was racing.

'Come with us, please.'

'Where are you taking me?'

'American headquarters, Salzburg.'

It had been months since Hans had last travelled that road. As they crossed the snow line down into the valley, he looked back up at the mountain, and thought wistfully of the few months he had spent there. Would he ever return? Stowed between his knees were his leather medical bag, and packed away safely in his suitcase, his leather briefcase containing his precious notes on mescaline.

Arriving on the outskirts of Salzburg, the jeep swung through the gates of a magnificent Baroque palace.

'Where are we?' Hans asked from the back seat.

'Schloss Klessheim, Dr Werner. Headquarters of the US Forces in Austria.' The jeep drove through a fine wooded parkland, finally arriving at the main doors of the palace. Hans was escorted inside, and shown into an office on the first floor.

'How do you do,' said a young American officer. 'My name is Major James Miller, and you are Dr Hans Vogel, I believe.'

· · ·

The interrogation lasted several days. Hans was not badly treated: his cell in the basement of the old palace had basic bathroom facilities and his meals were adequate. From the questioning, it was clear that Miller knew everything about the experiments, both his and Rascher's, as well as those of Claus Schilling. In the end, any denial seemed pointless.

'How did you find me?' Hans asked eventually, towards the end of the third day.

'It wasn't too difficult,' said Miller. 'Your wife mentioned your mother, and a possible link with Austria.'

'My wife... so you've seen Annaliese?' Hans' heart fluttered at the mention of her name. 'How was she?'

'She seemed very well. She cooperated – sensibly – and told us everything she knew, which was not a great deal.'

'I kept most of it from her,' said Hans quietly. 'For her own protection.'

'Very thoughtful, I'm sure, Dr Vogel. We spoke to your mother too. She seemed upset that you had run away. She expected more of you, she said.'

Hans visibly winced.

Miller continued, quoting from his notes. '"My son should have stood up for what he believed in, and faced the enemy, not run away".' Miller looked up. 'I almost admired her... her devotion to the ideology of the Third Reich seemed unshakeable, even now. She must have been a powerful influence on you.'

'Inevitably,' replied Hans. 'But not in the way you mean. If you think I became an SS officer because of my mother's conviction that Hitler was the saviour of Germany, then you're wrong. I thought both she and my father were slightly mad, if I'm honest. I despised Hitler. He was a brute and so were his henchmen. No, I joined his side for several reasons, not all of them bad. In fact, I believed I might do some good... crazy though that may sound.'

Miller looked puzzled, but Hans persisted in trying to exonerate himself. 'And as for my mother saying I should "stand up for what I believe in" – by the end I didn't believe in anything, except survival.'

Miller nodded. 'Well, that's honest, if nothing else. Your mother was useful in our search, though. It was through her that we found out about your aunt in Salzburg and then – the icing on the cake – we located your car, still parked in the road below her house. If that nice Mercedes of yours had been stolen, it wouldn't have been so easy to make the connection...' Miller smiled ruefully. 'As for your aunt – Charlotte... that's her name, isn't it? You'll be pleased to know she didn't give you away. But her neighbours were most helpful, and told us about her house in the mountains. Then, it was simple – we just asked around Alpbach, and everyone knew the charming Dr Werner... you're quite a hero up there.'

Hans smiled wanly. 'What's your plan for me now?'

'Well, you will be charged with crimes against humanity, tried, and almost certainly executed.'

'I see,' said Hans, his heart pounding. 'And what if I had something you might want?'

'Dr Vogel... I can't imagine you have anything the American people would want.'

Hans opened his briefcase, pulled out his research files, and laid them on Miller's desk.

Rather to Miller's surprise, word came down from his superiors that Hans was to be offered a deal. In return for access to his knowledge and research on mescaline, Dr Hans Vogel would be offered freedom from prosecution. Miller, a man of principle, objected, arguing it would set an unethical precedent, but he was overruled. The response from his superiors was emphatic – Dr Vogel was to be handed over to the Office of Strategic

Services because his research was cutting-edge, and could make an invaluable contribution to international security.

Five days after his arrest, Hans was escorted from his cell to Major Miller's office.

'It seems that your work has some powerful supporters,' said the major. 'Your research is considered to be of potential benefit to our country.'

Hans smiled. 'I thought it might,' he said quietly.

'However, I am formally required to offer you a choice between two options,' Miller continued. 'You can either stand trial for your crimes as Hans Vogel, or adopt a new identity and work for the United States government, completely under our control.'

'I think the answer is obvious, isn't it, major?'

'I have to agree with you, Dr Vogel.'

Over the following week, new identity papers and a fabricated past were meticulously created. Hans would henceforth be known as Dr Heinrich Schneider – ironically a Jewish émigré scientist and a refugee from Nazi persecution.

'You will work in a laboratory in America,' Miller told him.

'In America?' Hans, who had not considered this outcome, felt a momentary flicker of panic at the thought of leaving Annaliese behind. 'Can I ask why?'

'We will want to keep an eye on you. You will live and work at one of our top-secret sites. You won't be imprisoned, as such, but you will be under our control. You will be free to do your research and live a relatively normal life, in a house we will provide. But you will have no passport, and will be forbidden to travel anywhere without our express permission.'

Hans felt a vice-like sensation in his chest, as the harsh reality of his future sank in. He was no longer a free agent, as he had been in Alpbach – albeit a fugitive. For those few brief months in the mountains, he realised, he had actually thought he could get away with it. That he would one day emerge back into society, reclaim his life, his wife and their child. He had hoped the hunt for the SS elite would quickly die down... just melt away. But now he realised he had deluded himself.

He began to gasp, struggling to breathe.

'Are you all right?' asked Miller, rushing across to him. 'You're not having a heart attack, are you?'

'No,' replied Hans breathlessly, unbuttoning his collar. His forehead was beaded with sweat.

Miller held a glass of water to his lips. 'Drink.'

Hans took a few sips and his breathing began to ease. He wiped the sweat off his brow with a handkerchief. 'Is there any way you can get a message to my wife?' he said at last.

Miller sighed. 'I'm afraid not,' he said quietly. 'Contacting your wife is out of the question, along with any other friends and family. In fact, everyone must be convinced that you are dead. Do you understand?'

'But how will Annaliese live? How will she cope?'

'You must have thought about this, surely, before you left?'

'Yes, to a degree. She has the house and some shares – worthless now, sadly. I thought I'd be coming back to her, you see. I assumed I might only be away for a year or so...' He realised now how foolish that sounded, how absurdly optimistic. 'Can I transfer some money to her?'

'No, that won't be possible. It would be a clear signal that you were still alive. I'm afraid you'll just have to hope she'll be all right.' Major Miller looked him squarely in the face. 'Dr Vogel, we are offering you a deal, and with it, survival. But we are not your fairy godmother. The consequences of your decision to work with us are very clear – you will be cut off from your former life, and exiled. It's a punishment of sorts, but justified, given what you did.'

Hans nodded regretfully.

'I must emphasise that if you make the slightest attempt to communicate with anyone – including in particular your family – you will be immediately arrested, put on trial and almost certainly executed. Do I make myself clear?'

'Perfectly,' replied Hans.

Hans remained at CIC headquarters in Salzburg for a few more days. The day before his departure to the USA a suitcase of clothes was brought to his room, along with a temporary passport in the name of his new identity. At dawn one day in late November, he was escorted to an army jeep and, accompanied by Major Miller and two armed guards, they began the six-hour journey to Frankfurt. Their route took them through Munich, where Hans had to fight a visceral compulsion to escape and run back to Annaliese. The thought of leaving her forever, of not even saying goodbye, seemed unbearable. But the alternative was even worse. If he escaped now, he would certainly be caught and executed.

Approaching Frankfurt, the jeep drove straight to the airport, where the US Army had a military zone. Here, Miller suggested they share a farewell meal, before handing him over to the military police who would escort him to his new research post in America.

Standing on the tarmac, Miller shook Hans' hand. 'Goodbye... Dr Schneider. And good luck.'

'Goodbye, Major Miller – and thank you. Your government has shown great foresight. I feel sure I can do good work for your country.'

'I hope so, Doctor. I really do.'

30

DECEMBER 1945

One evening, a few days before Christmas, Annaliese was carrying Sasha upstairs to bed, when there was a knock on the front door. 'Marta!' she called out. 'Can you see who that is?'

As she laid Sasha in his cot, she heard a man's voice: 'Is Frau Vogel at home?'

Marta called up the stairs, her voice quivering slightly. 'Madam, it's that American officer again!'

Annaliese felt a frisson of anxiety. Marta must mean Major Miller... what was he doing there? She called back down. 'All right, ask him to wait in the sitting room, please. I won't be long.'

Annaliese came downstairs a few minutes later. 'Major Miller – Jimmy – how nice to see you! How can I help you?'

'I'm sorry to bother you, but I needed to see you urgently. I have some news, which I fear may come as a shock.'

'I see. What sort of news?'

'Perhaps I should pour you a drink...' He walked across to the drinks tray, poured out a large schnapps and handed it to her.

'What on earth is the matter?' she asked, taking the drink. 'Tell me... you're frightening me.'

He stood awkwardly in front of the fire, shifting from foot to foot. 'It's about your husband.'

'Hans – what about him?'

'You know I've been involved in looking for Nazi war criminals, in particular the doctors at Dachau.'

'Yes, you mentioned it last time we met. What's happened? Have you found Hans? Has he been convicted?'

'In the course of my enquiries, I came upon some... irrefutable evidence that your husband is dead.'

She stared at him in disbelief. 'Dead, you say? What evidence?'

'Perhaps you should sit down,' he began.

She sat on the sofa, looking up at him expectantly.

'It appears your husband was killed... by an SS colleague, when they were on the run. The fellow officer was captured a few weeks ago and confessed to me personally.'

Jimmy glanced nervously over at Annaliese. She was staring at him, clearly bewildered.

'Who is this man? What did he say exactly? Where was Hans killed, and how, and why?' She surprised herself by how upset she felt. She thought she had no love left for Hans, but the thought of him being killed – betrayed by another officer – distressed her. The truth was that while she had never felt passionately about Hans, she had cared for him, had loved him even, in the early days – before Hans had joined the Party, before he got lost in its wickedness.

'We believe your husband was threatening to go the authorities, and give himself up.' Miller explained. 'It was a final act of courage, I suppose... and something you should take comfort from.'

'Except this other man stopped him.'

'I'm afraid so.'

'Where is he – Hans, I mean? Can I see him?'

Miller ran his hands through his hair. He looked tense, Annaliese thought. 'I'm afraid not. You see... there is no body.'

'No body?'

'His body was destroyed. It was incinerated, apparently, to get rid of the evidence.'

'Incinerated?' She was standing up again now, and pacing the room, angry rather than upset. The story seemed bizarre and confused. Hans was resilient and clever. Whatever else he had done, she felt sure that he would escape capture. The thought of him threatening to give himself up seemed highly unlikely. Besides, he loathed his fellow officers. The idea that he might go on the run with one of them was utterly implausible.

'I realise it sounds strange,' said Miller, 'and it is. I wondered for several days if I should tell you at all. But in the end, I felt I had to. You and his mother deserve to know what happened. You need to be able to grieve for him properly and settle his affairs.'

She looked across at him. 'I can hardly believe it. It all sounds so... bizarre. Besides, Hans is far too clever to have allowed something like this to happen.'

'I'm sorry,' he said, picking up his cap. 'I should leave you now. Will you tell his family?'

'Yes, I suppose so. But wait,' she said, grabbing his arm, 'without a body, without a death certificate, how can we have a burial?'

'I'll organise the death certificate. And perhaps, rather than a burial, you could have a memorial?' Miller suggested. 'A memorial can be very comforting.'

'Comforting!' she exclaimed. 'What could possibly be comforting about this?'

'I'm sorry. Maybe I can call back in a few days – to see how you are.'

'Yes, if you like,' she answered abstractedly. 'Thank you for telling me...'

Annaliese dreaded giving Elisabetta the news. The following morning, she steeled herself to visit her at Hilda's house. She was shown into the sitting room by a maid, and found the pair engaged in a game of cards.

Hilda rose to greet her. 'Good morning, my dear. How delightful to see you. Do please sit down.'

Annaliese sat nervously on the sofa facing the two women and haltingly told the story of how Elisabetta's only son had died.

'I can't believe it,' exclaimed Elisabetta. 'Not Hans... surely not Hans.'

'He was going to give himself up,' said Annaliese, trying to comfort her. 'He was doing the right thing.'

'Who was this man who killed him?' demanded Elisabetta. 'I'd like to kill him myself.'

'I don't know who he was, but I suspect he's already been executed, or in prison waiting to stand trial.'

But Elisabetta was not to be comforted. She railed and howled, her hands flailing as if in agony. Finally, she sank down on the sofa and wept uncontrollably.

Annaliese looked on helplessly, until Hilda ushered her into the hall.

'Thank you for coming, Annaliese,' she said quietly. 'It must have been such a hard thing to do – to tell her about her son. I know she didn't make life easy for him, but she loved him so much.'

'I know,' replied Annaliese. 'Thank you for looking after her.'

· · ·

The day before the hastily arranged memorial, the front doorbell rang. Marta answered the door and called upstairs to her mistress. 'It's the post boy, madam. He says there's postage to pay on a card – it has no stamp.'

'All right,' said Annaliese, coming downstairs with her purse. 'How much?'

'Five pfennig,' said the boy. She handed over the money, and closed the door. Glancing at the card, she could see it was a picture of Frankfurt airport. Turning it over, scrawled on the back were the words: '*I will always love you, H*'. Beneath it were scrawled some numbers – most of them illegible.

She took the card upstairs and put it on her dressing table. As she brushed her hair, she studied the picture more carefully, with its odd message on the back. It had to be from Hans; there really was no other explanation.

The memorial service took place at the church where Hans' father was buried. The tiny Vogel family – consisting of Elisabetta, her sister Charlotte, Annaliese and Sasha – sat in the front pew. The rest of the church was empty, but to Annaliese's surprise, as the priest began, the church doors opened and Hans' oldest friend, Gunther, crept into the back row with his wife Ursula.

Snow lay on the ground, and a freezing wind blew through the churchyard, as the funeral party walked behind the priest, towards the family tomb. Hans' name had already been carved on the headstone, alongside the Hippocratic Oath: 'First do no harm'. It had been his mother's choice, and was a curious one, Annaliese thought, given the work Hans had been involved with. It struck her, as they stood staring at the headstone, that her relationship with Hans had begun in this churchyard – on this exact spot – and now, here she was eleven years later, putting it to rest.

Elisabetta, comforted by her sister Charlotte, sobbed loudly, but Annaliese stood silently, simply holding Sasha's hand. She was numb – almost in a state of disbelief.

Gunther came over and kissed her cheek. 'I'm so sorry, Annaliese. It must be a great shock.'

'Yes,' she replied. 'I can hardly take it in. But let's not pretend. We both know what he became. Perhaps his end was deserved, no?'

'I wouldn't say that,' Gunther replied softly.

Ursula took her husband's arm. 'Perhaps we should go.'

'No, don't do that,' said Annaliese. 'Come back to the house – I'd love to talk to you both.'

The wake was a small affair. Marta served the guests drinks and little slices of bread with smoked fish.

Elisabetta sat on the sofa with Charlotte and Hilda, while Annaliese chatted to Gunther and his wife. 'I'm so grateful to you both for coming. I know you and Hans didn't see eye to eye in the end.'

'I was once very fond of him, but I couldn't bear what he became,' said Gunther.

'I wish he had listened to you,' replied Annaliese bitterly. 'Life might have been so different.'

Gunther smiled sympathetically. 'In the end, we all have to live with our decisions, don't we? I personally couldn't stay here – we had to get out.' He smiled down at his wife. 'We have a wonderful life in Switzerland.'

'You must come and stay with us at our house on Lake Constance,' added Ursula.

'Thank you,' said Annaliese, 'I'd love that.'

After the couple had left, Charlotte guided Annaliese into a corner of the sitting room. 'We need to talk,' she said quietly, 'but now is not the time. I'm staying in Munich for a couple of days. Can I come back and see you – alone?'

'Of course, Charlotte. Any time you like.'

Despite the blizzard enveloping Munich, Charlotte returned the very next evening. When Annaliese opened the front door she found the old lady shivering outside, her fox fur hat covered with snow.

'Come in, come in. What a terrible night. Did you manage to find a taxi?'

'Yes, thank you.'

The sitting room was warm, a fire glowing the grate.

'Is the baby around? I'd love to see him,' said Charlotte eagerly.

'He's already in bed, I'm afraid.'

'Oh dear, perhaps I can see him another time.'

'Can I get you anything – a drink, something to eat?'

'A small schnapps would be nice – to keep out the cold,' Charlotte suggested.

They sat on either side of the fire, nursing their drinks.

'I wanted to talk about Hans,' Charlotte began.

'I thought you might. I know he spent a few days with you.'

'Yes. He told me about Dachau, and how he had hated it, and had been forced to work there. Was that true?'

'In a way,' Annaliese replied. 'In order to get on – professionally – he was... encouraged to work there. It wasn't too bad at the start, before the war, but once he realised what was really going on, it was too late to get out. He never talked to me about his work, but I could tell from his behaviour that he was deeply upset – almost traumatised. He became withdrawn, and his insomnia got so much worse.'

'Why did he never talk to you about it?' asked Charlotte.

'To protect me, I suppose – and himself. If I'd known at the start what he was really doing, I like to think I'd have tried to stop him. I feel guilty now that I had so little curiosity.'

Charlotte nodded. 'Would it really have been impossible for him to leave his job?'

Annaliese nodded. 'You have no idea the hold they had over people. Himmler was threatening him all the time. But still... he could have left Germany before the start of the war, like Gunther. I sometimes wonder what would have become of us if he and I had done that.' She looked up at Charlotte with tears in her eyes.

'It's never very useful wondering "what if", Annaliese, my dear. We all might have made different choices with hindsight.' She gazed into the fire, and sipped her drink. 'All of us are guilty to some extent of closing our eyes to the horror that unfolded in those years. Many people stood by watching Jewish shops being smashed, or Jewish families being rounded up, and said nothing... did nothing. Anyone who employed a foreign slave labourer, or cheered at a National Socialist rally, all bear guilt.'

'I suppose you're right,' sighed Annaliese.

'However, I didn't come here tonight to discuss our collective guilt. No, I thought you might appreciate hearing about Hans' visit.'

'Yes I would, thank you.'

'We spent a couple of days together, and it was clear he needed somewhere to hide away. I sent him to my cottage in the mountains. I was in two minds about it, if I'm honest. I seriously wondered whether I should hand him straight to the authorities the moment he arrived. On reflection, perhaps I should have done – he might still be alive today.'

'No, I don't think so – he'd have been put on trial by now, and executed, I imagine,' replied Annaliese sadly. 'Besides, he put you in a difficult position. He came to you for help and you did what you could. You were kind to him, but I worry that he put you in danger.'

'Oh, not at all. All that happened was that a nice young man from the American army in Salzburg interviewed me at home. I played the silly old lady card, and said I had put Hans up for a day or two, after which he left, without telling me where he was going. That was my only lie, but it seemed to work.' She smiled. 'Even when they found out he had gone to my chalet in Alpbach, they appeared to forgive me. He was quite nice, the American.'

Annaliese leant forward. 'Tell me, was he someone called Miller, by any chance?'

'Yes, that was him. How did you know?'

'I've met him two or three times,' explained Annaliese. 'The last occasion was when he told me how Hans had died.'

'Yes, I wanted to ask you about that. Elisabetta seemed incapable of explaining it properly, and it would have been insensitive to ask for details. She's still so upset.'

'Well, Miller told me Hans had teamed up with an old SS colleague, and was about to give himself up to the Americans, when his friend got frightened and killed him.'

Charlotte looked puzzled. 'You don't really believe that, do you? I can't see Hans giving himself up like that. He seemed so determined to avoid capture. Besides, he was alone when he visited me, so who was this "colleague"?'

'I don't know. It does sound rather unlikely, I have to admit.' Annaliese stood up. 'Wait there a minute – there's something I'd like to show you.'

She went upstairs to her room, and returned with the Frankfurt postcard, laying it on a side table next to Charlotte. 'What do you make of that?'

Charlotte put on her glasses, studying the card closely. 'What terrible writing... "I will always love you, H". How peculiar. I presume you think it's from Hans?'

'Who else?' said Annaliese. 'Although I wondered at first if it might be a joke of some kind.'

Charlotte looked across at her. 'Surely not – why would someone do such a thing? No, this is from Hans – even though the writing is rushed, it's definitely his style. But what are those numbers written under the message? I can't quite make them out.'

'I know... the last two are quite indecipherable.'

'A bank account number, do you think?' suggested Charlotte.

'Oh, I suppose it might be. But where? The bank told me he had closed the account.'

'How frustrating,' mused Charlotte. 'And I wonder why there's no stamp?'

'I agree, that is odd. He had money. Perhaps he just forgot to put one on.'

'It's possible, I suppose, but unlikely. Hans was nothing if not meticulous. Was he in a hurry, do you think? The card was franked at the airport, so it was clearly posted there. Maybe Hans was trying to tell you something... that he was going on a journey.'

'But if this was an attempt to communicate with me, why not just call me on the telephone, or write me a letter?'

'Maybe he couldn't. Perhaps he was being watched.'

'By who?'

Charlotte pondered, and took another sip of schnapps. 'That man Miller perhaps? He told me he worked for the American intelligence services. I remember seeing it on his card.' She paused, and leant forward eagerly. 'Might Miller be involved in this? Might the postcard be Hans' way of telling you he was going somewhere on a plane? Perhaps to a prison abroad?'

'But that makes no sense,' answered Annaliese. 'The Americans wanted all the Dachau doctors put on public trial, here in Germany.'

Charlotte sipped her drink. 'I don't know. It's all very mysterious – and perhaps it's best if it stays that way. Whatever happened to Hans, wherever he is, I suggest you don't look for him.'

'Do you think so? I have to confess... it was over between us, anyway.'

'Leave it that way, my dear. You have a death certificate, and a name on a tombstone. Let sleeping dogs lie – that's my advice – and get on with your life. You and your child deserve happiness. You've been through so much, it's time to look to the future now.'

31

The postcard preyed on Annaliese's mind. It sat propped up against a crystal perfume bottle on her dressing table. She studied it every time she brushed her hair, or put cream on her face, searching for clues. The photograph showed a plane parked in front of the airport terminal. Hans was clearly telling her he had flown somewhere, but where? Berlin, Paris, London?

His death certificate was neatly filed away in the top drawer of his desk in his old study. Legally, she was free to move on – even to remarry – and to claim whatever money he had left. That meant another confrontation with the bank manager. Before setting off for the meeting, she slipped the death certificate and the postcard in her handbag.

The bank manager was suitably grave. 'I'm sorry to hear of Dr Vogel's tragic passing. He was a charming man and a good customer for many years.'

'Yes, it's all been rather sudden,' replied Annaliese. 'But I'll come to the point, Herr Assel. I'm here to enquire about what might be left of his estate. Whatever is left of the funds he with-drew from our account last April is now legally mine. I wondered if you knew where it was? Perhaps you arranged the transfer to another account... in Switzerland, perhaps?'

'I'm afraid I am unable to provide any further information,' said the bank manager sympathetically. 'As for the existence of a Swiss bank account, I can tell you nothing.'

'But money doesn't just vanish, Herr Assel. There was over a hundred thousand marks in that account before Hans left. Such a large sum can't have disappeared into thin air. He can't have spent it all! Where is it?'

'The account was legally closed by your husband, and what he did with the funds is nothing to do with me. I'm sorry, but that's all I can tell you.'

The bank manager stood up, indicating the meeting was over.

'One moment, Herr Assel,' said Annaliese quickly. 'Can I show you something?' She took Hans' postcard from her handbag and handed it to him. 'I received this from my husband shortly before his death. Please look at these numbers on the back. The last two numerals are rather indistinct, I'm afraid. But, might it be a bank account number of some kind?'

The bank manager peered at the card, sucking air through his teeth. 'Mmmm... it's not one of our accounts. It could be a bank account, but quite honestly, I have no way of knowing. And as for finding it – it would be like looking for a needle in a haystack. You'd have to write to every bank in Europe, I'd imag-ine... impossible.'

In a strange way, the mysterious disappearance of Hans' money became synonymous with the disappearance of Hans himself. The money was somewhere, but she just didn't know where –

she felt the same was true of Hans. There was only one person who might hold the key to the mystery – the man who had informed her of his bizarre death – Major James Miller.

Annaliese decided to confront him. One morning, she took the tram to the US Army offices on Beethovenplatz. To her surprise, the reception area was filled with people – families with children, queuing up to enter a ground-floor room.

'Good morning,' she said to the receptionist. 'What's going on here? Why are there so many people?'

'Oh, we have a public library here now,' said the receptionist, pointing to a sign saying '*Amerikahaus*'. 'It has a reading room filled with books and magazines from the United States – to introduce the German people to the American way of life.'

'I see,' said Annaliese. 'Would you tell Major Miller that Frau Vogel is here?'

'I'm afraid Major Miller's section has moved.'

'But he asked me to come and see him if I had any information.' Annaliese placed Miller's business card on the reception desk.

'Well, I'm sorry, ma'am. He's no longer here, and the location of his section is now classified information. But I can take your name...'

Annaliese scribbled her name on a pad, and left the offices with a sense of frustration. Perhaps she would never understand what had happened to Hans.

A couple of weeks went by. Then, one morning, a letter arrived. Opening it, Annaliese saw it was from Major Miller.

Dear Frau Vogel,

I heard from colleagues at Beethovenplatz that you recently tried to contact me. I apologise for leaving without a forwarding address. My unit has been moved.

As it happens, I wanted to contact you – partly to see how you are, but also to find out if there was anything I could do for you. In particular, I'd like to offer you an opportunity.

You mentioned to me once that your husband's death had left you with financial concerns. I also know that jobs in Munich are hard to come by at the moment. I may have a solution – albeit temporary. Our army is looking for householders who may be prepared to offer lodgings to the many ancillary staff we are bringing over here to manage the American sector. Might you, with your large, elegant house, be open to the idea of providing a room or two? The rents are good, and our staff are charming people – nurses and doctors, even journalists sometimes.

I will leave it with you, but if you feel it's something you would like to do, please write to me at Beethovenplatz and I will make the arrangements.

I do so hope that you and Sasha are keeping well.

Yours ever,

Major James E. Miller

In so many ways, Annaliese thought, Miller's letter had arrived just in time. Her 'financial concerns', as he called them, were becoming acute, and she had no idea how she would pay Marta's salary that month.

As usual, she went outside to the garden to think. Looking

up at her splendid house, she realised she would like nothing better than for the rooms to be filled. And the money would be very helpful.

Sitting down to reply to Major Miller, she wondered if she should broach the subject of Hans' disappearance, but decided against it. He had been generous to offer her financial assistance, and it would be best not to rock the boat. Besides, even if he did know something, would he tell her? She wrote back by return of post, saying she would be delighted to offer two rooms to suitable candidates, and looked forward to hearing from him.

One evening, a couple of weeks later, two women in US Army uniforms arrived on Annaliese's doorstep.

'Hi, I think you're expecting us,' said a slim, blue-eyed blonde, speaking excellent German. 'I understand Major Miller's office told you we were coming... I'm Lucille.'

'And I'm Katy,' interjected a pretty girl with red hair and green eyes. 'We're both official army journalists.'

'Yes, I was expecting you,' said Annaliese. 'Please come in.'

The two girls followed Annaliese to the sitting room.

'Wow, you have such a beautiful home,' said Katy, gazing around.

'Thank you,' replied Annaliese. 'But it takes a lot of money to keep it going.'

'Is that why you're taking in lodgers?' asked Lucille.

'Yes, partly. I'm a widow and... well, money is tight, and we have a lot of spare rooms, so it makes sense.'

At that moment, Sasha toddled into the sitting room wearing his pyjamas, followed by Marta, who studied the American pair suspiciously.

'Oh, he's gorgeous,' said Katy, bending down to the little boy.

'This is my son, Sasha, and this is Marta – who helps me with everything!'

The two American girls smiled sweetly. 'Hi Marta,' they chorused.

Marta studiously ignored them. 'He wants to be read a story, madam, but he won't let me.'

'All right,' said Annaliese. 'Leave him here, Marta. I'll deal with him.'

Carrying Sasha on her hip, she showed the girls upstairs to their rooms.

'Oh, they're perfect, ma'am,' said Lucille.

'We'd love to take them,' echoed Katy, 'if you'll have us.'

'Yes, of course,' replied Annaliese. 'I think we'll get on very well.'

When they had gone, Annaliese put Sasha to bed and then went down to the kitchen. She found Marta noisily washing up, clanging dishes onto the draining board.

'Well,' said Annaliese, 'they seemed very nice.'

Marta swung round and glared at her.

'What's the matter, Marta?'

'I'm sorry to tell you, madam, but I've decided to leave.'

'Oh, no!' Annaliese sank down onto a kitchen chair. 'But why?'

'Well... I've been thinking about it for a while. There's been so much disruption lately – American soldiers coming and going, which I've found very frightening, to be honest. And then there are the shortages. It's not like it used to be when the master was here. And now, to be asked to look after more people for the same money, just doesn't seem fair.'

'Oh, I see,' replied Annaliese. 'So this is about the lodgers? Look, I'm sure we could come to an arrangement – perhaps increase your money a little. We've been through so much together, Marta, you can't leave now.'

Marta turned away and scrubbed at a saucepan. 'I know we've been through a lot, but I really can't see how you can afford to pay me any more than you do already.'

'I suppose you're right, Marta,' replied Annaliese phlegmatically. 'But it saddens me that you want to leave. You've been with me since the start of my married life. How will I cope without you?'

'I'm sure you'll manage, madam. As my mother always says, life moves on. And in any case, she would like me at home in Augsburg. She's missed me all these years, and she says there are a few jobs opening up there now.'

'Oh, I see. So you've quite made up your mind, then?'

Marta nodded awkwardly, her grey eyes filling with tears.

'I'll miss you,' said Annaliese sadly. 'And so will Sasha... you're part of the family.'

'And I'll miss you, I really will. But I have to think of my own future, now. I'd like to get married one day, and I can't do that if I'm living here with you, can I?'

'No, I suppose not.'

'So, if it's all right with you, I'll work till the end of the week, and then my brother will come and collect my things.'

Marta's departure was tearful. Her brother Karl arrived, monosyllabic and unsmiling, and carried her trunk down the stairs. He loaded it into the back of his old van and waited behind the wheel, a cigarette dangling from his mouth.

'I really hope you'll manage without me,' Marta said kindly. 'I'll think of you.'

'I'm sure we'll be fine,' replied Annaliese. 'But we will miss you – truly. And I hope you find what you're looking for – a nice husband and a well-paid job. You deserve it.'

'Before I go,' Marta began, 'I wanted to say... I hope you find happiness too.'

'Thank you.'

'You can't work in someone's house and not know a little of their business. I know you loved Sasha's father, and perhaps he'll come back to you one day...?' She smiled supportively.

They embraced on the steps of the grey house. But Karl was already tooting his horn.

'I'd better go, madam. My brother's got a terrible temper. Goodbye, madam, and good luck...'

'Good luck to you too.'

The following day, the two American journalists arrived. Soldiers from their unit carried their trunks upstairs, and the house was suddenly filled with noise and life as the two girls giggled and flirted with the young men.

Within days, the American pair had become an integral part of the household – they did the washing-up, played with Sasha and took care of their own laundry. They even insisted on helping to cook the meals. Over supper in the evenings, they sat together around the kitchen table, and encouraged Annaliese to learn English.

'I mean... who speaks German these days?' said Lucille. 'If you want a better job, or to leave your country one day, you have to learn English.'

'We'll help you,' suggested Katy. 'We can bring home some American magazines – they're a great way to learn.'

They arrived one evening with a basket full of magazines: *Vanity Fair*, *Life*, and a new arrival on the market, *Good Housekeeping*. Annaliese fell on them, fascinated. *Vanity Fair* focused on fashion and movie stars, who all appeared to live in stunning homes. *Good Housekeeping* was more concerned with recipes and how the American housewife could make life better for her family. *Life* magazine focused on 'real' people. Some of its articles were about the devastation of the war, and Annaliese was intrigued by the stories of brave Americans fighting for freedom in Europe. The photographs that accompanied the articles were stark and honest, and sometimes distressing. But one story particularly intrigued her. It featured Jimmy Stewart, the Hollywood actor, dressed in the uniform of a US army colonel. He seemed to sum up all that was good about America – an honest-looking man, handsome, brave and inspirational.

Reading the magazines not only improved Annaliese's English, they gave her a glimpse of the American way of life. She recalled how Alexander had often talked endlessly of one day moving to America, to a 'land where you can be free', he had said. Now she began to understand what he meant.

Now that she had enough income from her lodgers, Annaliese could devote her time to running the house and garden. With the arrival of spring, the garden had burgeoned into life, and the vegetable plot had quickly become a tangle of brambles and weeds.

One sunny morning, armed with a little trowel for her son, and her own garden fork, she led Sasha out into the garden.

'Let's start with this border here, Sasha. See these big weeds?'

He nodded earnestly.

'You need to dig that trowel down very deep under the weeds, and pull them out, because they have very long roots. Can you manage that?'

The boy pushed his trowel deep into the damp soil. By mid-morning, a big pile of dandelions and buttercups lay on the grass next to them.

Suddenly she felt a shadow on her back, as if a cloud had

crossed the sun. Sasha began to cry and ran to her, clinging to her legs. 'What is it, darling?' she asked, picking him up.

She turned, shading her eyes against the low spring sunshine. Outlined against the light stood a tall man, his hair glowing gold, like a halo.

'Who are you?' she asked. 'And what are you doing here?'

'Annaliese, don't you recognise me?'

'Alexander!'

It was not the emotional reunion she had dreamed of. He did not rush to embrace her. Instead, he stood back, as if there were an emotional as well as a physical distance between them.

She sat down on their old 'private' bench, but had to encourage him to join her. He had changed. He was fuller in the face and clean-shaven; his blond hair had grown and flopped elegantly over his forehead. Gone were the shabby clothes – he now he wore corduroy trousers and a tweed jacket, giving him the appearance of a young academic.

'He's a sweet boy,' said Alexander, watching Sasha busily digging up another dandelion.

'Like his father,' murmured Annaliese, reaching over and gently squeezing his hand. It was no longer the rough, chapped hand of a workman, but soft like that of a gentleman, she thought to herself.

Suddenly, Alexander pulled away and crossed his arms defensively across his chest. 'I'm sorry I couldn't accept the child when you came to see me at the factory. I was too angry.'

'You had every right to be angry. What Hans and I did was wrong. But I did love you, I promise you... and when I look at our son, I remember our love and how precious it was.'

He looked at her with his sharp green eyes. 'Yes, I think you really believe that.'

'I never stopped loving you.'

'Annaliese, you mustn't say such things...'

'Why mustn't I? My husband is dead. Perhaps you'd heard?'

Alexander nodded. 'Yes, I heard.'

'So... I'm free at last,' she said gently. 'Isn't that what we wanted all along?'

'It's what you wanted,' he said pointedly. 'I wasn't in a position to make my own decisions.'

She reached up to him, cupping his face in her hands. 'Didn't you ever love me? Look at me and tell me you didn't love me.'

Again, he pulled away. 'Annaliese,' he began, pushing his hands deep into his jacket pockets. 'I only came here today because your friend Jimmy suggested it.'

Annaliese was mystified. 'Jimmy who? Oh, do you mean Major Miller?'

He nodded.

'Major Miller's not my friend! I hardly know him. When did you meet him?'

'Didn't he tell you?'

'Tell me what?'

'He tracked me down last autumn. He asked me to testify at the Dachau trials. You must have read about it.'

'No. I try to avoid the papers.'

'Well, I gave evidence at the trial about the medical experiments. I was surprised not to see your husband in the dock.'

'I told you... he's dead, apparently.'

'Why do you say, "apparently"? Don't you believe it?'

She wondered what he would make of her theory about the postcard; he would probably think she was mad. Besides, did it matter any more? She had waited for him for so long and now he was with her. He had survived, they had come through their terrible ordeal, and now was not the time to talk about Hans. This was *their* time, surely – hers and Alexander's – and she wanted him to realise how much she loved him.

'Oh, I don't know,' she said. 'I suppose it's because I never saw the body. It's hard to accept.'

'It sounds as if you still love him.'

'No!' she insisted. 'How can you say that? You must know that's not true.'

He stood up abruptly. 'I should go. I didn't come here to have a fight.'

'No, no, please... please stay,' she pleaded, reaching down to Sasha and pulling him onto her lap. The boy stared curiously up at the strange man who was upsetting his mother. 'Don't you want to get to know your son? We are your family – don't you want us?'

Alexander stroked the boy's cheek tenderly. Sasha giggled happily, and held out his tiny hand to the man who was his father.

But Alexander turned away. 'I'm sorry, Annaliese. I only came to say goodbye. The Americans have given me a passage to the USA – a kind of reward for being a trial witness. I leave in a couple of weeks.'

'What? You're leaving?' Her eyes filled with tears, which spilled down her cheeks. 'Don't you care about us at all?'

'I can't stay, you must see that. I have to get away from here. I'll never move on if I stay in Germany. I hope you have a good life, I really do. And I hope the boy...'

'He's called Alexander – Sasha – after you,' she cried out.

'Take care, Annaliese,' he said simply, leaning over to kiss her. As his lips grazed hers, Annaliese inhaled his familiar scent and wanted to cling to him... to scream, 'Don't leave me!' But something made her hold back – pride, perhaps.

He suddenly backed away from her and turned. Helplessly, she watched him striding down the garden towards the road. He stopped and turned back to look at them both for a brief moment; he raised his hand, headed out into the street and was gone.

. . .

When the lodgers, Lucille and Katy, opened the front door that evening, the house was echoing to the sound of a wailing baby. Exchanging worried glances, the girls followed the sound, rushing upstairs to Annaliese's bedroom. Opening the door, they saw the outline of her body lying on the bed in the gloom, the child weeping pitifully beside her.

'Hey, Annaliese,' said Lucille, shaking her shoulders. There was spittle foaming out of Annaliese's mouth. She was deathly pale. Next to the bed were a bottle of pills and a half-empty bottle of schnapps.

Lucille looked up at her friend. 'You'd better call an ambulance. I think she's done something stupid. And take the baby with you...'

While Katy called for an ambulance from the hall, jiggling the sobbing Sasha on her hip, Lucille ran down to the kitchen and found a glass and a packet of salt. She poured an inch of salt into the glass, and topped it up with water from the kitchen tap. Back in Annaliese's room, she took a towel from the bathroom, laid it next to her and, cradling Annaliese's head in her arm, tried to force the salt water into her mouth. But it simply flowed down her cheeks and onto the bed.

Lucille began to panic. 'Come on, now,' she muttered at Annaliese. 'Don't you die on me.' She prised Annaliese's mouth apart, and poured the salty water down her throat. Suddenly Annaliese opened her eyes, coughed and retched violently.

A US military ambulance arrived within minutes. As Annaliese was stretchered down the stairs, she grabbed Lucille's hand. 'I'm so sorry. I didn't mean it. Will you take care of Sasha?'

'Of course,' said Lucille. Katy nodded. 'Don't worry, we'll look after him.'

. . .

An ambulance brought Annaliese home the following morning. The driver helped her up the steps to the front door. In the hall she stood for a moment, reflecting on what had happened, and how foolish she had been. She was relieved to hear the happy sound of the American girls chatting downstairs in the kitchen. There she found Katy making coffee, while Lucille was down on the floor playing with Sasha and his toy train. He ran to his mother, who picked him up joyfully; he wrapped his little arms tightly around her neck.

'I'm so ashamed,' said Annaliese, slumping down onto a kitchen chair, and desperate to explain herself. 'I can't believe I could have been so stupid. I didn't mean it. I had a drink or two, I admit, but I just wanted to get some sleep. Hans, my husband, had left some sleeping pills in the bathroom cupboard. I just took one, and then another. It was a mistake – you believe me, don't you?'

'Of course, honey,' said Lucille gently, handing her a cup of coffee. 'I almost did it myself once – over a guy. Was it a guy?'

Annaliese nodded. 'Someone I loved very much. He came to see me yesterday to tell me it was all over. I just felt so...'

She began to sob, and Lucille put her arms around her. 'There... just let it out. Men – they're the worst, aren't they?'

The following day, late in the afternoon, Annaliese was pottering in the kitchen, planning supper for the girls, when she suddenly saw a familiar figure through the glazed back door. She ran across the kitchen and flung it open. 'You came back.'

'I did.' Alexander held out his arms and clasped her to his chest. It felt so good to be held by him again. He kissed the top of her head. 'Are you alone?'

'Yes, apart from Sasha – he's playing in the sitting room.' She pulled him inside, and over to the kitchen table. 'Sit down. Do you want some tea – or a glass of wine, maybe?'

'No, I'm fine... I don't need anything.'

She sat down next to him, her heart fluttering. 'What brought you back here?'

He reached over and took both her hands in his and kissed them. 'You, of course... The other night, I got back to where I was staying, and I thought about what you said – about you and Sasha being my family, and I realised you're right. You *are* my family. And I also realised... that I love you.' He kissed her mouth.

'You do?' she asked, kissing him back. It seemed too good to be true. 'You really mean it?'

'Yes,' he said, laughing. 'We belong together. I'm leaving for America in two weeks. Come with me.'

'What?' Her heart was thumping now with excitement. 'I can't leave just like that.'

'Why not? What's to keep you here? You have no job, you have no family to speak of. All you have is a house that's nothing but a burden. Come with me. I'll look after you. They gave me a passport – I'm going to get work in America. I'll be a great architect, you'll see.'

'I believe you,' she replied firmly. 'I know you'll be a huge success one day. Your passion for life, for your work, it shines out of you. But are you sure, Alex? Can we really put everything behind us – the pain, the lies? Can you truly forgive me... forgive us, Hans and me?'

'Of course I can forgive you. As for Hans – that's easy. He's dead and I'm alive. It's a victory of sorts.'

She had a momentary thought of Hans – and his postcard upstairs on her dressing table – but she pushed it aside. 'A victory... yes. But first, you must tell me everything. How you managed to survive, and where you've been since the end of the war. You were in rags at the factory – and now, here you are, looking so well. What happened?'

'A few days before the Americans arrived in Munich, we

were marched east, into the countryside. At first we thought they were going to shoot us and throw us into a pit somewhere. But the more we went on walking, I knew somehow that I'd get away.'

'How?'

'The guards were useless – exhausted, and almost as hungry as we were. They had some well-trained Alsatian dogs with them to keep us all in order. But we outsmarted them. We got the dogs on our side, by feeding them what little food we had, slipping little pieces of black bread into their mouths. In the end, the dogs saw us as their friends. Then it was easy to escape. One night, we were ordered to spend the night on the edge of a wood. Everyone lay down on the ground. The guards were supposed to watch us, but they fell asleep. We had a tiny amount of black bread left and we fed it to the dogs. Pretty soon they fell asleep too. Then, in the quiet of night, five of us slipped away into the woods. We found an old cave and lived rough for a while, stealing clothes from washing lines in a nearby village, catching rabbits to cook over the fire, eating snails – anything we could find. But we survived.'

'I always knew you would,' she said.

'After a couple of weeks, we came across an American platoon and they put us in a field hospital. For the first time in months we were well fed, clean, clothed. Eventually we were interrogated – that's when I met Miller.'

He took Annaliese's face in his hands and kissed her. 'So that's my story. Now, what's your answer... will you come with me to America?'

Her mind raced. If she stayed in the house, she would never be free of Hans. This had been their home, and was filled with memories both good and bad. Whereas in America she could truly make a new start. But still... if felt like a momentous decision.

'I do love you with all my heart,' she began, 'but it will be complicated. I'll have to sell the house – and what will I do with all my furniture and possessions?'

'Sell them, or forget them. Start life again with me.' Alexander emanated such confidence that she was swept away by his enthusiasm. 'We'll make it work, you'll see. We'll be free and happy together, at last.'

'Free and happy,' she echoed, 'yes, you're right.' She took a deep breath. 'Of course I'll come.'

32

MARCH 1946

The house was quickly packed up. Items were labelled for auction, or to be sold with the house; one or two pieces were crated up to be shipped at a later date, and anything Annaliese couldn't bear to leave behind – the eau de nil bedspread and the cream linen embroidered tablecloth – were packed in a trunk with her clothes. Alexander contacted Jimmy Miller, who agreed to provide Annaliese with a visa to enter America, plus a ticket on the *Queen Mary*, due to sail from Southampton to New York at the end of the month.

Before leaving Munich, Annaliese had one final duty – to take Sasha to visit his grandmother. Elisabetta had finally found a new house in an elegant suburb near her old home. A maid opened the door and showed Annaliese through to the oak-panelled sitting room. The room was warm, the heat coming from a traditional Swedish-style stove, decorated with blue and white tiles. Elisabetta sat on a dark blue upholstered sofa, resplendent in lilac.

'Annaliese!' she said. 'What a nice surprise! Although, you should have called ahead.'

'I'm sorry... I didn't think. Things are happening so fast.'

'What do you mean, dear? Do sit down – you look worn out. Oh, and you've brought Max... how lovely. Come here, child.'

Sasha toddled towards his grandmother and allowed her to stroke his head.

'I wanted to tell you something,' said Annaliese nervously. 'I'm leaving Munich.'

'What?'

'I realise it might come as a shock – it's all been rather sudden. I'm emigrating.'

'Emigrating? Where?'

'To America.'

'America! Are you mad?'

'I've been offered a free passage, and I think I owe it to my son to take it. To begin a new life, free from all the sadness of the past.'

Elisabetta was suddenly dumbstruck, and her dark blue eyes began to fill with tears. 'But... I'll never see my grandson, or either of you, ever again.'

Annaliese went over to her and knelt by her side. 'Mama, I'm so sorry. It's obviously very upsetting for you. But try to understand. After all that's happened – Hans' death, his work at Dachau – I need to start again.'

'How will you manage? Financially, I mean.'

'I'll sell the house, and I have some shares. They're not worth much now, but they'll come up eventually, I'm sure. And I'll get a job,' she replied brightly.

Elisabetta studied her daughter-in-law's face intently, and then stroked the head of her grandson, looking down on him fondly. She suddenly stood up, and went over to her pale oak desk in the window. She opened a drawer, pulled out a cheque book, and quickly scribbled in it. Tearing it off with a flourish, she handed it to Annaliese. 'Take this.'

'Oh no, that's far too much.'

'Not at all – it's the least I can do. My son, your husband, let us both down. That money will go some way towards the boy's education, or help in some other way. Make sure you pay it into the bank straight away, and exchange it for dollars. I'll try to send more when you're settled. I know you and I haven't always seen eye to eye, but now Hans is no longer with us, you and the boy are all I have left.'

Annaliese kissed her mother-in-law's powdered cheek. 'Thank you, Elisabetta. I don't know what to say.'

'You don't need to say anything, my dear,' said Elisabetta, 'but write to me from time to time, and let me know you're all right.'

The following morning, once their luggage had been stowed in a taxi, the couple stood together on the steps of the house, Alexander holding his son in his arms.

'I can scarcely believe it's really happening,' said Annaliese, looking up at her lover. 'That you're here finally with me, and we're about to set off on a marvellous adventure together.'

He kissed her. 'Well, you'd better believe it.' He smiled and ran down the steps and into the taxi.

Annaliese turned back to face the house, gazing up at its fine facade. It seemed only yesterday that she had stood there for the first time, admiring the romantic Juliet balcony and the coloured glass above the door. It has been Hans' gift to her and she had thought she would live there forever...

'Come on,' shouted Alexander from the taxi.

She slipped the key through the letterbox and backed away down the steps. It was time to leave the house, and Hans, behind.

. . .

The couple arrived at Croydon airport, south of London, and arranged for their trunk to be sent ahead to Southampton by the boat train. Keen to visit the capital, they took a train to Charing Cross in the heart of the city. Late in the afternoon, searching for a hotel, they walked up the Strand and found themselves standing outside The Savoy, recently reopened after the war.

'This looks nice,' said Annaliese.

'It looks expensive,' said Alexander gloomily. 'We can't afford it.'

'No... we can. My mother-in-law gave me some money before we left.'

'Absolutely not,' he replied firmly, hurrying away from the hotel, wheeling the baby in his pram.

Annaliese ran after him and grabbed his arm. 'Please? I don't mind paying. It would be so romantic to stay somewhere lovely. Just this once?'

'All right,' he reluctantly agreed.

A uniformed doorman opened the glass doors with a flourish, and they entered the marbled entrance hall. Well-dressed men and women sat around on plump sofas arranged around a fireplace, sipping cocktails. It took Annaliese back to her life with Hans before the war. He would have enjoyed a hotel like this – he was always so confident in any social situation.

But Alexander, wearing his US Army-issue overcoat, looked uncomfortable in these surroundings. 'You go and see if they have a room,' he insisted, pointing to the reception desk. 'My English is no good.'

Annaliese walked purposefully up to the desk. In her fur coat she blended in with the other guests perfectly. 'We'd like a room for one night, please – with a cot.'

The reception clerk, dressed in a dark tailcoat, looked up

and smiled at the elegant woman in front of him. 'Of course, madam.'

Alexander wandered over to join her, rocking the baby in the pram. The baby chose that moment to cry noisily, and Alexander jiggled the pram to little effect.

'Just one night, you say?' asked the reception clerk with a touch of a sneer. 'We are very busy...'

'Please,' said Annaliese. 'We've come such a long way.'

The clerk gazed into her turquoise eyes. 'I think I may have something.' He turned the registration book towards her and clicked his fingers for a porter to take their bags. 'Sign here, please. And I'll need your ID cards... or passports, if you have them?'

She took her German passport out of her handbag, and Alexander handed over his newly acquired American passport.

The reception clerk looked askance at them, raising his eyebrows slightly as he noted the different names and nationalities. Annaliese flushed with embarrassment. She hadn't thought that being unmarried might cause such disapproval.

In the lift going up to their room Annaliese felt angry. The clerk had no right to judge them. But they would be married soon enough, she realised, and then no one would ever disapprove of them again.

They followed the porter down a long corridor and were shown into a room high up in the eaves, overlooking the Thames. The bedroom was small, with a bathroom on one side, and a little sitting room on the other. Here, a fire had been lit and a cot had been set up for Sasha. Annaliese tipped the porter, who laid their suitcases out on the bed.

'Is the restaurant open?' she asked.

'Yes madam,' replied the porter, 'but I'm afraid they don't allow children.' He smiled sympathetically. 'But you could order room service.'

Annaliese unpacked her small overnight bag, and ordered

their supper. As the food was wheeled in on a trolley, it struck her that this was not the romantic evening either had been hoping for. But when Sasha finally fell asleep, Alexander suggested they go downstairs, and have a drink in the bar.

'I'm sure someone at reception can check on the baby. Let's go and enjoy ourselves, Anna. Get changed – wear something wonderful.'

'I packed most of my good clothes in the trunk,' she replied. 'But I put in one cocktail dress, just in case.'

'You look beautiful,' said Alexander, admiring her in her blue silk knee-length dress. 'I've never seen you in anything glamorous before, isn't that strange?' He stood behind her, wrapping her in his arms, kissing her neck.

'You should change too,' she said, noticing he still wore the trousers and shirt he'd been wearing to travel. 'You have a suit, don't you?'

'Yes, but only the one the Americans bought for me to wear at the trial.'

He removed it from his suitcase and put it on. Made from cheap wartime grey serge, it was creased, and hung loosely from his broad shoulders.

'You look very smart,' she lied, trying to reassure him on their way downstairs.

As they entered the American Bar, Alexander looked around nervously at the other guests. 'I should be wearing a dinner jacket, like everyone else.'

'We could buy you one tomorrow,' she suggested brightly. 'Before we leave London, we'll go and get you some clothes. I noticed there was a men's outfitters down the road. Would you like that?'

'We can't afford it. I have to get a job first.'

'I told you – I have a little money. Let me pay for them. I'd like to.'

Although he agreed, she sensed he was uncomfortable she would be using her money, not his.

They boarded the ship in Southampton, travelling second class. Their cabin was small and claustrophobic, with Sasha's cot squeezed between their two single beds. The ceiling was so low that Alexander banged his head on his way to the tiny bathroom.

On their first afternoon at sea, he pulled the curtain across the cabin porthole, and sat gloomily on the edge of his bed.

'Don't you want to look at the ocean?' she asked.

'No,' he replied firmly. 'The water makes me uncomfortable.'

'Oh, I love the sea,' she said happily.

'I used to... before Dachau.'

'Oh.' She sat down next to him and took his hand. 'Does it bring back bad memories?'

'You could say that. All those hours... in the tank.'

'Oh, my darling,' she said, wrapping him in her arms. 'Look... let's get out of here – take Sasha and go upstairs. We can sit in the lounge and play cards or something.'

Up on deck, she was heading for the second-class lounge, when he suggested they sit outside instead. 'We should get some air.'

'But it's so cold... and what about the water?'

'I have to conquer this fear. It's ridiculous. We have days of this ahead of us. Sit with me.'

They chose a pair of deckchairs, and Annaliese settled down with the baby on her lap. It was windy and the ship was gently pitching in the waves. But she was aware that Alexander was becoming anxious – his hands were sweating, his breathing shallow and fast.

'Why don't we sing together to take your mind off it?' she suggested.

His eyes were wide with fear. 'I can't sing.'

'Everyone can sing.' She hummed the first few bars of a nursery rhyme, bouncing Sasha on her lap. 'Come on, join in, Alexander. It will help.'

But he was still sweating, his skin turning pale. 'I can't stay out here any longer.' He suddenly stood up and headed for the door that led to the lounge.

She followed Alexander inside, the baby on her hip, and found him already sitting in the bar, a glass of vodka in his hand.

'Are you all right, Alex?'

'Yes, thank you.' He smiled wanly, but she saw the fear in his eyes. 'I'll stay here for a while. See you later.'

They got through the next few days by avoiding looking at the sea wherever possible, and distracting themselves by playing cards and board games. Often, before lunch, Alexander suggested they went to the bar for cocktails; it was where Annaliese had her first taste of a Manhattan. But she began to worry he was drinking too much.

On their final night, and much to their surprise, they were invited to dine in the first-class restaurant. A steward promised to check on the baby during the evening and, as soon as Sasha was asleep, they made their way upstairs.

Alexander suggested a detour via the bar.

'Two vodka cocktails,' he told the barman. He drank his down in one draught. 'Don't you want yours?' he asked Annaliese, fingering her glass.

'Not particularly,' she said. 'Have it if you want, but do be careful, we don't want to be drunk when we arrive.'

He flashed her a dark look. 'I don't need a lesson from a German about how to behave.'

She felt as if she'd been punched in the stomach. 'I'm sorry...'

'No, I'm sorry,' he said, taking her hand and kissing it. 'I shouldn't have said that – it was unfair.' He stood up, draining the glass. 'Let's go.'

'You look wonderful in your new dinner jacket, by the way,' she whispered, as they lined up to meet the captain.

He smiled weakly. 'I'm glad you think your money was well spent.'

'Alex... don't say that.'

Over dinner, Alexander's lack of English put him at a disadvantage. Annaliese, reasonably fluent after her English lessons with the American lodgers, charmed the other passengers at their table, but sensed her lover's resentment.

In spite of the tensions between them, they made love that night with a wild passion, squeezed together in a single bed. Afterwards, as the ship pitched and rolled through the North Atlantic, they slept fitfully. But she woke in the middle of the night to find him sitting bolt upright, bathed in sweat.

'What is it?' she asked. 'Are you seasick?'

'No,' he replied. 'A bad dream. And it's always the same one.'

'Tell me,' she said, reaching out for him.

He lay back down in her arms, his head resting on her breast. 'I'm standing in the yard at Dachau, with those crazy Russians. The guard takes the man standing next to me, and then he looks straight into my eyes, and pulls me out of the line. We're shoved into the centre of the yard, where the gibbet is waiting for us. And I want to scream, "I haven't done anything wrong. I'm innocent!"'

He wiped his face with his hands, roughly brushing away the tears coursing down his face.

'Oh, darling, I'm so sorry.' She stroked his hair, holding him tight, feeling his tears on her skin. 'But that didn't happen, did it? You are alive... you survived. And now you're here, safe with me. No one is ever going to hurt you again.'

'That's just it,' he said. 'I survived, but so many others didn't. And I don't feel safe. I never feel safe, Anna. I worry I can never feel safe again.'

33

On the morning of their arrival in New York, Annaliese woke to find Alexander standing over her, grinning wildly.

'Get up, Anna,' he said happily. 'We'll be docking soon. I can hardly believe it.' He looked like a child on Christmas morning.

She packed their bags, dressed the baby and joined Alexander for breakfast. But while he seemed rejuvenated at the prospect of their arrival, she felt strangely nervous that their journey was coming to an end. These last few days had been a dreamlike, transitional state – a holiday from reality. But now it was over. She had left behind the old, familiar world, and there was no choice any more but to make this new world work for them all.

'Let's go up on deck,' he suggested. 'I want to see our new homeland as soon as possible.'

They joined the other passengers gathering by the railings, everyone agog, as they sailed into the heart of Manhattan.

'Look at that,' exclaimed Alexander, pointing to the skyline, gleaming in the spring sunshine. 'That's why I came here... for those skyscrapers. They are so powerful, so optimistic, don't you think?' He kissed Annaliese, who was relieved to see him happy, at last. 'We made it, Anna,' he said, 'we really made it.'

Immigration officers came on board to inspect the passports of the upper-class passengers, Anna and Alex among them. They clattered down the gangplank with Sasha in his pram, and were soon standing in line for a taxi into town.

'Can you take us to a hotel?' Annaliese asked the driver. 'Nothing expensive...'

'Sure,' he replied. 'My cousin has a place in Greenwich Village. Welcome to New York.'

Staring out of the cab window, Annaliese's initial reaction to her adopted country was bewilderment. The pavements were crowded and noisy; steam erupted from the streets, and the skyscrapers were oppressive. It felt so utterly different from Munich, with its peaceful roads and parks. New York, by comparison, seemed to run on adrenalin and aggression.

The hotel, as Annaliese soon discovered, was filled with a disparate collection of people: American travelling salesmen jostled with Hungarians, Irish, Italians and French – all refugees from the war in Europe. In the evenings, everyone congregated in the shabby dining room, where English was the only common language. Once again, Annaliese found herself grateful for her American lodgers' English lessons. They had even taught her a little New York slang, which smoothed her path with the Americans. She also made a decision – to change her name for good.

'I think from now on, Alexander, I'll call myself Anna. Annaliese is such a mouthful and so obviously German. Besides, you've always called me Anna and I think it would mark a break with the past – what do you think?'

'Whatever you say, Anna.'

In spite of her name change, the other hotel residents initially treated her warily. She suspected that her German accent and blond good looks made her appear to be a Nazi on the run, and it was only when she explained that she had risked death to be with her Russian lover that their attitude changed. Alexander, in effect, became her talisman – her right to exist in the land of the free.

But with the three of them squeezed into one room, the couple began to squabble. Without a garden for their little son to run around in, and no airy kitchen in which to draw and paint, Sasha grew tetchy and tearful. Alexander spent his days traipsing around architectural firms looking for work, while Anna focused on finding them somewhere to rent, where they could make a proper home.

As spring merged into summer, Anna finally located a third-floor apartment in an old brownstone in Brooklyn.

It had two bedrooms, a small living room, a kitchen and bathroom. Although unfurnished, it was comfortable enough, and reminded Anna of the flat she had lived in as a child. She paid the deposit with the money Elisabetta had given her and they moved in the following weekend. Anna bought a couple of beds from a thrift store, along with a chest of drawers, a table and some chairs, but the apartment still looked unloved and empty.

'You do like it, don't you?' she asked Alex nervously, sensing his disappointment. 'I can paint the walls. It would look better with some fresh paint, or wallpaper, perhaps?'

'It's all right. It's not what I would have chosen.'

'But it's better than the hotel, isn't it?'

'Sure,' he replied weakly. 'It's fine, Anna. I just...' He paused.

'What?' she asked. 'You just... what?'

'I suppose I feel guilty. To have brought you to this.' He looked miserably around the apartment. 'You must regret leaving Germany, don't you?'

'No!' she said, throwing her arms around him. 'Of course I don't regret it. After all, this is only temporary. Once the house in Munich is sold, once you get a job... everything will be all right, you'll see.'

'I hope you're right,' he said quietly. 'I can't bear the thought of being a failure.'

'You won't be a failure, my darling. We won't fail.'

Hoping to make friends, Annaliese knocked on the doors of neighbours. A young couple named Rita and Ricky lived on the floor below with their two small children. They had recently moved to the city from Ohio.

'What does your husband do?' Rita asked one day over coffee, as the children played by their feet.

'He's an architect,' Anna replied proudly. 'He's looking for a job.'

'I'm sure he'll find one here. There are new buildings going up all the time,' Rita said encouragingly. 'And if you ever need a babysitter, I'll watch Sasha for you.'

On the ground floor lived an old lady called Marion. Anna met her one afternoon as she returned home, bumping the baby's pram up the steep steps into the hall.

'He's a beautiful child,' Marion observed admiringly.

'Thank you.'

'You're married to the Russian, aren't you? I see him go off each morning.'

'Yes... well, we're not married yet, but we will be soon. I'm a widow, you see.'

'It's OK, honey,' replied Marion. 'You don't have to explain anything to me. This is New York. We're all starting over... Come in for coffee sometime. I'd love to chat.'

Gradually Anna began to feel at home in the big city. She grew used to the noise and the bustle, and the intense heat over the summer months. She scoured second-hand shops and antique dealers for small pieces of furniture to make the apartment feel more like home.

But she was surprised, and a little hurt by Alexander's reaction to her efforts at home-making. 'Why do you buy this junk?' he asked irritably one day, when a small Victorian mahogany side table was delivered.

'I like it, it's elegant. It reminds me...' She stopped herself, not wishing to provoke him.

'Reminds you of what... the house in Munich, I suppose. Perhaps you wish you'd never left?'

It was not the first time he had accused her of missing Munich. She had always denied it, but now, as she looked around their shabby little apartment, she realised that part of her did feel bereft. Her heart ached for the beautiful grey house, but she could never admit that to him. Instead, she did her best to reassure him. 'No, that's not true. Of course I don't wish that. We'll be happy here, you'll see.'

'I won't be happy until I get a job. And no one wants to employ a Russian.'

'It will happen,' she said firmly, praying it was true.

At night they still made love with passion. It was the one time they truly united – their bodies melding into each other. But in the middle of the night, he would often wake in a cold sweat, complaining his mind was racked by dark memories of Dachau.

Eventually, Alexander found a job with a large firm of architects. Anna hoped their problems were behind them. At the end of his first week, she cooked a special meal to celebrate. But sitting at the table in their cramped kitchen, he seemed far from happy.

'They have got me designing lavatory blocks, for heaven's sake,' he complained. 'Who do they think I am – a student? In Russia I was in charge of whole schemes.'

'They'll soon see how talented you are.'

But with each passing day, Alexander grew more irascible. He started coming home late, and often smelt of drink. When she tried to talk to him, he became angry. 'Don't tell me what to do,' he snapped one evening. 'I'm not your slave.'

The comment cut her like a knife. Adding to their troubles, money was short. Alexander's salary barely covered their bills, the money Elisabetta had given her had run out, and the house in Munich had still not been sold. There was a limited market for large comfortable houses, according to the German estate agent. Anna quickly realised that if they were ever to have the life they had dreamed of, she too would have to get a job.

Now, as soon as Alexander left for work, Anna would scour the 'jobs vacant' columns. After several failed attempts, she spotted an advert for a personal assistant to an interior decorator, working in Manhattan. She applied for the job and was thrilled to be invited for an interview. She left Sasha with Rita. 'It will just be for an hour or two,' she told her.

'No problem, sweetie. I'm happy to do it.'

Frederick Madison was from Tennessee and was already making a name for himself among the New York elite. His interior design style was considered 'eclectic', combining pared-down modern interiors with antique furniture. He had created a stir by designing an entirely white room for a well-known heiress, which had been featured in several of the high-society magazines. His showroom was on a quiet side street in mid-town Manhattan.

Anna arrived for her interview wearing her best turquoise suit – the one she had been married in, all those years before. It still fitted well and the colour brought out her eyes.

Madison, dressed in pale slacks and a silk shirt, shook her hand and then waved airily towards a gilded Louis XV chair. 'Do sit down, and tell me all about yourself.'

She explained that she had recently moved from Germany with her Russian husband. They had a child, were exiles from Europe, and loved America and the opportunities it provided.

Madison listened to her intently, smoking a black Sobranie cigarette, flicking its ash into a gold ashtray. 'You're very beautiful, I'll say that for you,' he said at last. 'And your dress sense is interesting. Wherever did you get that suit?'

'This? I've had it for years.'

'Hmmmm,' he said languorously. 'I rather thought so. It's old-fashioned, but charming, like you. Now, to business – do you know anything at all about interior decorating?'

'I decorated my own house... back in Munich. I love fabrics and wallpaper. I think I have a good instinct for colour. I visited Paris before the war and enjoyed the antique shops.' She paused nervously, aware she had been about to say 'on my honeymoon'.

'My husband is an architect – so, yes, I think I know a little about interiors.' It sounded strange referring to Alexander as her husband.

'An architect, is he? What sort of buildings does he design?'

'I'd describe him as a modernist. In Russia he was very well respected. But I prefer things that are more traditional.'

Frederick Madison raised his eyebrows. 'That sounds like a relationship disaster in the making,' he said, smiling. 'All right, Madam Vogel, you're hired. By the way – Vogel – it's not exactly a Russian name, is it?'

Annaliese blushed. 'No. The thing is, I was originally

married to a German.' She glanced down at her turquoise skirt, and was transported back to Café Luitpold and her wedding to Hans. 'Alex and I,' she went on, '...we are not actually married yet.'

'I really couldn't care less whether you're married or not,' replied Madison airily. 'As long as you're not an illegal alien, I'm happy. Now, the job – it's basic secretarial work mostly – invoicing, liaising with clients, that sort of thing. I think they'll like you. Your accent is pretty, you are pretty, there's something exotic about you. I'll loan you a little money to buy some new clothes. Go to Saks, or Bloomingdale's. The key is to look elegant, OK?'

She nodded, blushing again.

'You'll be out and about, meeting people, so you have to look good. From time to time you'll collect samples for me, or items I've bought from dealers. Do you think you can manage that?'

'Yes, yes, of course.'

'Good... you start on Monday.'

She rushed home full of excitement, impatient to give Alex her good news. She made dinner, put the baby to bed and opened a bottle of wine. But his reaction was disappointing.

'Thanks for the vote of confidence,' he said despondently. 'You're only getting a job because you don't believe I can look after you.'

'That's ridiculous. It's true that we could do with the extra money, but I've always wanted to work in interiors. I'm excited about it.'

'You never worked when you lived with Hans.'

'Things were different then... there was a war on. Oh, Alex, please try to be happy for me. I can't believe how selfish you're being.'

He sat back in his chair and stared at her. 'Selfish, am I?'

She heard Sasha crying from his bedroom, and got up from the table to go and comfort him.

'That's right,' said Alexander, 'walk away.'

'Our son is crying.'

'And who will look after him while you're playing "designers" in Manhattan? I'm not giving up my job.'

'I'm not asking you to. I'll find a nursery. Now, I must go to him.'

As she stood rocking Sasha in his room, she heard the door to the apartment slamming shut, and Alexander's footsteps retreating down the stairs.

Anna located a nursery a few blocks away, and Sasha was enrolled for the start of the fall term. She managed to scrape together the money for the deposit – her salary would arrive just in time.

She enjoyed her new job. Her boss Frederick could be tricky – he was petulant and demanding, and with a vile temper – but he also had great talent. Working for him opened up a whole new world for her, a world of rich and successful people, beautiful things, glamorous homes and expensive furnishings. She was sent out daily into Manhattan with a long list of errands – collecting fabric samples, or decorative items from antique dealers. She picked up Frederick's lunch each day from a deli a few blocks down. These trips out of the office gave her a chance to explore her surroundings. She got to know Manhattan well – the hotels, the auction rooms, the apartment buildings. She learned the best side of the park to live on, where to buy the most elegant clothes and the finest antiques. She delivered drawings and fabric swatches to his clients, waiting in the receptions of their grand apartment buildings, or, more rarely, being shown into their magnificent homes near Central Park. Usually met by butlers or housekeepers, she was occasionally introduced to the clients themselves; they all seemed to be fascinated by the exotic German blonde with turquoise eyes.

Beyond the glamour, she also learned the nuts and bolts of the business – about invoicing, how to plan and quantify a scheme, how to liaise with builders, plumbers and electricians. Frederick came increasingly to rely on her, even asking her advice. She began to feel that this was a career in which she could be successful.

'You should study design professionally,' he told her one afternoon. 'You have a real gift.'

She blushed. 'Oh, Frederick, I'm quite happy here working for you.'

'I'm not suggesting you leave, Anna. But if you did a course in technical drawing, for example, it would be useful to both of us.'

She went home that evening, wondering how Alexander would react if she told him she wanted to go to night school. In an ideal world, he would be proud of her, or at least pleased for her. But when he came home, he was his usual grumpy self, and Annaliese decided not to say anything.

As she prepared supper, she tried to analyse their relationship. Was he incapable of seeing her as an equal partner? Or was it a reaction against his time working as her slave? Perhaps he was determined to be in charge of their relationship, and any attempt she made to establish herself as an independent woman, who could contribute on an equal basis, knocked his self-confidence. She hoped that once his own career began to take off, he would be more prepared to allow her to follow in his footsteps.

The couple had been in New York for just over a year and Sasha's third birthday was approaching. Determined to give the little boy a birthday party, Annaliese asked Frederick for the afternoon off.

'When? he asked.

'At the end of the week – Friday.'

'Well, I suppose it would be all right,' said Frederick reluctantly, 'but don't make a habit of it. Now, let's get back to work... I'd like you to collect something for me – it's a blue and white Chinese vase. I was in a cab last night, and spotted it in the window of that dealer opposite Rockefeller Center. It will look beautiful on my desk.'

Anna was just coming out of the dealer's shop, clutching the vase, when she had a curious sensation of being watched. Glancing quickly around, she could see no one she recognised. She set off to walk the couple of blocks to Frederick's showroom, but the vase was too heavy.

Looking up the street for a cab, she caught a glimpse of a man in a raincoat, topped by a tweed trilby hat, disappearing around the corner. For some reason it reminded her of Hans – he often wore a hat like that, she remembered. In the taxi on the way back to the office, she couldn't stop thinking about it. The way the man had held himself, the angle of his hat – all seemed so familiar. But as soon as she got back to work, she put the episode out of her mind.

On Friday morning, before Alexander went to work, she broached the subject of Sasha's party that afternoon. 'Just a few friends are coming about three o'clock. I thought it would be nice – it will be our first party here.'

'I'm working,' he replied absent-mindedly, drinking his coffee.

'I know, but as I can't get away from work myself until after one, I wondered if you could you collect Sasha from nursery at lunchtime and bring him home? Maybe you could stay for the party?'

'OK, I'll bring him home, but I can't promise to stay,' he mumbled.

Anna had ordered a birthday cake from a smart bakery near her office. It was designed in the shape of a traditional colonial house, with four Georgian windows and a white front door – the kind of house she dreamed of living in one day.

She brought the cake home in a white box, tied with blue ribbon. It reminded her of the cake-boxes Elisabetta used to buy from Café Opera before the war.

Running excitedly up the stairs to the apartment, she found Alexander sitting at their small melamine kitchen table with his son. 'I'm sorry I'm a little late,' she told him. 'There was a queue at the baker's.' She ceremoniously placed the cake-box on the table in front of them, stroking her son's fair hair. 'How's he been?'

'Fine,' said Alexander, suddenly standing up. 'I'm glad you're back. I have to get back to work.'

'But what about his party?'

'I'm not interested in children's parties,' he said brusquely. 'I'll see you later.'

He gave her a fleeting kiss, and grabbed his corduroy jacket. She heard him thundering down the stairs, as if he couldn't wait to get away.

Standing at the kitchen window, Annaliese watched Alex as he arrived on the steps below. He lit a cigarette, inhaling deeply, and strode off down the street.

Sasha's birthday party that afternoon was a modest affair, with just a small handful of guests: Marion from downstairs, one or two friends from Sasha's nursery, and Rita with her two children.

At six-thirty the guests said goodbye. Anna tidied the apartment, expecting Alexander to return any minute – but there was no sign of him. Eventually, at eight o'clock, she put Sasha to bed, and poured herself a glass of wine. By ten, he had still not returned, so she took a shower and climbed into bed.

She woke at dawn, with the early-morning light filtering through the thin curtains. Her hand automatically went out to Alexander's side of the bed, but it was empty. Padding anxiously into the sitting room, she saw a cream envelope lying on the floor by the door. She picked it up and instantly recognised the handwriting. He must have come back in the middle of the night, and slipped it under the door.

She hardly needed to open the letter to know what it would say. In some ways it came almost as a relief: their relationship had been built on such rocky foundations from the start, it had always felt like a struggle. Nevertheless, it marked the end of something important, and her hands trembled as she read the letter.

I'm sorry, Anna,

I can't go on with this any more. I have to get out, get away. My head is filled with demons – and there are times when I think I will go mad with it. This is not the life I had envisaged for myself as I studied the walls of my prison cell in the labour camp. This is not the vision that kept me going as I weeded your garden, or stood for twelve hours in the factory. What kept me going then – what keeps me going now – is the idea of freedom. Total freedom. Do you understand? And this life – being with you and Sasha – it's not freedom. I feel imprisoned all over again.

I'm sorry. I know you'll be upset. I know I've let you both down, but I can't help it. I can't be the husband you deserve, or the father the boy needs. I am too damaged, too angry. I can't forget what your people did to me.

Forgive me, Annaliese. It's just no good.

With love,

A

PART FOUR

EXPOSURE

1984

34

JUNE 1984

Sitting on the train from Connecticut to New York, Anna opened the newspaper one more time, and reread the article:

Professor Hans Vogel will deliver the keynote address to the Global Conference on Vaccination to be held at the Waldorf Astoria Hotel on Park Avenue.

Her copy of the *New York Times* had been delivered at six that morning, as usual. Pete, the newspaper boy, had cycled up the drive of her Connecticut house, and thrown it onto the deck, where it had landed with its customary thud, waking her from a deep and dreamless sleep.

She climbed out of bed, hauled on her dressing gown, and went outside to pick up the paper. She put the coffee on the stove and flicked through the pages. Her eye was drawn to the name 'Vogel' immediately.

So Hans *was* alive.

To her surprise, she felt no shock. Somehow she had always

known... had always expected Hans to re-appear in her life – perhaps a chance encounter in a street or train, or even standing outside her front door. She'd been waiting for it all these years.

She ran upstairs and stood in the shower, her mind racing, her heart thumping. As she dressed, she smelt the acrid scent of burning coffee and ran back downstairs in her underwear, grabbed a dishcloth and yanked the pot off the stove and into the sink. 'Damn,' she muttered, turning on the cold water tap. The pot hissed angrily.

Back upstairs, as she sat at her dressing table, brushing her hair and applying a little make-up, she made a decision – to go to New York and confront him. She glanced down at the paper again. There was no indication of what time he was speaking at the conference, but she presumed he would be there most of the day.

Dressed in beige slacks and a silk shirt, she went downstairs to her study. Sitting at her desk, she removed the postcard from Frankfurt that had lain undisturbed in the top drawer for so many years, and put it, with the folded newspaper, into her handbag. She threw on a pale grey summer coat, locked the house and reversed her station wagon out of her drive. She caught the first train to New York.

The lobby of the hotel hosting the conference was filled with delegates, all wearing name-tag badges. If she were to blend in she would need a cover story and a badge. She waited around for a while, wondering what to do.

A delegate reception desk had been set up outside the main conference room. Anna noticed how the clerk ticked people off a checklist when she handed them their badge, which were all neatly arranged in alphabetical order. She looked up and smiled at Anna. 'Can I help you, ma'am?'

'No... no, thank you – I've already got a badge,' Anna said, patting her handbag.

She quickly backed away, and went to the ladies' room to think. She noticed a coat hanging on a peg with a delegate badge pinned to its lapel. With trembling fingers, Anna unpinned it and reattached it to her own jacket. She then walked briskly out into the lobby, and headed for the conference room.

Guarding the double doors into the room was another young woman with a clipboard. She looked at Anna's badge and then at her checklist. 'Welcome, Dr Prendergast... do please sit anywhere.'

Anna chose a place at the end of a row, near the back of the room, reasoning that it would mean less chance of someone talking to her and discovering her deception. The morning session began – with two speakers, lengthily discussing various vaccination issues.

At eleven, the conference broke for refreshments. Anna wandered out into the crowded lobby and took a cup of coffee from the buffet. Trying to keep a distance from everyone, she wandered over to a side-table, and noticed a pile of event itineraries. Her heart thudded when she saw that Professor Hans Vogel of Goethe-University, Frankfurt, was due to speak immediately after the break. She hurried back to her seat in the conference room, waiting nervously for him to appear.

'Excuse me... may I sit down?' A tall, middle-aged woman squeezed past her and sat down right next to her. 'I'm Gloria, nice to meet you.' She peered at Anna's badge. 'Oh, you work at New York City Hospital. I worked there a few years ago. How is Dr—?'

'—I'm sorry,' Anna interjected quickly, sweat breaking out on her powdered forehead, 'but you'll have to excuse me, I have a terrible headache. Would you think me very rude if we didn't chat?'

'No, not at all,' said Gloria, looking slightly puzzled. 'Forgive me.'

To Anna's relief, the lights were soon dimmed, and an elegant middle-aged woman mounted the stage. 'Ladies and gentlemen, it gives me great pleasure to introduce – all the way from the University of Frankfurt – Professor Hans Vogel.'

Anna joined in the polite applause, as the man who had once been her husband walked on stage to the podium. She was overwhelmed by a combination of horror and curiosity. He still had an upright bearing, and while his hair was unnaturally dark, it was certainly receding. He wore an elegant grey three-piece suit, which looked slightly too big for him, as if he'd lost weight.

He spoke in English, mostly without notes. His accent, she noticed, though obviously German, had a hint of the East Coast of America. She began to concentrate on what he was saying.

'One of the most serious issues we face,' he said, staring pointedly at his audience, 'is non-compliance. Mistrust of the vaccine industry is on the increase, and take-up of vaccines themselves is reducing. Consequently, pharmaceutical companies are increasingly reluctant to take the financial risk of developing vaccines, for fear of being sued – all for the sake of a few tragic bad reactions among the general public. Medical science has always had to find a path between harming a minority in order to benefit the majority.'

Anna had a sudden flash – a memory of Alexander's descriptions of the 'medical experiments' forty years earlier in Dachau.

'Clearly...' Hans went on, 'a solution needs to be found, and I believe that, increasingly, indemnity is the only way forward. Governments must be prepared to cover the costs of all medical injury claims against vaccine manufacturers. Only then can our industry progress and develop, creating new vaccines that will be of such benefit to the entire world.'

The audience applauded vigorously, and Hans bowed slightly in acknowledgement. He shook the hand of the moderator and descended the stage to the auditorium, walking swiftly up the centre aisle towards the main doors. Anna leapt to her feet, anxious not to lose sight of him.

Her neighbour looked up, surprised. 'Are you OK?'

'Yes, thank you. I just need some air.' She hurried towards the nearest set of doors. Outside she scanned the lobby, searching for him, her heart thumping. People began gradually to emerge from the auditorium, and she feared he would be lost in the crowd. But then she spotted him, standing awkwardly alone by the reception desk. A young woman approached him, holding a clipboard. Anna weaved her way through the crowd to get close enough to hear their conversation.

'Thank you so much, Professor Vogel. What a wonderful speech,' the young woman was saying. 'My name is Rebecca – I work for the organisers, arranging your accommodation and so on. Can I ask, are you intending to stay for the rest of the conference?'

'No, I don't think so,' he replied.

'Oh, well, is there anything I can do for you? The restaurant on the first floor is available for lunch if you'd like it. It's all paid for...'

'Thank you, that's kind, but no,' he said. 'I have to go.'

'Oh... all right. Well, thank you again, we're so grateful. I'll send a car to your hotel in the morning to take you back to the airport.'

'Yes, thank you. I'll be ready.'

He shook her hand and quickly headed towards the revolving doors leading outside to the street.

Anna ran after him. 'Hans,' she called out.

He turned around, his brow furrowed. 'Yes?' he said to no one in particular. When he saw her, he gasped. 'You!'

'Yes... it's me.'

He looked as if he might faint. He stumbled, clutching at a low table.

She grabbed his arm. 'Let's sit down somewhere.' She steered him through the rotating doors and out into the street, pulling him down next her on a nearby bench.

Hans smoothed down his thinning hair with trembling hands. It was something he always did when he was nervous, she remembered.

'How did you find me?' he asked quietly.

'There was a piece in this morning's paper about your speech.'

He looked ill, she thought – his eyes were slightly yellow at the corners, and his skin was pale and paper-thin.

'In an odd way, I wasn't surprised,' she said. 'I'd been told you were dead, but I never really believed it.'

He smiled a little, and gazed at her, as if he couldn't believe she was there with him.

'I'm sorry. It's obviously a shock to see me.'

'A shock, yes, it's a shock.' He reached over and took her hand. 'How are you?'

'I'm well, thank you.'

'How's Max?'

'Max?'

'Our son.'

'Oh, Sasha, you mean. He's very well. He's an architect now... here in New York.'

Hans winced, as if he'd been hit in the face. 'I see.' They sat for a few moments in silence. 'Why did you come today?' he asked eventually. 'Do you want something?'

'No... of course not. I just had to see you.' She blushed, embarrassed suddenly at having to explain herself, and began to babble. 'I don't live in the city any more – I spend most of my time in the country. So I just jumped on a train and came here.'

'Impetuous, as always,' he said, with a smile.

'I needed to understand... to know what had happened to you, all those years ago.'

'I see.'

'They told me you were dead, but I never believed it.'

'No? Why not?'

'It just seemed so unlikely – you being killed by another SS officer. You were far too clever for that. And then there was the postcard...'

He smiled faintly. 'So you understood, then?'

'Yes, I think so...'

He looked around, clearly uncomfortable at the crowds of people ebbing and flowing in and out of the hotel. 'If you want to talk, perhaps we could go somewhere quieter?'

'We can go to my apartment. It's only a few minutes away by cab.'

'Your apartment? I thought you said you lived upstate.'

'I have a place in town too.'

He allowed her to guide him to the taxi rank; he seemed so frail, she thought. 'East 69th Street, the junction with Park,' she ordered. Once there, she shepherded him into the lobby.

'Good afternoon, Mrs Vogel,' said the doorman when they arrived. 'Good to see you again... long time no see.'

'Yes, Arthur. I've not been in town for such a long time – the mail must be stacking up.' She took a key out of her hand-bag, unlocked a metal post box on the wall, and removed a thick pile of letters. She took her former husband's arm, and led him over to the elevators.

It felt awkward being alone with him in such a confined space. Anna was the first to break the silence, chattering nervously. 'I used to live in the city all the time. But when Sasha was a teenager I sent him to school in Connecticut. I fell in love with the countryside, so I bought an old clapboard house up there.'

There was an awkward pause.

'The doorman called you Mrs Vogel... did you never marry again?'

'No.'

The elevator juddered to a stop, bringing an end to the conversation. They walked in silence along the corridor to her apartment.

'It's charming,' he said, as she ushered him inside. 'But you always were very good at making rooms look beautiful.'

'It's been my job for the last thirty years,' she said, removing her coat. 'And I've done rather well at it. Can I get you anything? I have no food in the house, I'm afraid, but I have coffee somewhere, or tea?'

'Do you have any whisky?'

'Yes, of course. Please sit down.'

He gratefully sat down on her plump peach-coloured sofa, while she poured two glasses of whisky from a crystal decanter. 'Here,' she said, offering one to him.

'Thank you.' He downed it in one draught.

'Another?'

'Yes please.'

She sat opposite him, sipping her own drink. 'So, let's talk about the past... What actually happened the day you left Munich?'

'It's such a long time ago, I struggle to remember.' He grimaced slightly, as if in pain.

'Are you unwell?'

He smiled. 'Something like that.'

'Another whisky?'

He held out his glass. She refilled it and he took it in both hands, leaning back heavily onto the sofa. He sighed deeply, as if preparing for a long story.

'I lay low at the start,' he began. 'I didn't know what I was going to do at first. Pretty quickly I realised I needed to get out of Germany...' As he told the story of his life on the run and his eventual capture by the Americans, she studied his face. The pain that had been so visible when he first sat down, seemed to recede a little, as he recalled his post-war escapade. He told the story as if narrating an exciting spy novel.

'...It was while I was being interrogated that they made an approach.'

'An approach?'

'Yes. It turned out the Americans were interested in my work. They offered me immunity if I agreed to work for the intelligence services.'

'How... on what?'

'To continue my research on mescaline and other truth drugs. They brought me here to America. I worked in a lab in the south. I was quite well paid and lived a quiet life. They protected me well. But by the mid-fifties the research was pretty much done, and I asked if perhaps they might ever allow me to return to Germany. At first they refused, but over the next two years they came round. By then I'd acquired some academic prestige and they came to an agreement with the German government. They offered me a professorship at Frankfurt University, where I've been ever since. I switched my attention to vaccine research.'

'So, in the end, you got to fulfil your dream... of getting an academic position and the chance to save the world.'

'I suppose you could say that.'

'But going back for a moment... did you know the Americans were going to lie about you being dead?'

'Yes. I'm sorry about that – it was their idea.'

'But then you sent me the card.' She opened her bag and laid the now faded Frankfurt postcard on the table between them.

'You kept it all this time?'

'Yes. I don't know why. Somehow I knew I'd see you again.' She paused.

'Something that troubled me for such a long time were these numbers.' She pointed to the line of illegible numbers beneath his message.

'Oh yes.' He ran his bony finger along the line. 'It was the number of my Swiss bank account.' He looked up at her. 'I wanted to make sure you had enough money.'

'I thought it must be something like that... but I couldn't read the numbers.'

'I didn't know that – I'm sorry. I was being watched all the time, and just grabbed a card and wrote it in such a rush. And once I got to America I was forbidden to contact the bank. How did you manage?'

'It's a long story,' she said, picking up the card and putting it back in her bag.

She topped up their drinks. 'It's just occurred to me – you didn't seem surprised to find me here... in America, I mean.'

'No, that's because I saw you once, here in New York.'

'You did? When?'

'Oh, back in the late forties – a year or so after I'd been relocated.'

'How did you know I was here?'

'I didn't, it was purely chance. I'd come for a meeting with the intelligence people at Rockefeller Center. I saw you coming out of an antique shop. You had a vase under your arm and were hailing a taxi.'

'I remember now. How strange. I had an odd feeling I was being watched that day.'

'I was desperate to speak to you, but they told me when I came here that if I ever tried to contact you the deal was off, and I'd be prosecuted for war crimes.'

'I see.'

The two fell silent. He shifted uneasily on the sofa, and shot her a look. 'Did you ever see the Russian again?'

'Yes. That's what brought me here to America.'

He looked surprised.

'He was asked to give evidence at the Dachau trials, and in return was offered American citizenship and his passage across the Atlantic. I came with him, but it didn't work out. The past was too painful. He could never get over what happened to him – what you did to him – what we both did. It ate away at our relationship.'

'I'm sorry.'

'Are you? I'm not so sure, Hans. I think the postcard was a way of binding me to you. I was your wife and you wanted to keep it that way.'

He drained his glass; she leant across and refilled it.

'That's a rather uncharitable view. I was just trying to tell you I was still alive – that I loved you. I hoped one day to come back to you.'

She gazed at him, wondering if he was telling the truth. His eyes told her that he was. 'Do you still work for them?' she asked. 'The secret service, I mean?'

'Do you think I would tell you if I was?' He smiled again. 'Besides...'

'Besides, what?'

'I'm dying. So it really won't matter in a few months.'

'I'm sorry. What's wrong with you?'

'Cancer.' His tone was matter-of-fact. 'It has spread every-where now... there's no hope.'

'I am sorry. Really, I am.'

'Are you? Why should you be?'

'Did you never marry again, Hans?'

'Of course not. I was still married to you.'

'I just thought... you'd have found someone else.'

He shook his head. 'I'm surprised *you* didn't remarry, though – you're still as beautiful as ever.' His grey eyes softened as he gazed at her.

She blushed. 'Oh, I've had a few boyfriends, of course –

when Sasha was away at school – but I wanted him to have a stable background, to know there was someone he could always rely on. I provided a good home for him. I had a good career and enough money. I didn't need a man.'

'So you became a thoroughly modern woman.' He smiled. 'Did you ever see my mother at all?'

'Yes, a few times, before I left Germany. After I came here, I tried to stay in touch with both her and Charlotte. I wrote to them both until their deaths.'

'I felt guilty about leaving my mother,' he said sadly.

'More guilty than about leaving me?' she asked teasingly.

'I thought you were keen to be rid of me.' His expression switched from mild amusement to sadness. 'When did she die, my mother?'

'A couple of years after I came here. Charlotte wrote to me about the funeral... she's buried in the tomb with your father.'

'Ah, good... she'll be at peace there. She hated life without him, really. I was never an adequate substitute.'

'She loved you, I'm sure of it.'

'Perhaps.'

'She left some money in trust for Sasha when she died – that's what I used for his education. It was very kind of her.'

'Good... I did love the boy, you know, even though he was not mine. I often thought of you both and wished things could have been different.'

'Did you? I'm not sure our marriage could ever have survived what we went through.'

'Perhaps,' he said sadly. 'But you've been happy... haven't you, darling?' With that one word, it was as if they were suddenly reunited, a married couple who cared for one another.

'Yes, of course,' she assured him, leaning over and taking his hand. It felt thin and feeble in her own strong grasp. He held it to his lips.

'I'm so pleased,' he said, kissing her hand. 'And so glad

everything worked out for you and the boy, really I am.' He stood up suddenly, rocking slightly on his feet.

'Are you OK?' Anna asked. 'Would you like to lie down? My bedroom's just through there...'

'Thank you, no. I should go back to my hotel. I have a plane to Frankfurt early in the morning.'

'But we could have supper?' she suggested. 'I could show you some photographs of Sasha and his family.'

'No... but thank you.'

'At least, let me have your address, or a phone number.'

'What's the point, Annaliese?' His voice was weak now; he sounded exhausted.

'We may want to keep in touch.' She felt almost panicky at the thought of never hearing from or seeing him again. They had found one another after all this time, and to her surprise she didn't want to let him go.

But he was firm. 'No, you won't want to keep in touch. Why would you? After what I did, after all I put you through, and the hideous work I was involved in, why would you want to see me again? I've been lucky all these years. I got away with it... more than Rascher did.' He smiled briefly. 'Take care of yourself, and don't look back, Annaliese. And, please don't feel sorry for me.'

He walked towards the door, but turned as he reached for the handle. 'I'm so glad you survived, darling... and thrived. You were always a better person than me. Goodbye... my dearest wife.'

35

CONNECTICUT

SEPTEMBER 1984

The phone rang early. Anna glanced at the bedside clock. It was some time before her usual, informal wake-up call by Pete, the paperboy. She stretched across her bed and picked up the phone.

'Mom.' It was Sasha.

'Good morning, darling. This is rather early for a social call – what can I do for you?'

'Have you seen the paper?'

'The paper? No, not yet. It doesn't arrive until six. I'm still in bed.'

'Well, when it arrives, look at the obituaries and call me back.' He rang off.

She pulled on her dressing gown and went downstairs. It was five minutes after six. The paper still hadn't been delivered. Cursing the paperboy for his uncharacteristic tardiness, she made coffee and was standing at the window when he noisily threw the paper onto the deck.

'Thanks, Pete,' she called through the window to his retreating figure. He waved his hand without looking back.

She flicked through to the obituary section. The lead item was that Professor Hans Vogel of Frankfurt University, a pioneer in vaccine research, had died of cancer. Reading on, the obituary revealed something of his past life. He had been involved in an American government research programme known as MK Ultra, working on interrogation techniques for the CIA. Earlier, from 1935 until the end of the war, he had been a camp doctor at the Dachau concentration camp.

Annaliese put down the paper, and felt a fleeting moment of sadness. Their last meeting had lingered in her mind for some months. And now she wondered who might have been with him when he died. She hoped he had not been alone. He had done some bad things, but he was not an evil man. He had been good and kind when she had first met him.

Rereading the article, it seemed odd that there was no mention of her, nor indeed of any personal information. As for the rest of it, she wondered how the paper had managed to find out so much about him. Perhaps the American government had supplied he obituary – controlling the information until the end.

The ringing of the phone jolted her back to the present. It would be Sasha. He had sounded upset earlier, and now she knew why. As far as he knew, his father had died years before, leaving her a widow. She picked up the phone.

'Have you seen it yet?' His tone was cold.

'Yes, I've seen it.'

'And?' He paused.

She could think of nothing to say.

'Was this man my father? You told me he was a doctor in Germany, and he has the same name as us, after all.'

'Yes, it's the same man.'

'Did you know he was still alive?'

'No, not until a few months ago.'

'What?' He sounded furious. 'So you *did* know. Why didn't you tell me?'

'Oh, Sasha... it's all so complicated.'

'I'm so disappointed, Mother. I can't believe you kept it from me all this time.'

'We need to talk. I can explain.'

'Can you?'

'Yes, but I can't do it over the phone. Can we meet?'

'I'm busy.'

'Please, Sasha... if you want to understand, at least do me the courtesy of coming to see me.'

'I'll drive up after work. I'll be there around six.' The phone went dead.

Just before six, Anna sat down on the veranda to wait for her son. The sun was casting long shadows across the lawn, and the maple trees along the boundary were already turning a brilliant shade of vermilion. She had laid out a tray of drinks on the table in front of her, and had poured herself a small whisky to steady her nerves.

Sasha swept up the drive in his Mercedes estate. He walked across the lawn, and bounded up the wooden steps, kissing his mother on both cheeks. She found this one simple expression of affection comforting – perhaps he would forgive her after all.

'Good of you to come, darling. Was the traffic bad?'

'No, it was fine.'

'Drink?'

'Yes... I think we'll need one, won't we?'

He looked strained, she thought, as she poured him a whisky.

'First I need to explain,' she began nervously, 'that I only found out that Hans was alive a few months ago. I'd always believed he had died at the end of the war. You might remember... we went to his funeral.'

'No... I have no memory of that.' Sasha looked so pale and anxious, and Anna felt a wave of guilt at hiding the truth from him for so many years.

As the sun went down behind the trees, she began to unburden herself of a lifetime of secrets – the type of man Hans had been when she met him, and who he later became. A man who, because of his desire to be a scientific success, had found himself trapped as a doctor at Dachau.

'So... Dachau – was that like Auschwitz?' asked Sasha incredulously.

'Yes, sort of.'

'He actually worked there? Doing what?'

Anna bit her lip. 'Medical experiments... trying to find a cure for malaria, initially. Then he moved on to researching truth drugs, which is why the Americans were so interested in him.'

Sasha shook his head in disbelief.

'But you have to believe this,' she went on, 'that he hated what he had to do... I promise you that. He had gone to Dachau originally because he thought he was going to do important work to help humanity. It turned out to be anything but.'

'Geez... and this guy was my father.' Sasha sounded both mystified and appalled.

Anna drained her glass and cleared her throat, steeling herself before revealing the final, shocking secret. 'There's something else you need to understand... Hans wasn't your real father.'

Sasha rocked back in his chair, stunned. 'What? Well, if he wasn't, who the hell was?'

'A Russian... a man Hans had brought to work for us in the garden. He was a prisoner of war, who'd been released from Dachau to work in the factories.'

Alex stared open-mouthed at his mother. 'You had an affair with a prisoner?'

'Yes, but you have to understand... he wasn't a criminal, he was a soldier who'd been captured. He was an intelligent man. Kind, thoughtful, sensitive. He was an architect.'

'My father was a Russian architect?' Sasha stared wide-eyed at his mother. 'OK... now things begin to make sense.'

She nodded, tears in her eyes. 'You have to believe... I fell in love with him, you see. He was a beautiful man... like you, darling.'

Sasha sat for a long while, staring into his glass. 'Mom... there is so much to process, I hardly know what to think.'

'I know, and I'm so sorry, Sasha. Perhaps I should have told you all this before, but what good would it have done?'

'So, what happened to this Russian?'

She sat for a moment considering what else she should reveal. Some things were best left unsaid, surely.

'After the war, Hans disappeared. I was told that he was dead, but as we now know, he had actually been recruited by the CIA. Alexander, your real father, was finally released from the labour camp, and turned up at our house in Munich.' She smiled at the memory. 'I was so happy to see him. He'd been offered a deal by the Americans in return for being a witness at the Dachau trial. The deal was his passage to America and a passport. It had always been his dream to come here. He persuaded us to join him.'

'So what happened? I have no memory of him, either.'

'It just didn't work out between us. It was no one's fault. We did love each other, but he just couldn't handle it – living with us, taking responsibility for us both. He'd been through so much as a prisoner... pain, humiliation and suffering. And living with me just reminded him of all that. He left us when you were three years old... on your birthday, in fact.'

'He left us?'

She nodded, tears coming into her eyes.

Sasha put down his glass and went over to her, wrapping her in his arms. 'I'm sorry, Mom. That must have been really hard.'

'It was,' she said, wiping her eyes.

'How could he do that? Leave you alone like that in a strange country...'

'Don't think too badly of him. After all he'd been through, he was like a frightened animal – he just had to get away.'

'Where is he now? Is he alive?'

'I really don't know. He didn't stay in touch.'

'You didn't look for him?'

She shook her head. 'There was no point. It was over between us, I knew that. Perhaps it was over before it even began. I had to pull myself together... to make a life for us. And I believed I'd done that. You've been happy with me, haven't you, darling? I did everything I could to make your life a success.'

'I know that, Mom, and I'm really grateful. I've had a great life, it's just... there's always been this hole where a father should have been.'

'I'm sorry,' she said, 'I didn't realise you felt that way. I did my best... I always did my best.'

Later, Sasha called his wife from the phone in the hall; Anna listened to brief snatches of their conversation as she made supper in the kitchen.

'I'm going to stay here tonight, honey... It's been a bit of a bombshell... Mom needs me... There's so much to discuss.'

Mother and son sat up talking late into the night. There were still aspects of her story that she could never reveal: that Sasha's father had been a slave, for example, or that he was the result of an 'arrangement' between her and Hans. That would have been too much for him. Surely all that mattered was that he was loved, and was the much-loved child of a loving relationship.

The following day she watched him drive away, feeling exhausted, but in a curious way relieved that her son finally knew the truth, or at least part of it.

EPILOGUE

JUNE 1996

Sasha put his arm round the shoulders of his wife and two children as he led the party away from the cemetery.

'You OK, honey?' asked his wife, Louise.

'I will be. But it's hard.'

'I know.'

They drove back to Anna's house – his house now – where a few friends were due to gather after the funeral. Louise had arranged for caterers to serve drinks and canapés, and while she went into the kitchen to oversee the staff, Sasha wandered around the ground floor of the house, touching all the things his mother had bought over the years, as if he could somehow summon up her presence through the feel of a sofa's linen cover, or the wax polish on a side table.

The mahogany table in the dining hall had been laid out with his mother's favourite cloth – cream linen, embroidered with white stars – and the best silver. Louise had picked some pale pink and white roses from Anna's garden that morning, and now their scent filled the house. It was very elegant, Sasha thought, just like his mother.

Their two children, Mike and Annabel, now both grown-up college kids, hovered awkwardly in the entrance to the kitchen, chatting to the hired waiting staff.

'You two, go and welcome the guests,' their mother told them. 'Introduce yourselves, be polite.'

Sasha suddenly felt he needed to be alone, so he wandered upstairs to his mother's room. Laid out on his mother's bed was her favourite eau de nil bedspread – something she had owned for as long as he could remember. He lay down on it, and could still detect a trace of her favourite perfume, lingering on the bed linen. Tears streamed down his face. His mother was gone.

They'd had so many conversations over her last few years, and he'd learned so much of what she'd gone through – her upbringing in the shop, being orphaned in her teens, her marriage and, ultimately, what the two men in her life had put her through.

He had finally come to a place where he could be at peace about it. But he had a lingering desire to understand more about what happened, and to know who his father really was. That need to meet the man himself, to talk to him, dominated his thoughts.

'Sasha...' It was his wife outside on the landing. 'People are arriving, honey. You should come down.'

'Sure. I'll be right there.'

The dining hall was already full as he came downstairs. Several old friends from New York had made the journey. There were fellow decorator colleagues of his mother's, grateful clients and locals. As so often with these solemn occasions, the drink began to flow and the conversations turned from hushed tones to laughter and happy memories. His mother would have liked it, he thought – she loved a party. Sasha circulated among the guests, and came across an elderly man he didn't recognise, chatting to his son.

'Hello,' he said, his hand outstretched. 'I don't believe we've met before. I'm Sasha, Anna's son.'

'Hello, Sasha. We have actually met before, but it was years ago, back in Munich. You were just a tiny child.'

Sasha's heart missed a beat. Was this man his father?

'My name is James Miller,' the man went on, 'and I visited your mother once or twice at the end of the war. I was with the American Army of Occupation, you see.'

'Oh, she never mentioned you,' said Sasha.

'Well, she would have had no reason to... we only met once or twice. But I'm so sorry she's gone. She was a remarkable woman.'

'Did you keep up with her when she moved to the US?'

'No, but I wish I had. I'm sorry about that too.'

Sasha's wife, Louise, called out to their son: 'Mike, could you take the bottle round, honey? People's glasses are empty.'

'You'd better go, son,' said Sasha. 'Your mother needs you.'

He turned back to Miller. 'I'd really appreciate talking to you a little longer, if you have time. You see, you might be able to help me. I'm trying to find my father. My mother finally told me a few years ago he was a Russian called Alexander Kosomov. He might have been in Munich at the same time as you. Did you know him?'

Jimmy looked down awkwardly. 'I did meet him, yes.'

'You did!' Sasha said excitedly. 'You're the first person I've ever met who knew him. What was he like? Might he still be alive somewhere – do you know where?'

'No, I'm sorry,' said Miller, backing away, 'I really ought to be going now – it's a long drive. I just wanted to pay my respects to your mother.'

'Please don't go yet.' Something in Miller's demeanour suggested he knew more than he was letting on. Sasha took old man's arm and gently guided him outside onto the porch. 'I don't want to put any pressure on you, but I really need to find my father. So if you know anything at all about him, please help me.'

Jimmy Miller ran his hand through his greying hair. 'Look, all I can tell you is that I arranged for your father to get to the States. It was part of a deal.'

'Ah... my mother mentioned Kosomov's "deal".'

'We arranged for their passage to New York,' said Miller, 'but that was the end of our involvement. I heard your father moved out west... LA, I think. I kept in touch for a while. He started an architectural practice over there.'

'OK, LA – that's very useful. Thank you so much. I'm sorry to ask you so many questions, but now my mother's gone, I have no one else to turn to. My real father is an enigma and I have to find him.'

'Be careful,' said Jimmy.

'What do you mean?'

'I don't know how much you know, but many strange things went on during the war. Without understanding the context of those times, things can seem inexplicable... bizarre, even. All you need to know is that your mother loved you very much. And she was a wonderful woman who coped with very difficult circumstances. Let that be your memory. You should be very proud of her.'

'I am proud. But it won't stop me trying to find my father,' replied Sasha firmly. 'Look, perhaps I could have your contact details?'

'Sure,' said Miller, reaching into his jacket pocket and producing a business card. 'Here.'

'You're a professor... at Princeton?'

'I'm emeritus... retired,' said Jimmy with a smile. 'Good

luck, and I'm sorry again about your mother... she was a lovely woman.'

Over the next few months, Sasha spent many hours searching for his father – checking professional registers of architects in the West Coast, searching for any architectural practice with a vaguely Russian name involving either 'Alexander' or 'Kosomov'. Finally, one morning, he received an email from an architectural company called AK Designs.

> *Good morning,*

> *My name is Alexander Kosomov. I am told you want to contact me.*

Sasha's heart stopped. He tapped a reply.

> *Hi, Mr Kosomov. Thank you. I think you knew my mother – Anna Vogel. She was originally called Annaliese.*

The reply email came back within minutes. It contained just a phone number. Sasha dialled it.

'Hello.' The voice was deep, with an unmistakable foreign accent.

'Is that Alexander Kosomov?'

'Yes, who is this?'

Sasha took a very deep breath. 'My name is Alexander Vogel – I think you might be my father.'

They arranged to meet a few weeks later at Kosomov's home in Los Angeles. Sasha hired a car at the airport and, following his emailed instructions, left the smog-filled city behind, heading deep into the Hollywood Hills.

The route took him from a long winding road into a canyon, where half a dozen houses were built into the sides of the hill. The road grew rutted, finishing in a dead end, where he spotted a mailbox marked with the address he had been given. He pulled up at the side of the track, searching for the house and caught a glimpse of what looked like a huge glass box, hidden in the trees, perched on one side of the ravine.

He pulled into the parking area below it, climbed out of the car and stood for a moment, admiring the modernist vision; it was like a highly sophisticated child's tree house, glinting in the sunshine.

Leading up to the house was a set of steep steps in grey slate, which he tentatively began to climb.

A dog barked above, a glass door slid back and an elderly man emerged into the sunlit treetops. Tall, tanned and muscular, wearing faded blue jeans and a white linen shirt, he ran down the steps with his hand outstretched. 'You must be Sasha.'

'Yes, sir.' He shook the old man's hand; his grasp was surprisingly firm and strong. The two men studied each other with curiosity – each seeing himself in the other. Both had bright green eyes, the same Roman nose, and wide generous mouth, although the old man's blond hair was now heavily flecked with silver.

'It's so good to finally meet you, sir,' said Sasha eagerly.

'It's good to meet you too, Sasha.' Patting the young man's shoulder, the older man gestured up the stairway. 'Come upstairs.'

Waiting for them in the first-floor living room was a sleek chocolate-brown pointer lying at the feet of an elegant woman in her sixties. Tanned, with grey hair tied up in a messy chignon, she stood up as Sasha and Alexander arrived.

'Katja,' said the old man, 'this is Sasha Vogel.'

'How nice to meet you, Sasha.' Katja smiled broadly. 'I'll leave you two alone together...' She kissed the old man's cheek, and snapped her fingers for the dog to follow her out of the room.

'Sit, sit,' said Alexander. 'Are you hungry, thirsty?'

'A drink would be great, thank you, sir.'

'What would you like?'

'Anything – wine?'

The old man returned a few minutes later with a bottle of white wine and two glasses. He poured out a glass, and handed it to Sasha.

'So,' Sasha began. 'It's so good of you to see me.'

'Not at all... I was intrigued. You are my son, after all.'

Sasha gazed at the old man, basking in the words 'my son'. 'I don't want anything from you... money or anything,' he said hurriedly. 'I mean, that's not why I came. I'm quite successful as an architect... I have a family and so on. I just wanted to meet you – to understand.'

'Of course,' said Alexander. 'What would you like to know?'

Sasha took a big gulp of wine. He suddenly felt very nervous. This man seemed so open and easy, but he felt embarrassed quizzing him. 'I suppose I would like to know... if you loved my mother.'

The old man smiled. 'Yes. I cared for her, certainly. I did love her. She was a great beauty, and so vulnerable and yet at the same time, immensely strong – she was fascinating.'

'I know so little of how you met. All she told me before she died was that you worked for her and her husband.'

'"Working" is a rather polite way of putting it,' said Alexander, smiling. 'I was a slave.'

'I'm sorry – what did you say?' Sasha put his wine glass down on the coffee table with a clatter. 'A slave?'

'Did your mother not tell you?'

Sasha shook his head.

'Ah... always there are secrets,' he said ruefully. 'Well, I was a prisoner of war, and we were required to work for no pay. So, yes, it was slavery. For a year or so, I was lucky to work as a gardener for your mother. But I was still a slave.'

'But she told me how much she loved you. That you had an affair.'

'Yes, she did love me, that much was true. But our "love affair" was arranged, you know.'

'I'm sorry, I don't understand.'

As the old man revealed the whole story, Sasha sat aghast.

'Hans Vogel *forced* my mother to have an affair with you? I can't believe it.'

'Well, "forced" is perhaps the wrong word, as it suited them both,' replied the old man. 'Hans Vogel got the child he needed. And your mother, who was hopelessly in love with me, had the affair and the baby she yearned for. I did care for her too, but you must understand that I had no free will in that situation. I was not in a position to truly return her love. I felt controlled, manipulated.' He sighed, and refilled their glasses. 'After the war, we tried to make it work. She came to America with me and we lived together for about a year. Do you remember?'

Sasha shook his head.

'Frankly, the relationship was never going to work. You were about three, I think, when I left. I'm sorry about leaving you – I just couldn't cope. I couldn't rid myself of the bad memories, the abuse. I felt too angry and resentful.' He sipped at his glass and stared out of the window for a moment, as if collecting his thoughts. 'But I was unkind to your mother when we lived together... and I drank too much. I'm sorry about that too. In the end, I just had to get away. Do you understand?'

'I think so.'

'I feel bad for you because none of this is your fault. And I can see you are a credit to your mother. It says a lot for her that she never tried to find me, after I'd gone. She probably knew it was hopeless. I came out here to LA in 1946, and began working for another architect. I eventually took over his practice. I've had a lot of therapy, and come to terms with what happened. I've been happy here.'

'And happily married too? Was that your wife I met earlier?'

'You mean Katja? Oh no, she's not my wife. I never married. We just live together. She and I met back in the seventies. She's a psychotherapist, so she understands that I can't... I can't be tied down.'

'So you have no children?'

'Apart from you, no.' He smiled, and Sasha felt a faint glow of pride.

'Don't you think it's curious,' said Sasha, 'that I became an architect, like you?'

'No, not at all... genetics will out. Katja would hate me saying that.' He laughed. 'She believes in nurture not nature.'

'I'd really like to get to know you. I wouldn't tie you down, I promise.'

'No, I don't think you would,' replied Alexander, smiling at him. 'Come, bring your drink, we'll go to my office. I'd like to show you some of my work.'

'I'd love that. I'd love that more than anything.'

A set of slate steps led to the office on the top floor. Alexander took the cover off his drawing board while Sasha wandered out onto the terrace overlooking the canyon. 'Wow! What a view.'

'Yes, it's very therapeutic, being up here above the smog line. Here... this is something I'm working on.'

Alexander laid out his designs for a futuristic house, much like his own, made of glass and steel.

'I love that,' said Sasha. 'That's my style too. Unfortunately, I spend too much time designing houses for clients in New

England who want a pastiche version of an eighteenth-century house. All clapboard and cosiness.'

'You need to encourage your clients to be brave,' said his father.

Soon, Katja announced that supper was ready. They ate on the terrace, overlooking the canyon, watching the sun going down over the russet hills.

'I've brought some pictures with me,' Sasha said tentatively. Pulling a small packet out of his jacket pocket, he removed a set of photographs, laying them on the table. 'They're mostly of my mother, and a few of my wife and kids – do you want to see them?'

'Of course.' Alexander picked up a photograph from the top of the pile. It was of Annaliese standing on the porch of her house with her two grandchildren on either side of her, their arms wrapped around her. She was beaming happily into the camera, her turquoise eyes sparkling.

'They're beautiful, your kids,' said Alexander. 'What's the boy's name?'

'That's Michael, my eldest. He looks a little like you, doesn't he?'

Alexander nodded. 'When was it taken?'

'Oh, a couple of years ago.'

Alexander traced his finger around Annaliese's figure. 'Your mother was still very beautiful. I remember those eyes so well – they were like pools of turquoise water. And she was so tall, athletic and blond... the Aryan dream, the ideal German wife.' He looked up at Sasha and smiled ruefully. 'She looks happy. I'm glad about that.'

'Oh, yes. She was happy most of the time. In fact, I would say she had an extraordinary capacity for happiness. Mom often said she was the luckiest woman alive. Now I understand more about what she went through, it makes that comment even more remarkable.'

The night sky was blue-black, illuminated by a bright crescent moon, hanging low over the canyon. 'It's late,' Sasha said, standing and gathering up the photographs. 'I've taken up too much of your time already – I should go. I've booked a hotel downtown...'

'No, don't go,' said Katja, reaching up and taking his hand. 'Stay here with us. I've made up the spare room.'

She looked over at Alexander, who nodded. 'Yes, do stay, Sasha. I'd like that very much. Stay as long you like, my son.'

A LETTER FROM DEBBIE

Thank you for choosing to read *The German Wife*. I hope you enjoyed it, and if you would like to keep up with all my latest releases, just sign up at the following link. Your email address will never be shared, and you can unsubscribe at any time.

www.bookouture.com/debbie-rix

I wrote much of this novel through the long months of lockdown in 2020 and 2021, and in many ways the rhythm of going to my desk each morning was the one thing that kept me sane. Like so many other people going through that extraordinary experience, lockdown gave me a valuable insight into how it might be to live under an authoritarian regime. To be 'forbidden' to visit friends or family, or even drive any distance, was a frightening and upsetting control over our lives. But we were encouraged to believe that these controls were for our own benefit and for the protection of others.

The Nazis' control over their population was done in order to enact a new world order – one where Jews were initially branded as threats to health, for example. Anyone who spoke out against the regime was imprisoned or even murdered. It was also a world where medical experiments could be conducted on human beings without any thought for their welfare, treating them as mere laboratory animals – all for the sake of the greater good.

The Nazi defeat in 1945, and the subsequent trials at

Nuremberg that brought their crimes out into the light, was a milestone in history, forbidding medical procedures without people's informed consent.

If you enjoyed reading *The German Wife*, I'd be really grateful if you could write a review. Firstly, because I'd love to hear what you think, but also because it could be useful for people who are new to my books. I'm always delighted to hear from my readers; you can get in touch via my Facebook page, through Twitter, Goodreads or my website.

Thanks,

Debbie Rix

www.debbierix.com

 facebook.com/DebbieRixAuthor
twitter.com/debbierix

HISTORICAL NOTE

I was inspired to write this book by a photograph I saw in the Munich Documentation Centre for the History of National Socialism. I was in Munich to research my previous novel, *The Secret Letter*, and my eyes fell upon a photograph of a beautiful young man – a Russian 'slave' – who had been executed for having an affair with his employer. Strung up on a gibbet, his death was witnessed by many other slaves, forced to watch this atrocity, presumably as a warning to other rule-breakers. These rules stated that no slave – either male or female – should have any social interaction with their employer.

As I read about the slave system in wartime Germany, I was both surprised and appalled. I hadn't realised before how widespread slavery actually was. Literally millions of people were forced into slave labour for the German Reich.

That struck me then as a compelling starting point for a future novel. As part of my research I visited Dachau, the concentration and labour camp north-west of Munich, whose original buildings still largely survive today. The highly informative exhibition there illustrates daily life at the camp, and does not spare accounts of the appalling atrocities that took place for over a decade, until its liberation by the American invading forces in 1945. Dachau was not only the very first German concentration camp, it was also the first to specialise in medical experimentation. In the Dachau museum, I learned – with growing horror – the details of the experiments and their astonishing cruelty. Many of the inmates were forced to suffer horrendous fates as human laboratory animals.

It was at Dachau that I also discovered the bizarre background story of the infamous Nazi experimenter, Dr Sigmund Rascher, who plotted with his wife Karoline to become child kidnappers. Somehow, I knew I had to weave it into my novel.

The kidnapping story is totally genuine. Rascher's wife really did steal four baby boys and try to pass them off as her own, in order to be seen to fulfil her husband's duty to produce Aryan children for the Fatherland. The couple's deception was finally discovered in 1945, and despite their close friendship with Heinrich Himmler himself, they were both executed – Karoline at Ravensbrück concentration camp and her husband at Dachau, only days before the camp was liberated by the Americans.

My central character, Hans Vogel, is based on another real historical character: Dr Kurt Plötner. He was the first doctor to be employed at Dachau, where he worked on malaria research. He was a homeopath – a style of medicine much favoured by Hitler who believed in 'volk medizin' (roughly translated as 'the people's medicine'). Plötner later began to research mescaline at Dachau, and when the Americans arrived and arrested the Dachau doctors, Plötner was whisked away to continue his research into these 'truth drugs' for the American OSS, the forerunner of the CIA. In my novel, Hans Vogel is sent to America for ten years, but in fact Kurt Plötner never left Germany. In 1945 he was moved to Schleswig Holstein where he worked for the American government under the name of Schmitt. The French attempted to track him down and have him prosecuted in 1946, but the Americans lied to them, saying he had disappeared, probably into the hands of the Russians. Astonishingly, in 1952, Plötner was allowed to resume his real identity, and was taken on by the University of Freiburg, becoming a respected Associate Professor of Medicine, which is how he ended his career. It was as if the war crimes he committed had been literally forgotten.

I have attempted, with this novel, to try to understand how such a man – a doctor who had spent years training to do good to people – could possibly bring himself to inflict such cruelty on his fellow man. Without doubt, some of the doctors – Sigmund Rascher at Dachau, Josef Mengele at Auschwitz – were ruthless sadists. But Plötner struck me as somehow different. In particular, his interest in homeopathy implied a benign 'first do no harm' attitude to his patients. In the character of Hans Vogel, I have tried to explore his painful personal dilemma of how to pursue humanitarian medical research within a murderous regime.

As for Annaliese, the 'German wife' of the title, how could a normal woman cope with living with someone as appalling as a Nazi doctor? It seemed to me that she could only deal with the horror, if she simply didn't understand what he was doing, until it was too late.

This is a fascinating period in history, and we would do well to remember the lessons learned – most particularly those of the Nuremberg Trials, in which twenty Nazi doctors were brought before the international court. Their indictment was as follows:

- Committing crimes against humanity.
- Performing medical experiments without the subject's consent.
- Performing mass murder against both prisoners of war and civilians as part of the Euthanasia Program.

Their trial led to the publication of the 'Nuremberg Code', a list of ten principles that are now required to guide the administration of all medical interventions and treatments. The list is too long to print here, but the first principle is perhaps the most important: that anyone agreeing to a medical procedure must be made aware of its possible dangers, must never be coerced or forced to give their consent, and should have the legal right to withdraw their consent at any time.

Finally, let me point out that my novel, although its context is as factually based as I can make it, is essentially a work of fiction. My characters, the events in their lives, their motivation, emotions and relationships, have all arisen from my imagination.

ACKNOWLEDGEMENTS

As always, huge thanks go to my publisher, Bookouture. In particular, I want to thank my editor, Natasha Harding, for her unwavering support and brilliant instincts. The relationship between a writer and her editor is extremely important. The editor must nurse the writer through all the stages of researching and writing a novel, providing feedback, notes, reactions. In Natasha's case, this also meant encouraging me to take the first draft of this novel completely apart, and refocus the story on Annaliese and her husband.

I would also like to thank my family. My daughter and husband accompanied me on my visit to Dachau in 2020, and their interest in the subject I was researching spurred me on. My husband, especially, is both a valuable sounding board and great enthusiast for my novels.

Finally, this book would not have been possible without the information I found in two museums: The Munich Documentation Centre for the History of National Socialism, and The Dachau Memorial Museum. In spite of the fact that the exhibits reveal great suffering and appalling abuse, they are nevertheless done with enormous sensitivity and grace. Both are filled with fascinating information, which is very well displayed and catalogued, and I encourage anyone with an interest in the Second World War to visit both.

Made in the USA
Middletown, DE
04 September 2023